Sworn to the ......

The Wisdom's Grave Trilogy, Book One

by Craig Schaefer

Cover Design by James T. Egan of Bookfly Design LLC.
Author Photo ©2014 by Karen Forsythe Photography
Craig Schaefer / Sworn to the Night
ISBN 978-1-944806-09-5

Contents

Prologue 1

Act I 6

One 7

Two 14

Three 20

Four 26

Five 31

Six 38

Seven 45

Eight 52

Nine 60

Ten 67

Eleven 73

Twelve 80

Thirteen 85

Fourteen 92

Fifteen 99

Sixteen 106

Seventeen 113

Eighteen 120

Nineteen 127

Twenty 134

Twenty-One 141

Twenty-Two 147

Twenty-Three 151

Twenty-Four 158

Twenty-Five 164

Twenty-Six 170

Twenty-Seven 178

Twenty-Eight 186

Twenty-Nine 192

Thirty 199

Thirty-One 205

Act II 209

Interlude 210

Thirty-Two 213

Thirty-Three 218

Thirty-Four 225

Thirty-Five 232

Thirty-Six 240

Thirty-Seven 246

Thirty-Eight 251

Thirty-Nine 257

Forty 263

Forty-One 269

Forty-Two 274

Forty-Three 281

Interlude 284

Forty-Four 287

Forty-Five 293

Forty-Six 300

Forty-Seven 306

Forty-Eight 314

Forty-Nine   319

Fifty   328

Fifty-One   334

Fifty-Two   341

Fifty-Three   347

Fifty-Four   354

Fifty-Five   360

Fifty-Six   366

Fifty-Seven   371

Fifty-Eight   378

Fifty-Nine   384

Sixty   389

Sixty-One   397

Sixty-Two   406

Sixty-Three   410

Interlude   416

Sixty-Four   418

Afterword   421

Also By Craig Schaefer   423

Prologue

Carolyn had been kidnapped twice in the past month, which was twice more than most people in a lifetime. Still, she didn't complain. With a burlap sack over her head and the muzzle of a very large gun pressed against the back of her skull, she didn't think her latest abductors were interested in hearing her grievances. They shoved her into the back seat of a car, squeezed between two men with cold, callused hands. She listened to the rev of the engine as they squealed away from the curb outside her house. An hour on the highway, then a second car, then—guessing from the whistling thrum of the blades and the lurch in her stomach as they lifted off—a helicopter.

"I've never actually been on a helicopter before," Carolyn said. "Would you mind taking the bag off my head so I can look out the window?"

Nobody answered her.

"I'm a writer, you see. Learning from new experiences is very important in my line of work. Readers know if you get the details wrong."

No response. She shrugged, sat back, and rested her handcuffed wrists in her lap. They hadn't given her headphones to protect her hearing, but the chop from the rotors was only a faint droning vibration above her head. *Reinforced cabin*, she thought. *Expensive.* Ahead of her, from what she assumed was the pilot's seat, a man finally spoke up.

"We have geomantic telemetry lock. Goetic wards online, firing in the ninety-percent range. Prepare for transition effect in three...two...one."

The universe slid sideways. Carolyn's stomach jolted, churning, as her seat jerked hard to the left and the engine screamed like a vacuum cleaner with a broken gasket. She smelled burning popcorn and spilled diesel. Then another scent, slipping vaporous fingers under her nose.

Roses.

The men were shouting at each other, their voices swallowed by the whining engine, and the helicopter slammed hard to the right. She couldn't make out the words, couldn't focus as the cabin began to spin. A riptide of adrenaline coursed through her veins and her flesh prickled, hot and wild like the flame from a butane lighter. The engine screamed louder, its mechanical roar blotting out the world as the cabin spun faster and faster, free-falling, then—

—nothing. Utter silence.

They weren't moving. At all. The helicopter sat perfectly still. As her senses slowly returned, head reeling, she heard the blades spinning down. Carolyn breathed deep and fought a wave of nausea.

The men didn't speak. They dragged her off the helicopter, shoving her head down, out onto the landing pad. The floor felt like plates of corrugated steel rattling under her sneakers as they marched her away. The air was chill, like the sterile cold of a museum, and it smelled like hospital antiseptic. They marched her through a doorway. A chair scraped back. Rough hands shoved her down. Then they ripped the hood away and she squinted at the sudden flood of light.

She recognized the room from every TV detective show she'd ever seen. Steel table. Steel chairs. Crumbling brick walls, and an overhead lamp that blazed hot enough to cause a sunburn.

"An interrogation room," she said, "lovely. I assume that makes you my interrogator?"

The man in the corner, bald, with a hooked raptor-beak of a nose, wore a shoulder holster over his black turtleneck sweater. He crossed his arms and nodded to someone behind her.

"That's all. Leave us."

A heavy metal door whistled shut at her back. Then came the *clank* of a lever sealing them in. The interrogator stared her down.

"Carolyn Saunders," he said. Like it was an accusation.

"You'd better hope I am, or you just kidnapped the wrong person." She held up her cuffed hands. "Is this really necessary?"

"You're more dangerous than you look."

She snorted. "Please. I'm a sixty-four-year-old woman who writes fantasy novels and listens to NPR. I had a tuna sandwich for dinner with a glass of white zinfandel. How dangerous could I possibly be?"

He pulled back the chair on the far side of the table.

"You're a storyteller." He sat down across from her and spread his hands. "So tell me a story."

"I can do that. One of mine, or one of the classics?"

"The Witch and her Knight."

Carolyn pursed her lips and dropped her gaze to the table. She could see her reflection in the brushed steel, distorted and blurred.

"You want a fairy tale."

"We want to know what happened. The truth. All of it."

"Fair warning, then," Carolyn told him. "This isn't some sweet Disney bedtime story. This is a *real* fairy tale. With death, and blood, and suffering. And I never promise a happy ending."

"Do you know where you are?" the interrogator asked.

"I don't know where I am, but I suspect I know who you work for."

The overhead lamp flickered, humming and browning out, and a guttural shriek echoed in the distance. The scream of a man having his life torn away, inch by bloody inch. When the room dipped into darkness, the interrogator's face wasn't the same.

In the dark, he had no eyes. Just two black, ragged sockets.

The light flooded back in. The scream died. The interrogator gave her a calm smile and folded his hands on the table.

"If you know that," he said, "then you know this: we don't care for happy endings around here."

Carolyn swallowed, her throat suddenly bone-dry. Under the table she squeezed her hands together to drive away a tremor.

"You understand, I wasn't there for most of the story," she said. "I had to put it all together myself after it was over. Research, recollections. Interviewing the survivors, the few I could find, the ones who were still sane. I assembled the facts like the pieces of a jigsaw puzzle."

The interrogator's chair scraped backward. He rose from his seat, brow furrowed, his gaze boring into her.

"Tell me how they did it," he said.

He leaned in and loomed over her.

"Tell me how they killed God."

Carolyn unclenched her cuffed hands and laid them flat on her lap. Her fingertips riffled against her legs, like a piano player getting warmed up for a performance.

"I do hope you'll indulge an old artist. I'm fond of so many literary techniques. I've been known to break the fourth wall now and then. Sometimes I employ an unreliable narrator or two. I might even, if the story merits it, bring in a *deus ex machina* for the grand finale. But I always try to play fair with my readers."

"The truth," the interrogator said. "If you attempt to lie to us—even a single word—we'll *know*. And you don't want that."

"Then I suppose I'd better tell the truth," she replied with a slight pause, "and nothing but the truth. Now then, if you want to know the story of the Witch and her Knight, I have to start at the beginning."

He sat back down, staring in expectant silence. Carolyn took a deep breath.

"We should do this properly," she said. "So: once upon a time, in a magical kingdom, there lived a valiant knight. But she didn't know she was a knight, not yet, any more than she knew that she was fated to die. And in this same kingdom lived a witch who would have been peerless in wit, power, and wickedness, but she'd fallen under a vile sorcerer's spell—"

"Get on with it," the interrogator told her, glowering.

"Never rush a storyteller." Her eyes narrowed at him. "If you do, you might miss an important detail. So listen closely. And here...we...go."

ACT I

BABY BLUE

One

The knight stood on a windswept hill overlooking the walls of Mirenze, the once-proud city in smoking ruin. Sunlight glinted off her steel armor, and she resolved herself to the mission ahead. There would be no turning back when she met the enemy, only death or glory—

Marie jumped as a hard knock on the car window jolted her from her daydreams. She closed her dog-eared paperback—*Swords in the City of Coin*, by Carolyn Saunders—and tossed it in the glove compartment while the window hummed down. The sounds of the street poured in: distant horns, a jackhammer pounding old pavement into dust, a cheap radio blaring top-40 rock from a second-floor window. A warm breeze carried a smell like soggy newspapers and cooked liver. Just another morning in East Harlem. A slim hand reached through the window and shoved a paper cup in her face.

"That fantasy crap's gonna rot your brain," Tony told her. "You ever read that Val McDermid book I gave you?"

Marie took the cup, lifted the plastic lid, and took a sniff. The scent of fresh bodega coffee, rich and roasted and black, kicked her brain into gear. She reached for the seat belt. Her shoulder holster bumped the seat, snug under her wool blazer.

"Murder mysteries." She rolled her eyes at him. "I don't get it. It's like a bus driver reading stories about...driving buses."

She blew on her coffee while he circled their car, an unmarked Lincoln sprouting rust marks like a teenager sprouted pimples, and hopped behind the wheel. He set his own cup in the console between them and shifted the car into gear.

"Not the same thing," he said. "In a good murder mystery, you've got a perp, you've got a chain of clues, and the hero always gets the bad guy in the end. Everything makes sense and wraps up clean."

"Oh," Marie said as they pulled away from the curb, "so in other words, fantasy."

"Smart-ass. So what's on the morning agenda?"

Marie nodded to the dashboard. She'd taped up a photograph there, about the size of a Polaroid, captured from a website and run through a grainy printer. The young woman in the picture pursed her lips at the camera. She'd dyed her hair to match her neon-blue latex halter, front zipper pulled down to dangle below the valley of her breasts.

"I want to take a run at Eddie Li," Marie said. "We know he was her last client. Alibi or not, he's gotta have something we can use."

Tony puffed his cheeks and blew air between his lips. He nudged the car into a stream of slug-slow traffic.

"We have other cases, you know."

"It's not far from here. Won't take us long."

He didn't reply. She looked his way.

"It's important, Tony."

He drummed his fingers on the steering wheel.

"Fine," he said, "fine. But then we spend the rest of the day working cases we can actually solve, all right?"

They headed east on 135th Street. The sun crested over the Harlem River, looming ahead of them like a sizzling egg yolk, and cast a hard morning glare down through the city canyons. Marie flipped the sun visor and drank her coffee. They rode in silence, listening to the occasional squawk of the dashboard radio. Dispatch calls and numbers. License plate checks and ambulance call-outs. The same-old rhythm of a same-old day. They rolled up on the shop, cherry neon sign reading Nails behind a glossy plate-glass window, and Tony circled the block looking for a spot to park.

"Place is jumping," he said.

Marie glanced down at her own fingernails, unpolished and chopped short. "Springtime. It's sandal season."

The salon had just opened. The waiting area was full, clients watching television and sipping cucumber water. Marie made a half-hearted attempt at fixing her hair; a gust of stale wind had caught her on the way in, turning it into a tangled blond mop. Eternal bed head, her family curse. Tony was the Felix to her unkempt Oscar: lean, dark, suave, and accenting his chocolate-brown suit with an orange silk necktie like an urban peacock. That, and the gold shield clipped to his belt. Marie pulled her jacket aside to flash her badge at the front counter and asked in a low voice for a word with the owner.

Eddie Li received them in his back office, a shoe box with a cluttered office-surplus desk. A Tsingtao beer calendar hung tacked to a lopsided corkboard alongside a flurry of old schedules on curled pink paper. Eddie had a beer gut, a hairline in full retreat, and the guiltiest eyes Marie had seen all week.

"Thanks for seeing us," she said, shutting the door on their way in. "I'm Detective Reinhart, and this is Detective Fisher."

Eddie smiled too desperately, waving them toward the chairs on the far side of his desk with fluttering fingers. "Of course, of course, I always have time for New York's finest. What can I do for you?"

She set the photograph on the desk in front of him. The girl in blue gave Eddie a seductive smile, frozen in time. The blood drained from his face.

"I already, I mean, I already talked to those other officers. They *know* where I was—"

"Your alibi checked out," Marie told him. "That doesn't mean you're innocent. Her pimp kept exhaustive notes, Mr. Li. You were her last client the night before she disappeared. You were one of the last people to see her alive."

He shook his head, but he couldn't take his eyes off the picture. "Look, I made...I made a mistake, hiring an escort, but I barely knew anything about her."

"You hired her twenty-seven times," Marie said. "Twenty-seven times and no pillow talk? She never dropped anything about her personal life, trouble she might have been having? Not even once?"

"My wife is leaving me." Eddie squinted at the picture, shook his head again. "I'm already ruined. I don't want any more trouble."

Marie and Tony shared a glance. He leaned back and crossed one leg over the other, cool and casual.

"Eddie, c'mon, man. We know you're a law-abiding citizen at heart. Like, I'm sure your bookkeeping is impeccable. If we checked, I bet we'd find you dot every *i* and cross every *t*. No shortcuts, no funny business."

"Oh, no doubt," Marie said. "There's zero chance he's hiding cash, or saving money by buying his salon supplies on the illegal resale market. Which is good, because if he did and we found out about it, that'd really jam him up."

Tony tapped his chin. "Good point. And if the IRS got involved? That'd be a lot of lost revenue. I mean, it is sandal season."

"All right, all *right*." Eddie threw up his hands. "There was something...look, this can't come back on me, okay? My name has to stay out of this."

Marie leaned toward him. Hard and hungry-eyed, like a hawk spotting a mouse as it bolted for cover.

"Spill it," she said.

"Baby Blue is—" He paused, his fingers tracing her photograph, the curve of her cheek. "Electric. That's the only word for it. She's not like other girls, you know? She's a goddess."

Marie nodded. They'd talked to every man on her regular client list. They'd all said the same thing, in almost the exact same words.

"I wasn't her last client that night. She had a thing. A party."

"A party?" Tony asked.

"Some kind of a private club deal. I don't know, dancing maybe. See, I tried to get her to stay the night. I did that sometimes when I had the cash, but she already had this other thing lined up. And it was a *lot* of cash. I guess her—her, uh, manager didn't know about it."

Marie's hand tightened on the armrest of her chair.

"She's been missing for a week," she said, "you had information that could have helped us find her, and you're *just now* deciding to share it?"

Eddie screwed up his face. "Look, all I got is an address. She didn't exactly give it to me, not in so many words. I was worried about her, so..."

"You were stalking her," Tony said.

"I was *worried*. But these people—this isn't some low-rent massage parlor where you get a rubdown with your rubdown, all right? These are serious people. Connected."

"Connected?"

"Connected. Like the kind of people you don't rat on unless you want a good look at the bottom of the Hudson. That's what Baby Blue said, anyway. She was scared. Just not scared enough to turn down the money."

"These parties," Marie said. "Where?"

Eddie took a deep breath, held it, then let it out in a resigned sigh. Deflated, he opened his desk drawer and pulled out a crumpled slip of paper.

"Near Monticello. A house off NY-17, middle of nowhere. Good enough? We done here?"

Marie stood, snatched the paper from his fingers, and picked up the photograph. She held the picture in his face, giving him one long last look.

"You better hope she's there, *alive*, Eddie. Otherwise? You're going to see me again."

* * *

Out in the car, Tony drummed his fingers on the steering wheel.

"You know we're looking at a two-hour drive there, two-hour drive back, right?"

Marie buckled her seat belt.

"We can pass this tip along," he said. "Let the locals check it out. We don't have to do all the legwork ourselves."

Marie opened her wallet. A trio of rumpled photographs snuggled next to a yellowed library card and a few small bills. She took out the photographs—headshots, young, pretty—and held them up one by one.

"Vicky Wagner. Disappeared. Two weeks later, found butchered in a dumpster. Lottie Holmes. Disappeared. Two weeks later, found butchered in a dumpster. Letisha—"

"I get it," Tony said.

Marie held up the photograph of Baby Blue.

"She's running out of time. I don't care what the brass says, Tony. We've got a serial killer preying on sex workers. You know it, I know it, and nobody seems to give a damn. So no, we're not 'passing the tip along.' I'm not trusting the locals to do shit. This woman is counting on us, and I will *not* let her down."

The sedan's engine thrummed to life, rumbling under the squawk of the radio. Tony threw the stick into drive and eased into traffic.

"You can't save 'em all, you know."

Marie folded her arms and stared straight ahead.

"Have to try," she told him.

They drove north, then northwest, breaking away from the curve of the river and leaving the urban sprawl at their backs. They rode in the shadow of the Catskills past summer homes and villages, old resort towns clinging to life, bits of rust nestled in the bloom of spring. Past a barely marked exit and a dirt access road, the sun filtered through the boughs of wooly hemlock trees.

The house at the end of the road stood alone. It leaned this way and that, its second-floor arches sagging under the weight of weather and time. Scraps of bone-white paint clung to the rotten wood like memories of a happier age, most of the siding gone the color of cigarette ash. Some of the windows were broken, smashed by rocks, others caked with dust.

"Oh yeah, this place is party central," Tony said. "I think our pal Eddie might *possibly* have been full of shit. How do you wanna play this?"

Marie stared at the front door, thinking it over. "No cars out front. Let's see if anybody's home. If not, we can peep through the windows, see if we spot anything interesting."

They pulled up the drive. As they stepped out of the car, a pinched, frightened face loomed behind one of the second-floor windows. Marie held up her badge and smiled.

"Good afternoon! NYPD. Could we have a moment of your time, please?"

The front door swung open. The man behind it, a stringy-haired seven-foot giant in filthy overalls, stumbled out onto the porch and squinted at the sunlight.

He leveled the shotgun in his hands, taking aim at the detectives, and pulled the trigger.

Two

Marie dropped low behind her door as the shotgun roared. Buckshot tore into the sedan's hood and splintered the windshield. She had her pistol out in a heartbeat, her training taking over, reaching around the car door to snap off a couple of wild shots. Tony lay low across the front seat and shouted into the radio.

"Ten-thirteen, we are under fire. Repeat, we are *under fire—*"

The shotgun boomed and he jerked his face down, pinned under a sudden rain of shattered glass. The next shot hit Marie's door, shredding metal and making buckshot dance off the dry dirt inches away. More glass broke—not the car this time, one of the house windows—and the thudding clack of a revolver joined the fray as someone on the second floor opened fire.

Marie looked across to Tony, both of them huddled low. "Wait for it," she said through gritted teeth.

Buckshot raked across the bumper, peppered the grill, blew out the left tire in a hiss of dead air. The sedan slouched on three wheels and Marie and Tony came up from cover as one, unloading on the giant, aiming for center mass. The shotgun clattered to the porch and he staggered back as gunshots punched into his dirt-encrusted overalls. He grabbed the edge of the open door as he fell, leaving a slug-smear of blood across the rotten wood.

Marie ducked again as another round cracked over her head. The second shooter was inside the house. She popped her empty magazine, reloading fast, fingers driven by muscle memory.

"Cover me," she said. "I'm making a run for it. Gonna see if I can find a rear entrance and come at him from the other side."

Tony's eyes bulged at her from the driver's side of the car. Another bullet drilled into his door and rattled the battered sedan.

"Are you crazy? Wait for backup!"

"We're in the middle of nowhere," she said. "These are the guys, Tony. She could be in there *right now*, and I'm not giving this asshole a chance to start killing hostages."

He took one look in her eyes and let out an exasperated sigh.

"Fine," he said. "Call it."

"On three."

At the end of the silent three-count, Tony popped up from behind the car door and laid down a blistering stream of fire. The sniper dropped, pinned, blind for a few precious seconds. Marie broke from cover and streaked across the lawn. Her heart pounded, her vision narrow as a subway tunnel, hemmed in by walls of darkness. Everything was shades of gray at jet-engine speed. There was the back door. Rotten wood shattered under her shoe. The rusted lock snapped like a chunk of peanut brittle. She sprinted inside, weapon braced in both hands. A dusty lilac rug threatened to slide out from under her feet, but she got to the stairs and took them two at a time. The muzzle of her pistol swept over empty doorways. She heard the shooter up ahead, gunshots echoing, faint, everything sounding like she'd plunged a hundred feet underwater.

An old, pinch-faced man crouched beside his broken window, taking shots at Tony and the car, his back to her. Boxes of ammunition lay scattered across the bare wood floor alongside a couple of rifles, enough firepower to hold off a small siege. Marie trained her gun on him and roared, "*Police*, drop the fucking gun. Drop it *right now!*"

He spun, surprised—*no*, she thought, *terrified*—and his jaw dropped. The revolver, tight in his grip, twitched at his side.

"Had t'do it," he drawled, his lips puffy and cracked.

"Drop the gun."

"King comes a-callin', gotta dance. Gotta dance to the tune he plays."

Marie held him in her sights. "Drop. The gun. *Now*."

His lips twisted into a broken smile.

"Goin' home now."

He put the revolver to his head, yanked the trigger, and blew his brains across the dirty window.

Marie stood there, silent, staring as his corpse tumbled to the floor. She was frozen in time, one endless moment, watching trickles of crimson roll in slow motion down the fractured glass and pool on the windowsill. Then a deep rumbling, somewhere under her feet, pierced the silence and jolted her into motion. It sounded like a machine bigger than the house, some great engine, turned on and then quickly turned off again. She hunted the sound.

The cellar stairs leaned into darkness. She moved down, smooth, fast, weapon ready. She stopped at the foot of the steps.

The cellar was filled with people. Maybe twenty or thirty in all. Shadows, standing perfectly motionless in the dark around a hospital gurney in the center of the room.

Marie's finger rested on the trigger, her other hand reaching out to turn on the lights.

"Freeze! Nobody move, or—"

The overheads flicked on, fluorescent tubes popping and buzzing to life, washing away the darkness.

The room was empty.

She'd seen them. She knew she'd seen them. But as she walked across the cracked concrete floor, the lights humming above her head, she was alone. Alone except for a clutter of cardboard boxes shoved against one cold brick wall, and the dead man on the gurney.

He was naked. Pale. And open like a book. A tray of autopsy tools stood beside the gurney, blades and calipers and rib-crackers coated in congealed blood. They'd ripped him apart from his throat to his belly. Skin peeled back from snapped ribs. His internal organs had been snipped and sliced, rearranged like a puzzle made of flesh. From the ligature bruises on his wrists and ankles, he'd been alive when they did it.

Marie took his arm, turning it, feeling his wrist for a pulse just to be certain. He had a tattoo there, about the size of a silver dollar, a glyph of some kind, jagged and spiraling and strange. She pressed her fingertips over it.

The dead man's eyes snapped open and he seized her hand with an iron grip.

"Marie," he wheezed. His glassy, pale-blue eyes locked onto hers. "Hell is watching you."

He collapsed. His eyes fell shut. His hand went limp, arm dangling off the edge of the gurney.

Marie took a shuddering step back. Her throat felt like she'd swallowed a lump of ice. Upstairs, Tony shouted her name, and it took a second before she could remember how to speak again.

"Downstairs," she called up. "It's...it's clear."

She reached for the corpse's wrist a second time, slow, like grasping for the head of a sleeping rattlesnake. No pulse. She rested his arm at his side and, on instinct, took out her phone. She snapped a quick close-up of his tattoo, then stashed the phone as Tony rushed down the cellar stairs.

"You okay?" he asked, breathless.

"No girl. She's not here, Tony."

"This guy is, though." He walked up to stand beside her, shaking his head at the dead body. "Jesus, what kind of freak show did we crack open here?"

She didn't have an answer. Tony skirted the gurney and tugged open one of the cardboard boxes with the tip of a pen.

"Holy shit, *score*. At least we know what line of work these guys were in. Check it out."

Marie stood at his shoulder, grateful for something else to look at, and peered inside. The box was filled with baggie after translucent baggie of tiny black pebbles. On the news, they called it "the new crack." In their daily briefings, it was "the epidemic," a new designer drug that had hit the East Coast by storm and flooded west like a gold rush.

On the street, they called it ink.

"Gotta be ten, twelve boxes, ready to sell," Tony said. "Nobody can find the pipeline, and we just took down a goddamn stash house. By accident. How do you like that?"

She didn't have an opinion. She silently brushed the back of her hand, her fingers curling over the skin where the dead man had touched her. Marie felt like a ghost as she drifted up the cellar steps and through the house, vacant room after vacant room. A quartet of Monticello police cruisers rumbled up the dirt road with their light bars flashing.

It was a long afternoon. She watched the sun crest, then slide behind the hemlocks, while she sat in the passenger seat of their ruined sedan. Baby Blue stared at her from the dashboard, her smoldering eyes rendering silent judgment. The scene in the cellar played out in her mind's eye again and again: the disappearing shadows, the dead man speaking her name. *Adrenaline*, she told herself. *Stress under fire. You were hallucinating. It happens.*

Ambulances came. Paramedics hauled out the shooters under white sheets. Flash bulbs crackled in the fading light, documenting every angle of the gunfight. Eventually another unmarked sedan rolled up, caked in spring pollen, and Captain Traynor took Marie and Tony aside. He wore a shabby raincoat over his pinstriped shirt and needle-thin black tie, and he spoke in low, easy tones.

"We should be helping with the scene—" Marie said, and Traynor silenced her with a gentle wave of his hand.

"You can't work the scene, Detective. You *are* the scene. Listen, both of you, this is how it's going to be. You're going to go home and write your reports while everything is still fresh. *Don't* turn them in. You're on administrative leave, starting now, for at least four days.

Once you've had some time to think things over and compare notes, maybe you'll want to revise those reports a little."

Tony put a hand on his hip. "It was a righteous shoot, Captain."

"And I believe you. But it's IAB's job to find trouble where there isn't any. So take your time, and think real hard about what you're going to say." Traynor glanced over his shoulder at the stream of locals tramping in and out of the bullet-riddled house. He ushered the detectives back a few feet. "Don't want to embarrass you, but...you know how this goes. Badges and weapons. C'mon."

They handed them over. Traynor held up their gold shields for a moment before pocketing them.

"You'll get these back once you're cleared for active duty again. You *will* get these back. You'll have to face a panel and answer a whole lot of stupid questions, and you'll have to get a psych eval. I'll call you both tomorrow and we'll get into the details."

"I don't need a shrink," Marie said.

Traynor arched an eyebrow at her. "You ever drawn your piece outside the firing range, Detective? You ever pulled the trigger on another human being before?"

Her gaze dropped. "No, sir."

"I have. So believe me when I tell you this: you *will* want somebody to talk to about it. Maybe not tonight, maybe not tomorrow, but you will. Now go home. You've done all you can tonight."

He called up a squad car to give them a ride back to the city. Marie paused at their sedan, leaned inside, and peeled the picture of Baby Blue off the dashboard. The photograph went into her wallet, alongside the three dead women she'd been too slow to save.

Not one more, she told herself.

Not one more.

Three

There were quiet places in the city, tiny sanctuaries, if you knew where to look. Vanessa Roth had found hers in Inwood Hill Park, on the northern tip of Manhattan. She could imagine dinosaurs prowling the ragged, primeval wood, long-billed scavengers picking across the cool salt marshes. She'd found herself a cozy spot on the edge of nowhere, away from the hiking paths and bicycle lanes.

Her eyes blazed like sharp sapphires behind her glasses, the rounded, owlish lenses almost too big for her face. An eager smile played on her lips. Today was the day, she was sure of it. This time it would work. She knelt on a patch of dew-damp grass with a hardbound book open on her lap. The faded type on the yellowed, brittle page read "The Game of Finding a Guide."

For furtherance of skill, it is essential that the cunning Student of the Art seek a guide, who will teach the virtues of Power and Freedom. This guide may take on the form of a beast of the wild and must be greeted with respect and a proper sacrifice...

Nessa's offering, a small mound of fresh pecans and beechnuts, sat upon a stone disk carved with a five-pointed star. She'd arranged every nut with precision, carefully turning and placing the food like a Michelin-starred chef plating a celebrity's dish. Then came the chant. Words rippled from her lips, a song in a dead tongue, so familiar now she barely needed the lines in the book to guide her. They seemed to take on physical form, wafting through the air as a pale vapor, stretching and searching. A warm wind kicked up across the marshes and ruffled her coal-black hair. She tasted salt on her lips and caught the faint scent of blackberries.

Her fervor grew. Beckoning, calling, begging with words she couldn't even understand, trying to reach out with her heart and her voice. Then she came to the end of the page. The last word of the spell died on her lips. It thudded like a brick in her lap.

Nothing.

She waited there, still daring to hope. A rustling from the underbrush made her eyes go wide.

A white-tailed doe stepped into the clearing. Small, timid, barely older than a fawn, she took a hesitant step toward Nessa. One hoof brushed the moist grass, then yanked back.

"That's right," she said softly, "come to me. Come to Nessa. It's all right."

Another trembling step. The doe's big caramel eyes studied her, uncertain.

"You're my guide," she told the deer. "You're here to help me. Come closer. I...I brought an offering."

She gestured to the stone pentacle. The doe sniffed at it, nose twitching, but held her ground.

"Please," Nessa said. "I did everything right. I followed the rules, all the instructions, to the letter. Now give me what I asked for."

The doe snorted. She took a shambling step back and ducked her head. Nessa sprang to her feet, her anxiety taking over, frustration shattering her concentration.

"Give me what I need! *Please!*"

The doe wheeled around and bolted into the brush. Nessa heard light, scattered hoof beats, then...nothing.

Her shoulders sagged. She gathered up the book and the stone, bundling them into a canvas tote bag. She left her offering for the scavengers. On her way back to the trail, a fallen feather caught her eye. Long, tawny, and speckled, frayed at the edges. She slipped that into her tote bag, too. A little piece of the wild to join her in the long, empty walk—and a longer subway ride, alone and in silence—back to civilization.

*   *   *

Civilization was the West Village, a stone's throw from the Hudson River. Civilization was an $11.5 million townhouse from the nineteenth century with a restored brick facade, squeezed shoulder to shoulder with neighbors clad in mud-brown and bone. Civilization was plank hardwood floors, three fireplaces, and an oil painting of Nessa and her husband placed above the mantel in a sitting room neither of them ever set foot in. She came home to the aroma of roast beef wafting through the house. Gerta, the maid, puttered and clanked pans around in the kitchen. Nessa drifted past the open doorway and climbed the mahogany staircase, bound for her little nook at the back of the house.

The windowless, octagonal room was the size of a walk-in closet—their *actual* walk-in closet in the bedroom was bigger—but this room was hers. It was cluttered with easels and never-finished canvases, a collection of half-imagined grotesques in oil and charcoal. A wrist in chains here, ending at a bent elbow, the rest of the figure waiting to be drawn. A single trammeled wing, bound in cord, and a baleful eye drawn as a smear of ocher pigment. She'd abandoned that one too, her initial burst of inspiration fading to a tepid trickle.

Her latest attempt had come further than the others, but not by much. She wasn't entirely sure what she was painting. It was a chaotic storm of black and gray, a vague, angry flurry. She'd taken to picking up stray feathers, adding them to the canvas with a glob of black paint to fix them in place. The new feather joined the others: she placed it on instinct, a scatter of quills rising from the canvas in a pattern that felt right. She reached for her palette, then stopped. She wasn't feeling the muse, not today.

She hadn't heard the front door, but the hallway floorboards groaned under heavy footsteps. Her husband, Richard, walked in while he loosened his silk tie.

"Hey, hon," he said, leaning in to land a perfunctory kiss on her cheek. "Have a good day off?"

Nessa bristled at the intrusion, but she forced a smile. "Fine. How was the meeting?"

"Top notch. Looks like the Tribeca deal is a go." He paused, glancing at the feathered canvas. "You take your meds this morning?"

Nessa bit her bottom lip and swallowed the first response that came to mind.

"Yes," she said. "I did."

He gave her a wink and a smile. "Just gotta check on my girl. So, uh, what's with the feathers?"

"Trying something new. Playing with textures."

Richard shrugged. "Can't you paint something *nice* for once? Like a pretty landscape or something? Something we could hang up in the house and show our friends."

Your friends, she thought.

"Maybe next time," she told him.

*   *   *

Dinner. Nessa and Richard sat at opposite ends of a long glass table in the dining room, Richard's end festooned with piles of paperwork, folders, and brochures. He worked while he ate, flipping through photocopies and blueprints, sucking down a bottle of abbey ale. Nessa picked at her plate. Rare roast beef steamed on the square ceramic dish, leaking blood beneath piled spears of asparagus.

"So I may be taking on some more work at the college," she said.

"Huh," he replied, not looking up.

"They're expanding the anthropology track. So I might end up teaching another class or two. It'd be a good opportunity for me."

"Huh." He flicked his gaze toward her, just for a heartbeat. "Did you take your meds?"

Nessa stared at him, her eyes cold, as she set the unlabeled prescription bottle down next to her plate. She shook it, louder than she needed to, and tapped a pair of tiny pink pills into her open palm. Her eyes never left Richard's downturned face—his attention already back on his paperwork—as she tossed them into her mouth and washed them down with Perrier.

"I'm working on a new paper," she said. "Studying the impact of tourism upon the Jarawa tribe in the Andaman Islands. Dr. Milbourn thinks it could be a milestone for me. It's important work. Might even lead to tenure."

"That's nice," Richard mumbled through a mouthful of roast beef.

"I've been thinking about going on a killing spree," Nessa said.

"Huh," he said.

After that, she didn't bother saying anything at all. They ate in silence, and she was about to get up and leave, pushing back her half-finished plate, when he noticed her again.

"Almost forgot," he said. "I'm gonna be gone for a couple of days. Leaving tomorrow afternoon. Lodge trip."

"Lodge trip?"

"Yeah. Just, you know, bunch of guys getting together, doing guy stuff."

"And what kind of"—she paused—"'guy stuff' do you have planned this time around?"

He finally met her gaze and gave a defensive shrug.

"You know. Stuff. Just a bunch of guys hanging out at a hunting lodge, drinking beer and swapping stories. It's good for business: a lot of my contacts are lodge members. A lot of good prospects, too."

She didn't reply. He smiled, a nervous laugh bursting from his lips.

"C'mon, hon, it's how business gets done. You learn more on a golf course than you ever do in the boardroom. It's not like I'm having an affair or something. You...do know I'm not having an affair, right?"

She wasn't sure what bothered her more: that he probably was, or that she didn't really care anymore.

"Have fun with the boys," she said.

Then she retreated to her small room and considered the canvases. One she'd started last week. It called to her now, a sketch in charcoal. Three faceless figures, draped in flowing robes, danced around a black bonfire. No matter how she drew the lines, though, endlessly sketching and erasing and smudging with the heel of her hand, the dynamic of movement eluded her. The women were supposed to be wild, ecstatic, mad with dance and wine and freedom.

She knew what that had felt like, once. She just couldn't remember. And when she looked into her own heart there was nothing but a leaden gray stillness.

Nessa couldn't even remember what had inspired her to start working on the picture. She wasn't sure who the women were supposed to be. But they felt important. She picked up a charcoal pencil and tried again.

Four

A slate-black sky cast a shroud over Detroit. Full dark, new moon, no stars.

The Mourner didn't mind the dark, but she didn't care for the murky weather. Her home was west, in the arid desert deeps. She wore a gown of ivory white, a wide-brimmed hat, a lace veil, opera gloves. Her fingers were too long for her hands—too long for anyone's hands—and they wriggled bonelessly like worms as she glided down a back alleyway.

She stood at the heart of the alley, and her voice emerged from under her veil as a slithering hiss.

"By the pricking of my thumbs..."

"Do *not* finish that line," called down a voice from above.

Steel-toed boots rattled off rusted metal as a young woman jaunted down the fire escape. She wore an olive utility jacket over a worn chambray top. Her skin was dark, her eyes a faintly glowing brown, like flashlights shining behind a pair of stained-glass windows. She slid along the handrail for the last flight of stairs then jumped down the ladder, flipping her legs over a rung and dangling upside down in front of the Mourner. Her dreadlocks swayed like woven serpents.

"You're in my house now," she said. "Save the bullshit for that cave you live in."

"Dora," the Mourner said in an icy rasp. "Always a pleasure."

"If it was a pleasure, you'd come and visit more often. You've been hiding away from the world, sister. That's not good."

"It's not the world I hide from. The creature who once thought himself my master is on the move once more. The Kings of Man are machinating."

"*Ink*." The dangling woman turned her head and spat onto the concrete. "Yeah, that shit's been flooding the streets out here. Smells like magic, tastes like poison, and it's got the Kings' fingerprints all over it. You ever get a good look at an ink junkie?"

"They...vibrate in a disconcerting manner," the Mourner said.

"They *comply*. It's not like a heroin nod. Ink junkies forget how to ask questions. Whatever you tell 'em to do, they do it. They're open locks for whoever knocks. It's the motherfuckin' status quo in a syringe. You think that's why she called for a sit-down?"

"I suspect we'll learn anon. She never conjures without grave cause. Though I'm troubled by the implication."

Dora shot a questioning glance at her. "The implication?"

"The last time she summoned us," the Mourner replied, "this coven had *three* members."

A fog drifted in.

Cold tendrils of gossamer mist wound around them, carrying the peaty musk of graveyard soil and incense. Wild dogs brayed to the night, their howls rising over the purr of a motor.

"And yet, even with our strength diminished, we will be as we must," the Mourner said in a low whisper.

Dora looked to the alley mouth and murmured her reply. "Bloody, bold, and resolute."

The long shadow of a Rolls Royce limousine prowled into sight. The smoky-silver heirloom car stopped on a dime and its back door swung wide. The Lady in Red emerged.

She was a vision of a golden age, as sleek as her ride, draped in vintage scarlet. Her long, dark hair flowed behind her, kissed and braided by fingers of fog. Around her throat, dangling on a slender chain, she wore an antique iron key.

"How now?" asked the Mourner.

Even silent, the Lady carried traces of dark laughter in her eyes. Amusement and the promise of malice. Dora uncurled her legs from the fire-escape railing. She tumbled in midair and landed on her feet like a cat. The young woman crouched low for a moment, a subtle bow, before rising to her full height.

"Where we would revel in chaos and freedom," the Lady said, "our enemies would fetter every human soul in stagnation and rust. But I have seen portents, I have divined, and I know things. The table is set for a grand game. All the pieces are present. Would you like to play?"

"Speak," Dora said.

"Demand," the Mourner added.

Dora folded her arms and gave the Lady a hard nod. "We'll answer."

"After centuries of waiting," the Lady said, "my eldest daughter is here. Reborn on this world at last, and already hurtling toward her doom. She has no concept of who she really is, *what* she really is. And the wheel turns, as it always has."

"You wanna wake her up?" Dora asked.

"I want to break the wheel."

"Break the wheel," the Mourner echoed. "You speak of changing the fabric of the universe."

Dora broke into a grin. "She speaks of flipping some goddamn tables and whipping some moneylenders. *Finally.* I'm in."

The Lady favored her with a faint, cold smile and raised a finger.

"Patience. We can't afford a direct confrontation, not yet. We've endured this long by evading the eyes of the Kings and the courts of hell alike. We will begin with my eldest. We'll guide her from the shadows. Train her. Test her. Lead her to the crucible and toss her inside. If she survives, she'll be our finest weapon. Now then, a fledgling witch requires her tools."

"She'll need the powers of air and fire," the Mourner mused, "to evade, fly, and sear those who hound her. A Cutting Knife, then."

The Lady nodded. "There are four Cutting Knives in this world.

The man with the Cheshire smile has corrupted one to his service. *Adam* has corrupted another. The third is veiled from me. Now the fourth...that one might be reachable. It rests in the grip of a fool, but a well-guarded one, locked away."

The Mourner's veil rippled. "I have a key for that lock, one we've both made use of in the past. Faust owes me a debt. I will call upon him and collect."

Dora glanced sidelong at her. "Really? *Daniel* Faust? We're working with gangsters now?"

"Every witch has her favorite instruments. He's one of mine. And what of you, sister? What will you toss into the cauldron?"

"She can't fight and fly if she can't see or hear. She needs a witch's mirror, a *good* one." Dora snapped her fingers, turning to the Lady. "The Oberlin Glass. I've been keeping tabs on that beauty for a while now. I was going to make it a gift to you, but under the circumstances..."

"A gift to my daughter is a gift to me. Open her eyes. And as for my part, I'll buy sand for her hourglass. I'll send an ally to act as a stumbling block in her hunters' way." The Lady's gaze went distant, searching. "I know the name of every living witch, and I know the bones of the dead. Yes, she'll do. The agent. Harmony Black. She will serve as my champion in this matter."

"Her?" the Mourner said. "She's never bent the knee to you, never acknowledged you as her rightful queen. Why grant her the honor?"

The Lady chuckled. "She has lessons to learn. So I'll send her in the right direction with the wrong clue and a spur for her righteous pride. Standing at her shoulder, I will whisper honeyed words of poison into her ear, and she'll never know I was there. I'll employ her, punish her, and teach her, all at the same time."

"Damn." Dora arched an eyebrow. "You're hard on your kids, you know that?"

"You turned out all right."

"True," Dora said.

"You have your tasks." The Lady flung up her hand, pale fingers curling as if to snatch the blackened sky. "I am for the air. Scurry and scatter, both of you."

"When shall we three meet again?" the Mourner asked.

"Before the battle's won," the Lady said, "in a storm of our own brewing. I will provide the lightning."

"I'll bring the thunder," Dora said.

The Mourner turned her gloved hands. Her long, boneless fingers squirmed.

"It will rain in the desert before our work is complete," she hissed, "and the noonday sun will hide its face from our deeds."

"As it should," the Lady replied.

Five

In the borough of Queens, as the sun dipped low and Astoria's bars lit up neon blue and white, Marie sat on the edge of a cheap Ikea futon and huddled over her overheating laptop. Home was a cramped apartment in a second-floor walk-up over a convenience store, the bars of a cherry-red fire escape looming outside her narrow window. The building's decor hadn't been updated since the 1950s, all exposed brick and vintage nickel, though somewhere along the way "old and outdated" had magically transformed into "warehouse bohemian chic." Same apartment, five times the rent.

Marie was lost in the screen, hunting down property records, pecking through databases. On the opposite side of the futon, her roommate Janine had her head buried in *The Mycroft Encyclopedia of Heraldry, Seventh Edition*—a hardbound beast of a book that could double as the world's biggest doorstop.

"Don't drop that thing," Marie muttered. "You'll break your foot."

"The sacrifices we make for proper historical recreation." Janine lay back on the futon and sighed dramatically, stretching in her fluffy argyle sweater. "So when are you finally going to come to an SCA meet-up with me? The kingdom has need of bold warriors, Lady Knight."

Marie tapped at the keyboard. There it was: the kill house outside Monticello, with a listing for the owner. *Roth Estate Holdings*, registered with a Manhattan address.

"Not my bag," she said.

Janine tilted her head. "Like heck it isn't. You've had your knighthood...thing for as long as I've known you. You're seriously going to pass up the chance to wear real armor and lug a sword around?"

Marie fumbled for words, trying to explain. While she talked, the screen flooded with listings of other Roth properties. Almost all of them in NYC, mostly in parts of town where she couldn't afford to breathe the air.

"If it wasn't the right liege, if it wasn't the right cause, it wouldn't be real." Marie glanced over at Janine. "This is normally the point where I'd hold up my badge and say I've already found my liege to serve, but they took that. So."

Janine closed her book, watching her. "Yeah. So...you okay? I mean, I saw the news before you got home. Sounded pretty nasty."

Nastier than that, Marie thought. As far as she knew, the news had only talked about a couple of cops coming under fire. The drug stash and the tortured corpse in the basement were still officially under wraps, pending investigation. Nothing she needed to tell Janine about. She changed the subject with a nod at her roommate's book.

"Isn't that a reference copy?"

"Perks of the job." Janine hugged the enormous book to her chest. "Librarians can take home reference books any time they want."

"I'm pretty sure they can't."

"It's a secret librarian rule. You wouldn't know. Seriously, are you okay?"

Marie's phone buzzed against her hip. She pulled it out, shooting Janine a look.

"Tabling discussion of your petty larceny for a later date." She thumbed the screen and put the phone to her ear. "Reinhart."

"Detective," said the woman on the other end, her aged voice tinged with a faint Irish brogue, "it's April Cassidy. Is this a bad time?"

Marie was on her feet in an instant, cupping her hand over the phone as she moved to her bedroom door.

"Not at all, Doctor. Thanks for calling me back."

"It's my pleasure. I had a chance to look over those reports you sent me."

Cassidy had been a founding member of the FBI's Behavioral Analysis Unit, a Bureau superstar—at least until a killer with an ax put her in a wheelchair. She'd been in private practice ever since. Reaching out to her had been a long shot. Marie had been surprised April even answered her first e-mail, let alone offered to help.

"That means a lot to me. I tried getting the BAU involved, but—"

"But your superiors are loath to speak the dread words 'serial murderer' within earshot of the press, knowing the firestorm they'll invite. And kowtowing to federal agents is no one's idea of fun." April chuckled lightly. "I assure you, Detective, I'm very familiar with your plight. I'm happy to do what I can to help, though I wish I had better news for you."

Marie shut the door behind her. Her room was barely bigger than her single bed, with a razor-thin closet and a low bookcase stuffed with paperbacks. A European longsword, dull-bladed and bought off the Home Shopping Network after a night of too much chardonnay, hung on one wall. On the other, a print from the cover of her favorite novel: a woman in polished green steel sitting astride a warhorse, a long spear dangling in her grip as shadows drooped toward a hulking, shapeless behemoth on the horizon's edge.

"What's your take on the case?" Marie asked.

"Well, I concur. You're dealing with a single perpetrator in all three crimes. Possibly all four, assuming the latest abduction is related, and there's ample reason to think so. I believe you're looking for a sociopath. He'll be narcissistic, superficially charming, and have access to money and a secure vehicle. Likely, he'll have some form of an Axis Two antisocial personality disorder."

"Antisocial? Didn't you just say he was charming?"

"It doesn't have the same meaning in a psychological context.

People with specific Axis Two disorders have a damaged sense of empathy for other human beings. Antisocial, in that sense, means an inability to be socially integrated. They tend to have a grandiose sense of their importance and treat everyone else as a means to their own ends. Often they're married and may have children, but their spouses and offspring are just props to create a facade. He likely greeted his victims with a winning smile and they had no idea what they were dealing with."

Marie shook her head. "I've talked to the girls the victims worked with, out on the street. Spend enough time on the stroll and they can sniff out a weirdo or a cop from three blocks away. None of the victims were careless, at least that's what their friends told me."

"Suggesting he takes his time and builds rapport. I think they knew him, Detective. He likely visits them a few times, building their trust, becoming a regular. When he finally convinced them to bend from their comfort zones, he'd done half the work already. Once he got them to an unfamiliar location, one under his control, he could force their compliance."

A repeat customer. Marie's thoughts jumped to Eddie Li.

"What about the holding period?" Marie asked. "Why doesn't he kill them right away?"

"I believe you're dealing with a power motivation. He wants something from these women. Perhaps he frames it as love, or affection, or even worship, but ultimately it comes down to the same thing: he has a deep-seated insecurity complex and craves validation."

"Which they don't give him."

"Precisely," April said. "They probably play along once they realize they're in the hands of a killer, but eventually they'll say the wrong thing or try to escape. Then he feels lied to. Betrayed. And he retaliates."

Marie didn't have to look at the photographs anymore. Each crime scene was seared onto the backs of her eyelids. Bodies in garbage cans, chopped like mincemeat. Savaged.

"Hence the overkill," she said.

"An explosion of bottled-up rage. After the kill, he'll be pacified, probably even remorseful...for a little while. But then the urge returns. He'll need a relatively secure place to hold these women, again pointing toward affluence. If he's single, he'll keep them in his home, probably a basement. If he has a family, he's holding them somewhere remote. A rented storage unit, perhaps."

"Or a house out in the sticks."

"Or that. I heard about an altercation on the news. Is it reasonable to assume you were involved?"

"That was me, yeah."

"And the gunman?" April asked. "Your perpetrator?"

"Two gunmen, and no." Marie took a deep breath. She sat down on the edge of her bed, curling her free hand into a frustrated fist. "I think they're connected somehow, but...no. My guy is still out there. And he's still holding on to victim number four. Doctor, these freaks, do they ever team up?"

"How do you mean?"

Marie didn't answer right away. She was breaching all kinds of protocol just by talking to April, let alone laying her last card on the table. She did it anyway.

"It's not public yet, but there was a body in that house. A man, tortured to death with surgical instruments. The house is connected to my perp somehow, but that's not his kind of victim and that's not how he kills. Do serial killers ever, you know, get together? Cover for each other?"

"Not in my experience," April said. "While cases of collaboration do exist, it's almost always a dominant partner being assisted by a weaker, bullied one. They share the dominant killer's victim preference and killing style. I've only seen one exception to that rule, and it was a...special circumstance."

"Which was?"

"A cult," April said. "But cult killings are rarely directed against outsiders. They tend to transgress against people they've already isolated and cut off from their families. Easier prey."

Maybe it was street experience, maybe intuition, but Marie's instincts were tingling.

"All the victims in this case are street-level sex workers. Isn't that just as easy? I mean, they're already alienated and isolated by their profession."

"It's possible," April said. "Stick a pin in that theory. But everything you've shown me suggests this string of killings has one perpetrator in common."

Marie rested her chin on her curled knuckles. "Then I'm back at square one."

"You're fighting the good fight, Detective. Don't give up."

Marie swallowed a bitter laugh as she hung up the phone. Giving up was the last thing on her mind. Good fight or not, though, she couldn't box a phantom. And until she found a better lead, that was exactly what she was doing: standing alone in the ring, throwing mad punches at her own shadow.

She had a rainy-day bottle of Glenlivet stashed over the kitchen sink, and Janine was game to share it with her. Her mind was racing too fast for sleep, but two shots of scotch—then another two, and one more for the road—helped to ease her down.

She dreamed about Baby Blue. Standing on the edge of a dark country road, her thumb held out for a ride. Waiting.

*   *   *

The first ray of sunrise glinted off the cherry fire escape, sending a slow finger of dusty light across the apartment floor. Marie was back on the futon, back on the hunt, poring through the real estate listings again.

"It doesn't make sense," she muttered.

Janine trudged across the room with an electric toothbrush jammed in her mouth. Cartoon cats batted a ball of yarn across the front of her pink nightshirt. She glanced Marie's way, mumbling what sounded like a question around the whirring brush.

"Roth Estate Holdings," Marie said. "Their entire portfolio is high-end property. Mostly rentals, a few outright sales, but it's all really expensive stuff. Except for this one plot. Why does a company that makes bank selling midtown Manhattan condos to the rich and famous own a condemned house on a shitty little scrap of woodland outside Monticello?"

Janine leaned over the kitchen sink and spat toothpaste. She fumbled for a smudged glass and squinted, bleary-eyed, as she filled it with tap water.

"The real question is, how much did we drink last night, and how are you this awake right now?"

"That's two questions. A, we finished the bottle, and B, I've got work to do."

Janine leaned back against the kitchen nook's tiny counter. "No, I have work to do. You have a four-day mandatory vacation. Why are you even out of bed?"

"Clock's ticking." Marie shut the laptop and set it on the futon beside her. "I'm heading out. Don't wait up."

"You know you don't have a badge at the moment, right?" The front door jangled in Marie's wake, rattling on old hinges. "Or a gun? These are important things to have, Mar—you know what? Never mind. Just don't do anything stupid, okay? Rent's due next Tuesday."

Six

Marie strode through the precinct house like she belonged there. Just another day at the office, metal-bladed ceiling fans pushing sluggish air around and humming over the din of ringing phone, with too many people crammed into the bullpen and not enough desks. A row of hard-eyed kids sat cuffed on a wooden bench, waiting their turn for processing. Marie skirted past her own desk, a fat metal brick from the seventies with a swivel chair that drooped on one broken wheel. She poked her head into the break room.

Helena Gorski ran her fingers through her razor-cut hair and swore a blue streak under her breath. The light inside the snack machine flickered as the dented casing met the wrath of her steel-toed boot.

"Swear to God, if they don't fix this—" She paused, glancing toward the doorway. "Reinhart? The hell are you doing here?"

"Looking for you. Any idea who caught the Monticello case?"

"Yeah. Monticello PD. News flash: not our jurisdiction. I have been assigned as a courtesy liaison though, so thanks for that. I needed more work on my plate this week."

Marie stepped into the break room, shooting a quick look over her shoulder.

"So they're not connecting it to my case?"

"On what grounds? You've got a john who says one missing hooker—who you haven't connected to the *other* dead hookers—*might* have been at that house, *once*. They're a little more concerned about the corpse in the basement and, oh yeah, the boxes and boxes of drugs. Hell, we've been trying to find the ink pipeline for months. Everybody's dealing it, but nobody's got a name."

"Have they got an ID on anybody yet?"

Helena fed a dollar bill into the machine. It sucked it down halfway, sputtered, and spat it out again. She yanked it out and smoothed it between her fingers.

"Son of a—no, not yet, not the vic or the two shooters. House full of ghosts."

"What about the owner? This 'Roth Estate Holdings,' anybody looking at them?"

"Me," Helena said, "since they're a local outfit and the Monticello boys don't want to drive two hours to check it out. It's a dead end, anyway. Roth called *us*, about an hour after the shooting hit the news. Super happy to volunteer any help they can give us, long as we keep their name out of the press. According to the company, that property's been abandoned for years. The shooters weren't tenants, they were squatters. Company's owner is a guy named Richard Roth. I'm supposed to drop by and take a look at his records just to follow up and dot the *i* for the final report. You know, in my copious free time."

A shadow loomed at Marie's shoulder.

"Reinhart?" Captain Traynor asked. "Was there some confusion about the concept of 'administrative leave'?"

Marie spun on her heel, fumbling for an excuse. "Just...picking up some paperwork from my desk, sir."

He spread his hands. "This doesn't look like your desk."

The vending machine finally swallowed Helena's dollar. Behind the scratched Plexiglas, a bag of corn chips slowly edged toward the brink—then hung there, refusing to drop. The plastic rattled under Helena's bare-knuckled punch.

"Oh, you evil *bitch*—"

"Gorski," Traynor said, "stop assaulting the vending machine and get out there. I need everybody's ears for a minute. Reinhart, grab whatever you came for and *go home*. I don't want to see your face around here until I call you and tell you otherwise, understood?"

Marie started to reply but he was already gone, cutting waves through the crowded bullpen. She drifted in his wake and stood on the edge of the crowd next to Helena, watching as Traynor called for attention. The room fell into a curious hush.

"Listen up," he said. "By now, you've all heard about the bust up in Monticello. Most of you didn't wear a badge in the eighties—hell, half of you are too young to remember the eighties—but I was here. I saw what crack cocaine did to New York, firsthand. And this 'ink' shit is spreading even faster. We're not letting it happen again. Not here. Not in our city."

He walked to a corkboard. His knuckles rapped dead, pale faces, photographs of the shooters' corpses.

"Finding a link to the distribution pipeline is the biggest break we've had yet. I want an ID on these guys, and I want it yesterday. I want to know who they worked for, where they came from, who they supplied, and who was supplying *them*. Talk to your CIs. Squeeze 'em until they pop, if you have to. *Somebody* knows *something*."

Marie leaned close to Helena, murmuring soft. "You want to shut the ink pipeline down? Make a major bust or two?"

"Getting hard just thinking about it, metaphorically speaking."

"Let me take some weight off your shoulders, then. I'll talk to Richard Roth for you."

Helena gave her the side-eye. "You're on admin leave. And it's a waste of time, the guy's clean. Why stick your neck out for nothing?"

"Nobody has to know." Marie nodded back over her shoulder. "We'll keep it between you, me, and the vending machine."

Helena thought about it, but not for long.

"Anybody finds out about this," she said, "I had no idea. It's all on you."

Marie clapped her back and gave it a hard rub.

"Your hands are clean. Go get 'em, tiger."

*   *   *

"You want to do *what?*" Tony shouted. Marie had to pull the phone away from her ear. She stood on the hot sidewalk, pacing, a gust of wind ruffling her already-unkempt mop of hair.

"I want to take a run at the owner. It doesn't make sense, Tony. There's no reason Roth Estate Holdings even owned that land in the first place. The puzzle piece doesn't fit."

"Maybe you forgot, but we're on leave. No badges. No authority. And also it's *not our case.*"

"It's all connected," Marie said. "It has to be. Baby Blue was at that house. Those psychos had *something* to do with our perp."

"And you want to go after the guy who runs the real-estate company that owns the house. Who already said the place was supposed to be empty. And the only thread connecting any of this is Eddie Li—not exactly a model citizen himself—saying he *thinks* the vic was going to a sex party at that address, because he was stalking her. Are you hearing yourself right now? You realize how flimsy this is?"

Marie froze on the sidewalk. She took a deep breath, trying to steady herself.

"It's all I've got, okay? There aren't any other leads. Just...just this one thing, this one piece that doesn't fit. I've got to check it out."

"You realize how much shit we could land in if anybody finds out we were working a case while we're supposed to be on leave? People lose their jobs for less than this, Marie."

"This guy keeps his victims for two weeks before he kills and dumps them. Two weeks, at best. She's running out of time." Marie shook her head. "I'm going to talk to Richard Roth. You don't have to come, and I don't blame you if you say no. But I'm going."

A long silence. On the other end of the line, Tony let out an exasperated sigh.

"Fine. I'm in."

"I was hoping you'd say that," Marie told him. "I'm standing outside your building."

On the third floor, a curtain ruffled aside. Tony squinted into the hard morning light. From the sidewalk below, Marie looked up and curled her fingers in an awkward wave.

* * *

Their unmarked car was totaled and they couldn't requisition a new one until they'd been cleared for duty. So they hoofed it the civilian way: a crosstown train, then a city bus, making their way to the West Village. A quick call to Helena confirmed the address. Tony whistled low and stared up at the brownstone.

"Swank digs," he said. "I could afford about one square foot of this place."

"Sure." Marie stepped forward and rang the doorbell. "But the taxes would kill you."

A woman in her fifties, dressed in a demure maid's uniform, answered the door. Marie gave her a confident smile, inwardly praying she didn't ask to see their badges.

"Good afternoon, ma'am. Detectives Reinhart and Fisher, here to see Mr. Roth. I believe our colleague, Detective Gorski, called ahead?"

She ushered them inside, under the shadow of a crystal chandelier, down a hallway with floor planks stained mahogany-dark, and into a cold, austere dining room with a long glass table. They didn't have to wait very long. Richard Roth swept through the wide and open archway with a fat binder under one arm of his tailored blazer. He sported pristine teeth, a four-hundred-dollar haircut, and the kind of rugged physique only earned from putting in serious time at the gym with a personal trainer.

"Detectives, hey, hello," he said, setting his binder on the table and pumping their hands. His handshake was too hard, calculated to be too hard, laying down his alpha-male credentials right up front. Marie put her irritation aside and tried to study him unemotionally, like a scientist peering at a particularly interesting sample of fungus.

"Thank you for seeing us," she told him. "Obviously, we don't believe your company has any connection to the shooting incident at the property, but we're still trying to identify the men involved. Any information you can share would be very helpful."

Roth opened the binder. He flipped through page after page of eight-point type, flicking color-coded plastic tabs.

"Of course, happy to help. Unfortunately, as I told the other detective on the phone, that property was supposed to be vacant. We've had it for so long that the original paperwork is, well, *paper*. We've moved almost everything over to digital, but to be honest, keeping tabs on that particular lot isn't exactly a high priority."

"It doesn't seem to match up with the rest of your company's holdings," Marie observed, keeping her voice carefully neutral.

"It really doesn't, no. Reason is, and I'm a little embarrassed to say this, it was one of my first purchases when I inherited this company from my father. I was being a 'radical visionary,'" Richard said, hooking his fingers in the air, "and I was convinced I could buy some random lot in the middle of nowhere and flip it for a massive profit. Because I was a genius who knew everything, and also twenty-two years old. Which is basically the same thing."

"And it never sold?" Tony asked.

Richard laughed. "Have you *seen* it? Last time I set foot on that property was ten years ago, and it was a weed-infested eyesore then. Can't imagine what it looks like today. Hard to get to, lousy access road…once I finally got over myself, I mentally wrote the place off as a loss and forgot about it. Until yesterday, anyhow. Ah, here we go."

He waved them close, letting them read over his shoulder as he ran his finger down the cramped margins of a ledger.

"See, here's the original deed of transfer. Now, if I'd ever rented the property out, there would be follow-up information right here. In this big empty spot." He put his hands on his hips and shook his head at the book. "Ah, the follies of youth. Say, could I ask you a question?"

"Sure," Tony said.

"If I heard the news right, the squatters in the house opened fire when a pair of officers came onto the property. Why were the police there in the first place? Was there some kind of complaint?"

Something about Richard's routine had rubbed Marie the wrong way from square one, and it wasn't just the vise-grip handshake. Every word out of his mouth, as he showed them pages in a dead ledger, felt like stage patter. Rehearsed to a T, right up to the question he'd obviously been waiting to ask. While he looked at Tony, Marie slipped a photograph from her wallet.

"Her," she said.

When Richard turned around, he was staring right at Baby Blue. His smooth facade shattered like a wall of glass. It was only a heartbeat, just an instant, but he looked at the picture like a man caught with a bloody knife and a corpse at his feet. Then he blinked and the mask was firmly back in place, nothing but a trick of the light.

"I'm sorry," he said, "who?"

"A sex worker who goes by the street name Baby Blue," Marie told him. "She's gone missing. A confidential informant suggested she'd visited the property."

Richard pressed his palm to his forehead. "You're telling me people were bringing *prostitutes* out there? God, that's all I need, more bad press. You have to believe me, detectives, I can't tell you how much I wish I'd been paying someone to check up on the place. It was just a case of 'out of sight, out of mind.' I never imagined something like this could happen."

She almost believed him. He had slick moves and better lines than a used-car salesman, but nothing could conceal that first moment when Richard laid eyes on the photograph. She knew that look. She'd seen it on a hundred suspects' faces.

He had recognized her.

"Oh," said a woman's voice from the open archway. "You have company."

"Just the police, asking about the lot in Monticello," Richard said. "Detectives, this is my wife, Vanessa."

Marie glanced at the door. And then it was her turn to shatter.

Seven

For a moment, there was no one else in the room. Just Marie and Nessa, meeting each other's eyes across seven feet of mahogany floor. The others faded, the house faded, the world faded, swallowed by the swell of a string quartet. They stood on the edge of a mid-1600s ballroom, French, or maybe Spanish. It was white marble and gilded, the other dancers slow-spiraling shadows beneath murky golden light.

Ask her to dance, Marie thought. *Your entire life, this is the moment you've been waiting for.*

"Marie?"

Tony's voice jolted her from her reverie. The world slammed back into place, hard-edged and mundane, and Marie blinked, realizing she'd been staring. Nessa stared back. Her lips were slightly parted, a faint blush coloring her high cheekbones.

"I'm Marie," she said, then paused. "Detective. Marie Reinhart. Detective Reinhart. Good to meet you."

"Delighted," Nessa said. She looked like she was about to say something else, then fell silent.

"Are you...involved with your husband's company, Mrs. Roth?"

"No, I'm a professor at Barnard College. Anthropology."

"Fascinating field."

Nessa quirked a lopsided smile. Her blush, standing out on her pale skin, deepened a shade.

"I think so, but...not as exciting as your job, I'm sure."

Richard's gaze swung between the two women. His brow furrowed.

"At any rate, detectives, that's all the information I have for you. I'm sorry I couldn't be more helpful."

Tony stepped between Marie and Nessa, breaking their line of sight as he held out his hand to Richard.

"You were very helpful, Mr. Roth, thank you. We appreciate your time."

Richard slapped the binder shut and pumped Tony's hand. "Of course. Now, if you'll excuse me, I have a business trip to get ready for. If you need anything else, I'll be back in town in a couple of days. Feel free to leave a message and I'll get back to you as soon as I'm able."

Marie leaned around Tony's shoulder. Nessa stood on the other side of the open archway, her body half-concealed behind the wall. Light glinted off her oversized glasses as she slowly tilted her head to one side, peering at Marie, her lopsided smile growing. Then she disappeared. Soft footfalls echoed as she padded up the hallway.

"We'll do that," Tony said. "Detective Reinhart and I will—Detective?"

"Right," Marie said. "We'll be in touch."

Out on the front walk, the cold silence of the Roths' house swept away by the sounds of the city, Tony squinted at her.

"So what was that, anyway?"

Marie curled her arms over her chest, walking briskly. He scrambled to keep up.

"What was what?"

"*That,*" Tony said, jerking his thumb over his shoulder. "You and Roth's wife. Did you know her?"

Yes, she wanted to tell him, even though it wasn't true.

"No. Never seen her before."

"You weren't acting like it."

"How was I acting?"

Tony frowned. He skirted past a couple of slow-walking tourists. "I don't know," he said. "Weird."

"I haven't slept and I might be a little hungover," Marie said, searching for an excuse. Though she felt fine. Better than fine. "I'm probably not myself today."

"You've been saying that a lot lately. I don't want to tell you your business, but...maybe it's time you talked to somebody? I mean, you know, a professional? You don't wanna be self-medicating with a bottle. Cops have higher rates of alcoholism as it is, and I'm not even getting into the health risks—"

Marie threw up her hands. "Don't get Mormon on me right now, okay? I can't *have* you getting Mormon on me today."

Tony laughed. "Hey, I'm not pushing the religion, just the health benefits. No booze, no caffeine, my body is a *temple*."

"Yeah? When you took that waitress home last Friday night, did you show her around your temple?"

"Touché. Hey, slow down. Let me rap at you for a second."

They stood at the edge of the street beside a pair of battered newspaper boxes, out of the flow of foot traffic. Marie fidgeted, uncomfortable standing still.

"Real talk now," Tony said. "We had a lead, we checked into it, it didn't pan out. You gonna let this go and get some rest? I'm worried about you."

"I'm not sure we came up empty-handed. Roth reacted when I showed him that photograph. He recovered quick, but it startled him. I think he recognized her."

"Maybe he was startled because you jammed it in his face. You sure you saw what you think you saw? I mean, you just told me ten seconds ago that you're not you today. And considering how you were staring at the man's wife, I'm inclined to believe you."

"It's worth following up."

"How? Right now, we're safe. We made a routine appointment, had a nice talk, he did his civic duty, and he's got no reason to think twice about it. We're clean. You start stalking the man, all it takes is one phone call to the captain and we are *busted*. Leave Richard Roth alone, okay? It's not just your job on the line: it's mine, too."

Marie's gaze dropped to the sidewalk. Her shoulders slumped.

"Okay."

"Thank you." He squeezed her shoulder. "Go home. Get some rest."

He left her at the top of the subway stairs, getting lost in the crowd and disappearing beneath the city streets. Marie stood off to the side, uncertain, wondering if she could gin up an excuse to go back to the Roth house. Say she forgot something, dropped a pen on her way out. A pen? No. She was being ridiculous and she knew it. Still, as she waited at the bus stop and long streaks of wispy cloud grasped like straining fingers across the late afternoon sky, her head was filled with a vision of a dance that never happened. A dress she'd never worn, a room she'd never seen, and a woman she'd never met before today.

All the same, it felt like a memory.

*   *   *

Nessa sat cross-legged in her workroom, surrounded by canvases, her bestiary of half-finished grotesques. The black book—*her* book—lay open on her lap. She'd found it four years ago in a SoHo used bookstore, the last bits of worn-away gilt on the cover glinting as it poked out from a random stack of mismatched hardcovers. The gilt had caught the dim lighting just right, a lighthouse beacon flashing in her eye, like it had been positioned just for her. The title, *Games for the Cunning*, all but demanded she pick it up and take a closer look.

It taught her games, all right.

There were games to hear whispers in empty rooms and see fleeting faces in vacant mirrors. She learned games involving poppets made with twists of burlap and black iron nails and a splash of menstrual blood. Games involving jars filled with rusty razor blades and spittle, buried in just the right place. Sometimes her little tricks worked; often they didn't. Witchcraft was an art, not a science. But she could feel herself growing stronger, more capable. Every session with the book lured her closer to understanding. Then she ran headlong at the "Game of Finding a Guide" and hit a brick wall. Four times she'd taken her book and her offerings to Inwood Hill Park, and four times she'd failed miserably.

She couldn't skip ahead. Past that chapter, the second half of the book was gibberish. A cipher, all squiggly lines and uneven curves, glyphs in an alien tongue. *To the true witch*, read the final English words, *the means to understand are given. Once you have found your Guide, all will be made apparent.*

Maybe she wasn't a failure after all. *Something* had happened. Something had leaped between her and that detective, Reinhart, like a spark from the blue. Something that tasted like an impossible memory and a connection she couldn't begin to define.

Magic.

Nessa stifled a giggle as she flipped through the pages, looking for insight. Her heart was pattering, her head light. She wanted to run outside, track Marie down and talk to her for hours. *About anything*, she thought, *just to hear her voice again. What is this? I haven't felt this giddy since I was a teenager. What does it mean?*

A knock on the door jarred her from her thoughts. Richard poked his head into the workroom. She slammed the book shut and held it tight on her lap.

"Hey, hon. Uh, weird question. That cop, the woman, did you know her or something?"

"I don't believe so," Nessa told him.

He squinted at her. "Okay."

She stared back at him, silent.

"Oh, once I come home from my trip, we're hosting a party here at the house. Dad's flying in from DC and wants to do a meet-and-greet with some local boosters, so don't make any plans for that night." He paused, squinting at her again. "Are you putting on a little weight?"

"No."

"Well...just, maybe stick to salads for the next couple of days, okay?" He grinned and cocked finger guns at her. "If we don't look good, Dad doesn't look good, right?"

Nessa bared her teeth in the faintest imitation of a smile.

Once he finally left, she stole into the kitchen and came back with a ceramic bowl, half-filled with water. She set it down before her, with the book to her left, and killed the overhead light. She struck a match. The wick of a black candle sizzled to life, and she read aloud by the murky light, the instructions for "A Game for Conjuring Distant Sights" laid out beside her.

"By Cthonia," she whispered, "I call to my own concealed desires, my deepest currents. By Phosphoros, I call upon the majesty of illumination. Reveal unto me what I seek. Reveal unto me the truth. By Kleidoukhos, unlock wisdom, and I will learn."

She chanted, the words slow, serpentine, as she dripped calligraphy ink into the bowl from a slender vial. The midnight-blue droplets hit the water, spattered, and spread, turning it into a lapis mirror. Nessa saw the curves of her own face reflected like a shadow in the dark. As she chanted and stared, and fell into a waking trance, her image dissolved and vanished. She saw new things in the water now. Images floated in the haze, some like people, like distant buildings, like the curve of a farmer's sickle. This was as far as this spell had ever taken her, vague impressions that might have been simple tricks of the candlelight.

"Marie Reinhart," she heard her own voice whisper, unbidden. "Show me."

The ripples of ink turned to a gentle blanket of snow. A shadow play unfolded. A horse-drawn cart, rattling across a vast and trackless tundra. Two figures riding side by side. The cart filled the bowl, turning the water black, and then the vista changed. Now the outline of a woman in a flowing dress stood alone in the cold flurries. Behind her back, she cradled a long-handled knife.

A taller silhouette approached her. The second woman stood before the first and then gracefully knelt down in the drifting snow.

Static crackled in Nessa's ears. It was the sound of a distant radio trapped between stations. Snatches of syllables, words spoken over each other. This wasn't supposed to happen. The ink-scrying spell had always shown pictures, never sounds. Nessa leaned closer to the bowl. Her eyes widened behind her rounded glasses.

"*Hedy*," she heard a woman's voice—a voice almost like hers—say, "*hold the book.*"

The image in the bowl wavered and melted, coalescing in the shape of a lidless eye.

"*My name is Ness*—" A burst of static. A garbled shout. "*Not sure how this—but if you're receiving—*"

Streamers of black light twisted around the eye, faster and faster, sparkling in the dark. A squeal rose at the edges of Nessa's hearing, louder by the second, strident as a war horn.

"*Listen and understand,*" the voice said. "*You are in terrible da—*"

The candle blew out.

No wind, not even a draft, but the light died as suddenly as the impossible sound. Nessa slumped forward as an electric wave passed through her body, a jolting shock that stole her breath. The spell shattered, the moment gone.

She sat there alone, in darkness and in silence, perplexed.

Eight

Marie caught up with Helena Gorski at 5th Avenue and East 86th Street, right on the edge of Central Park. The price of Helena's company was an early dinner from one of the roving food carts that lined the sidewalk. Helena's partner, Jefferson, double-fisted his. The portly detective clutched a steaming taco in each hand, the grilled flour shells nestled in beds of aluminum foil.

"I'm not asking for much," Marie said. She tilted her head to bite into her taco. A pepper burst between her teeth, washing over the flavor of spiced meat and queso fresco.

"Not asking for much," Helena echoed. She jerked her thumb at Marie. "You believe this?"

Jefferson chewed fast, swallowing, and shook his head. "C'mon, Marie. Roth is a dead end."

"He's not right. Something about him isn't right, and I don't buy his explanation for the house in Monticello."

"Sounds pretty solid to me," Jefferson said. "Besides, of course he ain't right. Guy's a real-estate big shot. He's probably cheating on his taxes, his partners, his wife, and possibly, just possibly, not going to church every Sunday. None of which makes the guy a killer or a drug dealer."

"I'm just asking you to take a run at him. It's your case—"

"Correction," Helena said. "It's Monticello's case. We're just playing liaison. And we're all a little more focused on the drug stash and the murder victim. You're on leave, Marie. Go home. Get some rest. You're not doing yourself any good like this."

They walked along a sea of hexagonal paving stones between the woods of Central Park and the rows of cars on 5th Avenue. The traffic grew thicker as the shadows grew long, congealing like syrup in the city's arteries.

"Do you have any *better* leads?" Marie asked them.

"Nothing you need to worry about," Helena said. "It's not your case."

Marie honed in on the stress in her voice. "You do. What? You identify the shooters?"

"No."

Jefferson smiled with pride. "I IDed the torture vic, though."

Helena slapped him across the shoulder, giving him a glare that could melt steel. Marie got in front of him and stopped him in his tracks.

"Dish. Who is he?"

"Jefferson," Helena said, "swear to God—"

"Errand boy for the Five Families. Small-time scumbag, occasional messenger." Jefferson held one of his tacos like a gun, firing off an imaginary round. "Occasionally, messages written in lead. Or delivered with a baseball bat. Guy was a five-time loser, spent more time inside Rikers than out of it."

Helena leaned in on him. "Do you *want* to get us in trouble with IAB? Because this shit is exactly how you do that."

Marie ignored her. She tapped her wrist. "What about the tattoo? That didn't look like a Mafia thing."

"No idea." Jefferson finished scarfing down a taco. He crumpled the foil into a ball and pitched it into a waste bin on the corner. "Ran it by Gang Crimes, but they didn't have a match in their system. He probably just thought it looked cool."

"Working theory is that the mob is running the ink pipeline," Marie said. "They killed one of their own guys? Why?"

"Well, if you ask me—"

"*Nobody* fucking asked you," Helena said, "because we're not here and we're not having this conversation. Marie, *go home*. You can put your career on the line if you want, but don't drag us down with you."

She grabbed Jefferson by the sleeve of his twill jacket and gave it a hard yank, pulling him past Marie. As they walked away, leaving her behind, Marie caught the words Helena fired at her partner in a low hiss.

"Don't encourage her," Helena muttered. "Everybody knows she's fucked in the head."

Marie stood by the trash can, her half-eaten dinner getting cold in her hand. A gust of wind kicked across the street, carrying the smell of truck exhaust and smoke, ruffling her ragged hair. She forced herself to put on a smile and pretend that nothing could hurt her. Then she went home.

*   *   *

"You sure the sound isn't bothering you? I can put on headphones."

Marie and Janine sat on opposite ends of the futon, each of them engrossed in their laptop screens. Janine was streaming a sitcom, but the words and the laugh track barely registered in Marie's consciousness. She was a million miles away, staring at the vast white plain of her word processor and the expectant blink of a waiting cursor. Pecking slowly at the keys, she typed: *Baby Blue, Revised Timeline. 1. Eddie Li is last confirmed customer. Says she refused money to stay the night, scheduled for sex party at house in Monticello. Per Li, her pimp was unaware.*

"It's fine," she told Janine.

"Whatcha working on?"

"Just...trying to get some things straight," she said. "I'm missing something here, I know it."

She typed: *2, per initial interview with pimp, she stopped answering his texts. Waited 48 hrs, filed missing-persons report.*

"Did you see that therapist, so you can go back on duty?"

"I put it off," Marie said. "Couple of days, I'll get around to it. Doesn't matter until Internal Affairs clears me anyway."

Janine curled her lip, biting at the corner of her mouth as she looked at Marie.

"Yeah, but...I mean, I know you have to go, but maybe...you might *want* to? I mean, it could help. Having somebody to talk to."

"I've got you. And Tony."

"Yeah, but...a professional."

Marie kept typing. *3, Baby Blue was indigent, living at transient hotel, paid cash. Search of her room turned up $20 in small bills, no other known resources.*

"I'm just saying," Janine said, "you've got some stuff to work through."

Marie didn't look up. The crisp black Courier font hovered in front of her, the letters becoming a labyrinth.

"I defended myself in the line of duty. It happens. I'm not *happy* about it, but they opened fire on us. It was either him or me and Tony. I'm fine."

"That's not the stuff I mean."

Now Marie looked at her.

"I don't talk about that. Ever."

"I know," Janine said. "I think you need to."

For one shaky heartbeat, Marie's world went sideways. And she was gone.

Hiding under her bed, hands clamped over her head, looking at the open doorway. Feet, dirty shoes, tromping past. From downstairs, her mother's scream.

"Where the fuck is it?" shouted a man with a guttural voice.

"I don't know," her father groaned. "I don't know who you think we are—"

"Do you want me to start cutting on this bitch? Is that what you want?"

Marie squeezed her eyes shut. She took a deep breath. One hand patted the futon, patted the loose keys of her laptop, reminding herself. *I'm here now.* She got up and strode to the kitchen nook and ripped through the cabinets. Glasses clanked as she shoved them aside, slamming drawers shut.

"Where the fuck is the Glenlivet?"

"We drank it last night," Janine said. "Remember?"

Marie froze. She blinked. Then she walked back over, dropped down, and slumped on the futon.

"Yeah."

Janine stared at her, silent.

"What?" Marie said.

"I'm worried."

"About what?"

Marie picked up the laptop and typed, *4. Sex parties for big $$ on the side? No evidence, no money. So, a lie, or was that her first time, first trip to house in Monticello?*

"You've done this as long as I've known you. You get...fixated on things. Obsessed. But it's been getting worse."

"It's called doing my job," Marie said. She squinted at the screen, looking for a hidden sign between the letters.

"Tony's my friend, too, you know," Janine said. "He isn't like this. None of your cop buddies are like this. You push yourself until you drop, over and over again. Like you blame yourself for everything."

"Told you, it's my job," Marie murmured. She traced a fingertip across the screen, drawing invisible lines between points she couldn't see.

"And you get these...rages. I mean, you're fine, then all of a sudden it's like..." Janine trailed off. Hesitant, before finishing her thought in a softer, smaller voice. "I'm afraid you're really going to hurt somebody, Marie."

Marie glanced away from the screen. For the first time, she noticed Janine's tight body language, the look in her eyes, the way she hung at the far end of the futon, out of arm's reach. *She's afraid of me.*

Everybody knows she's fucked in the head, she remembered Helena muttering.

"You don't think I'd hurt you," Marie said. "Do you?"

Janine gave a tiny shake of her head. "No."

Marie wished she could believe her.

"Will you do something for me, Marie?"

"Sure," she said.

Janine pointed to Marie's bedroom door.

"Go to sleep? It's late, you're exhausted, I can see it all over your face. Are you really going to solve any mysteries tonight?"

The words on Marie's screen twisted and flickered, taunting her like electronic serpents. Marie rubbed her eyes. Then she shut the laptop.

It would keep. For now.

*   *   *

Tossing, turning, restless, Marie's dreaming mind pulled her into a desert. It was a wasteland of hard, cracked earth. As far as the eye could see, nothing but rust-red dirt under the glare of a green-tinged sun.

She rode on the perch of a wagon, reins loose in her hand, a rifle slung over one shoulder. The creatures pulling her along weren't horses. They were hairless, pale and lumpy beasts, cadaverous and skeletal, bloated with tumors the size of softballs. If they were in pain, it didn't show. They gamely marched along, bony hooves crunching the dirt.

Marie's clothes were ragged. Her worn overalls had been patched and mended a dozen times. She wore a plastic pauldron on one shoulder, like a football player's pads. Her rifle was a piecemeal contraption of copper tubing, PVC pipe, and duct tape, and it stank of dirty gunpowder.

"You've been quiet," Nessa said from behind her.

She looked back. Nessa wore a gown of midnight black, accented with lace, sitting cross-legged in the wagon under a black crepe parasol. A heavy book lay open in her lap. The pages were inlaid with diagrams and symbols that made Marie's eyes blur.

"I had a strange dream," she heard herself say.

"Dreams can be portents. Tell me, what did you see?"

"I dreamed of the before-time," Marie said. "Before the fires, before the cities died. It felt so real."

"I've read you stories of the before-time," Nessa replied, placidly turning a page in her book.

"No, but...I was *me*. At the same age I am now. I wasn't even born then. I had another life. I had a home."

"Interesting. And what were you, hmm?"

"A woman of laws," Marie said. "Not a bounty hunter, but a...I don't know the right word for it."

"Perhaps you were. I've long theorized that there are other worlds than this. And if there are other worlds, might we not have lived in them?"

Marie turned back to the pulling beasts. Her hand tightened on the reins.

"A world that lived?"

"Or just died later. Time is a fiction, Marie. Something our brains invent so everything doesn't happen at once. And where the veils are thin, worlds and times can overlap. Tell me, did you enjoy this other life?"

"You weren't in it yet," Marie said.

"A lamentable tragedy."

"I had...it's hard to remember now, some kind of problem. A puzzle to solve. And a woman was going to die if I couldn't solve it."

Nessa snickered. "Ever the crusading knight, even in your dreams. Too bad I wasn't there. I could have helped."

Marie looked back again over her shoulder as Nessa turned another page. She recognized the symbol in Nessa's book at once. The same jagged, looping glyph as the tattoo on the dead man's wrist. She tried to speak, to ask what it meant, but the words wouldn't come out. She was a passenger inside her own head, and a different question altogether emerged from her lips.

"Do you think we could get back to Wyrmont before the summer months? It's cooler there. They have water in Wyrmont, water for everyone."

Nessa looked up from her book, arching an eyebrow in annoyance.

"It's on the far side of the Cheshire lands and the mad-tribes are in heat. No. Not without an armed caravan, and we've no scrap to trade for passage. We'll summer in the Low Salt. It'll be fine."

Marie's shoulders sagged. "I hate the Low Salt. Everything is *foul* there. We could make real scrap in Wyrmont."

"Well," Nessa told her, "as soon as you figure out how we can get there without a penny in our purses, let me know, hmm? I'll be looking forward to your discovery. For now, my scarlet butterfly, hold the reins fast. We've miles to go before sundown."

Marie's eyes snapped open.

Her hands gripped sweat-cold sheets. The stucco ceiling of her bedroom swam in hazy light, drifting in around the edges of her curtained window. The sound of early morning traffic rose up from the street outside.

She threw back the sheets and strode into the living room. Her laptop was right where she'd left it on the futon's edge. She powered it up, tapped in her password, and read the numbered list she'd written the night before.

"*Got* you," she breathed.

Nine

Back in his hometown of Abilene, Kansas, Beau Kates would have been a regular Al Capone. By New York City standards, he was barely qualified to be a bottom-feeder. He'd gone down a few times for pimping and pandering, once for stolen goods, and once on a drug-possession charge. He'd managed to plead out by dropping a dime on his dealer. The last couple of years he'd spent coasting under the radar. Running girls out of his "modeling agency" and collecting the money they earned on their backs made up the bulk of his cash flow. Then Baby Blue disappeared, which put him back on the NYPD's list.

Worse for him, it put him on Marie's list.

She had reluctantly bought his alibi, his claim of being worried about Baby Blue—after all, he'd filed the missing-persons report himself. Now, in the hard light of a new morning, she wasn't so sure.

Marie ducked under an open bay door and into a garage teeming with faded black cars. There were a few limos, mostly town cars, a couple up on lifts and missing their wheels. A grinder whined at the back of the garage and spat a shower of sparks across the oil-stained concrete. The cherry-red sign out front read A+ Motor Services. The boss of the show was a hard-eyed woman named Jackie, with kerchief-wrapped hair and fifty years of nicotine stains on her fingers.

"Knock, knock," Marie said, standing in her office doorway.

Jackie's eyes narrowed. "You again? I thought I answered all your questions last time."

"Just a quick follow-up. One of your drivers, Harlow: I need to see his vehicle log."

"You got a warrant?"

Marie stepped into the tiny, cluttered office, with a window overlooking the garage floor. She shut the door behind her. The stagnant air stank of stale smoke and engine exhaust.

"Do I need one?"

Jackie snorted. "Yeah. You can't pry through my books, I know my rights."

"You want to take a second, think that through?"

"I already thought about it." She nodded to the door. "Get out."

Marie didn't budge. She gave Jackie a thin and humorless smile.

"Jackie, Beau Kates is your best customer. Something like seventy percent of your drivers more or less work for him. Shuttling sex workers all over the city, all hours of the night."

Jackie shook a cigarette out of a crumpled foil pack. She cursed under her breath as her thumb flicked her cheap plastic lighter, kicking three times before she finally got a spark. She held the cigarette to the feeble flame, a faint tremor in both of her hands.

"Prove it in court," she said.

"You don't think we can? Beau's out on bail, pending trial. You apparently don't know his history: he upholds a proud tradition of diming out his co-conspirators at the drop of a hat. Conspirators. As in conspiracy charges, which is what you're looking at right now."

Jackie's hand fumbled. She nearly dropped the lighter, caught it, then slapped it down on the desk like she'd meant to do it. "What are you talking about?"

"Beau Kates operates a criminal enterprise. You are instrumental in supplying vehicles and drivers in support of that criminal enterprise. Were you under the impression that's a slap on the wrist? In New York State, owning or managing a prostitution business is a class D felony. And if Kates goes down on felony charges, you're taking the elevator down with him. You could be looking at seven years in prison, Jackie. Seven years, and you're not exactly a healthy woman. Do you really want to die behind bars for *that* asshole?"

It was a bluff. Kates was bending over backward to cooperate, seven years was the far, *far* end of a class D, and even if they could prove Jackie knew what she was doing for him—knowing she knew and proving it in court being two very different things—she'd be looking at reduced charges, probably a year's probation at worst.

But Jackie didn't know that. And from the haunted look in her eyes, she was vividly imagining her future in prison orange.

Five minutes later, Marie was leafing through a handwritten driver's log. Harlow was Baby Blue's regular escort—her driver, and if a john got rough, impromptu muscle. He'd taken her on her last date with Eddie Li.

And he'd made one more trip, later that same night.

"He didn't list a destination, or a client." Marie tapped her finger on the two empty lines.

"Yeah," Jackie said, standing at her shoulder. "And until such time as I get an explanation, he's not doing any more driving for me. I raised all kinds of hell when I saw that. The odometer's right, though."

At the edge of the blank spaces, a pair of numbers in black ink and initials were scribbled. Marie glanced back at her. "How do you know?"

"Odometer gets recorded at every vehicle turn-in. That's for keeping on top of maintenance, tire rotation, oil changes—I got religion about that. Hell of a lot cheaper to stay on top of maintenance than it is to replace a blown engine. Odometer readings are done by me, or the manager on duty if I'm not here."

Jackie took an unsteady drag from her cigarette. Acrid smoke clouded the air between them, and bits of ash fell like dirty snow onto the logbook as she gestured at the initials.

"That's my manager. No idea where Harlow took the car—I got

no record of a call coming in, and he's still pretending he 'doesn't remember,' but I guarantee that number's right."

Marie knew where he took the car.

Baby Blue barely had a dime to her name. Kates made sure of that. Keeping his girls utterly dependent on him was the cornerstone of any pimp's game. There was no evidence that she used ride-sharing apps, and like over half of the people in New York City, she didn't own a car. Nessa's words from the dream drifted back to Marie. *As soon as you figure out how we can get there without a penny in our purses, let me know, hmm? I'll be looking forward to your discovery.*

The night Baby Blue went missing, Harlow's odometer read 99,486. The check-in after that, it was up to 99,702. Two hundred and sixteen miles. Just about the distance from New York to Monticello and back again.

"I'm going to need Harlow's home address," she told Jackie.

* * *

"I already told you everything," Harlow said.

He was a big man with fat cheeks and tiny eyes. Tiny eyes that roved like they were trying to escape his head. Like they'd bounce out of his skull and roll across the grimy linoleum floor of his Bronx kitchenette, if it meant they could avoid Marie's gaze.

She looked straight at him, though. He sat on the far side of his folding card table. The space between them lay cluttered with dirty plates and an empty pizza box. More plates piled up in the sink. His plastic garbage can, stuffed to overflowing, stank like its contents had begun to compost. No air conditioning. The kitchen window was open, just a crack, letting a wave of humid alley air flutter through the cramped apartment. A bead of sweat pooled at the base of Marie's neck.

"Tell me again."

"I took her to see Eddie Li. Always the same place, this boutique hotel up in Harlem, near West 124th. She was in there two, maybe three hours. Then I'd take her home. I remember because I never had any trouble on those dates. Eddie didn't pull any shit, like some of these guys do. She always looked, you know, okay after."

"I'm touched by your concern for her well-being."

Harlow's baby face tensed up, his tiny eyes squinting. "I *was*, okay? Baby Blue was a friend of mine. You don't spend that much time driving these girls around without caring a little."

Marie leaned a little closer and set her palms flat on the card table.

"You said 'was.' Twice."

He bit his bottom lip, looking like a guilty kid in the principal's office.

"I saw your logs," Marie told him. "You made one more trip that night. What was it, Harlow? She had a side thing, a chance to make some money and get out from under Beau Kates's thumb. But she didn't have any way to get to Monticello on her own. So what happened? Did she ask you for a ride? Offer to kick you some cash under the table, a little win-win?"

"It ain't like that." His bottom lip trembled now, the big man almost on the verge of tears.

"What's it like, then?" Marie asked. "Tell me."

He finally met her gaze.

"I had no idea. You got to understand that. I had no idea, not until after. She was a *friend*."

"Tell me."

"I want immunity," he said.

"Not my call. But if you cooperate, that'll be in my report. If you got sucked into something, if you weren't part of whatever happened to Baby Blue, I'll believe you. I *want* to believe you, Harlow. But you have to help me out."

He swallowed hard and nodded.

"I think it was a lie. I dunno who hired her, but she wouldn't go all the way out to Monticello for a cheap date. She told me to keep it to myself, not to say nothin' to Beau. Like it was a side thing and she was gonna keep all the cash for herself, you know? Maybe she was looking to build up a nest egg, get out of the life. Only...I don't think she was ever going to get a dime."

"How do you know?" Marie asked.

"I took her to that house. She went inside. And then Beau called me. He knew all about it, knew exactly where I was and where I'd taken her. He said...he said to just leave her there, that 'the client' would drive Baby Blue home when the party was over. It was weird. I mean, I knew it was weird, but I still didn't think anything was *wrong* weird. Just business, right?"

"And then?"

"And then she never came home." Harlow slumped in his chair. His gaze dropped to the table. "A couple days later, I went and talked to Beau. I asked him, you know, why he didn't tell the cops about Monticello when he reported her missing. He told me..."

He fell silent. The bead of sweat at the back of Marie's neck became an icy finger, trickling down her spine.

"What did he tell you, Harlow?"

The big man clasped his hands. A penitent in prayer.

"He told me he reported it so he wouldn't look guilty. Just in case somebody figured out that Baby Blue wasn't *never* coming back. And if I didn't want the same thing to happen to me, I'd keep my mouth shut, too. He told me that it wasn't him I had to worry about. That these people, they could get at me. They could get at me in my bed, in a cell in Rikers. There wasn't no place I'd ever be safe again."

Marie's chair scraped back on the dirty linoleum. She rose to her feet, her heartbeat steady and strong. Her pulse pounded like a war-drum beat calling her to battle. She had gasoline in her veins. The thought of Beau Kates, free on bail and hiding the truth while Baby Blue's time ran out, was a lit match.

"Your cooperation will be noted in my report," she said, her voice tight as she turned away. Her hand was on the doorknob when he called after her.

"You ever been tested, Detective?"

She paused, looking back at him.

"Tested?"

"Most times," he said, "life is easy. You do what you're good at. I'm a big guy. I don't mind throwing down, because I usually win. But I got that shit all wrong. See, I thought that made me a *tough* guy."

"What does it make you?" she asked.

"My momma, she said there comes a time in everyone's life when the Lord gives you a test. That moment when you go up against the wall and you find out what you're really made of, deep down inside. It ain't about winning or losing, it's about learning. Because once you've seen the truth of what you are, you can't *never* run away from it."

He took a deep breath, let it out, sagging in his chair.

"Me? I found out I'm nothing but a coward. That girl's gone because I let Beau tell me what to do, because I was too afraid to speak up."

Marie opened the door. "She's not gone yet. I'm going to find her. And I'm going to bring her home."

"I hope you are, Detective. Because something tells me...you about to get tested, too."

Ten

Nessa stared at the pink rejection slip on her desk blotter, the hastily-torn envelope from the *Quarterly Journal of Anthropological Review*, as if she might just be reading it wrong. As if she could read it one more time and the block letters on the page would magically transform into a letter of acceptance.

Her office at Barnard was small, barely bigger than her secondhand desk, but at least it was hers. She'd appointed it with tiny comforts: a lavender-scented candle warmer on the edge of her blotter and a wall calendar with landscape art of the Scottish moors by moonlight. The pink slip was a jarring intrusion. She picked up the phone.

"Jeffrey? It's Professor Roth, over at Barnard. I'd like to talk to you about this form letter I just received."

A long-suffering sigh echoed over the phone. "Yeah, I...I figured you'd be calling."

She picked the slip up in her free hand. Her fingers crumpled the corner on impulse, the paper rustling. She felt more confused than angry, but the anger was still there, a low simmer in the pit of her stomach.

"I mean, this is a *form rejection*. How many years have you been publishing my papers? You've had dinner at my house. I think I deserve a little better than that, don't you? Was it a mistake? If it was a mistake—"

"It wasn't a mistake."

She fell silent, listening to him breathe.

"And?"

"Look, Vanessa, your early work was brilliant. Some of the best papers we've ever published, and I stand by that. But in the last couple of years you've...fallen off. The quality, the depth, it's just not there anymore."

"What are you saying? That I peaked? I haven't *peaked*, Jeffrey."

Another sigh. "This happens sometimes. A lot of female scholars—they get married, they start thinking about having kids, and the quality of their work drops. They're just too distracted for the kind of academic rigor it takes to stay on top. It's not uncommon."

Her jaw clenched.

"Are you joking?" she said, her voice dangerously soft. "In what universe do you think it's okay to say something like that? What decade do you think we're living in? And I am *not*, for the record, having children."

"You might not be actively planning on it, but let's be honest, you're in your thirties and the biological clock isn't just an abstract—"

She hung up on him.

Nessa crumpled the rejection slip into a tiny ball, along with the envelope it came in. Her gaze flicked to the clock on the wall. Time for class. She'd deal with this later. For now she could bottle her emotions and force a smile. Always smile, that's what Richard told her. Nothing more important than keeping up appearances.

She crossed paths with Dr. Milbourn, the Anthropology department chair, in the corridor outside her classroom. The older woman hurried past, books clenched to her chest, silver-gray hair pulled back in a ponytail. She paused at Nessa's voice.

"Sorry," Nessa said, "don't mean to interrupt, but you haven't gotten back to me? About my email?"

Milbourn winced. "I...right. Look, Professor, yes, you're doing excellent work here, and the college is proud to have you on staff."

Nessa tilted her head, sensing the unspoken *but*. She waited for it to drop.

"But we only have so many tenure slots," the president said. "And in the end, they have to go to the best of the best. To the professors who really fight for it, who show they're here to go the distance."

"I...thought I was doing that," Nessa said, her hopes fading like a dying battery.

"I'm sure that you're trying your best," Milbourn said and gave her a smile of abject pity.

For just a moment, Nessa thought about the letter opener on her desk blotter. She wondered what it would feel like to ram it straight through Milbourn's throat. She imagined the administrator's expression changing from condescension to terror. The arterial blood spraying between her clenched fingers as she fell to her knees at Nessa's feet. Right where she belonged.

Milbourn took a halting step back. "Professor?"

Nessa blinked, the fantasy shattered. "Yes?"

Whatever she'd seen in Nessa's eyes, it rattled her. She quickly sidestepped, head down, books clutched tight like a protective amulet. "Nothing. Never mind. I have to be going, I'm sorry. We'll talk more later."

*   *   *

There was nothing Nessa enjoyed less than reading her day planner and seeing the line *1p.m. – Dr. Neidermyer*. Down in the glass canyons of Manhattan, she walked against the flow, fighting the tide of post-lunch-break workers heading back to the office and the milling, slow-walking tourists with their cell phones pointed at billboards and marquees. Nessa kept to the side and dodged one oncoming pedestrian after another. She felt like a ghost, like none of them could see her.

A man in a power tie was coming her way, straight as an arrow. There was a gap in the foot traffic and they both had plenty of room to move. On a sudden whim, she didn't. *You move*, she thought.

He collided with her, hard enough to knock her aside, and kept on going.

"Watch where you're walking." He barked the words, bristling and offended.

"Sorry," she said. The apology came out as a reflex. Something angry and primal uncoiled in her belly. She didn't know what to do with the anger except turn it loose on herself, so she swallowed it down and kept walking.

Ten minutes later she was up in Dr. Neidermyer's office, a discreet and quiet room just off a discreet and quiet corridor. Floral photographs decorated the walls. A pristine box of tissue offered comfort on a glass table, beside his white leather therapy couch. He'd told her at their first session that the couch was largely an affectation. Most of his patients opted for the chairs on the other side of his desk, so they could talk eye-to-eye.

Nessa preferred the couch. It was a chance to get off her feet for twenty minutes or so, and that was about the only tangible benefit she got from talking to the man. He sat beside her, a notebook on his knee, his pencil making low scratchy sounds over the air conditioner's hum.

"And your...manic episodes?" he asked, the questions ritual by now. "You haven't had any flare-ups?"

"Why don't you ever ask me about my depression?"

The bald man, his cheeks sallow, hunched over his pad. Scribbling.

"It's easier to check on the effectiveness of your medication if we focus on treating your mania."

"Explain," she said.

"Well, it's...easier to quantify. Many people experience periods of sadness, of unhappiness, of simple *dissatisfaction* in life, and mistake those feelings for chemical depression."

"So you're telling me," Nessa said, "that I'm not qualified to tell you what I'm feeling."

He looked up, eyes wide. His head shook like a sped-up metronome.

"Not at all, not at all. Only that self-diagnosis carries the risk of self-deception. Which is why I'm here, to help shepherd you to wellness. Let's talk about your hobbies, shall we? Your husband is concerned. He says your artwork has taken a turn toward the morbid."

"Does it ever bother you," she asked, "that discussing my treatment, and my therapy, with my husband is a gross breach of medical ethics? Sort of like the pills you slip me under the table."

He squinted at her. "You've never objected in the past."

"Maybe I should have."

"Yes, your treatment is a bit unorthodox, Vanessa, but considering your familial situation—"

"Oh, yes. My husband is a very important man. His father is a very important man." She lolled her head to one side, gazing at him with heavy-lidded eyes. "Wouldn't do for me to be seen picking up my prescriptions in public. Can't let anyone know Senator Roth's daughter-in-law is crazy-cakes."

Neidermyer set down his pencil. "You are *not* 'crazy,' Vanessa. We don't use that word here. Tell me about your day-to-day. What are your aspirations?"

"Right now?" She turned her head again, looking up at the ceiling. "Most of the time, Doctor...most of the time I just want to be loved. To be adored. Cherished. I'd like to know what that feels like."

"Your husband loves you."

"Really?" she asked. "Is that your professional opinion based on careful analysis? Is he one of your patients, too?"

Neidermyer plucked a tissue from the box. He put it to his mouth and let out a wet, hacking cough. He shifted in his chair.

"No, but...but I know him, and I can hear the concern in his voice when he asks about you."

"I'm pretty sure," Nessa said, "that he just left to spend the weekend with a younger and prettier woman. The funny thing is, what bothers me isn't the deed, it's that he won't just tell me outright. It's been two years since the last time we had sex, did you know that?"

He rose from his chair, crossing to his desk, and tossed the crumpled tissue into a waste bin. "I'm not sure that's—"

"I think the miscarriage, that was the moment when everything went sour. When they told me that my insides were…well, that I wouldn't be giving him a child. Apparently, that's a deal-breaker in the Roth household. So that's how it is. He prefers the company of his right hand, I prefer the company of a good book."

"You said you want to be loved 'most of the time,'" Neidermyer said, red-faced. "What else do you want?"

A faint, reptilian smile rose to Nessa's lips.

"Every once in a while, I think it might be nice to rule the world."

"I think everyone daydreams about that sometimes," he said. "It's a very common fantasy—"

"I would be terrible, I think."

Neidermyer chuckled. He fished in his desk drawer. An unlabeled bottle of pills rattled in his hand.

"Well, it's just a fantasy. That's a good mental exercise, though: instead of fearing you'd fail, imagine yourself as a successful leader."

She turned her head and locked eyes with him.

"The word *terrible*, Doctor, has more than one meaning."

His gaze flitted to the clock on his desk.

"Right, well, that's…that's all the time we have for today. Let's keep you at your current dosage, and we'll reevaluate in a few weeks. And please, Vanessa…trust your husband. Richard is a good man. He only has your best interests in mind, believe that."

Eleven

The Vandemere Zoo in upstate New York had never been much of a tourist attraction. Bequeathed to the county by a dead industrialist with too much money and too few heirs, it had been built out of loyalty to his faded hometown instead of anything resembling good business sense. Nobody was surprised when the backwater zoo went bankrupt less than a decade after it opened, all the animals sold off to wealthier, better-run attractions, leaving the park a desolate wasteland. Now the terraced walkways stood empty, the amphibian tanks drained, the enclosures long vacant but still bearing the faint, clinging stench of soiled straw and dung. A skeleton crew of workers, paid for by the zoo's new owners, came through once a month to trim back the weeds and groom the maze of pebbled paths.

At the heart of the zoo stood a lodge, fashioned like a vintage log cabin. Once a visitors' center and rented banquet hall, it now played host to an elite few. Their club had named themselves the Vandemere Lodge in honor of their new digs, but they'd had any number of names throughout the years. Names were a formality to be changed and shed as their needs demanded. Only their core values, and the strict bar to entry, remained.

Dress code at the Vandemere may have been business casual, but nobody was slacking when it came to sartorial indulgence. Savile Row blazers and designer sweaters were the order of the day, spruced up with a few lapel pins or school ties here and there, just to spur the occasional bout of Harvard-versus-Princeton rivalry. Beneath rustic timbers, under the glassy eyes of a twelve-point buck's head mounted over the crackling fireplace, Richard was in his element. He navigated the pine-patterned rugs and the swirl of conversation, cradling a crystal glass of cognac in his hand. There were maybe twenty men in all, mingling in the lodge hall, and another handful out on the elevated deck overlooking the abandoned zoo. He could see them through the wide windows, catching the pumpkin-orange sunset and taking out lighters. The faint tang of cigar smoke wafted in through the propped-open door on a cool evening breeze.

"The Rothster!" called a voice to his left. "My *man*! Wasn't sure you were gonna make it."

Scottie Pierce, lantern-jawed and whipcord-lean in a pinstripe vest, swooped in with a leering smile. They clasped hands, then fist-bumped.

"As if I'd miss it. Christ, between the job and the wife, I *needed* this trip. Not to mention this Monticello bullshit."

"Hear you loud and clear, good buddy. So is the Tribeca thing still happening? Because I just cut an import deal with this Saudi trust-fund kid. His family's all up in the oil biz, and he's looking for property in the city. I'd love to play matchmaker, hook you guys up."

"Done deal," Richard said. "Hey, on that note, got a little present for you."

He waved Scottie off to the sidelines. They stood in the glow of the hearth, pinned between the fire's heat and the cool wind blowing in from the deck.

"Rehabilitation Dynamics of America. Buy. Go in big."

Scottie tilted his head. "You nuts? Their stock's been in the toilet for months."

"Word is, certain friends of our friends got involved, know what I mean? The feds are about to renew their contract and they'll be opening five more facilities in the next couple of years. The announcement is next week, so grab as much stock as you can before the inevitable bounce-back."

"Booyah." Scottie snapped his fingers. "Thanks for the tip. Good money in locking people up. People who aren't us. People in general, you know, I don't discriminate."

A bear of a man in a powder-blue jacket threw his arms around their shoulders. He wore his thinning hair in a spiky, stringy comb-over.

"Brothers!" Tucker boomed. "That's what makes this fellowship of learned gentlemen so great. No discrimination."

"It's true," Scottie said. "We're a bastion of tolerance, and social justice, and whatever else I have to say to get college chicks to blow me."

"'Chicks' is sexist," Richard told him. "The proper term is 'unpaid intern.'"

"I stand humbly corrected. Tucker, why are you gracing us with your body-spray-laden presence?"

"Just got back from Havana. If you guys feel like indulging in some top-tier and entirely illegally imported stogies, join me out on the deck later."

"Yeah, we'll do that." Scottie watched Tucker leave, waiting until he was out of earshot. "Bro. Seriously. Cuban cigars have been warmed-over dogshit for years. They overworked the damn soil. 'Aw, look at me, I just went to Cuuuba! My dad's an ambaaasador! I had dinner at the Whiiite House!'"

"You do not like that man," Richard observed, sipping his cognac.

"Lodge legacy, got everything handed to him on a plate. Guys like us had to make sacrifices to get to the top. We put in the *hours*. Also, I think he wants to sleep with me."

"You think everybody wants to sleep with you."

"It's *true*." Scottie pantomimed grabbing his crotch, batting his eyes at Richard. "C'mon, you want a piece of this and you know it, big boy."

Richard rolled his eyes and deadpanned, "What happens at the lodge, stays at the lodge..."

The overhead lights dimmed.

"Aw, shit," Scottie said with a chuckle. "Speaking of, looks like it's popping off now."

The last of the men shuffled in from the deck and shut the door in their wake. The gathering milled in eager, restless silence, waiting. One stepped forward: Westwood, a thin-faced man with hair the color of sand, a crimson stola draped over the shoulders of his tailored jacket. The nod to old-world culture held swirling designs in gold thread along its length. Astrological symbols and images drawn from books on renaissance alchemy added a hint of the mystical. He raised his hands high with his fingers spread wide.

"Hail, brethren!"

Richard raised his glass, joining the full-throated shout from the gathering. "*Hail, Orgiophant!*"

"We gather as those who seek and those who dare," Westwood intoned, "those who risk all to pierce the cosmic veil and plunder the riches of the unseen world. Do you vow to uphold the creed of our ordo and defend your fellow brethren against all who oppose them? To stand strong and without fear as we make our will manifest?"

"*I do,*" came the solemn response.

Westwood smiled and fiddled with his glasses.

"Well, let's get this show on the road, then," he said. "Oh, hey, first order of business. If you haven't yet, get in on that shrimp spread at the banquet table. Brother Steve's restaurant did the catering tonight, and it is the fucking *bomb.*"

"Truth," Scottie murmured, "that is some damn fine shrimp cocktail."

Westwood's smile faded. "Second order of business. You've all heard about the situation in Monticello. Needless to say, that property is radioactive now—"

"Yeah," Richard called out from the back, "thanks for that, *assholes.* Somebody want to tell me who decided to make a snuff movie where we hide our shit? That lot is in my company's name. I've got cleaners working around the clock to clear out the other three stash houses before anyone comes sniffing around."

Tucker raised a sheepish hand.

"It wasn't for kicks," he said as every eye looked his way. "I was on site, overseeing the new ink shipment, and the caretakers caught this guy snooping around the grounds. So we brought him downstairs and asked him a few questions."

"And what have we learned?" Westwood asked him.

"He was a shooter for the Five Families, but he had one of those tats on his wrist, the kind Prince Berith's servants get. Half of those mob guys are working for the courts of hell these days, whether they know it or not. He knew it. That's all he knew, though—he was prowling around on nothing but a rumor, no evidence, trying to sniff out our pipeline."

Scottie slapped his palm to his forehead. "So you tortured the guy to death, then left his body ten feet from our drug stash? Jesus, Tucker, you're a bigger moron than the caretakers. At least *they* had the brains to go out in a blaze of glory."

"*Sorry*," Tucker said, glowering.

"As Brother Richard noted," Westwood said, "we're currently in damage-control mode. All of our remaining ink supplies are being moved here, for safekeeping—"

"I thought we didn't shit where we eat," called out a man from the crowd.

"In a perfect world," Westwood said, "we don't. This is a temporary measure. Our loss, thanks to the confiscation, was in the six-figure range."

Scottie snickered. "For some of you poor chumps, that's real money. *Tucker*."

"Hey," Tucker said, "let's put the blame where it belongs, huh? The cops didn't come to Monticello looking for the drugs or the dead guy. You know exactly why."

Scottie stood closer to Richard, a protective gesture, and shook his head.

"It's handled," he said. "I've got somebody on the force. The kind you can buy that *stays* bought. That investigation is going nowhere."

"And if you're wrong?" Tucker demanded.

"If I'm wrong, I'll know about it the second the wind changes. We aren't the *mafia*, boys. We don't need to ask anybody's permission to light up a nosy cop or two. Or three. Or five. Whatever. Point is, the investigation's stalled. The case is limper than somebody's steroid-shriveled impotent dick." Scottie paused. "*Tucker.*"

Tucker spun on his heel. He waded through the crowd, balling his hands into fists. Scottie grinned and curled his fingers in a beckoning gesture. A pack of their lodge brothers got between them fast, pushing Tucker back until he calmed down. Westwood's shoulders slumped as he grimaced.

"Please, brothers," Westwood called over the simmering din. "It's time for tonight's ceremony. We must stand united to earn the favor of our patrons. They who have blessed us, enriched us, and showered us with bounty."

A hush fell over the lodge. Tucker shook off the last of the men holding him back. He turned to face Westwood and smoothed his jacket's lapels.

"Hail," Westwood called out, "to all the Kings of Man. Blessed be their works and mysteries. Blessed be their delicious ruin."

"Blessed be," responded a roomful of voices in unison.

Westwood hooked his raised fingers into claws. The brethren did the same, every arm held high.

"And hail, first and foremost, to the King of Wolves," Westwood proclaimed. "Hail to our lord and master, our glorious teacher, he who separates predator from prey, who separates conqueror from the conquered. May our hunt be a glorious one and pleasing to his turquoise eye."

He whipped down his hands and clawed at the air. The gathered men did the same, moving as one, sleeves rustling swift and sharp.

Westwood walked to a flat-screen TV mounted on the wall beside the crackling fireplace. The screen flickered to life. The television gave a security camera's view of a cell, gray-walled and cramped. A woman in a ragged cotton shift sat crouched in the corner, her back to the wall, knees drawn up tight to her chest. Her long black hair was matted and stringy, her cheeks stained with tear-streaked mascara. She rocked from side to side. No sound, but her lips moved in an endless babbling prayer.

"Tonight's offering is a prostitute from Hoboken," Westwood said. "Early twenties, addicted to heroin but currently two weeks from her last dosage and recovering quite nicely. No other infirmities. For the gambling sportsmen among us, I will now open the betting pool."

Twelve

The Hunting Wall stood in what used to be the zoo's monkey house. A long rack of aluminum, hung with hooks and wires and tiny shelves, bearing a cornucopia of death. Mallets, meat cleavers, butcher knives. In silence, by tradition, the brethren lined up in order of seniority to choose their weapons. Scottie's favorite was waiting for him: a kendo bokken, the long wooden sword carved from stout oak. Richard's bokken hung right below it, each blunt blade seared with their initials at the base of the hilt.

"You follow my lead on the betting? The four-to-six-minute bracket?" Scottie whispered as they plucked their weapons from the wall.

"Yeah," Richard murmured, "what's the angle?"

Scottie shot a wicked grin over his shoulder. "Just watch. It was my turn to set up the course for tonight. Had a little brainstorm."

As Westwood led the procession out into the night, Scottie strolled alone through the monkey house. He passed a steel door secured by a keypad lock, then strolled down a long corridor. Old animal cages lined the hallway, converted into tiny prison cells with Plexiglas walls. Another keypad beeped and a cell door whispered open.

"C'mon out," Scottie said to the woman in the corner. "It's okay. C'mon."

She looked up at him, teary-eyed. He held out a reassuring hand. She didn't take it.

"Look," he said. "You can either die here and now, or you can take a chance. You take a chance, maybe you can go home tonight. You'd like that, wouldn't you?"

She blinked. "H-home?"

"Home."

She reached out. He took her hand, gentle, and eased her to her bare and unsteady feet.

"See," he said softly. "It's okay. C'mon."

He walked her down the corridor, past the empty Hunting Wall, and outside. She squinted up at the stars and sucked down the clean night air.

"Why are you doing this?" she asked him.

"Trust me, you wouldn't understand. I mean, you literally don't have the capacity to understand it. But it's all for a good cause. Now, here's what's going to happen: you're going to run. We're going to give you a thirty-second head start."

"And then?"

"And then," Scottie said, "me and twenty or so of my best buddies are going to hunt you down. And we're going to kill you. But hold on! No tears, there's a silver lining. The zoo gate is unlocked. If you cross the line, make it to the parking lot...you win. We'll let you go."

It was his favorite lie. Twice, a sacrificial offering had actually made it to the gate. The look on their faces when it didn't budge was priceless. Scottie pointed to the left, toward a rare spot of light in the gloom, somewhere on the far edge of the zoo.

"Fair is fair, so I'm going to give you a tip. See the spotlight? Right in the middle of the light, there's a revolver. You know how to use a gun?"

Her head bobbed a little, her entire body trembling.

"It's a risk-reward deal, get it? If you go for the gun, we'll see you. But, hey, you'll have a gun. None of us do." He patted his wooden sword. "Just blunts and blades. The kind that won't kill fast. Or easy. So, up to you whether to go for it or not, but if I was in your place—and thank fuck I'm not—I'd want an edge to even things up. Just remember: there's only six bullets and twenty of us, so you'd better make each shot count."

The revolver, that part was true. The gun was even loaded. What was a hunt without a little risk? *Worst-case scenario*, he thought, *I'll just stand behind Tucker*.

"Okay," he said, "time to play. Go on. Run."

She wavered on her feet. "Please. Don't...don't do this. You don't have to do this—"

Scottie's face contorted into a mask of feral rage. He grabbed the bokken in both hands, swinging it high above his head as he screamed, "*Run!*"

She ran. Scottie broke into a snickering laugh, tugged his phone from his pocket, and tapped the icon for a custom app. The zoo speakers crackled to life all over the park, vibrating with a booming bass-horn drone. Then an automated voice began a countdown: "*Thirty. Twenty-nine. Twenty-eight.*"

At the count of zero, cackles and raw animal howls split the air. The lodge went hunting. Tiny packs and lone wolves spread out along the pebbled paths. They swept wide, pantomiming blade slashes and gnashing their teeth in anticipation. The men wore their true faces now. No need for civilization, no need for social structures or play-acting. They were beasts. This was their hunting ground. Fresh meat was on the run.

Scottie and Richard ran together in silence. They always did. They had the wind in their faces and their weapons in hand, tracking their prey by the rustle of her footfalls and the scent of her skin. Words weren't necessary.

*   *   *

She was going to make it. Every stumbling step was agony, the rough walk biting into her bare feet, each ragged breath a burning stitch in her side, but she wasn't going to give up. She'd never given up in her life, through the worst the world could throw at her. She'd survived. She had a beautiful baby girl at home, waiting for her, and damned if she wasn't going to live to see her smile again.

Men hooted behind her, footsteps fast and pounding along the tangled maze of pathways. The gun. She needed the gun. No, she couldn't kill them all, but one shot and the rest would scatter. She could hold them off long enough to reach the gate. It was her only chance.

Up ahead, there it was. A small stone pedestal stood centered beneath the circle of light, in a patch of overgrown grass. The revolver, a heavy .357 with a taped grip, shone like the holy grail. A hundred feet to salvation. She closed in fast, digging deep. She was going to live—

The bear trap, hidden in the grass just outside the circle of light, slammed shut with a bone-shattering *snap*. She shrieked as she fell to the ground. A streak of raw agony burned up her leg as the rusted steel teeth tore skin and chewed at her marrow. Looking to the pedestal, she still didn't give up. She clawed her way across the grass, pulling herself on her hands, straining inch by torturous inch.

Scottie stood in front of her. He looked down and shook his head.

"I said the gun was here. I never said it'd be easy to get." He glanced up, past her, as the thunder of footsteps closed in from all around. "Hey! Watch your footing, there are ten other traps scattered all over the grass. Careful now."

Her head sagged. Her last candle-flicker of hope died. She didn't have the breath to weep.

"For what it's worth," Scottie told her, "you lasted five minutes and twenty-seven seconds. That's not bad. Better than most. Westwood, you want to do your thing?"

The older man stepped up, hands raised in benediction.

"King of Wolves, we commend unto you this sacrifice. Receive it in lust and delight, and smile upon our enterprises, that we may continue to prosper in fortune and power."

Scottie raised his wooden sword high.

"A-fuckin'-men," he said and brought it crashing down.

*   *   *

They took their time with her. Panting, exhausted, their hunger slaked, the winners of the hunt earned handshakes and patted backs from the brethren who arrived too late for the kill. It was their duty, as the losers, to clean up the scene and prepare the victim's body for disposal.

The King of Wolves had taken his meal and enjoyed his sacrifice. What remained was nothing more than garbage to be dumped.

Richard crouched over a rubber hose in the monkey house. He sprayed down his bokken, washing away blood and matted clumps of hair. He watched it all sluice down the floor drain as his hands faded from scarlet to ruddy pink. In these moments, after a victorious hunt, he felt...quiet. Satisfied. The only time he really did, he supposed. Life was good. His world was good.

He tapped in the keypad and took a stroll down the corridor of cells. Most of them stood empty, waiting for fresh offerings. All but the one on the end.

She was a rare one. She hadn't broken, hadn't given in to fear or despair like most of the others. She spent most of her waking hours pacing the tiny straw-scattered floor. Getting ready for a fight, he supposed. Good spirit. The ones before her, the broken ones, had given up and sat starving in their own filth until the hunt began. This one had eaten every scrap they'd tossed her, like a feral animal, and had torn pieces from her shift to clean herself. He stood outside her cell, a wall of reinforced Plexiglas between them.

She turned his way, eyes fierce, and tossed back her mane of cobalt hair.

"Baby Blue," Richard murmured and pressed his palm to the glass. As if he could touch her across the distance.

He couldn't hear her, but there was no mistaking the obscenity she spat at him. He smiled. This was what he wanted. Real prey. A real hunt.

"Don't worry," he said. "Just you wait. You'll get your turn."

Thirteen

Marie took the subway. She clung to a metal bar, standing room only, packed in like cattle as the train whistled its way across the city. She didn't notice the people around her. She didn't take in the stench of unwashed armpits and cheap cologne, or the body heat that sucked the air out of the train car. All she saw was the light at the end of the tunnel.

Literal light. The train broke out into sunlight and rattled along the tracks. Her phone buzzed against her hip. Tony calling. She almost let it go to voicemail.

"Yeah?" she said.

"Hey, where are you? I stopped by your place, wanted to see if you were up for grabbing lunch or something, but Janine says you took off early."

"Going to see a man about Baby Blue," she told him.

"What? Marie, we had an agreement. What are you doing? Please tell me you're not harassing Richard Roth again."

"It's Beau Kates, Tony. The bastard knew. He knew all along. He knows exactly who took her and where she is. And he's going to tell me."

"Marie, *wait*. Jesus, you're on admin leave. You don't have a badge. Nothing you get out of him is gonna be admissible, and you'll be damned lucky if you don't get brought up on charges."

The anger that had simmered in her veins since her visit with

Harlow, had ignited in the open air, kindled by the sun and stoked into a searing fire. Now the train dove and she was back underground, in the belly of a steel serpent, slithering through the veins of the city.

She was the serpent. Pregnant with venom, and burning to bite.

"She's running out of time," Marie told him and hung up the phone.

Beau Kates's "modeling studio" was a hole-in-the-wall, a former dance studio on the third floor of a building that should have been condemned years ago. Marie walked up, her shoes crunching on discarded food wrappers and crumpled carry-out bags, rounding corners fast as she climbed a stairwell painted the color of split-pea soup. She flung the studio door open. A young woman jumped to her feet. The particleboard on her reception desk was rotted, and an oversized whiteboard calendar on the wall hadn't been updated in months.

"You can't go in without an appointment! Ma'am?"

"*Leave*," Marie hissed and kicked open Beau's office door.

Grimy windows lined the narrow loft, casting dusty sunlight across uneven floorboards. Standing lights ringed a photographer's nook, where a camera on a tripod focused on an empty bed fitted with frilled pink sheets. On the other side of the room, Beau—his arms etched with prison ink, his body the kind of skinny you only get from a serious heroin habit—blinked and stirred from his nap on a cracked leather sofa.

"Detective?" he said, rubbing at one eye as he clambered to his feet. "What are you—"

She took a running start. She grabbed onto his shirt, swung him around, and threw him into a standing light face-first. It crashed down, the bulb exploding and spitting glass across the floorboards, and he sprawled on top of it. She got her hands around his throat. She pulled him up to his knees, squeezing hard as she yanked him close.

"Baby Blue. Where is she?"

"I told you last time, I got no idea—"

She heaved him to his feet, put a hand on the small of his back, and shoved him straight into the camera tripod. Beau went down with it, careening onto the floor, and the expensive rig shattered under him. He rolled onto his back and clutched his shoulder.

"You can't *do* this," he groaned. "I got rights!"

Marie straddled his chest, pinning his spindly arms under her knees. She drew back a fist and raised it high above his face.

"I'm not a cop today," she said. "You called Harlow. You told him to leave her at that house. You knew she was going to disappear. You *knew*. Who took her, Kates? Who are they?"

"No way." His eyes bulged with terror. "I tell you that, I'm a dead man."

Her fist thundered down, splitting his lip, knocking a front tooth loose. He drooled blood as she dragged him back to his feet. She shoved him backward, bracing her forearm against his chest, and rammed him up against a window. The back of his skull hit hard enough to crack the glass, leaving a smear of scarlet as his head lolled.

"*Who took her?*" she roared.

"I don't...swear to God, I don't know," he said. "These guys, I just knew they were connected. Super connected, okay? Not the kind of guys you say no to."

"Names. What did they look like?"

"I don't *remember*. I mean, I was pretty fucked up when I made the deal. I was on the ink trip, you know? Baby Blue was getting lippy, a real fuckin' problem, like she was gonna walk and take half my stable with her. These guys, they came to me and said they wanted a girl. One with *spirit*. So I..."

He fell silent, his body trembling. She pulled him almost nose to nose.

"You what, Kates?"

He sniffed, his nose running, snot mingling with the trail of blood leaking from his split lip.

"So I sold her to them."

Marie stared into his eyes. Then she grabbed his shirt and threw him back to the floor. "Sold her for what?"

He flinched, then pointed, waving his outstretched finger toward a filing cabinet by the sofa.

She pulled open the bottom drawer. Ink. Baggies of the tiny black grains, piled high in a shoebox, just like they'd found at the kill house in Monticello.

"Drugs," Marie breathed, her voice hollow. "You traded her for drugs."

"Yeah. I...I mean, I had a problem. They had a solution."

She turned and loomed over him.

"She was a *human being*."

Beau shrank back in fear.

"Look, you're pissed, I see that. We can work something out! I can get you some good shit—"

Two of his ribs snapped under Marie's heel. He rolled onto his side, howling, and clutched his chest. She strode to the open cabinet and grabbed a handful of the plastic baggies. Then she walked back over and planted one knee on his chest, pinning him flat. She dropped the scattering of baggies next to his flailing head and tugged one open while he squirmed under her knee. The black seeds fell into her palm.

"Open your mouth, Kates."

"W-what?" He shook his head, frantic, lips clamping shut.

Her other hand closed around his lower jaw. He pressed his hands against her, desperate, trying to shove her back.

"You ever see a man die from an ink overdose, Kates? It's a bad, bad way to go. *Open your fucking mouth.*"

"*Marie!*" Tony shouted from the doorway. He scrambled across the wasteland of broken equipment and grabbed her wrist. He hauled her off Beau. "Jesus, what are you doing?"

Beau rolled up onto his knees. He sputtered, rubbing at his throat and spitting blood onto the floorboards. Tony kept shoving Marie back, trying to keep them apart, looking as afraid as he did angry.

"You bastards," Beau croaked. "I'm gonna sue the living shit out of you, your department. I'm gonna own your asses—"

Tony stuck a finger in Marie's face.

"Stay. Put." Then he turned, towering over Beau. "No. You're not going to say a word to anybody about this."

Beau looked up at him, running the back of his hand across his mouth. "Yeah? Why's that?"

"Because that stash of ink sitting in plain sight? That's more than enough quantity for a distribution charge."

"What? I don't deal, that's just for me."

"I know. But the law doesn't give a shit," Tony told him. "So here's how it's going to play if you lodge a beef. We came on a tip about you peddling drugs out of your little studio here. You attacked my partner. We reacted in self-defense and slapped the cuffs on, just another scumbag dealer taken off the street. We get commendations, you get twelve to twenty. Or, we walk, you keep your mouth shut, and you get to keep your drugs *and* the rest of your teeth. Pick one."

Beau looked away. "Fine," he said, sullen.

Tony patted him on the shoulder. "Thought you'd see it my way."

He grabbed Marie by the arm and steered her out the door.

*   *   *

They didn't talk. Tony found a Starbucks. He sat Marie down and let her stew in silence while he went to the counter. He came back with a couple of coffees—iced and decaf for him, black for her—and set them down on the tiny table. His chair rattled on the tile floor.

"I don't want to know," he told her, "but I have to."

She met his eyes. Her rage had petered out, leaving her looking tired and lost.

"What?"

"Marie," he said. "Were you going to murder that man?"

She pulled the lid off her coffee and blew across the brim. Curlicues of steam rose between their faces.

"I was just trying to scare him." The words sounded hollow, heavy with exhaustion.

"Really? Because it looked to me like you'd just beaten ten shades of hell out of the guy and you were about to kill him. If I had showed up five minutes later, would you be telling me the same story right now?"

"Late is the point, Tony. There's a pattern. Each victim is only held for two weeks. Baby Blue is—"

Tony slapped his palm against the table hard enough to draw looks from across the coffee shop. He fought to keep his voice down.

"We are not vigilantes, Marie. And contrary to that fantasy crap you fill your head with, we aren't crusading knights, either. We're *cops*. We have *rules*. And thanks to that stunt you just pulled, everything we might have learned is totally inadmissible in court. Do you want these scumbags to walk?"

"I want to save her life. I'm not thinking much beyond that."

"Well," he said, "maybe you should."

They drank their coffee.

"You know," Tony told her, "it's one thing if you're a little rough with a perp once in a while. When we busted that chomo who was running a kiddy-porn website, nobody cared that he 'accidentally' fell down the stairs on his way to the squad car. Hell, I didn't even have to cover for you that time. But this? You've got to get this shit under control, because it's getting worse. Maybe you don't see it, but I do."

She didn't have an explanation for him. She stared into her coffee cup, as if she could divine an answer in the swirling wreath of steam.

"Sometimes I feel," she said, "like a roaring flame. A force of nature, burning everything in my path. And there should be...something focusing me. Controlling my fire, channeling it. Like there's part of me missing. And I don't know what it is, or where it is. I only know that it's missing."

Tony shook his head.

"You need therapy. I say this as your partner and your friend. You need professional help. Okay? I'm not putting you down. I care about you and I want you to be okay. But you need the kind of help I can't give you."

"I never asked you to. I never asked anybody for anything."

Tony lifted his cup. "I know. I'm asking you. I'm asking you to take care of yourself. For once in your life, Marie, take care of *yourself*. Not everybody else, like you always do. Put yourself first and get the help you need."

"I'll try," she said.

Tony cracked a smile. "Hell, if you 'try' the same way you go at everything else, I guess that's a guaranteed success."

She mirrored the smile, but she didn't feel it. Her mind was a million miles away. She combed through the half-remembered tatters of her dream and pictured Nessa's face. And her book, with the image of the dead man's tattoo.

Fourteen

On the other side of the country, stranger dreams were made and ruined every single night. The Las Vegas Strip was a neon-backed dragon in the heart of a desert, inviting all comers to dare to test the odds. Some walked away flush, while most ended up with broken wallets or broken hearts. For others, the outcome wasn't even the point. They were just in it for the pleasure of the ride. For a bold few, the real action wasn't found in the resort casinos and gambling parlors.

If you wanted the real rush and the real money, you had to go underground.

For a trio of heisters out of Reno, that was all too literal tonight. Las Vegas was built in a natural basin, which was fine except for the one or two times a year that the sky opened up and drenched the deserts with rain. To keep their investment from washing away, the city's founding fathers had constructed a spiderweb of storm tunnels under the streets. Between the homeless and lost, the black widow spiders, and the chittering tides of roaches, it wasn't a place anybody went without a damn good reason.

"This is bullshit," one of the trio muttered, clutching a briefcase. They'd carefully stuffed it with stacks of newspaper cut in the shape of cash, each stack topped with a real hundred-dollar bill. One of them had seen it done in a movie. The trick hadn't *worked* in the movie, but they were confident they could pull it off.

"Patience." Mason was their unspoken leader, by virtue of being quicker to throw a punch than the other two. The newspaper thing was his idea.

"I don't think these guys are even gonna show up," said the man on his left. He wore a cheap cotton blazer over his T-shirt, a .45 jammed down the back of his pants.

Footsteps echoed from the dark. A lean shadow took a slow, easy walk up the dank concrete tunnel, coming their way. Italian loafers splashed through murky puddles of stagnant water.

"They aren't," said the shadow.

He emerged into sight, stepping into the beam of Mason's flashlight. He had a flyaway wave of chestnut hair and a cruel slash of a smile. His tailored Brunello Cucinelli suit wasn't the right attire for slinking around in storm drains, and he wore his wry irritation on his sleeve.

"Your business partners aren't coming," Daniel Faust told them. "They're dead."

One of the trio took a hesitant step back. "Don't know what you're talking about. We're just...hanging out, that's all."

Daniel gave him a dubious glance.

"When you came to Vegas, you were told the rules," he said. "Don't cut your product with fentanyl. Don't deal to kids. Always—*always*—kick five percent of your take up to Jennifer. Oh, and a very important one. *Don't. Deal. Ink.* We don't want that shit in our city. As of tonight, you three rubes have managed to break every single one of those simple rules. Seriously, did you think it was a *checklist?*"

"We weren't—" the guy with the gun in his pants stammered. "We weren't really going to *buy* their shit. I mean, we were gonna rip 'em off—"

"Shut it," Mason snapped, then glowered at the new arrival. "This ain't any of your business, Faust. Shove off before you get hurt."

Daniel chuckled. The sound echoed off the vaulted tunnel walls and wrapped around the three men like the knot of a noose.

"The Commission has made a decision, gentlemen. I've been asked to deliver the message: your Las Vegas privileges have been permanently revoked. Leave town, drive in any direction you like, and never come back. Consider this your one chance to walk away from the table with your winnings intact. What do you say?"

The thug in the sweat-soaked blazer snaked one hand behind his back. His fingers curled around the grip of his gun. "You talk pretty tough, considering this is three against one."

"That's all this guy is," Mason sneered. "*Talk*. Everybody whispering about you, Faust, like you're some kinda bogeyman. Piss-scared over fairy tales. We don't scare that easy."

Daniel shrugged, nonchalant. "I'll admit my reputation is a little exaggerated for dramatic effect. When faced with out-of-towner yahoos determined to test our rules, for example, it's easier to scare them into behaving than it is to clean up the mess when they don't."

"You callin' us yahoos?" Mason said.

"And I was afraid that might fly over your head. Yes, you three are the yahoos I was referring to. And the mess. To be cleaned up, if you don't walk away. You see, I was trying to make a subtle point and give you one more chance to..." Daniel shook his head with a sigh. "You know what? Some people just can't take a hint. Let's get this over with."

He flicked out his left hand. In a riffle of pasteboard, a deck of playing cards leaped from his breast pocket, a serpentine stream that landed in his open palm. His right hand slapped across the deck, lightning fast, and snatched up three cards. He held them up in his fingers—three aces, the backs of the cards engraved with the image of a red dragon—like a spread of throwing knives.

The briefcase hit the tunnel floor as loud as a gunshot, bouncing, splashing in a puddle of dirty water as Mason and his boys reached for their steel. The thug in the sweaty blazer was the first to clear his piece. He was the first to die, too, as the ace of spades flew across the tunnel like a razor-edged wasp. The playing card bit into his throat hard enough to knock him off his feet. He landed flat on his back, gurgling as his jugular spat blood.

Mason got off a shot with his automatic, booming loud enough to burst eardrums. The king of hearts soared from the top of Daniel's deck and met the bullet halfway. The card fell dead with a crumpled slug buried in its royal face. Daniel's retort whined across the tunnel, two more aces with a killing edge. Mason and his other partner dropped like rag dolls. Their weapons clattered to the concrete alongside their twitching bodies.

Daniel stood over them for a moment and watched the three men bleed out. Then, with a tired sigh, he held up his empty right hand. The three aces, the cards glistening scarlet, leaped back to his outstretched fingers.

He left the bodies and the guns and the briefcase behind. What the human scavengers didn't take, the animals and insects would.

*   *   *

Getting lost in the tunnels, especially this close to an access door, wasn't something that normally happened to Daniel. And yet, here he was. He navigated by a light clipped to his breast pocket, strobing the beam off faded wall plaques and gossamer spiderwebs. Distant, baleful red eyes watched him from the dark, skittering away from the hated light.

He rounded a bend, expecting to see moonlight, and now he wasn't in the tunnels anymore.

Not in the Vegas storm tunnels, anyway. The walls transformed from smooth gray concrete to rust-red desert rock. From a level passage to a mouth leading down, and around, twisting as it narrowed. Bleached white bones littered the dirt at his feet. Down and around, and around again, and the tunnel opened onto a vast and murky cavern. Bats fluttered overhead on leathery wings, then fell silent. Daniel's pocket light sputtered and burned out.

At the heart of the cave, a small iron table waited with two ornate chairs. A ring of white candles pushed the gloom back to the edges of the rust-stone walls. The Mourner sat before a tea set, the kettle steaming hot. She turned her white lace veil toward him and beckoned him closer.

"This is different," he said. "Last I checked, your cave was about a hundred miles outside the city limits. Didn't know the storm tunnels stretched that far."

"They don't," the Mourner replied. "*I* do. Come, sit. Join me for tea."

As he pulled back the other chair, her gloved and boneless fingers unfurled like the petals of a rose. She poured a splash of tea—hot, brown, and carrying the scent of hyssop on tendrils of steam—into both of their cups. Daniel eyed his teacup, wary, not reaching for it just yet. She lifted her own and snaked it under her veil. Slurping sounds echoed from her concealed lips.

"Drink," she hissed. "I didn't bring you here to slay you. And if I did, you wouldn't be able to stop me. So be polite and drink."

He weighed his options and settled on courtesy. The tea was an herbal blend, rich and woodsy.

"Given that you just conjured me across the Sahara, I assume this isn't a social call."

"I have a task," the Mourner said. "One needing your wit. And if your wit fails, your cards, your wand, and your gun."

Daniel sipped his tea. "Since when do you get involved in the outside world? People come to you, not the other way around."

"Times are changing. And needs must. You are familiar with a man named Andre Lefevre?"

"The guy from the Cooking Channel?" Daniel leaned a little closer, staring at her veil. "I assume you mean a different Lefevre."

"No. That's the one. Our celebrity chef has come into possession of a special knife. You will steal it for me. Mark this sight, and mark it well."

She lifted the lid of the teapot. A gust of steam billowed out to form a white shimmering curtain in the air between them. With a twirl of her long, squirming fingers, the steam coalesced. It took on color and form, becoming a three-dimensional image that hung, slowly turning, in the open air. It was a kitchen knife, one that had fallen on hard times. Its wooden handle was cracked and wound with black tape, the blade pitted with rust.

"I hope he's not chopping veggies with that thing," Daniel said. "What's the deal? Enchanted?"

"In a manner of speaking. This is a Cutting Knife."

Faust sat back in his chair. His eyes narrowed. He sipped his tea.

"I've dealt with one of those. Recently."

"Yes," the Mourner said. "And I'm told you succeeded admirably. The reward for good work, as the saying goes, is more work. You should be honored: there are only nine true Cutting Knives in all of creation, amid any number of lesser imitations, and you'll have had the honor of wielding two of them. This particular one has been missing for centuries."

"Yeah? So how'd Mr. Heart Attack on a Plate get his hands on it, then?"

"Ill luck and happenstance, and machinations from strange quarters. He has no idea what it's truly capable of. Once you have the knife, bring it directly to me. You'll likely find it concealed in his home. If not...well, this sort of thing is your specialty. Find it and take it, by trickery or force. You may enlist the aid of your allies, if you must, but you will not reveal a word we have spoken here, nor will you reveal who you are working for."

"That's a lot of conditions for a job I haven't agreed to do yet," Daniel said. "Let's talk about my fee."

A slithering chuckle emanated from beneath the Mourner's veil. The lace rippled on a puff of hot breath.

"You will bring the knife to me and be rewarded as I see fit. Or you will fail and die. Or you will refuse and die. Do you wish to die, Daniel?"

"Honestly, I've been hoping to put it off for as long as possible," he said.

"Given that your name is marked among the damned," the Mourner mused, "a wise choice on your part. Consider this task a step toward redemption, for you have been chosen to play a small part in a grand and wondrous design. Go. Hunt. And return with the knife."

The ring of candles died, snuffed out in a sudden gust of white-hot wind, and plunged the cavern into darkness.

His pocket light flickered back to life. He sat in the ornate iron chair, all alone, in the middle of a storm drain. The vaulted concrete tunnel stretched dead ahead, farther than his light could shine, while fat black widows crawled slowly along the tunnel walls. Daniel took a deep breath, tasting the musty air, and let it out as a sigh of resignation.

"Well, shit," he said. He stood up and started walking.

Fifteen

Marie stopped at a liquor store down the block from her apartment and picked up a bottle of gin. A note from Janine waited for her at home, pinned to the refrigerator with a magnet shaped like a strawberry. *Game night*, it read, *don't wait up. Chinese leftovers in the fridge if you want.*

Underneath she'd doodled a heaping bowl of rice, cartoon waves of steam rising up. Marie smiled. She had a little reheated rice and General Tso's, the chicken and broccoli melting into a goopy but edible mess. Then she dug around in the cluttered fridge for something to go with the gin. A can of diet Sprite made a decent enough mixer.

Janine's mammoth and probably stolen book of heraldry sat on the futon, a bookmark with a sketch of the dead man's tattoo jutting out from the thick pages. Marie had asked her to do a little research in the hopes of finding a historical meaning behind it. So far, no luck.

A few fingers of gin performed alchemy, muffling Marie's stress, transforming her anxiety to wistful longing. She rummaged through her bookshelf, tugging an old favorite from the row of dog-eared paperbacks—*Swords Against Madness*, by Carolyn Saunders. She'd read it a dozen times; the text held no mysteries, no new surprises, but the words wrapped around her like a warm and familiar blanket. It was comfort food for the soul. She sipped her gin and leafed through the pages, letting the story wash over her.

A voice emerged from the hollow, she read, *dripping with cold malice and amusement. Even in her green-steel armor, her mother's sword riding on her hip, Talia fought a sudden shiver of fear. The swamp seemed to close in around her. Dangling tree boughs dripped down like black fingers, reaching for her.*

"Who ventures into my home?" asked the voice. "Who dares to disturb the Witch of the Challs?"

Talia swallowed, her throat dry, and raised her chin. "A knight-errant, on a holy quest."

"Holy?" A faint chuckle echoed through the dead trees. "I see no symbol of the father church upon you. I see no brand of the Sacristines. By what god do you claim right of passage?"

She touched her throat, tugging at the silver chain around her neck and fishing the symbol she'd been given out from under her breastplate. She held it high to catch the moonlight: a skeleton key, forged in cold iron.

"By no mere god at all. It is the Lady of the Crossroads, the Lady in Red, who sends me forth to battle."

The response came on a whisper of acrid wind. "Well chosen. And you would pay a witch's price for the wisdom you seek?"

"For the knowledge to save my people," the knight said, "I would pay any price."

Marie poured herself another glass of gin.

She thought back to her dream, to the tattooed symbol in Nessa's book. Of course Vanessa Roth wasn't a witch. There was no such thing, not in real life. But she was an anthropologist. She knew things. Marie didn't dare go near Richard Roth again, at least not until she had her badge back, but nobody had said she couldn't pay a courtesy call to his wife to ask for her academic insight.

Besides, maybe she just wanted to see her again.

*   *   *

The next morning, Marie felt like an interloper as she walked the campus of Barnard College. She was more than a decade out of college herself, though she didn't like to count the years. Walking among the crowds of younger women, hearing them talk as they roved in clustered packs, was a strange flavor of time travel. When she was their age, she was convinced she knew everything. In hindsight, she wanted to crawl under a rock and hide when she realized how little she knew about anything back then.

And in ten more years, she thought, *I'll probably look back and marvel about how I didn't know anything in my thirties. And ten years after that...*

A couple of helpful students played tour guide, pointing her way to the right classroom. She poked her head in, hearing Nessa's voice for the first time since they'd met at her brownstone in the Village.

"—August 14, 1791, a secret ceremony was held at Bois Caiman. One of the attendees was a woman named Cecile Fatiman, a *mambo*—that is, a priestess of vodou."

Marie stepped into the classroom and closed the door softly behind her. She lingered at the edges of the half-empty seats. While she'd looked like a fashion plate at home, Nessa at work was a figure just slightly out of time. She wore a long vintage skirt, a prim blouse, and a thin black silk scarf knotted into a dangly bow tie at her throat. Her eyes widened behind her owlish glasses when she glanced Marie's way, and she smiled as she went on with the lecture.

"Cecile, allegedly possessed by the goddess Ezili Dantor, sacrificed a pig while the crowd was regaled with prophecies of rebellion and freedom." Nessa held up her right hand, her palm to the classroom like a court witness being sworn in. "The celebrants drank the pig's blood and washed their hands in it. A symbol of their readiness to fight."

A few students stifled giggles, rolling their eyes at the melodramatic gesture. Nessa lowered her hand, casting another quick glance at Marie before turning back to her class.

"That was the start of the Haitian Revolution, the most successful slave revolt in recorded history. One week after the ritual at Bois Caiman, tens of thousands of slaves rose up to join the fight. Less than a year after that night, rebels controlled nearly half of the island, thousands of slave owners were dead, and almost two hundred plantations had been burned to the ground. Now, what does that teach us? Anyone?"

No hands went up. Nessa arched an eyebrow, cocking a lopsided smile.

"Whatever the culture, whatever it's called," Nessa told them, "witchcraft is the traditional tool of the politically dispossessed. A court of last resort for those who have no other means of exerting power. If you're looking for a revolution, look for a witch."

One student raised her hand. "But...Professor Roth, you're not saying that the ritual actually *worked*, are you? I mean, the sacrifice didn't magically make the revolution happen."

"Good question. And I'll ask you one in return: does it matter? The ritual took place, and whether it worked by some sort of crowd hypnosis, the sheer fervor for freedom whipped to a boil, or, sure, 'magic,' the results were very, very real. And I believe we're at the end of our time for today. Ladies, please read Leyburn, chapters eight through twelve, for Wednesday's class. I'm not saying there's going to be a quiz, but there's going to be a quiz."

She smiled at the chorus of mock groans and stood behind her desk with folded arms, watching her students shuffle off. Marie walked against the tide, making her way toward the front of the class. Hesitant, heart pounding, her mouth suddenly dry.

This is ridiculous, she told herself. *I'm a police officer making a professional consultation. I've done this a hundred times.*

But not with her.

As she neared the desk, Nessa looked almost as nervous as Marie felt. The professor's eyelashes fluttered, and she awkwardly fiddled with the scarf at her throat.

"Detective," she said. "This is an unexpected pleasure. If you're looking for my husband, I'm afraid he's still out of town."

"No, it's...it's you that I want. To speak to. I mean, um, if it's not a bother, I could use your professional expertise."

The professor's demeanor shifted, a change in her eyes. She

stepped around her desk slowly, her formerly anxious motions turning feline, graceful.

"Do tell."

Marie produced a sketch on scratch paper. She had copied the curves and lines of the dead man's tattoo with careful precision. Nessa snatched it from her outstretched fingers, unfolding it, peering closely through her glasses.

"This was a tattoo on a suspect's wrist," Marie said, "and I'm not sure if the symbol means anything, but my gut says it's relevant. I thought it might be a gang affiliation thing at first, but our gang-crimes division came up empty."

The classroom door drifted shut, leaving them alone together.

"A tattoo," Nessa echoed. "And the circumstances it was found under?"

"I can't go into any more detail, I'm afraid. It's an active case. Still, Professor Roth, any help you could give us—"

"Nessa."

Marie tilted her head. "Hmm?"

"Not 'Professor Roth.' Nessa, to you. We don't have to be formal here."

Keep it professional, Marie told herself. *Keep it professional.*

"All—all right, Vanessa. You can call me Marie—"

"No."

The professor closed the gap between them. Stepping into Marie's personal space as easily as popping a soap bubble. She lingered there, as if she could sense Marie's sudden discomfort. Savoring it.

"Not 'Vanessa,'" she said. "Nessa. My friends call me Nessa."

Nessa moved an inch closer, looking up at the taller woman. A delighted little smile played on her lips.

"Say my name, Marie."

Since the day she put on her uniform blues for the first time, long before she earned her detective's shield, Marie had been threatened more times than she could count. She had faced off against rampaging tweakers, pumped well-armed gang members for information, and had even piled onto a four-hundred-pound PCP addict and helped wrestle him into cuffs. Getting into trouble, and getting out of it in one piece, was part of her job description.

Despite all that, she'd never felt like she was walking a razor's edge quite like she did in this moment. Her assertiveness training from the police academy told her exactly what she needed to do: reestablish boundaries, and politely but firmly assume command of the interview.

"Nessa," she whispered, standing perfectly still.

Nessa nodded and took one step back. Allowing Marie some breathing room, a reward for her correct answer.

"Of course I'll help you." She looked back at the paper, squinting. "I have to say, it's not familiar at first glance, but I don't mind cracking the books for a good cause. I'll call you as soon as I have something. Give me your phone."

"My—" Marie started to say. She'd arrived with her usual confidence. Shields up, professional mask firmly in place. By uttering just a few words, glancing her way, and controlling the distance between them, the professor had managed to throw her into a tailspin.

"Give me," Nessa said, holding out her hand, "your phone."

Marie handed it over. Nessa turned the screen toward herself, humming happily as she tapped away. She gave it back, showing Marie the new entry she'd made in her contact list: *Nessa*, followed by a phone number.

"That's my personal cell," Nessa said. "And I texted myself your number, so I have it now. I'll be in touch. Soon."

* * *

Nessa sent Marie away, the detective looking bewildered and blindsided. As the classroom door swung shut at her back, leaving Nessa alone, she stood frozen for a moment.

Then she clutched a balled-up fist to her chest. She beamed and shifted from foot to foot in an impromptu, giddy dance.

She'd spent the entire morning in a downbeat haze. Between

yesterday's insults, the denial of tenure, her rejected paper, and the indignities of a new day—yet another batch of students who couldn't be bothered to *think*, compounded with the mental image of her husband in bed with some younger, prettier surrogate, not even having the respect to tell her he wanted an open marriage...she'd craved nothing more than to go back home, crawl under the covers, and sleep the rest of the day away.

Marie's arrival had changed all that. Nessa had started to convince herself that the odd spark between them had been a one-sided flight of fantasy. That there was no magic afoot, no strange connection, just Nessa's own loneliness and frustration playing tricks on her.

But she came to see me, Nessa told herself. *She came to see ME*.

She still didn't understand any of this. The euphoria she felt, the way she glowed when Marie looked her way. That delightful little fraying sound at the edge of Marie's voice when she whispered Nessa's name. But it was real. And it was wonderful.

Nessa spun into a pirouette as she danced around her desk, laughing, catching herself. She felt silly but she did it anyway.

"Something is happening, isn't it?" she asked the empty classroom. "Something special. Something that's never happened before."

She had never put much stock in gods or religion. Her own witchcraft was an agnostic and solitary pursuit. In that moment, though, she was certain of one thing: somebody was looking out for her.

Sixteen

Less than a year after it first hit the streets, experts were lining up to call ink "the new crack." It exploded into an epidemic overnight, from New York to LA, scouring the country east to west like a barbed-wire scourge. The usual suspects had clean hands, and they were bending over backward to prove it. Rackets from the Cali Cartel to the Five Families had issued bounties on ink dealers, as desperate to find the elusive pipeline as the law was.

Nobody liked having their profits stolen.

The warehouse in Dallas, baking in the springtime heat on the outskirts of the city, was run like a prison camp. Sentinels were on duty twenty-four hours a day, seven days a week. Snipers on the sheet-metal roof, and a dozen men with military-grade firepower on call and ready to kill to protect their secret. There was constant surveillance within and without, electronic countermeasures in play, and half the local cops were either on the take or blackmailed into silence. They'd built an impregnable fortress, a crucial hub of the ink pipeline.

Hence Bruno's surprise when he came back from a food run, carrying fat plastic sacks of wrapped sandwiches from the Subway a quarter mile away, and found the outer gate wide open.

Then he found the dead men lying in the dust, their unfired guns still clutched in their pale hands. Playing cards jutted from their throats like darts.

The sacks dropped from Bruno's arms. They burst, spilling sandwiches across the hot asphalt as he drew his snub-nosed pistol. He gripped it in both hands, trying to keep them from shaking. Bruno was a middleman, a nobody. He'd been recruited from a cushy management job in pharmaceutical sales, chosen for his easy access to base chemicals and his industry contacts. Despite the guns and the perpetually looming threat of violence, he'd managed to convince himself that this was just another white-collar job.

His mind raced, trying to remember his briefings. There was a number to call in case of a security breach. He was supposed to memorize it. Instead, he'd written it in a binder and forgotten about it. After all, his recruiters had told him the job was perfectly safe, hadn't they?

The binder was in his office. Inside the warehouse.

The barn door, for loading and unloading delivery trucks, hung wide open. He inched through, swinging the gun wildly, jumping at shadows. More dead men littered the floor, scattered among the maze of shipping crates. All his coworkers, the entire security force—everyone was dead, their blood spattering the concrete like a Jackson Pollock.

Not everyone.

A woman stood amid the carnage, draped in a scarlet gown. An iron key dangled at the hollow of her throat, suspended on a delicate chain. She looked Bruno's way and smiled softly, tilting her head.

"Take heart," the Lady in Red told him. "Your death is for a good cause."

She held up a playing card, twirling it in her fingertips, and flicked it effortlessly through the air.

It was the last thing he ever saw.

*   *   *

Two hours later, a strike team hit the warehouse gates like the fist of an angry god. Six black SUVs, sharks with tinted windows and armor plating, blasted into the parking lot and squealed to a dead stop. The SUVs looked like FBI standard issue. So did the men and women who boiled out, badges on their belts and their Glock pistols braced for an all-out gunfight. Instead, they found a fresh graveyard.

Jessie Temple took the lead. She wore glasses a few shades darker than her skin, her frizzy black hair pulled back in a tight bun. She tapped her earpiece as she strode through the sweltering warehouse, glancing left and right, taking in the scene.

"Kevin," she said, "we've got a goddamn massacre here. Talk to me."

A teenager's voice crackled in her ear, carried on a burst of static. "Pulling feeds from my back door into the Helix spy sat, boss. This is...yeah, something. Couple of hours ago, logs show a *massive* burst of electrical interference. Something disrupted comms a mile in every direction for about fifteen minutes."

"What would cause that, an EMP?"

"I don't think so. Signatures aren't quite right. Harmony, you got any idea—"

"Magic," said the woman at Jessie's shoulder.

Jessie turned and tugged down her dark glasses. Her irises were pure turquoise, inhumanly bright and blue. She stared at her partner with an unspoken question in her eyes.

Harmony Black wore a three-piece suit the color of midnight, an ivory blouse, and a man's salmon necktie. She crouched over a corpse and touched her fingertips to his pale forehead. She closed her eyes for a moment, as if communing with the victim. Drinking in the scene.

Jessie raised her open hand as a pair of the tactical-team agents approached. "Hold up. Give us some room, our witch is doing her thing. You guys start searching those crates. I want to know what's here and what's *not* here, you get me?"

Harmony's palm followed the contours of the dead man's chest, hovering an inch above his blood-soaked shirt. Tiny, almost imperceptible sparks danced along her fingertips. Then she snapped her hand away. She curled it into a fist and unclenched it again. She wriggled her fingers as she rose to her full height, as if flicking away something foul.

"This place is drenched in raw magic," she told Jessie. "Not any normal practitioner, either. Whoever did this was *way* out of my league. Feels like a nuke went off in here. These men never had a chance; the fight must have been over in minutes, if not seconds."

Jessie nodded, poking her toe at a fallen submachine gun. "None of these have been fired. No stray shells, no collateral damage. It was a blitz attack fueled by occult power. High speed, high precision, no mercy. What does that remind you of?"

"The Network," Harmony said.

"Exactly." Jessie put a hand on her hip and sighed. "This has all the signatures of a Network hit. Which is kind of a big damn problem, since as far as we know, they're the assholes *making* ink."

The Network was a myth. A tale told by underworld scum looking to boost their reputation: everybody knew somebody whose brother's best friend's roommate did a job for the Network. A criminal organization, the story went, buried so far underground that the world's foremost law enforcement agencies couldn't prove they existed. They didn't even have a name; "Network" was just shorthand, a title of convenience. Ask nine out of ten FBI agents, they'd swear it was nothing but an urban legend.

Jessie and Harmony knew better. Then again, they weren't ordinary FBI agents. The government organization they really reported to, concealed five layers deep behind Washington cutouts and walls of red tape, had firsthand experience in this fight.

"Second-floor office," Jessie said, pointing up toward the back of the warehouse. "I'm gonna take a look."

Jessie made a running jump, grappled a wall of wooden crates, and effortlessly scaled them hand-over-hand. She raced along the row of boxes with her coattails flying out behind her, launched into an acrobatic flip, and sailed through an open office window to land in a graceful roll on the other side.

"Showing off much?" Harmony called up. "Perfectly good flight of stairs, you know."

Jessie poked her head out the office window. "My way is more fun."

Harmony prowled among the dead. Outstretched hands, wide and glassy eyes, a chorus of silent pleas for help that came too late. She had no sympathy for the fallen. All the same, they belonged behind bars, not in a grave. This wasn't justice; it was a blood-soaked ambush. Criminals murdering criminals.

And as she crouched beside a second corpse, studying his wounds, she knew exactly who was responsible.

A playing card had buried itself halfway into the dead man's skull, right between his eyes. She gripped it with her fingertips and slid it out slowly, wriggling it, feeling it give. It came out half-painted scarlet with a rivulet of blood dripping down the ace of hearts. She turned it in her fingers. On the back, a red dragon rampant.

She didn't see the Lady in Red standing silently behind her, a faint smile on her lips. Nobody did.

"Son of a bitch," Harmony breathed. She tapped her earpiece. "I know who did this."

From the office window, Jessie's head perked up. Harmony saw her lips move as her voice echoed over the earpiece. "Usually you're happy when you figure out who the bad guy is. You don't sound happy. What gives?"

Say it, whispered the Lady in Red.

Harmony held up the bloody playing card. "Daniel Faust."

"Faust?" Jessie tilted her head, looking down from the window. "He died in a prison riot."

"We *thought* he died in prison. I always thought it was a little too convenient. He probably arranged the entire thing as a cover for his escape."

"Are you sure? Harmony, let's get real, you've always been a little Captain Ahab when it comes to that guy. Are you sure you don't *want* him to be alive, so you can go after him again? Besides, weren't you saying this took massive occult power? Daniel Faust was just a gangster with a few card tricks."

The Lady in Red leaned close to Harmony, murmuring in her ear. *Only one man kills like this.*

"Only one man kills like this." Harmony flicked the playing card with her finger. "There are at least fifty human sorcerers in our target database, and *one* of them uses cards as weapons. Daniel Faust."

"Well, you're the one who crossed swords with him. If you say it's him, it's him. What's the motive?"

April Cassidy's voice broke in on the line. "We know a considerable number of the criminal underworld's more notable denizens are eager to find the source of ink. If our resurrected Mr. Faust is back to working freelance, or carving out an empire of his own, perhaps he's on the same trail that we are."

"Then we keep hunting," Harmony said. "We find the pipeline, we find *him*."

"Well, I've got some ledgers here that might point us in the right direction," Jessie said.

Harmony joined her in the office. Unlike Jessie, she took the stairs.

The ledgers were dense, half the details coded or in cryptic shorthand. They started with the computer database and shipping labels. With the aid of Kevin's expertise, and some highly illegal cracking programs, a picture started to take shape. The Dallas connection was receiving chemical components from Juárez to Winnipeg, but made outbound deliveries in one direction only: northeast, to New York City.

"Let's saddle up," Jessie said. "Looks like we're on the right track. Our best chance yet to shut this circus down and give the Network one hell of a black eye."

"We may be able to call upon some local assistance if we need it," April's voice said over their earpieces. "Do you remember Detective Reinhart? You met her at that bank robbery in Manhattan last year."

"Sure," Harmony said. She had found something of a kindred spirit in Marie Reinhart.

"I've been doing a bit of consulting on the side, helping her with a serial-murder investigation. No relation to our current case, but I suspect we could rely upon her if it proves necessary."

"Sounds good," Jessie said. "The more help, the merrier. I think we're due for a win."

"Two wins," Harmony said.

Her partner looked Harmony's way, curious. "Yeah?"

"Yeah." Harmony offered up a thin, hungry smile. "I've got a white whale to catch."

Seventeen

Marie was on the hunt for her own white whale. Her ship was foundering, taking on water fast. Beau Kates had sold Baby Blue for a shoebox full of chemicals, so stoned he couldn't remember what her kidnappers looked like. A revelation and a dead end, all in one. She still thought Richard Roth was dirty, but without her badge, she couldn't do anything about it. She couldn't show her face in the precinct without Captain Traynor jumping down her throat, so department resources were out of reach until she was cleared for duty again. And while she could always reach out to Gorski and Jefferson...

Don't encourage her, she heard Helena mutter, as vivid as when it happened. *Everybody knows she's fucked in the head.*

Her frustrations reduced her to pacing her tiny living room, recounting facts and dates like some dime-store Sherlock Holmes and getting nowhere fast, when her phone buzzed.

"Reinhart."

"Detective," said an unfamiliar raspy voice. "We haven't met. This is Jake Moretti. I work Homicide out in Jersey City. This a bad time?"

Marie's brow furrowed, curiosity getting the better of her. "Not at all. What can I do for you?"

"A little birdie tells me you've been working a string of dead hookers out in your burg. The kinda string that says 'serial killer,' but you've got no support from the brass to back that up."

"You've got some birds with keen hearing out in Jersey."

"What can I tell ya? We've got everything here. Paradise on Earth. Anyway, point of the matter is, I'm in the same kinda boat. Maybe the *exact* same boat."

Marie stopped pacing.

"More victims?" she said. "Jersey side?"

"And a fresh one just showed up this morning. Same MO. You ask me, your unsub and mine? Same guy."

Marie's heart skipped a beat. If there were more victims out there—if the killer, or killers, were dumping bodies on either side of the state line to throw off the scent...

"How many have you found so far?" she asked him.

"Nothing official, because my captain refuses to *make* it official, but off the record? I've linked four vics to this creep. I say 'off the record' because I've been told not to make this phone call. I'd just be opening a can of worms, they tell me."

"Can't go fishing without opening a can of worms," Marie said.

Jake barked out a laugh. "Yeah, see? We've got the same idea. I'm not a big fan of sitting on my ass while innocent kids are getting carved up, my future career prospects notwithstanding. I hear you've got the same sorta attitude problem."

"I've been accused of being a poor team player. Got to tell you before this goes any further, though, they pulled my badge and my gun. Officer-involved shooting. It was a good shoot, but until I'm cleared, I'm technically not a cop."

"And I'm technically a shitty pitcher, but they haven't tossed me off the department softball team yet. This is strictly on the down low. See, we got a guy in custody."

Marie held the phone tight against her ear. "Who?"

"Caught him dumping the body red-handed. He told the uniforms he's not the killer, he just got paid to drop the corpse in a junkyard and walk. I think he's telling the truth. The guy's gutter trash, a junkie who can barely tie his own shoelaces. Still, might know more than he's letting on. I want to team up, both of us take a run at him at the same time. See, I don't know the details of any of your vics. Jersey can't pull New York's case files—"

"And I don't know yours," Marie said. "But together we might get more out of him than either of us would get alone."

"That's a bingo. He ain't lawyered up yet and I want to have a go before he gets smart enough to invoke legal aid. What do you say? Wanna be a ghost in the room?"

Marie's hopes soared. She had a lead. She had an ally. She had a shot.

"On my way," she said.

She took a cab to the Port Authority Bus Terminal, then hopped the 119 to Jersey City.

*   *   *

Jake Moretti looked like his voice sounded: bedraggled, rough around the edges, burned by cigarettes and cheap beer. He was a thirty-year veteran of the homicide squad who had seen every horrible thing one human being could do to another. When they shook hands, Marie felt the sandpaper calluses on his palm.

"Anybody asks," he said in a low voice as he hustled her through the crowded precinct house, "you're the psych consultant I called in to assess the perp's state of mind. Barring that, just forget how to speak English and we'll figure something out."

Their suspect waited in Interview Room C, his wrists shackled to a ring in the stainless-steel desk. They paused outside the one-way window to study him before they headed in. He was a young guy, twenties, with long black hair like a wannabe rocker. He had a wannabe rocker's drug habit, too: that giveaway twitch, bouncing in his chair, too itchy to sit still.

"Sylvester Rimes," Jake said, taking a cursory glance at the coffee-stained file folder in his hands. "Born a loser, gonna die a loser. Got a string of petty convictions as long as my arm. Possession, burglary. So far, his greatest claim to fame was an attempt to commit armed robbery with a water gun."

"Looks like he just graduated to the major leagues," Marie said.

They didn't bother with good cop, bad cop. It was bad cop, bad cop from the second they hit the room.

"You fucked up, Sylvester," Jake told him, circling the table like a shark smelling blood. "You. Fucked. Up."

His shackles rattled. "I told you, I didn't kill her! I was just paid to dump the body, that's *all*."

"Sure, in two jurisdictions," Marie said. "Bad idea. See, we've got you tied to seven homicides—"

"*Seven?*" His eyes bugged out. "No, no, hey, that wasn't me—"

"Know how this works? You're a party to all seven, split across state lines," Marie said.

"Which means when we're done with you," Jake said, "we put you on a prison bus, send you across the GW Bridge, and you stand trial all over again."

Sylvester folded in on himself. His gaze darted between them, a drowning man searching for a life preserver.

"I wanna...I wanna make a deal!"

"With who?" Jake shrugged at him. "Any deal you make with our DA doesn't hold water on the other side of the Hudson. Same on their end."

Marie slapped her palm on the steel table to get his attention.

"You're going down for a long, long time, Mr. Rimes. Your best chance of survival, your *only* chance, is to come clean right here and now. Tell us everything, from the first contact with the men who hired you to the second the cuffs went around your wrists this morning. You do that, and if the details check out, *maybe* we can talk about some kind of leniency."

"Man," he stammered. "One man. And it was only two, swear to God, it was two bodies. I never even *been* to New York, you gotta believe me. I'm on probation, I ain't supposed to leave the state. My probie catches me in New York, that's an instant violation and I go back inside."

Jake loomed over his shoulder. "Who hired you? Give us a name."

"There aren't any names, man. Nobody's got a name, not where I come from."

"What about the payment?" Marie asked. "Don't even pretend they paid you up front. Nobody trusts a junkie. Where and when?"

He looked to her, forlorn. "An hour ago. Newport Station, near the lockers. He's gone, okay? I didn't show. That means he knows I got picked up. You ain't gonna find him. He's *smart*. Last time we met, he showed me where to stand and walk so the security cameras can't get a look at your face."

Jake glanced at Marie. "I'll pull security footage from the station, just in case."

Marie fished out her phone. She flicked through her web browser, rummaging through her history for the Roth Estate Holdings website. She magnified a photo of Richard Roth, smiling like a champion in the living room of a ten-million-dollar condo, and showed Sylvester the screen.

"Was this the man?"

Sylvester tried to rub at his eyes. The chain on his shackles shook, his wrists jerking short. He squinted.

"I don't...no, I don't think so. I mean, he had a nice suit like that, around the same age, but...no, that's not the guy."

Disappointed, Marie put the phone away. She couldn't shake her instincts about Roth. All the same, she was experienced enough to know better than to latch on to a hunch. Her first mentor had beaten it into her head over and over again: *follow the evidence. If the evidence disagrees with your gut, follow the evidence anyway.*

The mirror at her back slammed on its frame, the one-way glass jolting, sharp enough to send her shooting to her feet. A man screamed like a strangled cat. Another slam on the glass, and a hairline crack tore right down the middle.

Marie and Jake ran for the door. They burst from the interrogation room into sheer pandemonium. A grizzled man with a tangled beard and ragged, dirty clothes grappled with police out in the hall. Four uniformed officers clung to him like barnacles as he spat and fought and kicked. Another jumped on his back, struggling to bring him down to the checkered tile floor. His head swung in Marie's direction. He had the jaundiced skin and blown-out pupils of a late-stage addict, and the faint black lines etched around his chapped lips told her his drug of choice was ink. His tortured eyes widened in recognition.

"*You!*" he bellowed. "You. I see you. I've *read* you!"

The uniforms wrestled him to his knees, then onto his belly, planting him flat while they zipped two sets of flex-cuffs onto his wrists and ankles. As they carried him down the hall to the holding cells, he looked up and gave a leering grin.

"You're gonna die, Marie! I've read the ending. *I've read the ending!*"

He disappeared around a cinder-block corner, still screaming, laughing, his words devolving into garbled nonsense. Marie stood frozen, staring at the empty hall.

"Did you know that guy?" Jake asked, looking at her sidelong.

"No." She shook her head. "I've never seen him before."

"Huh."

He didn't have anything else to say. Neither did she. They went back into the interview room.

Their suspect wasn't alone. The new arrival was a prim, tight-lipped gentleman in a pressed gray suit, an alligator-skin attaché resting on the table before him. He rose sharply, almost mechanically.

"*Excuse* me," Jake started to say.

"No, sir, excuse me." The man flicked out a business card, holding it between perfectly manicured nails. "The name is Smith. Mr. Smith, Esquire. Legal counsel from Weishaupt and Associates, here to represent Mr. Rimes. You've been interviewing my client without his representative present. Unacceptable."

"He didn't ask for a lawyer," Jake said.

"Didn't he? And yet, here I am. Suffice to say, this interrogation is over, and I'll be lodging a formal complaint with your captain."

"Yeah," Jake said, "you do that."

The lawyer's head turned on a swivel, locking onto Marie. "And you are?"

Marie was focused on Sylvester. He didn't just seem nervous and erratic, like he had when they were questioning him. He looked absolutely terrified. And it wasn't the detectives he was afraid of.

"Leaving," she told Mr. Smith. "I was just leaving."

Eighteen

At the heart of a cavernous laboratory, under electric-blue lights, the Scrying Table clacked like a typewriter in the hands of a madman. It was a map of the world made from thousands of magnetic pins suspended in an oily black broth. The pins surged, rippled, and roiled, as if charting invisible earthquakes across the globe. Every jump of a pin ended in a metallic *pop* as it slapped back down again, splashing into the oil and striking the iron beneath.

Bloch stared at the table, his face pale, his cheeks lined with unshaven bristle. His lab coat was half buttoned and his hands hung limp at his sides. "Now we are all sons of bitches," he murmured.

"You're quoting Kenneth Bainbridge?" called a voice from above. "Now? Really? Shall I do Oppenheimer, then?"

A crane arm whirred, and Savannah Cross descended from the ceiling.

She wore a harness cabled to the crane, the device effortlessly swinging her across the laboratory. At her back, mounted on the harness, four robotic arms swiveled and snapped. The arms were engraved with spidery silver runes running from the harness to the pincer tips. She spun, twirling across the open air, half ballerina and half venomous spider. She floated past a bank of tables, checking on chemical equipment, adjusting a Bunsen burner with her human hands while one of the robotic arms snatched up a pencil in its yellow pincers and scribbled a quick notation on a pad of paper. As the crane winged her over to a steel slab, Savannah did a graceful backflip.

She typed on one keyboard while her extra arms hunted and pecked across two others, answering three emails at once. She talked to Bloch over her shoulder.

"Now I am become death, destroyer of etcetera, etcetera. You are *such* a drama queen. And ungrateful. We're doing cutting-edge work here, standing at the untold frontiers of science, and all you do is whine about it."

Bloch waved at the Scrying Table. The pins clattered and clacked.

"Have you seen these readings?" he demanded. "The project is going too far, too fast. We have to rein it in. We should go back to square one, start from scratch with new limited-release trials."

Savannah pulled on a pair of goggles. Tiny pin lights at the sides mirrored the sapphire blue of the overheads. She jumped back and the crane lifted her off her feet. Momentum spun her around, her lab coat flaring out behind her. She loomed over Bloch and raised her hands high. The four robotic arms, steered by her subconscious mind, struck a pose. An electronic Kali floating in midair.

"Oh, sure, the early trials. Watered-down ink, barely one-percent pure. And what did the test subjects do, once they got hooked? Mostly spray-painted graffiti about owls. Not productive."

"Doesn't it bother you that we don't even know *why*?" Bloch asked her. Savannah spun away, swinging down in front of a whiteboard scrawled with equations and occult sigils. She tapped her finger against her lips and studied her work.

"We know why. Memetic bleed from the Shadow In-Between. A glitch in the system."

"A 'glitch' we should have thoroughly studied before pushing forward. Fifty addicts with no connection to one another, from San Francisco to New York, all decided to write 'The Owl Lives' at nearly the same moment. Maybe we should find out what 'the Owl' actually *is*?"

"We will. That's what good science *is*, Dr. Bloch. We study, we experiment, we learn."

"We're risking a mass-casualty event. If this experiment slips out of our control, and I think it already has, the death toll could be catastrophic."

The crane arm hummed. She turned his way, arching a pert eyebrow.

"Of course it could. Your point being?" She shrugged. Her mechanical arms mirrored the gesture. "Discovery requires risks. No knowledge without sacrifice. You should try to be more like our sponsors."

"Our *sponsors*," he spat. "We made a deal with the devil. You know that, don't you?"

"For unlimited funds and access to the most advanced laboratory on the planet? That's a deal any *real* scientist would jump at. But for the record, Dr. Bloch, your assessment is incorrect."

She swooped in, hovering over him again.

"We made a deal with the Network," she told him. "They're the people the devil is afraid of."

Bloch clapped his hands to his ears as every speaker in the room, every device and machine, let out a piercing static squeal. The blue lights flickered and dimmed.

"Boss is coming," Savannah chirped, her lips curling in a tight bow. "Better look busy."

With a ripping sound, like scissors slicing through construction paper, the copper blade of a knife tore a crack in the world. The blade protruded from nowhere, leaving a glowing black line in its wake. Then the crack wrenched open.

Beyond it lay a lightless void, darker and colder than outer space. Papers ruffled and the map pins clattered in a panic as the howling void sucked at everything around it, stealing the oxygen, flooding the laboratory with the sound of clanging steel chimes.

A towering man stepped from the darkness, clutching the copper-bladed knife in one brutish fist. His bare feet touched down on the tile floor, his legs like fat steel pistons under a pair of black silk trousers. He had a bodybuilder's frame, but the muscles of his bare chest bulged in all the wrong ways, too many, misshapen, like serpents under his skin. His head was squat and bald, his ears boxy, his eyes dirt-brown and glinting with malice. He looked like a talented but untrained artist's first attempt to model the human form in clay: an ambitious disaster.

The crack in the world whipped shut at his back, leaving nothing behind but the faint scent of roses.

"Adam." Savannah offered a floating bow, then kicked into a somersault as her crane arm whirred. She spread her arms wide in greeting. "Welcome to the frontier of science."

"Dr. Cross," he rumbled in a gravelly voice. "Dr. Bloch. I've come to check on our investment."

"The ink trials are proceeding with maximum efficiency. Oh, except for the virus Dr. Bloch attempted to introduce into our database this morning."

Adam offered a faintly amused smile. "Did he really?"

"Hold on, now—" Bloch raised his hands, taking a defensive step backward.

"He'd rather wallow in the mud as a primate than rise up and dance with the Kings of Man." Savannah shook her head as she swung closer to Bloch. Her robotic pincers snapped at the air in irritation. "The only real sin in the universe is incuriosity, Dr. Bloch. I'm afraid it's a mortal sin, too."

Bloch's head swiveled between Savannah and Adam, his face lined with panic.

"We have to stop this!" He flung out an arm, pointing at the map table. The pins bounced and rippled. "If we continue at this rate, we're risking more than the lives of every single ink addict. We're endangering this entire *planet*."

Adam ignored him. He looked to Savannah. "Are you going to take care of this situation, Dr. Cross?"

Savannah flitted away. A ping from the workstations caught her attention, and she turned her back on the men as she rattled off a fresh email.

"Already did, twenty minutes ago. Poisoned his coffee. Should be kicking in any minute now."

Bloch stared at her, then looked at his empty mug in horror. "*What?*"

"Any. Minute. Now," she repeated, glowering at the clock.

Bloch began to cough. He fell to his knees, one hand pressed to his heart, the other clutching the rim of the map table. His eyes bulged as he collapsed to the floor, seizing, thrashing like a fish on a hook. He made wet, ragged sounds and retched dark blood onto the pristine tiles. Then he gave one last shuddering gasp and fell still.

"There we go," Savannah said. "He died like he lived: missing his cue."

"I'll have him removed," Adam said.

One of Savannah's robot arms shook its pincers from side to side at him, like a wagging head. The silvery runes engraved upon the steel glimmered under the blue lights.

"Leave it." She kicked away from the workstation, glided through the air, and landed beside the map table. "I can use it. Always need fresh bodies for something or other. I'm running ten experiments at once here. Twelve's my current record. Going for thirteen."

"Do as you please on your own time, Doctor, but there's only *one* project my masters are interested in. Give me an update."

Savannah's human arm swept across the map, taking it all in.

"We're maintaining real-time surveillance of geomantic frequencies. Essentially, monitoring the membrane between our world and the Shadow In-Between. As you can see, the stronger pulses are emanating from urban centers where ink distribution is on the upswing. Every addict becomes a living antenna."

Adam's brutish hands clamped down on the rim of the table. His beetle brows furrowed as he watched the metal pins dance. "So they transmit back to us."

"For now," Savannah said. "But that's the beauty of an antenna. They're primed to *receive*."

A fistful of pins shot up off the table, soaring from the bed of black oil. They hovered for just a moment before slamming down with an ear-popping squeal. The waters rippled and spat. Savannah put both hands to her mouth. Behind her, her robotic arms bent inward and wrapped her in a mechanical hug.

"Oh my," she said behind her hands. "This is interesting."

"I've learned to be very concerned when you use the word 'interesting,'" Adam told her, his voice bone-dry.

"We've had a spike of psychic power. A...mind-quake, you could say. In New Jersey, by the looks of it."

"We aren't running any operations in New Jersey," Adam said. "That wasn't us."

Savannah lowered her hands and beamed. Behind her, the robotic pincers applauded with tiny golf claps.

"Then we have a conundrum to explore! Delightful."

"I am not convinced," Adam said, "that you are approaching this project with the gravity it deserves. Magic is a primal force, Dr. Cross. It has little regard for your 'scientific method.'"

The crane whirred, lifting her high in the air. She floated around the laboratory and spun in a pirouette.

"Gravity is overrated. And so is magic. It's just another universal force, Adam, no different from electromagnetism, the strong nuclear, the weak nuclear, or...well...gravity."

She landed before him.

"And as humanity has proved time and time again," she said, "anything that exists can be quantified, studied, and understood. Magic is no different. By the time my work is done, people will master the powers of magic as simply and easily as they master the power of electricity now: with the flick of a switch, the push of a button."

Adam held up a warning finger. "Have a care, Doctor. You'd do well to remember the story of Prometheus."

"Stole fire from the gods," she said. "Gave it to the people. A fine role model for any scientist."

"And for his noble efforts, condemned to an eternal torment of being devoured alive." He loomed over her. His lips curled into a cold, predatory leer. "Just remember who you serve now. We *can* arrange that for you."

Savannah's eyes narrowed. She gave Bloch's corpse a petulant kick.

"Unlike my late and unlamented lab partner, *my* loyalty should be unquestionable."

"I question everyone," he said. "It's part of my job. And we are both charged with pleasing some very uncompromising taskmasters. Failure isn't an option, Doctor. We've invested too much money and too much time into this project. Random, unexplainable power surges do *not* reassure me."

"Nothing is unexplainable," she said. "There's only the explained and the not-explained-yet."

"I want you in the field. Take a team, go to New Jersey, find the source. I want an explanation. And a guarantee that this won't be a problem for us."

"Outside?" Her steel arms hugged her tight. The runes along the metal cast a faint glow across her worried face. "But...me? Outside? I can't take my arms outside—"

He cut her off with a glare.

"That wasn't a suggestion, Dr. Cross."

Nineteen

"I found something," Nessa said on the phone.

Marie's bus, battling its way through gridlocked traffic, rolled another few inches then jerked hard on its brakes. She jolted in her seat. Leaving the city was a lot faster than coming home again. Still, the sight of New York's canyons wrapped her in a strong and reassuring embrace. Everything about her visit to Jersey felt wrong, starting with the junkie screaming her name, and ending with a lawyer appearing from nowhere. She felt as though she'd been swimming in murky, black waters, and something had grabbed her by the ankle and hauled her under. Daylight, air, and safety were gone, and she was drowning in the strangling dark.

Then again, she supposed she'd been feeling that way for a while now. Today just drove the point home.

"That was fast," she told Nessa.

"Well, I am a professional. It's not much, I'll tell you that right up front. All the same...dinner?"

Marie blinked. "Dinner?"

"Yes, it's the third meal of the day, generally eaten in the evening. I just finished my last class. So come have dinner with me. Do you like Mediterranean?"

"I don't think I've tasted enough to say," Marie replied.

"Now is the perfect time, then. Meet me at Kashkaval Garden, on Ninth Avenue."

She changed buses at the next stop.

Kashkaval was over in Hell's Kitchen, on a street lined with rainbow flags, tattoo parlors, and psychic readers who catered to a hipster crowd. The restaurant was a cozy nook with a half dozen tables up front and a long oak bar running the length of the room. The faint scent of mingled spices hanging in the warm air gave Marie thoughts of the ocean. Nessa waited for her at a table for two, a thick hardcover book with a worn-away cover resting beside her water glass.

"You've had a long day," Nessa said.

Marie had to smile. "Is it that obvious?"

"Your true face is showing."

"True face?" Marie pulled out the chair across from her, settling in. A waitress swooped by and planted a glass of water on her left.

Nessa waved an idle hand. "Never mind. Tell me about your day."

As she sipped her water, ice cubes bumping her lip, Marie quietly marveled at the comfortable familiarity. She barely knew this woman. *Tell me about your day* was something you asked of a friend, a housemate, maybe a lover. But the question didn't seem strange at all. It fit like a favorite old sweater. It was strange for its lack of strangeness.

"Just...police business. I can't really talk about it."

"Really? But you're on leave."

Marie was reaching for the menu. She froze, her fingertips brushing the laminated surface.

"How do you know about that?"

Nessa cocked a lopsided smile. "Please. You came and questioned my husband. You think I wouldn't want to know why? The gunfight in Monticello made the news. Your name wasn't mentioned, but it didn't have to be. You were too...invested to simply be asking follow-up questions. So I made some phone calls. Discreet ones, I promise."

The mention of Richard Roth felt like a wedge; a curtain suddenly draped across the table, cutting a line between them. Marie's suspicions were a slow, swirling simmer. If Richard was involved in the killings—every bit of proof said otherwise, but she still couldn't shake her intuition—there was no telling what Nessa knew, what she'd done, where her loyalties lay. Dinner was a minefield. Marie wanted to kick herself. What was she doing, getting this close to a suspect's family? It was stupid, reckless. Dangerous.

But she was doing it anyway.

"I hope you don't play poker," Nessa mused, reading Marie's face over the top of her menu. "I'd clean you out."

"Thank you. For being discreet."

"Your secrets are safe with me. So. Why the badge?"

Marie picked up her menu. She ran her fingers down the list of choices. So many unfamiliar possibilities. She felt water closing in over her head again.

"What do you mean?" she asked.

"You're intelligent. Driven. I'm sure you'd be suited to any number of careers that don't involve people shooting at you. So why did you become a police officer?"

Marie gestured at the menu. "I'm lost here."

"I'll throw you a lifeline." Nessa turned her head, looking to the waitress. "We'll share the tapas. Just bring out a little of everything, hmm?"

"Tapas?" Marie asked.

"Small plates. Sure to be something you'll like. All of it, I suspect—this place is quite good. Hummus, baba ghanoush, tzatziki. I'm a firm believer in living deliciously. And you haven't answered my question."

Marie had a list of stock answers whenever her job came up. Those platitudes were a litany of bland and forgettable half-truths. None of them rose to her lips. Instead, she shook her head. "You'll laugh."

Nessa's smile vanished.

"Two rules," she said.

"You're making rules now?" Marie replied.

"My dinner invitation, my rules. One, I will never laugh at you. Two, you will never lie to me. Do you accept?"

"You know," Marie said, "most people don't establish rules for social events."

"Most people aren't me. And if I'm reading you right, I suspect you might take comfort in knowing they're there. Like a handrail on a speeding train. The only rules that matter, after all, are the ones you consciously choose to obey."

"That's not true," Marie said. "What about the law?"

Nessa smirked. "What *about* the law? You've been suspended, and you're still investigating a case. I'm fairly certain that's not allowed."

"On administrative leave. Not the same thing as a suspension."

"You're a cop," Nessa said, "not a lawyer. Don't forget it. Two rules: I will never laugh at you; you will never lie to me. Will you accept?"

"That's a rule for each of us. Don't we both have to accept?"

The light caught Nessa's owlish glasses, glinting.

"No," she said. "Because I'm the one making the rules. You are free to accept, or not accept. But you have to choose."

The room slowly spun. Marie drank her ice water. It didn't help. As strange as the conversation had turned, random and half-mad, she wanted to see just how far down the rabbit hole went. Maybe she was half-mad herself.

"I accept your rules," Marie told her. Nessa clapped her hands, once, as if sealing her words in the air.

"Very good. Now, with the safety of knowing you will not, in fact, be laughed at...tell me the truth."

Marie leaned back in her chair. Her gaze went distant, drifting to one side.

"I grew up in foster care. The first home they put me in...it wasn't a great place. They weren't bad people; they just had too many kids and too little time for any of us. So I spent most of my time alone, in my own head. One day I found a box of beat-up paperbacks in the basement. And there was a copy of *Le Morte d'Arthur*."

"The Knights of the Round Table," Nessa said.

Marie chuckled at the memory. "I read the hell out of that book.

Over and over, until the cover fell off. Then I discovered fantasy. Robert Jordan, Carolyn Saunders, Glen Cook. I'd read anything I could get my hands on, really, but what I loved most were stories about knights. I loved the idea of being a crusader, a...a force for cosmic justice. Having a liege lord and a cause, something I could devote myself to, swear my life to."

"I bet you were a terror on the schoolyard," Nessa mused.

"Let's just say bullies learned to run very fast when I was around." Marie smiled and recited, "'Thou shalt respect all weaknesses, and shalt constitute thyself the defender of them.'"

Nessa tilted her head. "The Code of Chivalry."

Marie nodded. "Bottom line, the strong have the duty to protect the weak. The funny thing is, Gautier's code is kind of a crock. He wrote it in 1883."

"Not many knights around in 1883," Nessa said.

"No. Real, historical knights...well, some might have lived up to the myth, but not many. I guess that's why I drifted to fantasy."

"And when you found yourself seeking employment," Nessa said, "the closest thing you could find to a worthy liege was the law itself."

Marie lifted her glass. "You got it."

The waitress came over with a basket of flatbread, the fresh-baked aroma filling the air between them as she laid out a cluster of round white plates. A medley of purees garnished with olives, shavings of eggplant, a small feast for the sharing. Nessa tore a chunk of bread in half and dipped one piece into a puddle of hummus.

"That raises another question," she said.

"Which is?"

Nessa chewed on her flatbread, giving Marie a critical eye.

"Why on earth would you think I'd laugh at you for that?"

"Because it's ridiculous."

"It's your dream."

"Doesn't mean it isn't ridiculous." Marie shifted awkwardly in her chair. "Knights aren't real. Storybook knights never were."

Nessa gestured at her with a chunk of bread. "Not a dream born in a vacuum. No. You were looking to fix something, weren't you? You mentioned *cosmic* justice. Something was set wrong in your world, from a very early age. Something grievous, something you longed to correct."

"Are you an anthropologist or a psychologist?"

"My minor was in psychology. What was it, Marie?"

Marie's gaze dropped to the table. She set down her flatbread. Her appetite withered and died.

"I don't...I don't talk about that. Ever."

"Maybe you'd feel better if you did."

"I can't," Marie said.

"I propose a new rule." Nessa set her phone on the table and tapped open a stopwatch app. "For the next five minutes, once I start the clock, you have no secrets from me."

Marie looked at her now. Her brow furrowed.

"That's...that's not a rule you can make."

"I just did. Your only choice is to accept it, or refuse it. If you accept, then for the next five minutes, you will answer any question I put to you with absolute candor and without hesitation."

"What," Marie said, "then...it's your turn?"

"No. Only you."

"That's not very equal," Marie replied.

Nessa smiled. "When did I say we were equals? Nobody in this world is *equal*, Marie. We all have our niches, our natures, our unique roles to play."

"And why would I say yes to this?"

"Because you spend all day, every day, making decisions. Many of them life-or-death, I imagine. It must be exhausting. Protecting everyone around you, taking care of everyone, probably never being thanked for it."

"It's my job," Marie said.

"Wouldn't it be nice, for just five minutes, to let me make the decisions for you?"

"This...sounds like a dare."

"Oh, it is." Nessa pushed her glasses up on her nose, pretending to be grave. "I'm daring you to try something new. Careful, now. You might like it."

"Five minutes?"

"Five minutes. *Any* question I ask. No secrets."

Marie stared at the phone. The glowing green timer, five minutes on the clock, waiting for the countdown. She imagined she was standing on the edge of a cliff and thinking about jumping, just to see what it would feel like.

"I accept," she said.

Nessa's finger tapped the start button. The numbers began to move.

"Tell me what happened to your parents."

Twenty

It was three days before Christmas.

Marie remembered the season in flashes and glimmers. The wood paneling in her family's den, the snow lightly falling on her father's powder-blue Buick out in the driveway. Strings of lights and sleepless nights, the giddy anticipation of presents to come. Decades later, after she'd spent a couple of years on the beat as a newly minted patrol officer, she knew all about the utter fallibility of memory. She'd seen firsthand how a witness could watch a fleeing man in a bright green sweater and swear—with absolute honesty and one hand on the Bible—that he'd been wearing black. The world was full of liars, but memory was the most insidious of them all, the only liar that lived in your head.

So she wondered, now and then, how much she really recalled. That half-glimpsed flash of presents under the tree, wrapped in glossy paper with images of Christmas bells, each parcel snuggled in ocean-blue twine—real, or something she'd seen on television? Did she really remember the way the doorbell chimed that night, a strident, sharp bell, or had time and distance made it louder than it was? Did the men even ring the bell, or did they knock on the door? Sometimes she could remember it both ways. One of her memories had to be wrong. Maybe both.

Her father's shout, that much she remembered.

It was a strange, high-pitched thing. Her father was big, with broad shoulders and a merry, rumbling voice. She would never have expected a sound like that to come from his mouth. In the movies, on television, men made deep, manly sounds when they were attacked. Grunts and curses and growls to show their strength. Real violence was messier. Real violence sounded like surprise and shrill outrage and unexpected, undeserved pain.

Violence wasn't supposed to come to your house three days before Christmas, in the middle of the nightly news.

Marie had been up in her room, coloring. That was one of the memories she'd lost. She knew she was coloring, but every time she tried to recall the page, she remembered something different. Sometimes she was coloring a car. Sometimes it was a clown. Sometimes she was holding a brick-red crayon when her father cried out, sometimes chocolate brown. She remembered the feeling and the place, just not the things attached.

She was sure she scampered to the second-floor landing, though. Staying low, dressed in her pajamas (sometimes she remembered them being white with flowers, sometimes solid blue), staring through the slats and down into the living room. Her father was on the floor, clutching his gut, writhing. Her mother was pressed to the wall, and the knife at her throat gleamed electric in the glow from the Christmas tree lights.

Sometimes she remembered her mother looking up, making eye contact, mouthing the word *hide*. Sometimes she remembered hiding on her own, trying to be as quiet as a mouse. She was almost certain the first one was the real memory, though. She remembered feeling that her mother would have done anything to protect her, if she could.

Marie was sure she ended up under her bed, belly pressed to the thin gray (sometimes beige) carpet, listening to the three men in ski masks.

She was sure there were three men. Not one detail ever changed when she thought of them.

"Where the fuck is it?" shouted one of the men.

A rib-shattering *thud*. Her father's groan.

"I don't know what you want," her father gasped. "I don't know who you think we are—"

"Do you want us to start cutting on this bitch? Is that what you want?"

Her mother screamed. In fear, at first.

Then there wasn't anything but screaming.

It went on, and on, until the only thing louder was the sound of the police siren outside the house. There were pounding footsteps, and shouts, and the bray of a gunshot. More shots, muffled, out on the lawn. A window broke.

Then silence.

When she earned her detective shield, Marie pulled a copy of the police report. She had one question, just one, that needed answering. Sometimes she remembered that it felt like five minutes passing between the first scream and the last. Sometimes it felt like hours. She just wanted to know (*how long they suffered*) how long she had been hiding under that bed. The report wasn't much help. Neighbors called in about the noise at 8:10 p.m., but they'd been out at dinner and just returned home. Neighbor on the other side was deaf as a post and never heard anything, or that's what he claimed.

The first patrol unit arrived at 8:22 p.m., the second one five minutes later. The sole surviving perpetrator was taken into custody at 9 p.m. or thereabouts. In the adrenaline aftermath of a gunfight, facts and figures got muddled.

Marie remembered the man in the uniform scooping her up in his arms, his strong hands holding her tight as he walked her down the stairs. He turned her face to his chest, her forehead pressed to his cold metal badge. *Don't look, honey*, he'd told her. Still, she'd caught a glimpse of the two bodies on the living room floor, sprawled around the Christmas tree, covered in white sheets. At least she remembered it that way.

The report included the coroner's summary. The wounds on her parents' bodies. She didn't know how long she had sat there, locked in a silent argument with herself. Eventually, she turned the page.

—apparently inflicted by a straight razor, it read. *Multiple cigarette burns (7), to the victim's—*

She shut the folder.

She didn't need the clinically detailed catalog of atrocities. It wouldn't give the memory any finer definition, wouldn't lend any clarity or closure. All it would do was make her angrier.

Marie was already angry, every waking hour of her life. She didn't need any more fuel for that fire.

*   *   *

Marie sat across from Nessa, her hands resting limp in her lap.

"At the trial, it turned out the men had gotten a tip about a drug dealer. They wanted to rob him. Except...the dealer lived at 821 Fairmont Road. Our house was at 821 *Fairfield* Road. The other side of town." Marie cracked a humorless smile, her eyes like frozen coal. "That was the punch line. They invaded the wrong house. Everything that happened...it was for nothing. No meaning. No purpose. Just this howling void where a family used to be."

"But if there'd been someone to help," Nessa replied. "A knight in shining armor, perhaps..."

Marie met Nessa's steady gaze.

"I couldn't do anything to fix my own fucked-up life. Damned if I was going to let it happen to anyone else. Only way I can tend my scars is to make sure nobody else has to wear them."

"Thank you," Nessa said.

Marie didn't know what to say to that.

"For sharing. How do you feel, letting that out?"

She wasn't sure. A little lighter. A little freer, maybe.

"All right," Marie said. "I feel...all right. Any other questions?"

Nessa gestured to the phone. The stopwatch read 0:00.

"The timer ran out four minutes ago."

"Oh."

"I'll guard your secrets," Nessa said. "Would you like one of mine, in trade?"

Marie nodded a little, curious. "Yes."

Nessa glanced over her shoulder. She leaned in, shifting to one side, eyeing the other diners.

"My husband and I have been married for five years. We fell out of love four years ago."

"Why do you stay?"

Nessa shrugged and tore a piece of flatbread down the middle.

"For him, it's appearances. Divorces make for bad press. The Roth family is all about appearances. It's a political dynasty—Alton Roth is his father."

Marie tried to place the name. "I don't know him."

"He's a senator out in Nevada. Senator for life, most likely, like his father was before him. Scruples and civic duty aren't really a thing in the Roth family, beyond their value as lip service. I'm fairly certain that if Mephistopheles appeared before him and offered more power in trade for his soul, Alton would jump to sign on the dotted line. Richard isn't much better. It's all about *things* with them. Acquiring them. Having them. Keeping other people from having them. And I used to be one of Richard's favorite things."

"So why do *you* stay?" Marie asked.

"I'd like to say I'm mercenary. You've seen where I live, Marie. You don't get a brownstone in the West Village on a college professor's salary. Richard and I generally lead independent lives. It's not a great burden to playact the dutiful wife, now and then, in exchange for the perks. To be honest, though? Chalk it up to simple inertia. I could live happily with far less than I have. It's just easier to stay than it is to leave. A comfortable rut. My husband would be happy to replace me with a younger, prettier model, if he could do it without making a stir or upsetting his father."

"I think you're pretty," Marie told her. She twisted her lips, suddenly awkward. She wasn't sure why she'd said it.

"Thank you," Nessa said with a faint chuckle. "But I'm not as young as I used to be. Besides, in the Roth family the purpose of a woman is, first and foremost, to provide a male heir. Something we've discovered that I am medically incapable of doing."

"I'm sorry."

"Why?" Nessa asked. "I'm not."

Marie drank her water.

"So," Nessa said, "now we each know a secret. There's power in secrets, you know."

"I always thought there was more power in truth."

"Spoken like a valorous knight. You're confusing truth with exposure, though. The truth is buried inside the secrets we keep."

"What you said when I came in," Marie said. "About my 'true face' showing—"

"I believe that we all have two faces. Our public face—the mask we wear, the persona we want the world to see—and our true face. The person we really are, when we're completely unguarded and our defenses are down. There is no greater intimacy than the truth, Marie. You can stand utterly nude before your lover and never show him anything at all. Nothing that truly matters. I know, I've done it. Your body isn't who you are."

"The corollary being," Marie mused, "I assume, that you can reveal to someone your deepest truths in the middle of a crowded restaurant."

"And no one, no one but your intimate companion, will know that you're naked as the day you were born," Nessa said with a smile. "A bit exhibitionist for my tastes, though. I find such conversations flow much better in privacy, on moonless nights."

"In the dark," Marie said.

"It's nobody's business what we do in the dark." Nessa put her napkin to her lips, coughing delicately. "I mean 'we' in the universal sense, of course."

Marie smiled. Her gaze came to rest on the untouched book at Nessa's side.

"What's that?" she asked.

Nessa's French-manicured fingernails rapped the dusty blue cover. It looked like the book had once been titled in gold leaf, but age and wear had scraped off all but a few slivers, leaving the ghosts of words behind.

"A little light reading. As I mentioned on the phone, I found a partial reference for that mysterious tattoo of yours. I'm afraid it won't help you, though."

"Why do you say that?" Marie asked.

"Because the reference in question is nearly four hundred years old." Nessa's hand caressed the cover of the book. "From 1627. The Würzburg witch trials, in Germany."

Twenty-One

"Würzburg was a bloody affair," Nessa said to Marie. "All of Europe was going through a bit of a witch frenzy in the early sixteen twenties, and Würzburg was the worst of the lot, largely owing to the Catholic reconquest of Germany. By the time the smoke cleared, and I mean that literally, as many as a thousand victims were executed on charges of consorting with the devil. The lucky ones were beheaded *before* they were burned."

"A thousand witches?" Marie asked. "That seems...steep."

"A thousand *victims*. Precious few of them could tell the difference between a supernatural hex and a bad dream brought on by undercooked sausage, I assure you. But when war and disease are on the doorstep and the wolves are circling, people crave simple answers, simple solutions. Life is bad? Find a witch to blame for it. Your life isn't magically better after you murder her? Well, obviously there are more witches out there. Keep hunting."

"And the tattoo?"

Nessa carefully shuffled the tapas plates off to one side. Marie helped her make some room. Then Nessa turned the tome, opening it to a page marked with Marie's scrap of paper, her copy of the dead man's tattoo. On the edge of the page, all dense type in a florid, antique font, was her drawing's twin sibling. A bit cruder, the woodcut blotchy and lacking the tattoo's precise swirls, but clearly the same glyph.

"It was described as a brand, in this case," Nessa said. She tapped the side of her hand. "Right here, on the bridge between thumb and forefinger. The accused was a local blacksmith whose 'cursed' shoes allegedly caused a clergyman's horse to bolt, throwing its rider into a bed of stinging nettles. Rather slapstick, until the smith was put on trial for the sake of the priest's wounded ego. Better to burn a witch than admit to being an incompetent horseman."

"That's...horrifying," Marie said.

"It was the sixteen hundreds. Anyway, the blacksmith—possibly realizing he was good and screwed, and hoping to avoid being tortured into a confession before they killed him—gave himself up. He presented himself before the magistrate with a fresh brand on his hand, this one, and proclaimed it was a mark of his fealty to the prince of darkness."

Marie blinked. "What happened to him?"

"Oh, they tortured him anyway. They tortured him a *lot*. Nobody likes a smartass."

It didn't make sense. She had her own torture victim to investigate, and he wasn't a village blacksmith. The man in the basement in Monticello had been a shooter for the mob, and for all of the Five Families' sins, they weren't known for practicing Satanism.

"Weird," Marie said. "Thanks for looking, anyway."

She reached out, her fingertip tracing the curves of the woodcut, looking for a clue. Nessa reached out at the same moment. Their fingers brushed.

"Oh." Marie jerked her hand back. "Sorry, I didn't—"

"No, no, that was—" Nessa shook her head, suddenly flustered. "I'll keep digging."

"You don't have to. I mean, I don't want to put you to any trouble."

"It's no trouble at all," Nessa said. "Now you've got me curious. I'll text you, okay?"

*   *   *

Home again. Marie locked the door behind her, flipped the

deadbolt, and listened to the sound of a laugh track playing over a tinny laptop speaker. She kicked off her shoes.

"Welcome home," Janine said. "How was work? Oh, right, you're on a mandatory paid vacation, but you went looking for work to do anyway, because you are a crazy person."

"Guilty," Marie said. She strolled into the kitchen nook, humming to herself, rummaging around in the fridge and plucking out a can of Dr. Pepper. Janine sat on the futon and stared at her.

"What?" Marie asked, looking back at her.

"You're *smiling*," Janine said.

"I've been known to do that occasionally."

"No. Uh-uh." Janine hit a key, pausing her show. "Not that kind of smile. That's a very specific vintage of smile, one I've not seen in a long time. I know your secret, Marie Reinhart."

She popped the tab on her soda can and took a sip, leaning against the refrigerator. "Yeah? Do tell."

"You," Janine said, "were on a hot date tonight."

Marie choked on her drink. Sputtering, she set the can down.

"Uh-huh. I knew it." Janine beamed with triumph.

"No, no I—it was *not* a date. It was just dinner, with a...this college professor who's doing some research for me. You know, about that weird tattoo?"

"Just dinner," Janine said.

"Just dinner. And research."

"I remain skeptical," Janine told her. "What's his name?"

Marie winced. "Um...George," she said, offering up the first name that jumped into her mind.

"And is Um-George cute? He is, isn't he?"

"I don't know." Marie fluttered a hand. "I guess? I think so?"

"Oh my God, you're turning bright pink."

"I am not."

"You are so." Janine grinned. "Go look at yourself. Did he kiss you? Did you kiss him?"

"He's married."

"Is it a happy marriage?"

"*Janine.*"

She shifted on the futon, curling her legs up. "I'm just saying, you're way overdue for a lover who doesn't run on batteries. It's a small apartment, Marie. Thin walls."

Trapped somewhere between mortification and laughter, Marie ducked her head and scurried across the apartment.

"I can't even handle you right now."

"You need to be handling *George* right now," Janine called out behind her.

In her room, the door closed, Marie looked in the mirror. She wore a blush on her cheeks, and something else: a light she hadn't seen in her own eyes for a very long time.

"What am I *doing?*" she asked her reflection. But she smiled when she said it.

*   *   *

At five minutes to eleven, Marie's phone rang. She stirred from an uneasy sleep, grumbling, and reached for it. She rubbed her eyes with her other hand. The display on her cell sharpened as she squinted at it. It was Jake Moretti, her new friend from Jersey City.

"Detective," she mumbled as she answered the call. "What's up?"

"Hey, sorry to wake you. We, uh, got a little problem here. The Sylvester Rimes situation."

"Don't tell me he got out on bail."

"Never had a hearing," Jake told her. "He's dead."

Marie sat up and clicked on the bedside lamp. "Wait, what? What happened?"

"He ended up in a holding cell with five other guys. CO came through on patrol, found Rimes dead on the floor with his brains painted all over the wall. Somebody beat him to death. All five guys say they didn't see a thing."

"Covering for whichever one of them did it," Marie said. "Typical. Everybody knows snitches get stitches. What about the recordings from the surveillance camera? You've got cameras in New Jersey, right?"

"Well, that's the thing." Jake paused; then his voice went deadly soft. "Cameras we got. Recordings we don't. The hour Rimes spent in that cell is *gone*. Erased. I saw it myself: there's a burst of static, then nothin'. Just a one-hour jump. One second he's fine, the next he's stone dead."

"How is that possible?"

"Your guess is as good as mine. This whole thing is a clusterfuck. The brass is calling half the department on the carpet, the Policemen's Benevolent is getting involved, and everybody's pointing fingers at everybody else. That ain't all. You remember how we left the interview room when that homeless guy had his little freak-out?"

"Sure," Marie said. "And that lawyer went in while we were distracted."

"I pulled that footage too, from the hall cam. Whole lot of people in that hallway. The homeless guy, five or six uniforms, you and me...but no lawyer."

A slow chill rippled down Marie's arms. She inched closer to the lamp, as if the softly glowing bulb could drive back the cold. A little pool of sanctuary in the dark.

"You're saying—"

"I'm saying," Jake told her, "that I watched that footage over and over again. And that lawyer, Smith, he's *not* in it."

"But he got into the interview room."

"That's right," he said.

"There was only one door."

"Watch your back, Detective. Something is very, very hinky about this whole mess, and I don't like it one bit."

"What are you going to do?" Marie asked.

"I'm gonna keep my head down," Jake said, "mind my own business, and be as invisible as humanly possible until this all blows over. You oughta do the same."

"I can't do that," Marie said.

"Whoever got at this guy, they did it in the middle of a secure lockup and walked away clean," Jake said. "You oughta be asking yourself one real important question right now."

"Yeah?" Marie said. "What's that?"

"If they could do that to Sylvester Rimes, what could they do to *us?*"

Twenty-Two

Marie didn't sleep much, or easily. She groaned as the alarm on her phone roused her with the dawn, flashing a reminder on her screen that she couldn't put it off any longer: today was her mandatory psych evaluation. She rode a crosstown bus, still waking up, wanting nothing more than to get this over with.

The shrink's waiting room held a bare Berber rug, magazines from a previous decade, and some very uncomfortable chairs. Marie thumbed through an old issue of People. She wasn't really reading. Her eyes wouldn't focus on the glossy pages.

She didn't object to therapy on principle. Some cops worried about being seen as weak for seeking help, but that wasn't a problem either. Mandatory was mandatory, nothing she could do but show up if she wanted to get her badge back, and nobody was going to judge her for it. It was just that therapists had this tendency not to help. Children who went through hell saw a lot of doctors, and none of them had been overly useful. Most had talked down to her about how it wasn't her fault, tried to help her overcome something that wasn't even bothering her, and given her more of a complex than she had to start with. Of course it wasn't her fault. She'd never been confused about exactly who to blame for her parents' deaths.

It had never been about that, and none of them understood. Then again, they were expecting a scared little girl, not a bloodhound catching her first scent.

The door swung open. Marie wasn't sure if she was in the right place, for a second. It wasn't that therapists had a particular dress code, but all of the ones she'd visited favored neutral cardigans and slacks that reminded her of Mister Rogers. This one didn't. Dr. Chen stood half a head taller than Marie, and she wore broken-in jeans and a white button-down. *Come to think of it*, Marie thought with a glance at the doctor's square-toed shoes, *she looks like a cop.*

"Come on in. Marie? You can call me Patricia, or Patty." She didn't wait for a response, just turned and headed inside with the surety that her patient would follow. It worked.

Once inside the room, though, Marie remembered a dozen offices with a smell just like this one and diplomas on the wall just like the ones behind the doctor's mahogany desk. Hesitantly, she managed, "Look, Doc, I know you need to do your job, but I'm really not that into talking about my feelings."

"That's good. I don't want to hear about them." Patricia sat down across the desk and took out a notebook and a pen.

"What?" Marie said. "Um. Okay. Well, if you want to just sign the paper—"

"Oh, we're going to talk. We're just not going to talk about your feelings."

Marie tilted her head, wary. She'd gone from irritated to curious in less than a minute, but this still felt like some kind of touchy-feely setup.

"O...kay." She settled a little more comfortably in her seat. "What are we going to talk about, then?"

"Behavior. Specifically, how your perception affects your behavior, and what tools you can use to control those perceptions and clear up confusion and anxiety." Patricia eyed a file on the desk. "I see you were involved in two prior incidents involving civilian deaths."

Marie nodded. She shifted in her chair.

"Yeah, back when I was in uniform, early in my career. Liquor-store shooting, and a domestic."

"You were offered nonmandatory counseling after both events.

You accepted the first time but only attended one session with...ah. Dr. Sinclair. You declined the second time."

"I didn't like him," Marie said. "He kept telling me how much he understood. Like a guy who's never worn a badge can understand what it's like to be first on the scene at a robbery gone bad. See, the perp and the cashier blew each other away and caught some customers in the crossfire. Four corpses on the ground and the only person still breathing was this stupid scared kid who was there to buy booze for his twenty-first birthday. Kid bled out in my arms while we were waiting for the bus to show up. Sinclair tells me 'I know what you're going through.' Pretentious prick."

"Sinclair is a good therapist, really. He's just not used to dealing with patients who have to confront mortality as part of their daily work. Patients who, for example, may have to put down a suspect to save a life. And he's much more of an emotional analyst sort." Patricia rested her palms flat on the desk. "I'm not. I work primarily in cognitive behavioral therapy. The focus is on your issues, where they come from, and what biases are skewing your perceptions. I help you get from point A to point Z with a few stops in-between."

"That's different." Marie still felt uneasy, but at least she didn't want to swallow her own gun to get out of there faster. This felt more like...maintenance. Like a trip to the dentist. Nothing anyone wanted to do, but you felt better when it was over and were glad that you went.

"It's useful in situations where moralizing just makes things less clear. Which is often true for police officers. There's a baseline of right and wrong, but it's easy to get stuck in a loop of what the *more*-right solution would have been. Should you have shot earlier? Should you have shot at all? Could you have somehow de-escalated the situation before it became lethal, or would that have led to more loss of life? Any time a gun comes into the picture, you're facing incredibly complex and life-changing decisions—for you and everyone around you—that have to be resolved in the blink of an eye. Nobody gets out of a situation like that unscathed."

Marie chewed that over. "Okay. I guess that makes sense. So you talk me through some stuff today, and I'm... What, equipped to go back out and shoot people?"

"Fuck no," Patricia said with a smile. "We're going to be seeing each other for a while. I'll sign off, but I have the ability to rescind that for the next three months before it clears your file. So you'll be coming to see me once a week. We can meet somewhere else if you'd be more comfortable."

"Wait." Marie started to stand up, a hand on each armrest. "I'm supposed to have one session, and then get back on the job."

"And you will. Then next week, you'll have another one. That's how it's supposed to work. I sign off, you go out into the world not murdering anyone or gambling or drinking yourself stupid, and we both show the brass how good at our jobs we are. Except I'm not a moron and I know nothing gets solved in an hour. I'm good at my job, Detective, and I don't rubber-stamp my patients through the process. You see more of this world's ugly face in a month than most civilians do in a lifetime. If you don't deal with it, it'll eat you alive."

"But you don't want me to talk about my feelings." Marie sank back into her chair, suspicious but a little intrigued.

"Not really. I want you to talk about your perceptions."

"You realize we tend to be wary of anything we say to our boss's in-house shrink, right?"

"Doctor-patient privilege doesn't magically disappear because you wear a badge, Marie. 'Confidential' means exactly that. Now then, I'm seeing that our hour has a good chunk of time left. Shall we talk?"

Marie pursed her lips. Doctors had always let her down before, but this...this felt different.

Worth a shot, she thought.

"Okay," she said, "let's talk."

Twenty-Three

Richard fixed his stance on the tatami practice mat. His navy blue robe shifted, the traditional fabric cut to his powerful frame, and his foot slid one inch to the right across a patch of densely woven straw. Eyes dead ahead, taking in the empty gymnasium, the rows of vacant exercise bikes, as his fingers curled around the hilt of his sword.

Standing on the mat beside him, Scottie mirrored his pose.

Richard's thumb pressed against the sword's laminated guard. Gently, slowly, the blade inched from its sheath.

Scottie didn't speak. He signaled with a short, sharp breath, a "*hnn*" hissed through gritted teeth.

Both men drew as one. Their katanas whistled from their sheaths as they raised the blades high in a two-handed grip, sweeping upward. At the apex of the swing they barely paused before bringing the weapons down in a killing blow.

They froze, knees bent, the tips of their swords shivering a quarter inch from the tatami mat. Another hiss from Scottie, and they rose.

The iaijutsu strike ended with the sheathing of the blade. Neither man looked down, relying on muscle memory and training to end the ritual. Scottie made it look easy, like a samurai from an old Kurosawa movie, the tip of his katana finding the narrow opening and sliding home. Richard hesitated, fumbling for a moment before following his lead.

"What time ya got?" Scottie asked.

Richard pulled back his sleeve and checked the glowing dial of his sport watch. "Shit, it's late. Quarter after eleven. We've been going at it."

"Nice thing about owning a gym, nobody throws you out at closing time." Scottie held up his clenched fist. Richard dutifully leaned in and bumped it.

"On the bright side, Vanessa should be asleep by the time I get back to the Village. I won't have to *talk* to her."

"Bachelor life, man. You and me, a penthouse in Manhattan, bitches on call twenty-four seven. Think about it."

Richard laughed. He dug in a sleek Nike duffel bag, pulling out a hand towel and mopping the sweat from his face.

"Yeah, that'd go over great with my dad. He's already got his 'presidential exploration committee' knocking on doors and running polls. One scandal and I'm good as disowned."

Scottie checked his phone, flipping through messages. "So you're stuck with the old ball and chain for the duration, huh? Y'know...there's always lodge night."

"Like I haven't thought about it? For one thing, she'd be a lousy sacrifice. You've met her; she's timid as a mouse. She'd probably be like that screamer we had a couple months ago, the one who absolutely refused to run? Just froze up until we put her out of her misery?"

"Yeah, that sucked. Even so, that's a price I'm willing to pay if it gets you out of marriage jail. Love you, bro."

Richard paused. He glanced sidelong at Scottie.

"I mean," Scottie said, cringing into an awkward shrug, "no homo. Like, you're my brother. We've been best friends for how long? I'm looking out for you, that's all."

Richard considered that, then nodded.

"Same here." He dug around in his duffel. "Anyway, the aftermath is a lose-lose. She goes missing or we dump the body, all the media's gonna talk about is her, pulling the spotlight *off* my dad. Nah, I've got my own thing underway. There are other ways to get rid of a wife. What I've got in mind should leave me smelling like roses."

"Whatever you need, just say the word." Scottie arched an eyebrow at his phone. "And hey, at least one problem is fixed."

"That screw-up in Jersey?" Richard asked.

"Yeah. Our buddies from Weishaupt and Associates took care of everything. Not for free, mind you. Fuckin' New Jersey, man. Carpet-bomb the whole damn state, nothing of value will be lost."

"No argument there, but what do you mean 'not for free'? Aren't we all on the same team?"

Scottie slid his katana into his own duffel, the hilt jutting out from one end, and zipped it up as far as he could before shouldering the bag.

"It's how the Network rolls," Scottie told him. "We're in the outer circle. Minor leagues. Everybody in the minors is compartmentalized. Cell structure, minimal points of contact with the inside, so if something goes sideways the whole organization doesn't come crashing down. The Weishaupt crew is inner, *inner* circle. Like 'they've got Adam himself on speed dial' inner circle."

"You ever meet that guy?"

"Adam?" Scottie mock shivered. "Yeah. Once. Once was plenty. Why do you think I let Westwood take up the mantle of lodge leader? *He* can deal with the nightmares. Anyway, the Network's outer circle gets run on the mushroom principle: keep us in the dark and feed us bullshit. So when Adam shows up and says 'hey, guess what, you're drug dealers now, don't ask questions...'"

"Not exactly a burden. That mess in Monticello notwithstanding, we've been making *stupid* money since the ink started flowing."

Richard killed the lights, dousing the gymnasium in shadows. Scottie held the front door while Richard tapped a string of numbers into the alarm pad. The pad beeped, lights flashing from green to red, and they stepped out onto the sidewalk together. Quiet night, quiet street, one lonely lamppost pushing back the dark.

Richard sorted through a thick ring of keys, locking up the glass door. Scottie glanced over his shoulder at him. "All the same, nobody collects baseball cards for minor-league players. I'm thinking we need to step up."

"Sounds like you've got a plan," Richard said. They started to walk, side by side.

"I know there's a factory pumping out ink somewhere in the city. Just not *where*. Now, if they were to have a catastrophic accident of some sort, the Network would need a capable, well-organized team in the area to take over operations fast, wouldn't they?"

Richard held up a hand and stopped him in his tracks.

"Wait a second," Richard said. "You want us to move up in the ranks by taking out another Network cell?"

"Hey, it's all in the scriptures, man. What does the King of Wolves teach us? You're either a predator or you're prey. Survival of the fittest. And we are the fittest."

"We'd better be. You know they'll kill us if they figure it out, right? I mean, we'll be *lucky* if all they do is kill us."

"And our footing's any better right now?" Scottie asked. "We're the ones sticking our necks out, drawing fire from the law *and* the mob. We need to work our way into the inner circle and let some other poor bastards do the heavy lifting for us."

They strolled down the sidewalk. Richard fell silent, mulling it over.

"We probably wouldn't be the first cell to climb up on the backs of another one," he conceded.

"It's the Network, bro. That's probably the *only* way to do it. They just won't say it out loud. It's something you're supposed to figure out on your own, you know?"

"Not saying I'm in," Richard told him, "but *if* I was in, what's our next move?"

"First thing we've got to do is find the warehouse. I've got an in there. You know my source inside the NYPD? They're also running interference for—"

He fell short, stumbling to a stop as a man darted from the alleyway on his right and planted himself in their path. He had wild eyes and greasy hair. The barrel of his matte-black nine-millimeter wobbled, swinging between Scottie and Richard.

"Don't you fucking move, not one *inch*," the man snapped. Scottie and Richard shared a look.

"Whoa," Scottie said, "this is different. When's the last time you got mugged?"

Richard shrugged, barely acknowledging the gun. "In this borough? Never. In general? It was...wow. The late nineties, maybe?"

"I know, right?" Scottie turned to the mugger. "You are a relic of an older time, my friend."

The man jammed the gun in Scottie's face and pressed the barrel to the middle of his forehead. Up close and personal, they got a good look at the swirling, jagged glyph tattooed on the inside of his wrist.

"I'm not your friend, *Mr. Scott Pierce*. And this isn't a mugging, it's a message. You think you can peddle your shit in this city without paying out to the Five Families? Yeah. We know. We've been watching your ass for months and you finally slipped up."

Scottie glanced sidelong at Richard. "See what I mean? If we were on the inside, somebody else would be in this situation."

"Nice tattoo." Richard nodded at the gunman's hand. "Are you really repping the mafia, or do you answer to a *lower* power?"

"You two trust-fund pricks should be a lot more nervous right now," he said. "You think this is some kind of joke?"

Scottie and Richard stood there, beacons of calm, while the gunman worked himself up into a lather. His bloodshot eyes went wider as he pressed the gun's muzzle against Scottie's forehead and thumbed back the hammer. The streetlight caught the sweat glistening on his forehead.

Scottie rested his hand on the hilt of his sword, jutting out from his duffel bag.

"Man asked you a question," Scottie said. "If you don't feel like answering, I'll ask you another: are you familiar with iaijutsu?"

The gunman blinked. "Ia-what?"

"Iaijutsu. A key component in the training of a bushi, or warrior, in feudal Japan. It's the art of the quick draw. One draw, one slice, one kill. A true master of the art, it is said, could draw his blade, cut a man down, and resheath it, all in the space of a heartbeat. I'll admit, I've been kind of a Japanophile ever since I spent a summer there in my college days, on break from Cambridge. None of that anime bullshit, though. I'm a cultural scholar, not a weeaboo."

"Also you like banging Asian chicks," Richard observed.

"True. True. I do have my preferences."

"What the *fuck*," the gunman hissed, "are you *talking* about?"

Scottie smiled.

"Nice pistol," he said. "I'm guessing it's not a custom job. Standard pull-weight. You could blow my brains all over the sidewalk if I'm not careful. So I'm wondering...do you think I could draw my sword and kill you before you have time to shoot?"

The gunman didn't answer. He locked eyes with Scottie, trembling, and his finger curled around the trigger. Tugging it just the tiniest fraction of an inch.

The katana ignited with blue fire as it lashed from the scabbard. Scottie's hand spun in a figure-eight blur, the burning blade moving faster than the eye could follow, leaving smears of light in its wake.

The blade whistled back into its sheath.

The gunman hit the sidewalk in four pieces. Cut in half at his hips and through his torso, one arm sliced in half, the wounds bloodless, scorched black and cauterized.

"What an asshole," Scottie muttered.

Richard nudged a chunk of the corpse with his shoe. "You totally cheated."

"It's not cheating if you win. And that makes two mafia hitters with tattoos reading 'property of the courts of hell.' One too many for a coincidence."

"And they've got your name," Richard said. "Meaning they're a heartbeat away from my name and everybody else's. You feel like going to war with the Five Families?"

"Screw that. Let's move up in the ranks and make somebody *else* do it. C'mon, let's get out of here before a cop rolls by. We need to talk strategy. Besides, we haven't finished our earlier conversation."

"Yeah?"

"Yeah." Scottie grinned at him. "Now I'm curious. I want to hear exactly how you're planning to murder your wife."

Twenty-Four

Nessa and Richard slept on the opposite edges of a California king bed. On their sides, each facing away and into the dark. The span of mattress between them was a demilitarized zone. Vast and empty and bleak, and the border lined with silent cannons.

Nessa stirred when Richard came home. She heard him climb into bed, she heard him shift and turn. She pretended to be asleep until he started snoring. She had been dreaming, she thought, something about dinner, something about Marie, but she couldn't put her finger on it beyond a vague feeling of fuzzy warmth.

She slipped out of bed.

Down the hall, in her private workroom, she clicked on the light and hit the books. The mystery of the tattoo was marginally compelling; she was inquisitive by nature, and history was a rich bouquet of mysteries waiting to be explored. She didn't even try to lie to herself, though. Finding more information meant a justification for seeing Marie again.

Nessa didn't have many friends. She had colleagues, friendly coworkers. She had Richard's friends, but they were Richard's friends. Marie was different. With her, she felt...comfortable. Like she could be herself. Like they could share, and talk, and she didn't have to be afraid of rejection. If anything, Marie seemed more afraid than she was. Though she'd visibly relaxed once Nessa had set a few tiny rules for her. That idea was born of a hunch, a spark of Nessa's intuition, and it had worked quite nicely.

After the dinner, after she came home alone, that was when the worry set in. Had she pushed Marie too hard, talked too loudly? Been overbearing? Obnoxious? She couldn't count the number of times Richard had used those very words, generally before demanding to know if she'd taken her medication. You could only be told how socially inept you were so many times before you started to believe it.

She couldn't just text her to say hello. No, she needed a professional pretense. Then she could see how Marie responded—if she talked to her as a police contact or as a friend. That was the smart approach. The careful approach.

So, the books.

Surrounded by her half-finished canvases, her gallery of grotesques, Nessa pored over yellowed and moldering pages. She cross-referenced historians, followed up on footnotes from the Würzburg witch trials, traced the timeline.

A little before one in the morning, she found a lead. Eager, her heart thudding, she scooped up her phone and started a text. *Hello there*, she typed, *it's me. I know you won't get this until the morning, and you don't have to respond if you're busy. I assume you're busy—*

"Ew, no," she said and started over.

I found something about that tattoo. You might be interested. Promise I won't make you sit through dinner again, ha ha, unless you want to—

"No," she muttered and deleted it.

Hello, detective friend! I hope I'm not bothering you—

"Ugh." She groaned and erased that too. She stared at the blank window, the blinking cursor.

Marie, she typed, *I don't care if you're busy. Drop whatever you're doing and respond to me immediately.*

Nessa's finger hovered over the Send button. Daring herself to do it. No. She liked that one—it felt like her secret voice, the one she kept hidden deep down inside. But it was too much. She erased it.

She got up and paced the tiny room, her hands clenched at her sides. Nessa looked to the canvas in charcoal and the three shrouded women dancing around a gray bonfire.

"Why can't I just be normal?" she asked the picture. "Why can't I just act like a normal person for *once? Stupid.*"

She dropped back down on the floor in front of her scattered books, crossed her legs, and stared at the phone again.

Hi Marie, she typed. *I enjoyed dinner. I hope you did too. I know you won't get this until the morning, but I may have found something about that tattoo. Drop me a text when you have a second?*

Adequate. She hit Send before she could second-guess herself again. Casting the die.

*   *   *

Marie was awake. Her session with the department's shrink had left her head swimming, but not in a bad way for once. She was almost looking forward to her next appointment. Almost. Her mind was too busy to sleep, and she'd turned to the pages of a rumpled paperback in the still hours of the night. Her phone chimed. She glanced to her side, her head propped up on two pillows. She slipped a bookmark between the pages, set her novel aside, and reached to the nightstand.

Nessa. Marie smiled, just seeing the name on her screen. She'd been worried after dinner. Dropping a bombshell like she had...Nessa had asked about her parents, after all, and she'd asked for honesty, but it still didn't make for casual conversation. Marie's last boyfriend had ghosted on her after three months of dating, right after she'd opened up to him about her past. She half-expected Nessa to vanish, too.

But here she was.

I'm awake, she texted back. *Shouldn't be, but I am.*

Insomnia? I get that sometimes.

Nerves, Marie replied. *IAB appointment tomorrow. The shrink says I'm good to go, so I've just got one last hurdle before I get my badge back.*

IAB? Nessa asked.

Internal Affairs. The police who police the police. I'm Certified Not Crazy according to the doc. Now I need to be a Certified Good Cop, too, or I don't go back to work.

I think you're a good cop.

Marie rolled onto her stomach, holding the phone in both hands in front of her, and muted the volume. Janine's remark about thin walls was fresh in her memory; she didn't need to be interrogated in the morning about who she was up late texting with.

Great. Tell the IAB investigator that. I could use the support.

No answer. Marie wondered if Nessa had fallen asleep. Then her phone gently vibrated as the response came across: *What's their name?*

Marie laughed, putting one hand over her mouth to muffle the sound. *You are NOT calling Internal Affairs.*

No, Nessa's next text read. *But I want to know their name.*

Why?

Another pause.

Curiosity. My husband gives generously to the police foundation. If they don't clear you for duty, I might be able to make a few phone calls. If.

Marie had to dig into her emails, flipping through a week's worth of spam and random memos to find her appointment listing.

Antoine Carson, she replied. *But you don't have to do that.*

Don't have to. Want to.

This is crazy, Marie texted, *having to keep things quiet, so my roomie doesn't hear me. I feel like a teenager in algebra class, passing notes.*

I had a teacher who would read the note in front of the whole class if he caught you. Mortifying.

Marie grinned at the screen. She bent her knees, kicking at the air.

Me too. Maybe that's what made it so irresistible.

What did? Nessa asked.

The feeling of danger, she replied.

* * *

Huddled over her phone, surrounded by open books, Nessa snickered. She couldn't help herself. She reached for a wire-bound pad of drawing paper, tore off a sheet, and grabbed one of her pencils.

Nessa quickly scribbled a note and took a photograph, sending the picture to Marie.

The result mimicked any number of countless furtive classroom notes, an old classic passed down through the decades. A simple scribbled line and a pair of empty check-boxes: *Do you like me? Yes / No.*

The second she hit Send, her delight deflated like a popped balloon. She wanted to kick herself. That was stupid. Too forward. If she hadn't done anything to scare Marie off yet—and it was just a matter of time—that was going to do the job.

No response. A minute passed. Then another. Nessa hugged herself and gritted her teeth. "Fucking *stupid*," she hissed. "You never learn. You *never* learn."

Her phone chimed.

She didn't look right away. She couldn't. She knew what the razor-blade bite of rejection was going to feel like, and as long as she didn't look, she wouldn't suffer the sting. She could just stave off the moment forever like this. The response wasn't real until she read it. Schrödinger's abandonment.

She peeked at the phone.

Marie had sent a picture of her own. She'd copied Nessa's note on the back of a rumpled receipt, in faded ballpoint pen.

The word *YES* was check-marked, circled, and underlined. Twice.

Nessa beamed. She bit down on her knuckles to keep from squealing and thumped her slippered feet on the floor.

What time is your appointment tomorrow? she texted.

I face the firing squad at 10AM sharp, Marie replied.

Nessa glanced at the time. *Which doesn't give you much of a full night's sleep. What I found will keep for later. Let's face this hurdle first. I want you in bed, lights out, in two minutes.*

Already in bed. Just reading, want to finish this chapter.

Nessa eyed the phone. Could she push this? Just a little?

Marie, she texted, *I wasn't asking. You need to be at your best in the morning. I want you to go to sleep. Now.*

She held her breath until the response chimed in. Marie sent her an emoji of a yellow happy face sticking its tongue out, followed by: *Yes, ma'am.*

Nessa closed her eyes and let out a contented sigh.

We'll talk tomorrow, she replied. *Sweet dreams.*

Then she put down her phone and gathered her supplies. She'd told a tiny lie to get the information she needed; she didn't have any pull with the authorities.

What she had was witchcraft. And her special book, open to a page that read "The Game of Binding an Enemy's Tongue."

Twenty minutes later, Nessa sat in a ring of silver candles, their flames rippling in the dark. She'd inscribed Antoine Carson's name on a sheet of parchment, inked in black, drawn on a precise grid both horizontally and vertically. A sketch of the ouroboros, a serpent eating its own tail, encircled the words. Nessa's fingers carefully, methodically worked with a long string of black wool yarn. She curled the strand around her fingers, looped it, and felt a spark of heat as she jerked the knot tight. Thirteen knots for thirteen letters in the investigator's name.

"You will bend to my will," Nessa whispered to the shadows. "Or you will break."

Twenty-Five

"And you understand," Lieutenant Carson said, "that you can have your union representative present for this interview."

The investigator's office was clean. Cold. Bland. Aggressively empty, like he was just borrowing the place and had to return it in pristine condition. The air smelled like Pine-Sol. A tape recorder bore mute witness, sitting on the desk between him and Marie, its reels slowly turning.

"I told you what happened," Marie said. "Twice. My story should match up with my partner's perfectly. Haven't said anything that'd jam me up, as far as I can tell."

The investigator—clean, cold, bland—studied her. His pen rapped against his spiral-bound notebook.

"And why are you confident that your stories will line up perfectly?"

"Because it's the truth."

He offered a noncommittal *hmm*. Then silence, inviting her to fill the void. Interrogation 101. Marie could play that game too. She sat, still and sullen, until he decided to speak again.

"You left your jurisdiction."

"To follow a lead," Marie said.

"You could have passed the lead to Monticello PD."

"And they could have sat on it. And a woman could have died."

Carson checked his notes. "'Baby Blue.' Who wasn't at the aforementioned house you left your jurisdiction to investigate."

"They moved her before we got there. But she *was* there."

"And you know this how?"

She bit the inside of her cheek. She knew it because Harlow, the limo driver, confessed to taking her there. She knew it because Beau Kates admitted selling the woman for a shoebox filled with drugs.

And she'd learned both of these truths while she was suspended, with no badge and no legal authority. Not to mention bouncing Kates off half the furniture in his office and handing him grounds for a lawsuit.

"A confidential informant," she said. "My CI is reliable."

"I see," he said, sounding like he didn't. Or didn't want to.

"I don't understand what the problem is here. It was a righteous shoot. We came under fire, we responded with appropriate force, and we uncovered a homicide scene and a stash house in the process. Why don't you just tell me what you want me to say, I'll say it, you can sign off on my paper, and I can get back to work."

"That isn't how this works," Carson said.

Again, he stopped talking. She'd broken perps the same way, using people's natural discomfort with a silence to spur them on. She'd seen suspects babble themselves into a full confession more than once.

She wasn't a perp. But he was treating her like one. Marie's anger simmered, a rising boil in the pit of her stomach.

"Then tell me," she said, her words carefully measured, "how it works."

He turned a page in his notebook and took a cursory glance.

"Would you be surprised to find out that your story *doesn't* match up with your partner's?"

"It doesn't?"

"Would you be surprised?" he repeated.

Interrogation 102. Separate two suspects. Put them in different interview rooms, don't let them compare notes. Tell each one that the other guy is singing a different tune, and see how fast they change theirs.

"I'd be very surprised," Marie replied. "Considering I'm telling the truth and Detective Fisher has no reason to lie."

"If there's anything that either of you are omitting," Carson said, "anything that might cause a problem down the road, it's generally a good idea to be the first one to come clean about it. For instance, if he were to reveal details that you kept hidden, for whatever reason, it'll go a lot easier for him. And vice versa, of course, if there's anything you'd like to tell me."

Interrogation 103. "*Your buddy is in the next room, selling you out. First one to confess gets a deal from the DA.*" Marie's short-cropped fingernails dug into her knees as her shoulders clenched.

"Lieutenant," she asked, "were you given this post because you were a failure at real police work, or was it an aspiration? When you were a little boy, did you dream of joining the rat squad when you grew up?"

He sat forward in his chair. "*Excuse* me, Detective?"

"You've got zero reason not to clear me for active duty. Zero. And while we're dicking around in here, people out there need my help."

Carson folded his arms. "Is that so?"

Marie opened her wallet. She slapped the picture of Baby Blue down on the desk.

"This woman has been abducted. The suspect is a serial murderer who holds his victims no longer than two weeks before butchering them. And I'm the only person who can save her. So while you're—"

"Why?" Carson asked. "Why only you? There are thirty-four thousand police officers in New York City, Detective Reinhart. Why are you the *only* one who can save her?"

Marie's jaw tightened. "Because nobody else is trying."

"You like analyzing people, Detective? Sounds like a fun game. Let me take a turn." He unfolded his arms, leaning in, aggressive as he flipped through his notebook. "You've got a hero complex. Even your partner characterized you as a 'crusader,' and he was being nice. A regular knight in shining armor."

"Sign my paper so I can go back on active duty."

Carson sneered at her. "You're living in a fantasy world, Detective. It's a shield, isn't it? You're always looking for that next damsel in distress, that next hit of being a hero, so you don't have to deal with your own shit."

He rapped his finger on Baby Blue's photograph.

"This isn't the first vic you've carried around in your wallet, is it? I bet you've done it your entire career. One obsession after another. Some people would say you're sick in the head, *Detective*."

Marie's eyes narrowed to slits. "Fuck. You. Sign my paper and let me get back to work."

"What will you do if I don't?" Carson asked her.

Under the desk, out of sight, Marie's hands curled into fists.

"Don't push me," she said.

Carson studied her like some kind of lab rat. "What happens if I do?"

Marie's stomach churned. She felt like throwing up. She felt like jumping over the desk and slamming Carson against the bare office walls until she wiped that smug look off his face. She felt like bolting for the door and just running, running down the stairs, running outside in the warm air, running until she dropped from exhaustion. Being anywhere but here.

"I've got you pegged," she told Carson. "You're getting off on this, aren't you? You get cops in here, good honest cops, and their careers, their *lives* hang on your signature. You like that, don't you? You're the sick one, not me."

"Is this career your life, Detective? What would happen if you never got your badge back?"

"Fuck you. Sign my paper."

"What would you do? Can you think of a life without it? Have you ever thought of—"

Marie jumped out of her chair and slammed her fists on the desk.

"*This is all I have!*" she roared.

Carson didn't even flinch. His cool, steady gaze cut a hole in Marie's rage.

Marie sank back down into her chair. Withering, her sightline drifting to the desk between them.

"This is all I have," she said again, soft now.

He didn't answer right away.

"It's my job," he said, "to protect the integrity of this department. You can call me a rat if it makes you feel better, but at the end of the day, we're on the same team. As it stands, there are certain outstanding irregularities in the Monticello shooting. Enough irregularities that I can't in good conscience—"

Carson fell silent. He blinked. His lips moved, but no words came out. Marie squinted at him, her brow furrowed.

"Lieutenant?"

Carson's eyes went wide. His hand went to his throat. He took a deep breath, trying to speak, but all that emerged was a froglike croak.

Marie shoved her chair back, on her feet in an instant. "Are you choking? Do you need help?"

Carson shook his head wildly. He croaked again. Biting his lip, his face drawn as if racked with pain, he stammered, "N-nuh. No. Under...under the circumstances..."

He opened another folder and tugged out a yellow form, slapping it down on the desk. His movements were stiff, robotic, like a puppet dancing on piano-wire strings.

"Under the circumstances," the investigator said, "I can see...I can see no reason not to clear you for active duty, effective immediately."

Marie watched, puzzled, as Carson scrawled his signature on the form. He shoved it across the desk, hand fluttering, wordlessly begging Marie to pick it up.

"Thank you," Marie said. The words came out as a question, sounding as befuddled as she felt.

Carson slumped against the desk. He rested his head in his hands, breathing heavy.

"Lieutenant? Can I get you some water or something? Are you sure you're all right?"

"I'm fine." Carson spoke into his hands, his voice muffled, eyes squeezed shut. "I have...I have another appointment coming in. Please leave."

Twenty-Six

It was the weirdest thing, the text read. Nessa smiled contentedly at her phone as she adjusted the hem of her dress. She paused to tap out a quick response.

Well, the important thing is we got what we wanted.

We? Marie responded.

You think I wasn't cheering for you?

Ha ha, true, Marie texted back. *I guess I wasn't alone in that room after all.*

Nessa looked to the mirror, taking herself in. For once, she liked what she saw. Her hair was pinned up, her body adorned in jet-black Christian Dior, a sheath dress with a stylish drape of silk at the neckline and one short sleeve slightly longer than the other.

"You have no idea," she murmured to her reflection.

This felt good. This felt right. Nessa hummed a happy, tuneless song as she sifted through her jewelry box, looking for her favorite silver earrings. Then Richard poked his head into the bedroom.

"You're not wearing that," he told her.

She glanced up, catching his reflection in the mirror, the look on his face like a kid being told to eat his broccoli.

"Why not?"

"Seriously? Come on, Vanessa, you look like you're going to a funeral. This is supposed to be a party. Bright colors, festive, donors with open wallets. You know Dad likes everything colorful. Put on that orange dress, the one I bought you in Aruba."

She slammed the lid of her jewelry box.

"Sure," she said, her voice bone-dry. "Then I'll check on the caterers again, ensure the house is pristine, and play the perfect hostess while you and your father smoke cigars on the deck."

He gave her a thumbs-up, missing her tone by a mile. "Great! That's all I'm asking. Thank you. Did you take your meds?"

Her gaze drifted to the unlabeled prescription bottle sitting on the edge of her vanity.

"Not yet."

"Please. Nessa. C'mon. I can't handle you when you're—" He shook his head. "Tonight is really, really important for Dad, okay? So just...don't be weird. Take your meds."

He vanished. Nessa glowered at the mirror, her confidence crumpling like a house of cards in a gust of wind. She trudged over to the walk-in closet, looking for the orange dress she hated.

The bottle of pills sat on the vanity, untouched.

* * *

As night fell over New York, the skyline igniting to push back the dark, the crème de la crème of the city descended upon the Roths' brownstone. Politicians, moneymen and bankers, a B-list celebrity or three, everyone there to bask in the spotlight. And at the heart of it all, holding court and cradling a glass of champagne, stood Senator Alton Roth.

He was a big man with expansive gestures, the kind of politician who looked like he was born wearing a Stetson and a flag lapel pin. His hair was silver at the temples, his eyes falcon-sharp. He glad-handed his way across the room and back again, at ease with everyone, cracking focus-tested jokes and boldly taking only the most crowd-approved stances. While Richard trailed in his father's shadow like an obedient puppy, Nessa played the role of the dutiful wife and hostess. She milled around the edges of the room, making small talk when she had to, watching the caterers to ensure the drinks and finger foods kept circulating.

She avoided her reflection. She looked like a frilly tangerine in Richard's favorite dress, some parts too loose, some too tight, the outfit making her feel like an unbalanced mess. The bright color was a spotlight calling everyone to stare at her ineptitude. Trying to distract herself, she focused on Alton's entourage. He'd brought a handful of men to the party with him, some clearly working private security—they lingered at every doorway, silent and steely-eyed—and others were aides who occasionally cut into the senator's conversations with messages and whispers.

Then there was the odd one out: a tall, dark man in a tan linen suit, cut perfectly to his lanky physique. He hovered on the fringes, just like her, a silent phantom in the social swirl. He regarded his surroundings with an air of quiet amusement. Nessa circled the room, spotting him on the far side before losing sight of him in the crowd of partygoers.

Then she turned and nearly bumped into him.

He leaned against the wall, faintly smiling. His smile grew as he looked down at her.

"Not your scene either, huh?" he asked in a slow, basso rumble.

"Oh," Nessa said, "I can't complain."

"Sure you can. Everybody's got the right to sing the blues." He offered her his hand. "Webster Scratch, at your service. My friends call me Calypso."

His hand was smooth as silk, with a gentleman's touch.

"A pleasure, Mr. Scratch. You work with my father-in-law?"

"Mm-hmm. Director of Campaign Communications, though I'm really more of an all-around troubleshooter. So, how do you feel about becoming part of the First Family?"

Nessa gave him an appraising look. She pitched her voice a bit lower. "Do you really think Alton has a shot at the White House?"

"I'm a rambler and a gambler, Mrs. Roth. Do you know the two keys to being a good gambler?"

She shook her head.

"Number one, never hitch your wagon to a losing horse. Number two, cheat." He gave her a sly wink. "In all certitude, though, it's a long road just to reach the primaries. But I think our boy Alton's gonna go the distance. Time will out the truth, it always does."

One of the aides swooped in, cutting between them. He held out a small tablet for inspection. "Sir," he said.

As he offered up the tablet, the aide's tailored sleeve slid back, baring a sigil tattooed on his wrist.

It wasn't the same as the one Marie had asked her to research, but easily a kissing cousin, all sharp angles and jagged loops, something primal and cold. Then it was gone, and the aide gone with it, leaving Calypso holding the tablet. His eyes darkened as he flicked the screen with his fingertip.

"Mm-*hmm*," he rumbled.

"Something wrong?" Nessa asked.

"No, ma'am, just a tiny bump in the road. If you'll pardon me, I haven't said hello to your husband yet."

*   *   *

The alley behind the house was as pristine as the street out front, if lonelier and poorly lit. Richard was glad for both, for the moment. He needed a few minutes of peace to catch his breath. He felt like he was being strangled twice, once by the crowd, all grasping hands and need, and twice by his father's thinly veiled disapproval.

"Never fucking good enough," he grumbled, fishing out a cigarette. It dangled in his lips as he flicked his lighter. It sputtered, failing to spark. Then again.

A thin, dark hand dropped in front of his face. A silver lighter ignited, the sudden flame dazzling Richard's eyes.

"Allow me," his unexpected guest said.

Richard blinked, startled, then pursed his lips in an attempt to hide it. He put the tip of his cigarette to the flame until it sizzled then nodded his thanks.

"Appreciate it. You're...Mr. Scratch, right? You work with my dad."

The tall man smiled, but his eyes were chips of black ice.

"We're family. No need to stand on formalities. You can call me Calypso."

"Calypso." Richard nodded, uncertain, and took a drag on his cigarette. "That a nickname or…"

"Oh, I've got plenty of names. That's just the one I like most right now. Names are like faces. Everybody's got two or three of 'em."

Richard chuckled. "Pretty sure I only have one face."

"Do you now? Richard, you seem like a quick study. So I'm gonna lay some wisdom on your doorstep and trust you to pick it up. Your father is going to formally declare his intention to run for the presidency next month."

"Yeah, I know. Dad told me—"

"He's going to get the party's nod, he's going to win the primary with minimal opposition, and then he's going to win the electoral vote. In a landslide, in fact."

Richard forced a smile. He realized, as a trickle of gray smoke rose between their faces, that he hadn't seen Calypso blink once.

"Getting a little ahead of yourself, aren't you?"

Calypso shook his head.

"No," he told Richard, "I'm not. Some very important people are very heavily invested in your father's success. And what we can't have, what we absolutely cannot afford right now, is any hint of a scandal. That'd be bad for everyone. Do you dig what I'm saying?"

His shoulders sagged. "Oh, God. Did Vanessa say something to you? Is she being weird? Look, I'll talk to her—"

"Your wife? She's sweeter than a Georgia peach. No, I'm more concerned about you, son."

Richard took another drag. He turned his head and exhaled a thin plume of smoke, an excuse to tear away from Calypso's gaze.

"Me? What about me?"

"I get it, you know. We've all got our little peccadilloes, our…extracurricular activities that some might find distasteful. But you and your playmates, well, you're getting sloppy. And I can't *have* sloppy, son. I won't abide it."

Richard squirmed like a worm on a hook. "I...I don't know what you're talking about."

"You know, Richard, while he has a hard time showing it, I know for a fact that your father loves you very much." Calypso loomed over him. His smile vanished. "I *don't*. And if you screw the pooch and sink your father's career, there won't be any place in this world or any other where you can hide from me. Clean up your act, son. Clean it up and keep it clean, because if I have to do it for you, well...you won't be a happy man."

Richard froze, staring up at him. They stood there, eye to eye, the air between them electric. Then Calypso shrugged. The amused smile returned, his affable mask firmly back in place. He patted Richard's shoulder.

"Stay clean," he said, "and you and me are copacetic, all the way to the White House. Great things ahead of you, young man. Great things indeed."

Calypso stepped back inside the house. Richard stared at his cigarette, dropped it, and snuffed it under his heel.

*   *   *

Nessa had been downgraded from hostess to messenger, courtesy of Richard's father. She walked the upstairs halls, looking for Richard after he'd vanished from the party below. She heard his voice, a strained and muffled shout, from behind his closed office door.

"No, I don't know who the fuck he is, Scottie! Just some guy who works for my dad. That's the point—"

She raised an eyebrow. Leaning close, she put her ear an inch from the wood.

"And I'm telling you," Richard said, "he knows. Okay? The dude knows. No, I don't know specifics. No, I didn't fucking ask him. He was leaning on me, all right? I played dumb. It didn't work. We need an emergency—yeah, okay, *thank* you."

Heavy footsteps on the other side of the door. Nessa scurried back a few feet, straightening her dress, freezing in place until the office door swung open. Then she walked past, pretending to be surprised when Richard loomed in the doorway.

"Oh, Richard, there you are. Your father is looking for you. He's downstairs."

Her husband looked like he'd aged a year since the last time she saw him. His face was pale, with a five-o'clock shadow starting to sprout on his cheeks. He ran nervous fingers through his hair and smoothed it back.

"Yeah, okay, I'll...yeah." He paused. "Hey, one thing. I'm gonna be heading out for a day or two tomorrow morning. Business trip."

Nessa shook her head. "You just got back. Where are you heading off to now?"

"*Business*," he said, stepping around her. "Jesus, Vanessa, just...don't start with me, okay? I'm under a lot of stress right now. It's hard enough dealing with my father without you adding your bullshit to the pile."

"I was just asking a question."

"Well *don't*," he snapped. "Can you just shut up and *support* me? For once? Is that too much to ask?"

He stomped down the stairs, leaving her to bristle in silence.

Nessa drifted to the bedroom. She couldn't go right back to playing her role at the party. She tried to put her mask on, but it wouldn't fit. Her reflection stared out at her from the mirror, this unhappy woman in her ridiculous orange dress, her pinned hair wilting.

"There has to be more than this," she murmured to the glass.

She looked at her phone, sitting on the vanity. She knew one thing that would bring her smile back.

We should celebrate your success today, she texted. *Come have dinner with me tomorrow night.*

The response came less than half a minute later, as if Marie had been waiting for her. She almost certainly hadn't, Nessa knew, but she liked the mental image.

I'd like that. Where at?

My home, Nessa replied. *Husband is gone on business. Just the two of us.*

Twenty-Seven

Richard left at seven in the morning. Nessa sent the maid home at noon, giving her the rest of the day off and a small wad of under-the-table cash to go shopping with. The brownstone was quiet.

Storm clouds rolled in a little after one, painting the sky with mud-brown smears and turning the sunlight a sickly shade of yellow. Nessa didn't mind. In the kitchen, as the first spatters of rain kissed the tall windows, she took stock of the pantry and the double-wide refrigerator. Plenty to work with. She laid out prep bowls and washed down the cutting board, bouncing with nervous energy.

Richard had spent an ungodly amount of money wiring the entire house for sound, concealing Sonos speakers behind recessed grills in every room. They used them once a month, at most, and always *his* music. Nessa quirked a smile, pulled up the control app on her phone, and flitted through her personal collection. With a tap of a button, the kitchen filled with the slow, ominous strains of a gothic rock song. Bauhaus, performing "Bela Lugosi's Dead." The warbling guitar droned like an oboe being played underwater, the staccato, scratchy drums banging a counterpoint to the tapping of raindrops against the windows. Nessa basked in the music and poured herself a glass of cabernet.

*   *   *

"You're going to see George tonight, aren't you?" Janine asked. She clung to the futon like a cat about to pounce.

It took Marie a second to remember who 'George' was. Right. The name she'd blurted out after coming home from dinner with Nessa.

"Huh? Why would you say that?"

"I dunno," Janine said. "Because you've paced through the living room three times in the last half hour, wearing three different outfits? And you're so nervous you're vibrating?"

Marie turned on her heel, stopping in mid-pace. She glanced down at herself. Her latest attempt was a casual floral top with a little ruffle at the waist and black skinny jeans. Simple, clean, noncommittal.

"He—George," Marie said, "found some more information for me. On the case."

"Ooh, of course. It's all about the investigation. Are you going undercovers together?" Janine fake coughed into her hand. "I mean, undercover?"

Marie winced. "Stop, just stop. It's only dinner. Friends having dinner."

"Why are you refusing to admit you're going on a date?"

"Because it's not a date!"

She swept into her bedroom, rummaging through her drawers, second-guessing herself again and not sure why. Janine hovered in her doorway.

"Okay," Janine said, "first of all? Stop. You look great."

Marie sighed. "Really?"

"Really. That top looks amazing on you and I want to steal it. And I probably will. Second of all? Let me do your makeup."

"I don't want to look like I'm wearing makeup," Marie said. "Really, it's not that kind of thing."

Janine rolled her eyes. "Yeah. That's why I said to let *me* do it, because you don't know how. Hello? Veteran theater geek here. I have secret and arcane skills. C'mon, let me help."

Marie thought about it. She gave in slowly, her resistance crumbling like a sandcastle under a steady tide.

"Okay, just...really light, okay?"

Janine clapped her hands together. "I'll get my brushes. You are going to look *so* hot."

"I'm not trying to look hot!" Marie called after her. "Absolute minimal hotness!"

*   *   *

By the time night fell, Nessa had taken to prowling the halls, fiddling with the music every five steps. From goth to classic rock to bouncy pop, the tunes changing as fast as her shifting mood. Her mind was a radio with a spinning dial. She remembered the first time she laid eyes on Marie and that *feeling*, like the ground was sliding out from under her feet. Anxiety and delight. It all surged back to her now as the clock counted down.

She settled on a satellite station that played classical. Chamber music, soft, filling the house with the dark strains of a lonely violin.

She popped into the bedroom to check her reflection one last time. Black Dior dress, on. Silver earrings, in place. Something was missing. Her gaze drifted across the cluttered vanity. Her pill bottle sat on the edge, just where she'd left it.

Did I— she thought. No. She'd changed last night, at Richard's command, and went downstairs without taking her pills. Then this morning she'd been treated to an encore of his raging-prick routine from the night before, and he'd talked to her like she was a child while demanding three separate times to know if she'd dosed herself. She hadn't, out of sheer irritation at that point, and then forgot about the pills altogether halfway through breakfast.

She hadn't been off the drugs for more than a day since she'd started her sessions with Dr. Neidermyer, not until tonight. And she felt...fine. Better than fine, really. She figured it was just the nervous excitement cutting through her usual brain fog, but she felt better than she had in ages. Nessa touched the bottle. She picked it up. Then she set it down again, unopened.

Not the missing piece. In a burst of inspiration, she tugged open a narrow drawer and picked up a long-neglected tube of lipstick. Her favorite, a deep and elegant plum. She'd worn it once in front of

Richard and he'd given her a half-hour lecture, telling her she looked like a moody teenager.

That wasn't what she saw in the mirror, though. Her dark eyes, high cheekbones, her black bangs artfully sweeping above one pert eyebrow. Her plum lips curled into an eager smile.

"Surrender, Dorothy," she said to her reflection.

The doorbell rang. She bounced down the staircase, almost giddy. She paused to strike a studied pose, the graceful lady of the manor. Then she took a deep breath, opened the front door, and—

"You're soaked!" Nessa's cool grace shattered and her hands fluttered, beckoning. "Come in, come in!"

A springtime torrent kissed the street outside, wind-whipped showers coming down in rolling wet waves, almost horizontal. Even with her blue folding umbrella, Marie looked like a drowned rat. She stepped inside, fast, droplets of rain pooling on the welcome mat.

"The bus stop looked closer last time, when it wasn't storming out," she said, her tone apologetic.

Nessa plucked the umbrella from her hand, collapsed it, and jammed the sodden mess into a brass stand beside the door. "Come with me. Bathroom. Let's get you some warm fluffy towels."

*   *   *

The towels were warm. And fluffy. Marie stared at her reflection in the bathroom mirror, beneath a softly humming art deco light sconce, and sighed. Most of Janine's careful makeup work was a wash, literally; at least she'd salvaged what she could, and she didn't look like a blurry raccoon. Her hair was a tangled mess, but then again, when wasn't it? She rubbed it down with thick Egyptian cotton. Nessa's bathroom was tiny but well equipped with spa towels and a heat lamp. The hard orange eye of the lamp chased away the cold of the streets.

With the towels, Nessa had passed her a dress on a padded hanger. It was nightingale blue, with an empire waist and bell sleeves. One glance at the designer's name on the tag and Marie realized it probably cost more than she made in a month.

"Our sizes are *fairly* close and this runs a little long on me, so it should fit you nicely," Nessa said.

"Oh, no, you don't have to—"

"Marie," Nessa said. "Your clothes are soaked. You'll catch your death. Put the dress on."

"Do you have anything less...fancy?"

Nessa tilted her head, studying her.

"Dry off and change while I finish making dinner. When you join me in the dining room, you'll be wearing this dress."

Marie had to admit, glancing at herself in the mirror and turning to the side, the dress looked all right on her. Damp but moderately dignified, she poked her head out into the hall.

"Nessa?"

"Up the hall," Nessa called out. "Archway on your right."

Marie followed her voice, stepping into the dining room. Silver candelabras glowed on the long glass table, casting shifting shadows across the hardwood floor. The high-backed chairs, normally posed at opposite ends, had been shuffled closer together on the table's left-hand side. Nessa positioned napkins and silverware, arranging everything just right, eyeing the layout like an artist. She glanced up and let out a nervous chuckle.

"I hope the candles aren't too much," she said. "I never really get to cook for anyone, or set table arrangements myself. I wanted it to be nice. And...oh, look at you. Perfect. That's my favorite color, you know. Well, besides black."

Marie shifted from foot to foot, awkward. "You didn't have to go to this much trouble. A restaurant would have been fine."

"Eh." Nessa folded her arms, giving Marie a dubious look. "Waiter overhears that you're celebrating something, next thing you know there are twenty of them clustered around your table, singing an off-key, off-brand version of 'Happy Birthday.' And honestly, after playing hostess to my father-in-law and his paper friends last night, I'm in no mood to deal with people in general."

"Paper friends?" Marie asked. "And aren't I people?"

Nessa held up her hand, flat, and wriggled it sideways.

"Made of paper," she said. "Two-dimensional. As deep as a mud puddle, at best. And you're a friend; that's not the same thing as *people*. I have very little use for large swaths of the human race. It's likely a good thing for everyone that I'm not running the planet."

"Nessa," Marie deadpanned, "Queen of the World."

Nessa held up a finger. "I'd put a lot of people to work in the salt mines. Are salt mines still a thing? If not, I'd make them build salt mines first. Then work in them. Come on, sit, sit. I'm trying a new recipe tonight."

The new recipe was a lush cacophony of greenery, a splash of wild color served up in black ceramic bowls. Marie took her seat at Nessa's right hand and leaned over the bowl, inhaling the aroma. Subtle, lemony, tart.

"It's an Asian fusion dish with cabbage, Chinese long beans, plum tomatoes, Persian cucumbers, and daikon shavings, mingled with roasted chicken marinated in lemon juice and kaffir lime leaves. The dressing is a medley of fish sauce, Thai chilies, and palm sugar." Nessa ducked her head, suddenly sheepish. "I make complicated salad."

Marie dug her fork in, taking an experimental bite. A long bean burst between her teeth, ripe with mingled flavors, the sweet and the tart slow-dancing together and concealing a little sting of heat behind their backs.

"It's good." Marie stared at her fork. "It's *really* good."

Nessa squinted at her. "You're not just saying that? You really like it?"

"I assume," Marie said with a tiny smile, "the rule about not lying to you is still in effect."

"And so it is. Good. I'm glad you remembered."

Marie took another bite. "If I forgot, I assume you'd send me to the salt mines."

"Or just put you over my knee," Nessa said. "Whichever is more convenient."

They both fell silent, eyes on their plates. Marie shifted in her seat.

"So," Nessa said, breaking the stillness. "You passed with flying colors, I assume? Got your badge back?"

"I...passed, I suppose. I get officially reinstated tomorrow, but as far as anyone at the precinct is concerned, it's already a done deal. My partner went in this afternoon and apparently he got the thumbs-up too."

Nessa reached for a wine bottle, tall and slender with a weathered sepia label. "And so we celebrate. Hand me your glass."

She poured for both of them, generous splashes of golden wine, and slid Marie's glass over before lifting hers in a toast.

"To our knight with the golden shield, reunited with the law, her steadfast liege."

Their gazes met, entangled, a silent caress by candlelight.

"Cheers," Marie said, and their glasses clinked together like crystal chimes.

Nessa took a sip and nodded approvingly. "This is a 2009 Zind Humbrecht pinot gris, by the way."

Marie shrank in her chair. "We mostly buy Two-Buck Chuck at my place."

"Once upon a time," Nessa said, "Richard had me playing hostess for his work friends, half of whom were avowed wine snobs. So I served them red wine from an eight-dollar cardboard box and told them it was a 2011 Louis Latour Batard Montrachet grand cru. Not one of them knew the difference."

"Saved some money," Marie observed.

"Oh, no, we already had the bottle. I drank it myself, later that night. My reward for putting up with their bullshit. It is, after all, the societally approved coping mechanism."

Marie regarded her over the rim of her own glass. "Meaning?"

"Our mothers took Miltown and Valium. We drink wine. Every generation of women has their own special numbing agent. Only difference being, they popped pills behind the bathroom door while we took our particular vice public."

"It sounds like you don't approve," Marie said, "yet we're drinking wine right now."

"Oh, I enjoy wine. What I don't approve of is the normalization of the ritual. We are told, day in and day out, by advertisements and television shows, that gathering to drink wine is simply what women *do*. That it's how we relax, how we cope. I don't object to vices in general; it's unquestioned and unexamined vices I detest. If one is going to drink poison for fun, as we're doing right now, one should at least be honest about it."

Marie cast an uncertain eye at her drink.

"Poison," Nessa said as she took a sip, "is the wellspring of so many of life's little pleasures."

Twenty-Eight

They had another glass, the bottle dropping low as they ate and talked by the candlelight.

"Your mysterious tattoo," Nessa said, "has a pedigree. I didn't find anything else in the historical record, so I delved into more esoteric sources. The *Grimorium Verum*, *Cultes des Ghoules*, the *Purged Testimony of Edward Kelly*."

"Sounds like some light reading," Marie replied.

"For me, it is. Turns out that particular symbol is linked to a cult of demon worship. The 'Court of Windswept Razors' it was called, with a particular affection for a creature called 'Prince Berith.' Near as I can tell, the cult wore out its welcome in Ireland and the surviving adherents hitched a ride on the pilgrim ships. The symbol pops up again here, in colonial-era New York, around 1771. After that, nothing. Well, until now, that is."

"Demon worship," Marie echoed.

"Not what you expected to find?"

"I shouldn't talk about this," she said, "but the tattoo was on the body of a man affiliated with the Mafia."

Nessa shrugged. She reached for the wine bottle and topped off both of their drinks. The last dollop of gold splashed from the bottle's mouth, a few scant droplets clinging to the glass.

"Would hardly be the first time members of organized crime dabbled in the occult. In the early nineteen hundreds, the Five Points

Gang and the Neapolitan Camorra both used the threat of death curses to scare shopkeepers into paying protection money. They'd import *streghe*—witches—from the Old Country, just to drive the point home." Nessa winked. "My maiden name is Fieri. I can talk about Italy for hours. Fun fact: the word *strega*, 'witch,' is etymologically derived from the word *strix*, or 'owl.'"

"You know a lot about..." Marie fell silent.

"Italy?"

"Witches," Marie said.

Nessa sipped her wine and smiled. The candlelight gleamed in her eyeglasses, painting the round lenses in shifting, molten brass.

"I have a passion for history," she said, "and all the best history is made in the dark."

Marie felt like she was toeing a line drawn by a silent dare in Nessa's eyes. She could back away, safe but her curiosity unfulfilled, or step across and take her chances.

She took her chances.

"Just an academic interest?"

"Marie," Nessa said, "I enjoy dancing too, but I prefer to use my body, not my words. Ask me what you really want to ask me."

"Are you a witch?" Marie blurted out.

"Yes."

Marie paused. She'd asked the question, gotten an answer, the simple word hanging in the air between them. Like a dog chasing a car, she wasn't entirely sure what to do now that the car had stopped.

"Does it work?" she asked.

"Sometimes," Nessa said. "It's an art, not a science."

She gazed into Marie's eyes, contemplating her.

"Would you like to see my workroom?"

Marie nodded, slow. Nessa eased her chair back and rose to her feet. She held out her hand.

"Come with me."

Marie eyed Nessa's outstretched fingers. Then, curious, wary, she reached out and took the other woman's hand. Nessa gently tugged her along, out of the dining room, into the hallway. The soft chamber music, playing throughout their dinner, had stopped. She hadn't seen Nessa turn it off. But it was gone now, extinguished, cloaking the brownstone in trembling silence.

Then a distant sound. Somewhere, a clock was faintly ticking.

Nessa paused by a glass credenza. She opened a small box, the outer lid and sides layered with tiny mirrors. Inside, nestled on a bed of velvet, lay an antique iron key. Marie's hand tensed around Nessa's, squeezing her slender fingers.

"That box," Marie said.

"Mm?"

"That wasn't there a second ago."

Nessa chuckled and scooped up the key.

"Sure it was," Nessa shut the lid and twisted the clasp, the mirrors reflecting the twirl of her dark-painted fingernails. "You just didn't notice it."

"No. I was looking *right at* the table. That box wasn't there until you opened it."

"You were looking," Nessa told her, "but you weren't seeing. Mirrors can be tricky things, after all."

She pulled Marie's hand, leading her up the narrow staircase to the black door on the second-floor landing. A turn of the key, a flick of the light switch, and Nessa guided her into her private sanctum. Marie turned in a slow circle, eyes wide, as she took in the easels and dangling, half-finished canvases.

"Did you draw all of these?"

Nessa gave her a tiny, sheepish smile. "Mm-hmm. I'm a bit of an amateur artist. I dabble. Not very skilled, but it gives my brain something to do."

"No," Marie said. "These are really good."

"You're sweet to say that, but I barely finish anything I start. I just...run out of steam, I suppose. My inspiration doesn't hold."

Marie paused at the charcoal sketch of the three women dancing around a bonfire of shadows.

"Who are they?" she asked.

Nessa peered at the canvas. Did it look more vibrant now? The dancers more energetic, with the sense of movement she hadn't been able to capture before? A trick of the light.

"I'm not sure," she told Marie. "They just felt important."

"So." Marie looked her way. "Show me something."

"Understand, this isn't like the movies. No special effects."

"Show me anyway." Marie's bottom lip was trapped between her teeth. "I want to see what you do."

*   *   *

Ten minutes later, the two women sat side by side on the floor, the only light glowing from the wick of a tall black candle. Nessa's special book lay open across her lap, a ceramic bowl of water before them. Calligrapher's ink dripped into the water, blooming in a nightingale cloud to fill the basin's depths. Nessa's spidery, whispered chant filled the room as Marie sat in frozen silence.

"Now look into the waters," Nessa murmured, "and let your mind float free."

"What should I see?" Marie whispered.

"There is no 'should.' You might perceive shapes, or faces, or shadows. You might see nothing at all. Don't force it. Just relax, and float." Her hand closed over Marie's. Their fingers entwined. "Okay?"

Marie glanced sidelong at her. "Okay."

Nessa gave her a lopsided smile. "Look into the waters."

Minutes drifted by, punctuated by the distant patter of rain on the brownstone's roof. Marie felt like she was losing herself. Slipping away, the waters closing over her.

And then she saw it. The ink swirled and took on form. A square became a box became a horse-drawn wagon, riding across a snowy tundra.

"Do you see that?" Marie gasped. Her fingers tightened.

"Scrying is a personal experience," Nessa whispered. "It's all filtered through your subconscious mind, like a dream. We'll likely perceive very different things. What do you see?"

"A...a cart. A wagon. Two women, riding through the snow." Nessa blinked.

"That shouldn't happen."

"What?" Marie asked.

In the bowl, the women—their faces blots of shadow—stepped down from the wagon and approached a stockade wall.

"We're seeing the same vision," Nessa told her.

A flurry of snow washed the scene away. An eye, vast, unblinking, rimmed with rippling blue fire, took its place. And then a voice, tinny and distant like an old radio transmission, crackled from the water's surface.

"*Hedy. Hold the book. Yes, just like that.*"

"Did you hear that?" Marie squeezed Nessa's hand tighter. "Am I hallucinating? Did you *hear* that? Is that *you*? It sounds like—"

"Shh," Nessa said. She leaned closer to the bowl, her gaze fixed on the unblinking eye.

The bowl rattled against the hardwood floor.

"*My name is Nessa Fieri,*" the voice said. "*Maybe yours is, too. I'm not certain how all this works.*"

The bowl rattled harder, turning in place, the ceramic vibrating in tune with the voice and the inky waters.

"Are you doing this?" Marie stared wide-eyed at Nessa. "How are you doing this?"

"Shh," Nessa snapped.

"*But if you're receiving this,*" the voice said as the bowl thrummed and shook, "*then listen and understand: you are in terrible danger.*"

Then a pause.

"*Marie,*" the voice said, "*go back to—*"

The bowl shattered.

Marie let out a shrill yelp as the ceramic burst into a dozen jagged pieces, like it had been dropped from five feet in the air, shards scattering and spinning across the workroom. Ink-stained water splashed across the naked floorboards. She let go of Nessa's hand and jumped to her feet, sprinting from the room.

Nessa sat perfectly still in the flickering candlelight, staring at the spilled water, the swirls of midnight-blue ink.

Twenty-Nine

"Tell me that was a trick," Marie said. Her back was pressed to the wall in the hallway outside Nessa's workroom, her eyes fixed on the open doorway and the shadows beyond. "Tell me it was a remote control. A hidden speaker."

"I've instructed you not to lie to me," Nessa replied. "I choose not to lie to you. No, it wasn't a trick. It was also not something I did on purpose. The last time I tried that spell, it was...well, it was right after we first met."

"And the same thing happened?"

"No." Nessa frowned. "I didn't get that far into the vision before it broke up. I think, doing it together, we...amplified it somehow. The bowl just couldn't contain the energy coming through."

"Coming through from *where*?"

"I don't know. I told you, witchcraft is an art, not a science."

Marie pointed a shaking finger at the doorway.

"Well it sounds like a pretty important message. To both of us, from *you*. And if you didn't record it, that means..."

She trailed off, leaving the conclusion unspoken. Nessa finished the sentence for her.

"I haven't recorded it yet."

"Time travel," Marie breathed. "And witchcraft. Jesus, Nessa, this isn't...this isn't *real*. None of this is real."

"You saw and heard the exact same thing I did. Two people can't have the same hallucination. Ergo, it was quite real."

Marie's shoulders slumped. The back of her head thumped against the wall and she closed her eyes.

"Nessa, you don't understand. I mean, I love fantasy novels. Novels. Stories. Not real. I live in a world of facts, and logic, and...and voices from the future giving warnings from bowls of ink *is not a thing that happens.*"

"It just did. Denial is not a refuge. So what are you going to do about it?"

"I don't understand."

"Marie," Nessa told her, "open your eyes."

She did. Nessa stood in front of her, half a foot away. Close enough for Marie to feel the warmth of her breath.

"Look at me," Nessa said.

"I am," Marie whispered.

"No. *Look* at me." Nessa gazed into Marie's eyes. "Your world of facts and logic just went away. Bye-bye. If you want, you can go chase it. The front door is right down the stairs. I won't stop you. You'll probably spend the rest of your life living a lie, wondering what's hidden in every shadow, wondering what you might have experienced and explored if you'd been brave enough to try, but maybe you're better at fooling yourself than I think."

"Or?"

Nessa's plum lips curled into a fishhook smile.

"Or," she said, "you stay. With me. And we dive down the rabbit hole hand in hand."

Marie's eyes flicked to the stairwell. Then to Nessa. Back and forth, lingering longer on Nessa's face each time.

"I want to stay," Marie said. "With you."

"Very good," Nessa replied.

"So...what now?"

"Now," Nessa said, contemplating the question. "Now, now, now.

Let's see. We've had a lovely dinner, a little magic...whatever am I
going to do with you now, Marie?"

Marie fell silent. Nessa leaned closer. Studying her, their noses
nearly brushing, as Nessa raised her hand. Her fingernails closed
lightly around Marie's jaw. Pinching, soft, like five tiny needles.

"The correct answer to that question," Nessa murmured, "which
I can see written clearly in your eyes, though I'm sure it hasn't yet
found the courage to reach your lips, is that I'm going to do anything
I want."

"Nessa," Marie stammered, forcing an awkward smile, "I don't, I
mean, I'm not...you've...you've got the wrong idea—"

"Do I?" Nessa let go of her. She took a step back and nodded to
the staircase. "Front door's right down there. I'm not holding you
hostage."

Marie's feet didn't budge.

"I mean," Marie said, "I *like* you, I mean, as a friend, but I'm not like
that. I mean, I don't..."

Nessa watched her, almost clinical, as Marie's stammered denials
sputtered into silence.

"All done now?" Nessa asked. "Finished? Did you get it all out?"

Marie's head bobbed once. A tiny nod.

Nessa closed in on her. Taking her time. She reached up and slid
her finger around a strand of Marie's dirty-blonde curls, toying with
her hair.

"I told you about lying," she murmured into Marie's ear. "This
once, just this one time, I'll let it slide. Do it again, and I'll have to
punish you."

Her other hand rose to Marie's chest and rested on her breastbone.
The thud of her heart felt powerful under Nessa's fingers, like the
pounding hooves of a racehorse. She chuckled.

"Oh, your pulse is racing. Can you feel that? It's okay if you're a
little afraid, Marie. To be honest, I think I like you being a little afraid.
But I'll tell you this much: I'm not going to do anything to you that
you won't enjoy, even if you're too ashamed to admit it."

Their cheeks brushed together, feline. Nessa pulled back and looked her in the eye.

"I understand, you know. Out there, fighting the evils of an entire city. Always on your guard, always in control." Nessa's smile broadened. "Would you like to know a secret?"

"Yes," she breathed, frozen where she stood.

"Inside this house, behind these walls, when it's just the two of us...you're not in control here. I am. And you will do as I say. But here's the real secret: that's exactly the way you want it. Watch, I'll prove it to you. See, I can do this, and you won't stop me."

Her finger, twined around a lock of Marie's hair, pulled a little tighter. An unspoken threat, or a promise.

"And I can do this," Nessa said, "and you won't stop me."

She let go of the curly lock and suddenly, swiftly dug her hand into Marie's hair and grabbed hold with her fist. Marie gasped as Nessa jerked her head to one side and pressed up against her, trapping her, pinning her to the wall.

Marie's lips parted, her breath ragged and fast. Nessa wore a smile of cold triumph.

"And I can do this," Nessa said, and kissed her.

Their lips met and Marie's paralysis shattered like a dam bursting wide. Every feeling she'd bottled up, every guilty longing, every buried hunger exploded at once and now she was nothing but her raw, aching need. She clawed at Nessa's back, bit at her bottom lip, trying to devour her. Nessa's grasping fingers slid up her thigh and yanked her body close. Her grip on Marie's hair tightened. She forced Marie's head back, baring the tender curve of her neck to Nessa's hungry kisses and her pearly, nipping teeth.

"Bedroom," Nessa hissed, "*now.*"

They stumbled together, staggering, wrapped up in each other's arms and careening up the hall. Then over the threshold. Nessa shoved Marie backward, the mattress jolting, and swooped down upon her like an owl diving after a scurrying mouse. She yanked out her hairpin and tossed it, letting it clatter across the floorboards.

They rolled across the bed together. Marie was on top, just for a moment, her desperate hands hiking Nessa's black dress up around her hips. Then she was rolling again, or the world was rolling around her, and they laughed together as Nessa straddled her waist and pressed her shoulders to the mattress. Giddy laughter, relieved laughter, hungry and mad laughter, and Nessa shot a gleeful look at the bedroom door and flung out her hand.

A gust of wind from nowhere, as hot and fast as the blood pumping through Marie's fevered heart, surged through the room.

The door slammed shut.

*   *   *

After they were spent, after the last strangled cry and the last kittenish whimper, Nessa watched Marie sleep. She'd drifted off in Nessa's arms, slipping across the river of dreams. Nessa smiled contentedly at the slow rise and fall of her lover's chest, her naked body sprawled beneath the Egyptian cotton sheets. *I imagine you don't sleep much*, she thought, *or well, when you do.*

You will tonight. I'll make sure of it.

Her lover. A phrase Nessa had never expected to use. She supposed she'd had designs on Marie—she supposed she had since the moment they met—but it wasn't a conscious plan. More like an invitation to the dance. She just let the music play and let her body move as it wanted. Everything about this felt...natural. Right. Like they'd known each other for years. Their lovemaking had a strange spark of the familiar, like she knew, on instinct, all of Marie's little secret places. The things that made her shiver and gasp in the dark. And Marie certainly had a natural talent for finding hers. Nessa shut her eyes and beamed, the fresh memory spurring a warm, tingling ripple in the pit of her stomach.

Life was uncertain. Life was chaos. But here was something uniquely, wonderfully *hers*. Something she could keep. Carving out a sanctuary in the heart of the storm, just big enough for the two of them. *You'll protect me*, she thought. Her fingers lightly trailed along the curve of Marie's bare shoulder, needing to touch. *And I'll protect you.*

A phone trilled. Not hers. Nessa frowned as Marie shifted and groaned, the tranquility broken.

"Let it ring," Nessa told her.

"Can't." Marie leaned off the side of the bed, fumbling for her phone, her other hand rubbing at her bleary eyes. "That's the ring tone I use for work. I'm on call, twenty-four seven."

Nessa crossed her arms and bit back a surge of jealousy.

"Reinhart." Marie fell silent as she listened. Nessa could make out a man's voice on the other end, chatty and quick. She felt a black mood settling in as their time together slipped away, stolen by Marie's devotion to the law. Their night was over, and Nessa wasn't done enjoying it yet.

"No," Marie said, "this is good, thank you. I really appreciate—yeah, I'll meet you there. Thanks, Jefferson."

She hung up. Nessa's eyes narrowed as she stared at Marie's naked back.

"You're leaving," she said.

Marie turned to her. She squeezed Nessa's hand.

"I have to. It's my job. I'm sorry." She paused, contemplating Nessa's expression, trying to read something there. "So was this...was this a one-time thing, or...?"

She's afraid, Nessa realized. She reached up and traced Marie's cheek with her fingertips.

"No," Nessa told her. "I'm keeping you."

Marie swallowed hard and smiled.

"We're a thing now," she said.

"Uh-huh," Nessa said. "We're a thing now. And if I could tell you what that means, or where we're going with this, I would, but honestly I'm just playing it by ear. It's like dinner. Complicated salad. We'll figure it out."

"Together," Marie said.

Nessa sat up in bed. She leaned close, kissing Marie's shoulder. Then her lips.

"You're going to need to find more time for me," Nessa warned her. "I don't like to share. The next time we spend the night together, I want *all* of it. Any more interruptions like this and I'm going to start making you wear a leash."

Marie laughed. She rummaged through their pile of rumpled clothes on the hardwood floor, hunting for her underwear. "Funny," she said.

"What's funny," Nessa replied, her voice dry, "is that you think I'm joking."

Thirty

After a few years on the beat, even before she'd earned her detective's shield, not much could shock Marie. She'd worked scenes with all kinds of corpses. Gunshot wounds, stabbings—after a while what was once stomach-churning became abstract. Her first month on the job, still wet behind the ears, she'd gotten called up to a tenement where a shut-in had died maybe a week earlier. One week, rotting in a sealed-up apartment with no air conditioning and a swarm of flies, in the dog days of July.

Looking back on it now, she was thankful: to this day it was the worst thing she'd seen or smelled in her entire life. Everything got a little easier after that. All the same, walking into a morgue always brought back a little of that revulsion reflex. The faint choke at the back of her throat, triggered by the smell of industrial antiseptic and the glow of the hot lights. Human shapes on gurneys, draped in white, hiding their faces and their secrets. A gallery of the violent dead.

Jefferson met her there. The portly detective came equipped with a plastic jar of Vicks VapoRub. He scooped up a dollop of cream and smeared it across his upper lip, just under his nose, before offering Marie the jar. She followed his lead.

"Thanks," she told him. "And thanks for calling me in. I mean it."

Jefferson hadn't spelled out his motives on the phone, but he talked around the edges enough to paint a picture. Helena Gorski's comment, out on 5th Avenue—he knew Marie had heard her say it, just like he knew he hadn't stood up for her. Apparently it had stuck in his craw, and when he saw a chance to make amends, he jumped at it.

"Hey, you know me, I just want to do right by everybody. My partner's a good cop, she's a good person—she really is. She just says some cruel shit sometimes. Speaking of, you gotta be in and out before Helena gets here, or it's *my* balls on the line."

"I'll be quick as a bunny. And I owe you lunch."

"Deal," Jefferson said. He gave her the side-eye. "Did I, uh, interrupt something when I called?"

"Only my beauty sleep. Why?"

"You're smiling. Like...a *lot*."

"Let's meet the stiff," Marie told him, "and see if I still have a reason to."

The medical examiner, a severe, thin-faced man who looked like he should be teaching at an English boarding school, led them to a gurney. He shot a disapproving look at the glossy cream under the detectives' noses.

"This may be troubling if you have *sensitive* dispositions," he said.

"Thanks for your concern, doc." Jefferson nodded at the white sheet. "Let's go."

The medical examiner unveiled the corpse. All four pieces of it. The naked man had been carved into fractions, a math problem solved in body parts.

"Jesus," Jefferson breathed. "What happened to the guy?"

The medical examiner gestured to the bisected torso, running a gloved hand over the seared and jet-black wound.

"I'm not remotely prepared to render a conclusion. These wounds are perfectly cauterized. From the lack of blood, I'd say they were burned shut almost immediately after the cuts were made. At the same time, in fact. Though I can't begin to guess how it was done."

Marie leaned in, furrowing her brow as she studied the dead man. "What was the weapon? A chainsaw?"

The medical examiner shook his head and pointed to another cut. "No. A chainsaw would have left tears along the tissue; it would pull as it ripped through the body. These cuts are almost impossibly clean. Again, far too early to say, but if I had to guess? You're looking at a very fast, very sharp instrument. Like a guillotine blade."

"A guillotine," Jefferson said, "which was on fire at the time."

A memory, a scene from one of her favorite books, sparked an idea. "What about a sword?" Marie asked.

"Possible," the medical examiner told her. "The problem is that most modern swords are reproductions for collectors; they're art pieces, not weapons. The blade that did this was *incredibly* sharp. And it still doesn't explain the cauterization effect."

"A sword which was on fire at the time," Jefferson said. He reached for the severed arm and looked to Marie. "Or a lightsaber. Maybe we should put out an APB on Darth Vader. Anyway, that's not what I invited you in for. The uniform who caught the call is a buddy of mine. He told me about—yeah, here we go."

Jefferson turned the pale arm. On the underbelly of the wrist, faded but clear, was a tattoo the size of a quarter.

"Exactly like the one on the vic in Monticello," Jefferson told her. "We don't have an ID on this guy yet, but I'll bet a Hamilton we find out he's got mob connections too."

"And the body was found out on the street?" Marie asked.

"On the sidewalk, literally. Some little old lady found him, walking her dog. Hell of a way to start your morning. But here's the kicker: Mr. Jigsaw here was just a few doors down from the Kissena Boulevard Gym. Wanna guess who *owns* the Kissena Boulevard Gym?"

Marie stared at him. "Roth Estate Holdings."

"Hell of a coincidence, huh?"

Marie pursed her lips, thinking fast. "Too much of one. We'll never get a search warrant. *Maybe* if the body was right on the doorstep, but it's just one business on a crowded street."

"All the same," Jefferson said, "two dead guys with the same tattoo found in or near a Roth building? I'd draw that connection in pencil, not permanent ink, but it's still a line."

"The Five Families are swearing up and down that they've got nothing to do with the ink trade. They want to find these guys as bad as we do. Given that the first vic was found murdered at a stash house, maybe the mob drew the same connection we did. Maybe they sent their errand boys to check out Roth's other properties and see what they could find out."

Jefferson shook his head at the corpse. "This guy found something, all right. Or it found him. Which doesn't say a lot for Richard Roth's innocence. Go snooping around his stuff, end up dead."

And I'm having an affair with the man's wife, Marie thought. *Complicated salad.*

"Exactly what the *hell* is going on here?" said a voice from the doorway. Helena, coming in with a full head of steam and a beet-red face. "Jefferson? I'm sorry, did you switch partners and nobody told me?"

Jefferson hunched his shoulders and ducked his head like a turtle trying to escape into its shell. Marie got between them fast.

"It's not his fault," she said. "I found out where he was going and invited myself along."

Helena jabbed her finger in Marie's face. "Maybe we're having a communication problem. This. Isn't. Your. Case. Nothing *related* to this is your case."

"That tattoo draws a connection to the murder in Monticello. The Monticello house has a connection to my abduction victim—"

"Oh my God." Helena gaped at her. "Seriously? We're chasing down a major narcotics ring, and you're still obsessed with some missing whore? You're a fucking train wreck. You know that, don't you?"

"Come on, Helena—" Jefferson started to say. She cut him off.

"No. Don't *you* even open your mouth. This is the kind of case that makes careers, and I am not going to have some crusading wannabe superhero stomping all over *my* scenes, endangering *my* investigation." She turned, aiming her wrath back at Marie. "One more time, and I go straight to the captain and lodge a formal complaint. And I'll tell him how you were harassing Richard Roth while you were on admin leave."

"Interviewed, not harassed. And you said I could."

"Did I?" Helena gave her an ugly smile. "I don't remember having any such conversation. But if you want to screw up your career *and* your partner's, go ahead and keep pushing me. I'm saying this as clear as I can possibly make it: stay out of this. Mind your own business. And do your fucking job."

Marie moved in close, toe to toe. Her voice was a cold and dangerous whisper.

"That's exactly what I'm going to do."

She turned and pushed her way through the morgue's double doors like an old west gunslinger on her way to a showdown. They swung back and forth in her wake.

* * *

Marie rode a crosstown train, chasing the dawn. The car was almost empty, rattling and swaying on the tracks as it hummed through the dark, and she curled her arm around a metal pole and smiled to herself. Life was crazy, or maybe she was, but it was all right. Every time she closed her eyes, she saw Nessa's face. She felt the memory of Nessa's touch, and how her skin was soft and smelled faintly like lavender under Marie's fingers, under her lips.

I'm having an affair, Marie told herself. *With a woman. With a married woman. With a married woman whose husband might be connected to a narcotics syndicate.*

"Definitely complicated salad," she said out loud. A few seats down, a grizzled old man in an army-surplus jacket gave her a curious look.

Still, treacherous as these waters were, she felt like she could sail to the horizon's edge.

Her phone trilled. She glanced at the screen, then picked up.

"Hey, partner," she said. "You back in action yet?"

Tony's voice was distant. Softer than usual.

"Yeah. Well, technically later today, according to the paperwork. You know how it goes."

"I hear you," Marie said, "and I hope you had a lovely vacation, but we are officially back to work. What do you say, wanna saddle up, go chase some bad guys?"

"I'm already...I mean, I got a call."

Marie's smile faded. "You okay, Tony? You don't sound happy."

"Listen." He sighed, a sound of quiet resignation. "There's a construction yard in Bushwick, over on Johnson Avenue. Meet me there, soon as you can, okay?"

"Tony? What's going on with you?"

"Just...meet me there."

He hung up the phone.

Thirty-One

Marie changed trains and changed direction, from Queens to Brooklyn. She hopped a cab and made it to the construction site just as the sun crested the city streets, shining the first light of a new day through the muddy clouds. A couple of cruisers were parked outside the wooden fence, a wrap-around advertising a new condo development. A uniform out front, a fresh-faced rookie, chewed on his bottom lip like it was made of bubble gum. He moved fast to stand in Marie's way.

"It's okay." She flashed her shield. "Detective Reinhart. I think my partner's already here?"

"Yeah." He shot a nervous look over his shoulder. "Yeah, he is. Go on in, Detective."

They'd barely broken ground on the condos. The construction site was bedrock and wet black dirt, piles of rebar and wooden pallets all soaked from last night's rain. And in the middle of the scene, under the shadow of a sunset-orange crane, a dead and broken body.

No.

She felt like a ghost, drifting across the yard, past cops reeling out crime-scene tape. Past an evidence tech who swooped around the body with his camera, snapping photographs that sounded like cannon fire. Tony rushed over in slow motion, looking like he hadn't slept, trying to get in her way.

"Marie, listen—" he started to say. She brushed past him without a word.

And stood over the corpse of Baby Blue.

Blood smeared her pale cheeks, painted her lips, dotted the tip of her nose. In death, her killer had made a clown of her. Stealing everything she had. Her clothes, her dignity, her life. Leaving nothing behind but cuts and broken bones.

Marie collapsed to one knee in the wet, cold dirt. Her shoulders tensed, her jaw rigid, fighting back the tears. She couldn't show weakness. Not here. Not now. Grief welled up like a torrent of razor blades and sliced her to ribbons inside. She'd failed Baby Blue just like she'd failed the other victims. Not coming to the rescue. Not saving the day. Not saving anyone at all.

"*I'm so sorry,*" she whispered. She searched for absolution in those glassy, blood-flecked eyes. There was none to be found.

Tony's hand touched her shoulder, feather-light, like he was handling nitroglycerin.

"C'mon," he said softly. "Marie, c'mon, they have to finish taking the pictures. Move back a little, okay?"

She rose, turned, and walked away.

As she walked, the agony in her heart simmered into a gathering rage. A storm cloud of fury rumbled on the horizon of her mind, black weather and lightning coming in fast. The law was her liege. That's what she always said. But she couldn't make herself believe it anymore.

She thought about Nessa. How she felt safe in the woman's arms, the rules Nessa set for her, Nessa's promise of keeping her. Nessa felt more real than her oaths and her badge ever had.

The law said "fair trials for all." The law said "bring the suspect in alive." That wasn't the liege she needed right now. She'd been on a quest: find Baby Blue and bring her home, safe and sound. She had failed. Now Marie had a new quest.

She was going to find the monster who did this. And she was going to kill him.

*   *   *

Nessa had spent the morning cleaning up all evidence of last night's indiscretions. Washing dishes, clearing away leftovers, changing the sheets. The bedroom smelled like torrid sex and while she could have happily basked in the scent, she flung open the windows and aired out the room. In her workroom, she'd swept up the broken ceramic bowl and mopped the floorboards, the wood stained in spots with faint swirls of deep blue ink.

She heard the front door rattle, her husband's heavy footsteps on the stairs.

Richard was all smiles as he lugged his rolling suitcase upstairs, meeting her on the landing. He leaned in for a kiss. "There's my girl. Did you miss me?"

The party had left him a tense, miserable grouch. One night away from home, though, and he was a transformed man, lighting up the house with his good mood. *Your lover must be good in bed*, Nessa thought, taking a little pleasure in her own cattiness. *Bet she's not as good as mine, though.*

She paused, gesturing at his collar. And the tiny scarlet smear she'd spotted there. "Is that blood?"

Richard blinked. He turned, catching his reflection in the hallway mirror.

"Oh, looks like it. Must have cut myself shaving. I have to run my dry cleaning over anyway. They'll get the stain out."

She scrutinized his face. "Where? I don't see a cut."

His smile wavered and he turned one cheek away from her. "I don't know, I mean, it was yesterday. Don't worry about it. Did you take your meds this morning?"

"Yes," she lied.

He rolled his suitcase into the bedroom, unpacking, laying out his travel kit on the bed Nessa and Marie had wrecked a few hours before. Fresh clean sheets and the morning spring breeze from the open windows had erased all traces of her treason. Nessa's gaze drifted to her vanity. To the plastic prescription bottle, and the drugs

Dr. Neidermyer so happily, so discreetly procured for her every month at her husband's direction.

She'd been off them for two days now and felt better than she had in years. Sharper. Clearer. And while she wanted to chalk that up to her delightful evening and the rush of new love, dark suspicions were brewing.

Now she was going to do something about it.

ACT II

TIME AFTER TIME

Interlude

Carolyn Saunders sat placidly at the interview table, the stark light of the interrogation room casting long shadows across her weathered face. She folded her cuffed hands on the table.

"I hope you're starting to understand how everything that happened was basically your fault," she said. "'You' in the general, collective sense of the word."

Her interrogator, sitting across from her, wrinkled his hooked nose like he smelled something rotten. "Explain."

"Let's see. For starters, you people created an occult drug, this 'ink' garbage, and flooded the nation with it before you really had any idea what it *did*. You still don't know."

"We know more than you think."

"If that was true," Carolyn said, "Dr. Cross and her team would have known what they were walking into. Instead, you had one Network cell acting as a distribution hub, another serving as a middleman between the hub and the street dealers—oh, and *that* cell was into kidnapping and ritual sacrifice on the side, not the most low profile of hobbies—and getting ready to murder their way into a better job."

Her interrogator cracked a rare smile. "Scottie Pierce's assumptions were quite correct. We *say* it's forbidden, but we do rather like it when our outer-circle teams test each other's strength.

The fastest way to rise in the ranks of the Network is over the broken bodies of your former superiors. It shows initiative."

"And with all that trouble brewing, the logical, brilliant, certainly not-at-all-a-raving-lunatic Savannah Cross was coming to town and armed for bear hunting. Well, coming to Jersey City, but we both know how that ended up. Badly."

"I wouldn't say that."

Carolyn rapped her knuckles on the stainless-steel table. "Ah, but you don't know all the nasty little details. If you did, I wouldn't be here."

"We're more interested in what happened after," the interrogator told her. "You're the one who insists on telling the whole story from the very beginning."

"Because you have to understand. You have to know who Marie and Nessa were, before you can understand what they *became*. Why they did the...things they did. This is the story of their initiation." Carolyn's cuffs rattled as she raised her hands, holding up three fingers. "A quote, from a piece I'm fond of: 'Spiritual initiations vary from culture to culture, but throughout the ages they have always been marked by three essential elements. Beyond ritual, beyond liturgy, a true initiation always involves pain, fear, and blood.'"

The interrogator mulled that over and gave her an easy nod.

"True enough, I suppose. One of your books?"

"No. 'Reflections on Global Initiatory Practices,' by Professor Vanessa Roth. It was the last paper she ever published. And it was true for both of them, each facing their own crucible. A fallen would-be knight, mired in misery and grief after her failure to save Baby Blue...oh, Marie Reinhart knew all about pain. She'd known about pain her entire life, since the night her parents were taken from her. And now she was learning how to turn it into a weapon."

The interrogator tilted his head. "And the Roth woman?"

Carolyn chuckled, but there wasn't a trace of humor on her face.

"That leaves us with fear and blood. And as she would soon prove, if there was anyone in this *universe* who knew all about fear and blood...it was Nessa Roth."

Thirty-Two

Nessa climbed from the back seat of a taxi at the edge of Inwood Hill Park, a canvas tote bag slung over her shoulder. Today was the day. She knew it.

Excitement put a bounce in her footsteps as she crossed the walking trails, leaving the well-traveled paths for the ragged, primeval wood on the northern tip of the park. It rested on the farthest edge of Manhattan's peninsula, barely touched by human hands or eyes, a spot of rare solitude in a city of eight million.

She stopped here and there along the way, pausing by clumps of wildflowers. Her ritual knife, a small and slightly curved blade with a wooden handle painted white, sliced at the roots of the choicest, most colorful plants. She gathered them in her hand like a bouquet for a date.

And that made her think of Marie.

Thinking of Marie made her think of Marie's desperate kisses, the way her body had writhed under Nessa's. She bathed in the memory of how Marie's wrists had twisted, helpless, trapped in Nessa's grip. The way they'd held each other close after, until Marie sank into a peaceful slumber. Warmth simmered in the pit of Nessa's stomach and spread out through her body like tingling lines of fire.

Getting that Internal Affairs detective off Marie's back had been a pleasure, not to mention a mark in the win column when it came to Nessa's growing prowess as a witch. But that was nothing compared to the scrying experiment. Both of them, side by side, witnessing the same vision in the inky water? It was such a triumph she could almost overlook the content of the message.

Almost.

She'd heard it clear as a bell, though: her own voice, telling her that she was in danger, just before the spell overwhelmed the vessel and the magic shattered along with the porcelain bowl. There was only one remedy for this.

She needed more. More magic. More power.

Nessa found her spot of perfect solitude on the edge of the shaggy line of trees, set down her tote, and laid out the tools of her trade: the smooth, round stone carved with a pentacle, a scattering of fresh beechnuts and pecans, the wildflowers sprinkled around her. Their vivid color was a lure. Her book, *Games for the Cunning*, lay open across her lap as she sat on the grass with legs folded. "The Game of Finding a Guide" was the final spell in the book, the halfway point before the strange tome became nothing but page after page of tangled, incomprehensible ciphers.

For furtherance of skill, the anonymous author wrote, *it is essential that the cunning Student of the Art seek a guide, who will teach the virtues of Power and Freedom. This guide may take on the form of a beast of the wild and must be greeted with respect and a proper sacrifice.*

Nessa read the chant, a hymn in a dead language that became a whispered song. The chant twisted in the air as the words left her lips. They seemed to take on form, shimmering like runes of gold in the crisp late-morning air and fading, echoing into the wood. She felt her power rising, spurred by her memories of Marie's eyes, her voice, her kisses, one desire feeding another until the heat in her stomach was a raging inferno that burned along her spine and ignited sparks behind her eyes.

The doe had returned. The timid creature stepped cautiously from the wood. She watched Nessa with deep caramel eyes.

Yes, Nessa thought. She held out her open hands. "That's it. You're my guide. You're here to teach me. Come closer."

The doe stood her ground, halfway between the safety of the trees and her offering. She turned her head toward the mound of beechnuts and sniffed the air.

"I'm ready," Nessa whispered, trying not to scare the doe away a second time. "I'm ready for the real magic, the real power. Give it to me. Please."

The doe extended one uncertain hoof, then pulled it back.

The more Nessa watched the doe, her head clearer than it had been since...well, since she could remember, the more wrong this seemed. This wasn't some harbinger of mystical enlightenment, some occult teacher and taskmistress. The doe was timid. Afraid. Inches away from what she wanted, and refusing to reach for it.

She looked into the doe's eyes and saw everything she hated about herself.

As if sensing her thoughts, the doe's head jerked up. She turned and bolted, diving into the trees, bushes shivering in her wake.

Nessa sat in deflated silence. The fire in her veins sputtered and died, going cold.

She gathered her things, bundled them into her tote, and emerged from the woods alone. Her phone chimed, reminding her it was time for her appointment with Dr. Neidermyer.

*　*　*

"And you've been taking your medication?" Dr. Neidermyer asked.

Nessa lay back on his leather couch, staring at the ceiling. Distressed over her failure, distressed over being stuck in this room with this over-degreed idiot, waiting for the clock to wind down. She thought about Marie. Despite it all, Nessa found a smile.

"Always," she lied.

"Your husband was concerned. He thought you might have missed a dose, before a party, I believe?"

"If my husband is so concerned, Dr. Neidermyer, maybe he should try being home once in a while."

"He has a very demanding career. You know he cares about you."

"I'm so glad," Nessa said, "that my appointments with my doctor allow me to have such reassuring conversations with Richard. It's almost like he's in the room. Does he pay you extra for this?"

Neidermyer pulled a tissue from the box on his desk. He blew his nose and tossed the rumpled tissue into a wire basket at his feet.

"Sorry," he said, "allergies. I only ask because you seem...different today."

"Isn't that the idea? That the treatment is supposed to make me different? Better?" She twirled one finger around her ear. "Less cuckoo for Cocoa Puffs. Less mad than your average hatter—"

"Vanessa, please."

She reached up and tugged an imaginary train whistle. "Less of a conductor on the crazy train, final stop: Batshit City. *Choo choo.*"

Neidermyer rested his forehead against his fingertips. "*Please.* You know we don't use words like that here."

She couldn't tell him what she really wanted to say: that since going off her meds, she'd felt sharper and more awake than she had in ages.

"I'm only bringing this up," Neidermyer said, "because at a certain stage of treatment—when the medication is doing its job and normalizing your neurochemistry—many patients are tempted to stop taking it. It's a common cycle: the treatment works, they feel better so they go off of it, and the original symptoms return in force. I don't want to see you fall prey to that."

"I'm fairly certain I know how I feel, Doctor."

He shook his head, folding his hands on the desk.

"But you don't. Vanessa, you are severely manic-depressive. An insidious element of some mental illnesses, including yours, is a common inability to gauge how you actually appear to the rest of the world. Aren't there times when you *believe* you're presenting as perfectly calm, and others find your affect...off-putting?"

Her thoughts had been jogging along, free and clear—and now she stumbled over a brick in her path. Flailing, her arms mentally windmilling, trying not to fall. Sure, she could think of times like that. A few hundred of them. Mostly involving Richard.

Tonight is really, really important for Dad, she remembered him telling her before the party. *So just...don't be weird.*

Don't be weird, Vanessa. I can't handle you when you're like this, Vanessa. An endless refrain, reminding her of how many times she'd embarrassed him with some awkward comment or by wearing the wrong outfit for the wrong party. Then there was the form rejection from the *Quarterly Journal of Anthropological Review*, her failure to earn tenure, everyone acting like her academic career had gone down in flames when she was sure she was at the top of her game.

Maybe Neidermyer was right.

He reached into his desk drawer, pulling out an unlabeled prescription bottle. It rattled in his puffy hand.

"I think we should raise your daily dosage by five milligrams," he said. "Just for a while, then we can evaluate your progress."

Nessa found herself out on the streets of Manhattan, alone in a crowd. Across the street, a homeless man in an olive army jacket and wool cap was stumbling, raving, his whiskered face flecked with spittle as he shouted at passers-by about the ants in his brain.

Could that be me, she wondered, *right now? He doesn't know what reality is. So how can I be so sure that I know? Maybe I'm screaming at the top of my lungs and I'm the only person who can't hear it. Maybe everyone just takes one look at me and thinks, "Stay clear, she's got crazy eyes."*

She thought about her night with Marie, and for the first time, wondered if any of it happened the way she remembered it.

She had to know. She called her. The phone rang seven times, then went to voicemail. She called again. Voicemail again.

A sudden fear gripped her by the throat. Was Marie ducking her? Trying to make a silent exit?

She had to know. Nessa stepped out at the curb, holding one hand high to flag down a taxi.

Thirty-Three

Marie wasn't taking anyone's calls.

It was two in the afternoon and she was still in bed, hair a tangled rat's nest, buried under the covers in her flannel pajamas. She'd taken a sick day.

Janine knocked on her door now and then, talking to her through the thin wood. Marie responded in terse monosyllables. One thing you didn't do as a cop, Marie had learned, was bring your work home with you. Sure, every once in a while she'd regale her roommate with anecdotes from the lighter, funnier side of the job. She'd share stories like the burglar who'd invited her and Tony to search his car, insisting he had nothing to hide, because he'd forgotten that he left a stolen necklace in the glove compartment. Or there was the time a purse snatcher had thrown everything he could grab at them, trying to slow them down during a foot chase—including his wallet, with his driver's license inside. Those were the things you could tell a civilian about.

You didn't tell them about the murdered and brutalized woman dumped like garbage in a construction site in Bushwick. Her body lay broken in Marie's memory, her eyes wide open and staring up with a silent question: *You promised you'd save me. Why didn't you save me?*

Marie pulled the covers over her head and curled into a fetal ball.

Out in the living room, she heard a knock at the door and a

muffled exchange of voices. Then Janine's response. "Hey, Tony. No, I...I don't think it's a good time."

More murmurs.

"Yeah, I'll tell her you stopped by. I think she just...well, you know. Sometimes she just has to sort things out."

The door closed. Footsteps shuffled across the living room.

"Hey, Marie?" Janine called through the bedroom door.

"Yeah," Marie said. Her voice sounded strange. Dry, cracked. Her head hurt, probably dehydrated. She knew she should get up, go to the kitchen nook, get a glass of water. She couldn't make her arms pull the covers back.

"Tony came by. He's wondering if—" She paused. There was another knock at the front door. "Huh, hold on."

Marie drifted in the dark, her head throbbing.

"Oh, hi. I'm Janine, her roommate. I'm sorry, Marie is...she's sick."

Now two pairs of feet were striding across the living room.

"*Sick?*" Nessa said. "Where is she? I need to check on her."

"You can't—you can't just come in here," Janine said, flustered. "She doesn't want to see anyone—"

The bedroom door flung open. Nessa was at Marie's bedside in a heartbeat, her voice laced with worry.

"Marie? What's wrong? Did you come down with something? What do you need? How can I help?"

Marie poked her head up from under the covers, looking past Nessa. Janine stood on the threshold, wringing her hands.

"It's fine, Janine. Thank you."

"Yes," Nessa said, an edge of annoyance in her voice, "*thank* you."

Janine looked dubious, but she shut the door. Nessa sat on the edge of the bed. Her hand curled over Marie's shoulder through the sheets, giving a protective squeeze.

"My room is a mess," Marie croaked. "I'm a mess. Didn't want you to see any of this."

"Stop listing things I don't care about." She pressed the back of her hand to Marie's forehead. "You're not running a fever."

"Not that kind of sick."

Marie sighed, shaking her head. It was going to come out, one way or another. Might as well rip the bandage off.

"That girl I was trying to save," Marie told her.

She didn't need to say anything else. The rest was in her silence. In the half-lit gloom, Nessa leaned in and held her close.

She gently kissed Marie's forehead. Her fingertip brushed Marie's mouth.

"Your lips are cracked," Nessa murmured. "You need something to drink. I'll be right back."

"You don't have to—"

Nessa's finger pressed harder against Marie's lips, silencing her.

"Let me take care of you," she said.

She came back a minute later with a tall glass of water. Marie wriggled her shoulders to prop herself higher on the pillows, sitting up in bed, and drank as Nessa watched her like a nurse. The cold water went down fast. She hadn't realized how thirsty she was.

"You weren't answering your phone," Nessa said. She took the empty glass from Marie's hand and set it on the nightstand, then sat back down beside her.

"I couldn't." Marie glanced down, wearing her shame on her face. "I didn't want you to see me like this. Nessa, last night was...I don't know *what* last night was, but it was...magic. And then this happened and I fell apart and I didn't want you to see me in pieces. I was afraid you might change your mind. About us."

"Never," Nessa whispered.

Marie tilted her head. Squinting a little, reading something in her lover's eyes.

"What is it?"

Nessa flashed her lopsided smile. "Nothing. I had a question. But you just answered it."

She looked around the room. To the cheap replica sword on the wall, the bookshelf stuffed with paperbacks. Her eyes fell on the framed print opposite the bed. She took it in, eyeing the knight in her green-steel armor and lance, facing a looming shadow on the horizon.

"I like your picture," Nessa said.

"It's the cover of one of my favorite books. *Swords Against Madness*, by Carolyn Saunders."

"One of those fantasy novels you grew up with? From that box in the basement?"

Marie nodded, her gaze distant.

"What's it about?" Nessa asked.

"A paladin—a knight of a holy order—is trying to save her city from a coming darkness. But her superiors don't believe her. They punish her for speaking the truth. Cast her out, strip her of her vestments, and even her god stops answering her prayers. But she's determined to keep fighting, even if it costs her life."

"Sounds like a fine role model for a starry-eyed girl."

Marie let out a tiny chuckle. "Maybe not. In desperate need of aid, the fallen knight goes to the Queen of the Witches. She kneels before her and pledges her service, becoming her coven's knight, in exchange for the aid she needs to save her people. Fighting evil with evil."

"Still, she fights. Does it have a happy ending?"

Marie thought about it.

"Bittersweet," she said.

Nessa shifted on the mattress. Her hand rested on Marie's hip.

"You're mourning today," she said, "and no one in the world could blame you. What happened...it hurts. Let it hurt. Don't deny it or shove your feelings in a box. *Hurt*, Marie. It's all right. But you have a decision to make. You're mourning today. What will you do tomorrow?"

Marie met her steady gaze. "I go back to work?"

"Are you asking me, or telling me?"

"I go back to work," Marie said.

Nessa patted Marie's hip and rose from the bed.

"You go back to work," Nessa said, "and then you text me immediately afterward and tell me how it went. Yes?"

"Yes," Marie said.

Nessa had her hand on the door when Marie spoke up again.

"When will I see you?"

Nessa looked back over her shoulder, sly. "Do you have plans for Friday night?"

"No."

"Yes, you do. You'll be with me."

She closed the door behind her. Marie lay in the shadows, staring at the artwork. At the armored woman she'd idolized as a girl, pretended to be on the playground, charging imaginary foes with a backpack for a shield and a fallen-branch lance.

She had a real shield now, issued by the City of New York. There was a real monster to hunt.

Marie was pushing back the covers, resolved to clean herself up and salvage what remained of the day, when an aroma drifted under the bedroom door, sweet, familiar, and warm. It could only mean one thing.

She poked her head out. "You made cinnamon rolls."

Over in the kitchen nook, Janine held up her oven-mitt-clad hand.

"I *know* you, Marie Reinhart. And when it comes to getting my roomie out of the dumps, I fight dirty."

Marie stumbled over, led by her nose and her rumbling stomach. "You do. Not fair. Not remotely fair."

A fat eight-pack of cinnamon rolls, glazed in gooey white frosting, cooled on a baking sheet. Janine brought down a couple of mismatched plates from the cabinet.

"What can I say? I'm a heinous bitch. These should be just about cool enough to eat by the time you get out of the shower."

"Is this your way of forcing me to take care of myself, or do I just smell that ripe?"

"Both." Janine waved her hand over the tray, wafting wisps of curling steam toward her. "Mm, it's Marie's favorite food, just *waiting* for her. *Mmm.*"

Marie threw up her hands in surrender and trudged to the bathroom.

*   *   *

Marie and Janine sat on the futon, plates and paper towels in their laps, fingers and lips sticky as they each dug into their second cinnamon roll. Marie was in the lead by half a bun.

"I am going to feel so bad after this," she mumbled as she chewed.

"But you feel so good right now," Janine shot back.

Marie closed her eyes and shivered. "I *do*. You're my best friend, you know that?"

"Duh."

"The calories, though."

Janine snorted at her. "Make up for it with exercise. I've seen cops on TV. Your entire day is, like, foot chases and parkour and jumping across rooftops."

"I have *never* jumped across a rooftop."

"Speaking of friends, that Professor Roth is kind of intense, huh?"

Marie smiled at her cinnamon roll. "Nessa is...unique."

"Nessa." Janine nodded to herself. "See, that's more fitting. I was saying to myself, funny, she doesn't *look* like a George."

Marie froze in mid-bite.

"George?" Janine said. "You remember, your research buddy? C'mon, Marie. I'm not stupid."

"How did you..." she asked, uncertain.

"For one thing, *not* that I was eavesdropping, the walls in here are made of tissue paper. But I didn't need to overhear anything. When she came out of your room to get you a glass of water? And when she left? The look on her face said it all. Why didn't you just tell me what was going on? I mean, you know I'm not homophobic, right? I'd hope you'd know that by now."

"No, of course not, I didn't think..." Marie shook her head. "It's just been a very, very complicated week. And weird. And every time

I think it's done being weird, it just gets *weirder*. And it's like, I'm not normally...I've never been, you know, with a woman. I've never leaned that way. I don't *think* I have."

"So you're not gay in general, you're just gay for her." Janine shrugged. "There's also this concept you may not have heard of. It's called 'bisexual.' It's a real thing. You can look it up."

"You don't say."

"Sex is weird, Marie. Relationships are weird. People don't fit into neat little categories, even if we want them to. Can I ask you one question?"

"Shoot."

"Are you in love with her?"

Marie set down the remnant of her cinnamon roll and wiped her sticky fingers on the paper towel. She leaned back on the futon, contemplating, staring out the window at the cherry-red fire escape. She looked back to Janine.

"Yeah." Marie nodded. "Yeah. I think I'm in love with her."

Janine leaned across the futon and punched her shoulder.

"There you go, then. That's all that matters. You've just gotta go for it. Trust your gut and take a chance."

Marie's popped the last bite into her mouth and chewed thoughtfully.

"Yeah. Still," Marie muttered, "weird."

"That's the thing about life," Janine said. "Just when you think you've got it all figured out, you find out that it can *always* get weirder."

Thirty-Four

Across the Hudson River, Jake Moretti finished a twelve-hour shift. The sky was full dark when he returned to his condo in Jersey City, the stars blotted out by the city's electric noise. His key rattled in the lock, and the sturdy old door groaned on its hinges as he let himself in. He reached for the light switch.

A hand clamped on his wrist and hauled him into the shadows. He stumbled, off balance, and a rock-hard fist plowed into his gut. The air gusted from his ruddy lips as he buckled to his knees. Hands grabbed on to his jacket sleeve, twisting his other arm back, plucking his service revolver from his shoulder holster. The sole of a boot slammed into the small of his back and shoved him flat on his belly on the cold linoleum floor.

The lights clicked on.

Pale hands held his wrists, forcing him onto his back. Others snatched at his ankles, yanking hard and held him spread-eagled. The narrow kitchen was filled with faces. Moretti had been expecting street-hardened eyes and gang colors, some crew he'd rumbled coming after him for payback. These were normal people. A teenager in a video game T-shirt. A construction worker, still wearing his orange safety vest and tool belt. Just a scattering of people you might see on any Jersey street, any time of day. An elderly woman in bifocals held his wrist in a grip as strong as the rest, too strong for her frail frame.

The crowd of intruders had two things in common. One, their skin was fish-belly white.

Two, they didn't blink. At all. And whatever their glassy eyes were staring at, it was a million miles away.

"Don't know what you people think you're doing, but you're makin' a big mistake." Moretti nodded his chin at his belt. "You see that? See that badge? I'm a *cop*."

No reply. They just stared.

"You hear me?" he demanded. "What do you want?"

"My qliphoth can hear you," said the woman rounding the corner, the hem of a pristine white lab coat swaying around her legs, "they just can't *speak*. Forced exposure to corrupted cosmic data has reduced their gray matter down to little clumps roughly the size of walnuts."

Savannah Cross tapped a button on one side of her goggles. Side-mounted beams, like laser pointers the color of shimmering sapphires, strobed over Jake's face. A projection inside the goggles spat scrolling data across the lenses.

"Really. Brains the size of walnuts." She shrugged. "I mean, what would they possibly have to *talk* about? I snip their vocal cords as a matter of expediency. Saves you from having to listen to all that pointless screaming. Not to mention, otherwise every now and then one of them starts speaking in four voices at once. The next thing you know half the lab is infected with extra-dimensional parasites and you've got to purge all of your interns. But I'm getting off track. Detective Moretti, my name is Dr. Cross. We need to have a word about what happened the other day."

His mouth hung open. He didn't understand a word she was saying. That wasn't strictly true. He knew the words, but the order she spoke them in left something to be desired in the clarity department. He only understood that he was in serious trouble—the kind of trouble the academy hadn't trained him for.

"What...what other day? What are you talking about?"

"Well, that's the problem. I'm not entirely sure. But *something* fascinating happened, and I've tracked it to your precinct. Can you think of anything unusual that took place, specifically, at 2:48 p.m.?"

Jake furrowed his brow. "Yeah. Yeah, the...the perp. We had this guy, serial-murder suspect, and we caught him dumping a body. A disturbance pulled us out of the interview room. When we got back, this defense lawyer was in there with him. Except nobody saw the guy come in. Nobody. He was just *there*."

Savannah frowned. She tapped her goggles again. The beams turned a sickly amber and a fresh flood of data spilled across the inner glass.

"Don't tell me," she said. "Mr. Smith, Esquire, from Weishaupt and Associates."

"Yeah." He blinked at her. "How'd you know?"

The silent, pale figures held him to the floor. She turned and started rummaging through his refrigerator, violently jostling bottles and cans around.

"I didn't, but I should have. This is what happens when the left hand doesn't communicate with the right. Could have cleared it up with one phone call, but no, I had to leave my laboratory and go to *New Jersey*." She poked her head over the refrigerator door. "Do you not have any pomegranate juice?"

"Pome...what? No. Why?"

She slammed the door shut, eyes wide and furious behind her goggles. She took a deep breath and counted softly to five as she let it out.

"Because daily intake of pomegranate lowers a hormone called cortisol. Very good for managing stress. Well, this...this is embarrassing. I'm very sorry, Detective Moretti. I appear to have wasted your time. If it's any consolation, your organs will be used to further the cause of science. You'll continue to benefit the community long after your death. I mean, not *this* community, but a community. Somewhere."

She reached into her lab-coat pocket and took out a scalpel. She tugged a plastic cap to expose the blade. Its edge, honed to a razor sheen, gleamed under the kitchen lights.

"Wait a second!" Jake shouted. He thrashed against the hands holding him fast. "Wait, that wasn't—there was something else!"

She paused. "Oh?"

"That disturbance, the one that pulled us out of the interview room? See, I wasn't alone. I had this detective with me, from New York. She was investigating a serial case on her side of the river, and I thought our vics might be connected. Some uniforms were bringing a vagrant shoplifter in for processing. A hardcore ink junkie. You know what that is?"

"Ink?" Savannah smiled primly. "I'm intimately familiar with it. And?"

"And, well, this guy spotted her through the one-way window, broke free, and rammed himself against the glass until it fractured. Took five guys to bring him down, and he was still trying to get at her."

Savannah tapped her goggles. The beams shifted to scarlet.

"Tell me *everything*."

"Not much more to tell. We ran out to see what was up, he locked eyes with her and started screaming. He shouted that he'd *read* her."

She tilted her head. "Like a book?"

"Yeah. Like a book. He said he knew she was going to die because he read the ending."

She put the cap back on the scalpel blade.

"Now that," Savannah said, "is interesting."

She clicked her tongue twice at one of the pale and unblinking figures. He shambled off, then returned with a teak box in his outstretched hands, just big enough to hold a Christmas ornament.

"I need to see what you saw," Savannah said as she took the box and crouched down beside Jake's head. "Your exact memories. It's important for my research. That woman, you see, she caused a, well, a minor earthquake in the fabric of reality. Which is wonderful. Unless she destroys the planet. Which...oh, who am I kidding?

That'd be wonderful too. Do you know how much we stand to learn from this? No. Of course you don't."

Jake shook his head, bewildered. Savannah reached into her coat pocket, trading the scalpel for a pair of sturdy blue latex gloves.

"I don't know what you're talking about," he said.

She pulled the gloves on, snapping the tight latex against her wrists.

"Yes. I'm aware of that. Which is why I need to take your memories directly."

She tugged open the lid of the teak box and dipped her fingers inside. Jake saw what was in her hand, held carefully between her thumb and forefinger, and he shook in her assistants' grip like a chew toy in a dog's mouth. They held him fast, pinning his wrists and ankles to the linoleum floor.

"What the *fuck?*" Jake shouted, craning his neck to pull his face as far away as he could. "What *is* that?"

Savannah gazed upon her prize with quiet admiration. It was a chunk of ash-gray rock, pitted and gnarled, like a miniature asteroid. Worms, fat and luminous and tinted vomit-yellow, poked their heads from its surface and squirmed over her gloved fingertips as they crawled in and out of the stone.

"Highly advanced technology, Detective Moretti. Not *human* technology, but what can I tell you? We're trying to catch up. These surprisingly precise instruments will harvest the tissue I require for my research." She paused. "I should say that the aforementioned tissue has to come from your medial temporal lobe, your hippocampus, and your ocular nerves. The important thing is, which I hope you'll bear in mind, that you're making an invaluable contribution to science."

He thrashed wildly on the floor, jerking his head back as far as he could, teeth gritted and forehead dripping with sweat as she loomed over him. The rock inched closer to his face. The glistening worms turned their blind heads toward him, rippling eagerly.

"You can trust me," Savannah told him. "I'm a doctor."

* * *

"I don't answer to you," Mr. Smith told her.

Mr. Smith, Esquire, she reminded herself as she breathed in the stink of diesel exhaust. It was five in the morning, a rest stop off the New Jersey turnpike. Early-morning traffic rumbled by, cutting through a wet bank of fog. The air had a cold and greasy feel to it.

"The ink initiative is my project," Savannah said. "Period. I should have been notified."

The bland-faced lawyer, in his gray suit and gray shirt and gray pocket square, nodded genially.

"I agree. You should have. By the Vandemere Lodge. They called me instead. You should cut them loose, Dr. Cross. They're sloppy. Reckless. Nothing but puffed-up serial killers with trust funds and investment portfolios."

Savannah shrugged. "Cultists of the King of Wolves are not known for their flawless judgment. Still, they're loyal and eager to serve."

"Eager to serve themselves. Fairly certain they're getting ready to make a play for New York's ink production facility. Inter-cell rivalry is always amusing to watch, but it makes for a lot of cleanup work. This cop, Marie Reinhart, she's edging too close to the truth and she's not going to stop. We should eliminate her before she can cause any more trouble."

"Is that your response to every fascinating anomaly? Kill it?"

"It's my job," Mr. Smith replied. "The Network won't tolerate exposure. We have endured for centuries by adhering to simple, basic rules. When the rules are broken—"

Savannah curled her lips into a sneer. "Provincial and petty-minded. That woman *caused* something. Simple proximity exposure to a late-stage ink addict induced a ripple in the fabric of reality. And you'd kill her without learning why?"

"It's my job."

"Hands off," she told him. "I'm going to New York today. Marie Reinhart is *mine*."

Mr. Smith folded his arms. Studying her, taciturn, as a line of semi trucks trundled through the fog.

"And you'll be doing what, exactly?"

"Science." Savannah leaned in and slapped the back of her hand against the lawyer's chest. "I'll be doing science. Stand back and watch me work."

Thirty-Five

Marie paced her sliver of open bedroom floor and got dressed while she talked. Her phone lay on the rumpled bedspread.

"Thank you for taking my call, Dr. Cassidy."

"Of course." April's faint Irish brogue drifted over the phone's speaker. "Have there been any new developments in your case?"

Buttoning her blouse, Marie grimaced. A flavor in her mouth more bitter than the aftertaste of her morning coffee.

"The woman I was trying to rescue…I was too late. But we have a lead. Last time we talked, you said something—that the one and only time you'd seen serial killers teaming up together was a cult situation. Can you tell me about that?"

April spoke slowly, carefully, like a poker player holding her cards close to her chest.

"It was a murder-for-hire arrangement," she said, "with the participants bound by shared religious beliefs. They consecrated their kills as sacramental offerings."

"Doctor, I don't think we're looking for *one* killer anymore."

"Then my earlier profile may be entirely incorrect," April said. "What changed your mind?"

"Are you familiar with this new designer drug, 'ink'?"

"Very. As it happens, I'm currently consulting with a Bureau investigation into the source of the malady. We're on our way to New York as I speak."

"Can we meet?"

"If time permits. Tell me about your lead."

"Nobody believed me when I tied Baby Blue to that stash house in Monticello," Marie said, sitting on the edge of the bed and slipping into her slacks. "But her driver confirmed she was there. Beau Kates, her pimp, was bribed to hand her over. They didn't pay cash; they paid him with ink. That's two points of connection to the ink cartel. The stash house was a Roth Estate Holdings property. We've also got two dead bodies with the same tattoo and ties to the Five Families, and the second corpse was found down the block from another one of Richard Roth's buildings. You know what that says to me? Turf war."

"You believe these murders are drug-related?"

Marie clipped her shield onto her belt.

"Street gangs use criminal acts as initiations. You know the routine. Recruits are told to pick out a stranger and commit an assault or a murder while the higher-ups watch. Proves the new blood is loyal and willing to get their hands dirty, and just as importantly, it proves they're not an undercover cop. What's throwing me is the pattern. The victimology, the holding period, and every murdered woman dies the same way. I mean, different weapons, but the overkill is the same. This doesn't read like an initiation. It's the same person—people—doing the deed every time. It feels...ritualized. Religious."

"Pack bonding," April replied.

"Like wolves."

April fell silent.

"Doctor?" Marie asked. "Are you still on the line?"

"Humans," April said, "are incalculably crueler than actual wolves, metaphors aside. But yes, bonding over shared criminal acts has been known to happen. Also, there are often commonalities between religious cults and tight-knit criminal organizations. Are you familiar with Santa Muerte?"

Marie scooped her wallet and keys off the dresser.

"She's like a...goddess of death or something, right? Down in Mexico?"

"A folk saint," April said. "Venerated by the poor and disenfranchised. It's a generally benign following—if heretical, according to the Catholic Church—but an increasing number of narcotics traffickers make offerings to her as well. There have been cases of Sinaloa Cartel associates performing human sacrifices to win the saint's favor, hoping for protection from the authorities."

"You think that's what we're looking at here?"

"Not that particular saint," April said, "but it could be a related phenomenon. And you need to be very, very careful, Detective."

"You got quiet when I mentioned wolves."

"So I did."

Marie frowned. "Dr. Cassidy, if you know something—"

"Out of curiosity," April said, "were any of the victims...cannibalized?"

Marie stopped in mid-pace.

"Why do you ask?"

"As I said, curiosity."

Marie narrowed her eyes. "Strangely random thing to be curious about, Dr. Cassidy. Which tells me it isn't a random question at all."

"It's premature to offer my assessment."

"Well," Marie said, "they weren't, that I'm aware of, but the bodies were all in pretty bad shape."

"It might be worth looking into. I'll call you when I'm on the ground in New York, Detective. Our investigations may be running on parallel tracks."

April ended the call. Marie dialed the medical examiner's office.

"Yeah," she said, "it's Reinhart. You still have my vic on the slab?"

"Which one? The human jigsaw puzzle or the one who had her face painted with her own blood? You're racking up mutilated bodies all over town. I'm getting carpal tunnel from writing all the reports."

"You want to compare your paperwork with mine? Trust me, mine is worse. Anyway, I'm calling about Baby Blue. Have you done the autopsy yet?"

"No, but I'd hope the cause of death was self-explanatory."

"Do something for me," Marie said. "Look for bite marks."

"Bite marks. You do realize that just notating the lacerations is going to take me all afternoon, right? There's barely a square inch on her that isn't cut or contused. On top of all that damage, a bite mark would be a needle in a haystack."

"Would you rather I put in a request to have the previous victims exhumed, and make you reexamine *all* of them?"

The medical examiner sighed. "You know you're a pain in the ass, Reinhart?"

"Yep. What would you do without me?"

She eyed herself in the mirror, ran a half-hearted hand through her bangs—her hair already a rumpled mess before she'd taken one step out into the springtime wind—and pulled a blazer over her shoulder holster. Out in the living room, Janine was finishing off the dregs of a pot of coffee. She looked Marie's way and whistled.

"Damn, look who's all bright-eyed and bushy-tailed. My cinnamon rolls are magic."

"They are," Marie said. "Don't wait up. I've got a lead to chase."

"Gonna go slay a dragon?"

Marie paused at the door. She looked back, flashing hard, determined eyes and the slightest trace of a smile.

"That's my job," she said.

* * *

A C-130 Hercules carved a path through the stormy sky. The cargo plane was bulbous and fast, a whale with shark's teeth. Inside the belly of the beast, a chunk of seating space had been replaced by a command-and-control suite. Banks of screens flashed with map data, triangulations, scrolling reports, and up-to-the-second news feeds.

April ended her call and gazed at the screens as she sat back in her wheelchair. Jessie Temple stepped up behind her. The plane rumbled, bouncing on a gust of turbulence. She put her hand on April's shoulder.

"Cannibalized?" Jessie asked. "That's a pretty big thing to let slip. And considering you're the woman who *never* lets anything slip..."

April pulled on her wheels, turning in place to face her.

"Ritual murders tied to organized crime? We've seen this before. And considering we already believe this new drug is a product of the Network, I think you can follow my reasoning."

"You think she's hunting a wolf cult," Jessie replied.

"As I said, we've seen this before."

Jessie tugged down her dark glasses, studying April over the rims. Her eyes, inhumanly turquoise, glimmered like radioactive gemstones.

"They don't always eat their victims," Jessie said. "My parents didn't."

"But they—and your mother's 'pack'—indulged whenever it was convenient. Devotees of the King of Wolves share certain commonalities. Among them being a compulsion toward group murder—the more brutal, the better—and cannibalism. Detective Reinhart is a civilian, so obviously we can't tell her the truth about what she might be walking into, but hopefully I can give her enough pause that she takes added precautions. She's one bad step away from walking into *our* world, and that would be a tragedy."

"You think she'll back off?"

"I think," April said, "that she's driven, devoted to duty, and displays personality traits I would characterize as obsessive. No, she won't back off. She'll follow this case to the gates of hell and beyond if it means capturing her quarry."

Jessie took a step back. She kept her eyes on the screen, watching neon blips flash across a wire-frame map of the nation as crisis reports filtered in.

"She's a good cop," Jessie said. "Let's get in there and see what the situation on the ground looks like. Maybe we can keep her from finding out just how real those gates are."

*   *   *

Tony and Marie had a new ride, courtesy of the motor pool, an unmarked prowl car with all the bells and whistles. On the outside it was a rust-spotted Ford that looked one good kick away from collapsing into a pile of scrap. Under the hood, it hid a turbo-charged V8 engine. Marie bought the coffee—one cream and no sugar for her, decaf for him. Tony drove.

"How are you holding up?" he asked.

"I just needed a day. Had to do some thinking."

He flicked the turn signal and eased into a clogged intersection.

"Are we good?"

She glanced sidelong at him, sipping from her cardboard cup. "Why wouldn't we be?"

"Because the last time we talked—the last time we *really* talked—was after you beat ten shades of crap out of Baby Blue's pimp. I wasn't all puppies and hugs about it."

"You weren't wrong," Marie said. "And you had my back at Kates's place. You've always had my back."

"No," he said. "I haven't."

They drove in silence, the dashboard squawking now and then with radio call-outs, while Marie waited for him to explain.

"I didn't believe you about the link between Baby Blue and the house in Monticello, about Richard Roth. Every time you pushed us to focus on this case, I pushed back. I didn't listen. Bitch of it is, I couldn't even tell you why." He hesitated, biting one corner of his lip. "That's not true. I thought you were going off the rails a little. Obsessing. You do that sometimes, you know? Like a terrier with a bone. Makes you a good detective, but sometimes I think...I think you're just dealing with a lot of shit. And maybe struggling a little."

"You mean you think I'm fucked in the head," she said, her voice flat.

"No." He shook his head. "I've never thought that. Just that you've got a lot on your shoulders. And I was wrong, anyway. After what happened, looking back, I see it clear as day. You're my partner. I should have listened."

The air between them felt clogged, curdled by Tony's need for forgiveness. Marie shrugged and gave it to him.

"That's because you're always thinking about your wardrobe, you damn peacock. Every time I open my mouth, you're a million miles away, shopping for new clothes."

The tension shattered under her partner's grin. "At least I don't dress in a closet with the lights off. Let me ask you something: the clothes you're wearing right now? Do you really think those colors go together?"

"Oh, I'm sorry." Marie's eyes were wide with mock reproach. "See, while you were attending fashion school, I was at the *police* academy. You know, that place where we go to learn how to solve crimes?"

"Is that where it happens? I knew I was missing something. Fortunately, the bad guys just can't resist confessing when they meet me, 'cause I'm so damn suave."

"You're my secret weapon," Marie said. "I'm like, 'Think you're a tough guy, creep? Prepare to meet my partner. Oh, he's not going to lay a hand on you. He's just gonna date your mom.'"

"They always start crying when I show them the pictures. Then I tell them to call me 'dad.' Breaks 'em every time."

"You know," Marie said, "we've still got this case. It's a homicide now, not a missing-persons, but it's still ours."

Tony drummed his fingers on the steering wheel.

"That we do," he said.

"And now we know Baby Blue and the other victims have a connection to whoever's been spreading this ink crap all over the city."

The sedan coasted to a stop at a red light. Tony looked over, meeting her eye to eye.

"Whatcha thinking, partner?"

"I'm thinking," Marie said, "we hit the pavement hard, kick down some doors, and terrorize street dealers until somebody gives up a name. And if that name is Richard Roth, we take a ride over to the West Village. Sound like fun?"

The light strobed green. Tony looked to the road ahead.

"Sounds like Christmas and my birthday all rolled up in one. Let's go make some trouble."

Thirty-Six

By lunchtime, Marie and Tony had picked up a passenger. The kid in the back seat looked like he'd picked his clothes out of a dumpster and smelled two days ripe. He shifted, wriggling, his eyes as restless as his body.

"I can't be *seen* with you people," he whined for the twentieth time. "You know what happens if people on the block start thinking I'm a snitch?"

The prowl car rolled slow down a side street in Flatbush. Tony shot a look at the rearview mirror.

"What? They won't invite you to go bowling anymore? We nabbed you with twelve grams of ink, plus a set of measuring scales and a box of plastic baggies. You know what that is, kid? That's intent to distribute."

"It'd be real smart for you to cooperate right now," Marie told him.

The kid slunk lower in the back seat. "Told y'all, I don't deal ink. The baggies and scales are for my weed business."

"You're not helping your case here," Marie said. "Are we close?"

The kid peeped over the back seat. "Yeah, yeah. Corner right up there. Shit, he's gonna see me."

Tony pulled over. The unmarked sedan nestled snug against the curb, camouflaged behind a string of empty cars. On the corner ahead, a sallow-eyed young man in a battered jacket too heavy for the spring weather was leaning against the wall of a Caribbean deli.

"That the guy?" Marie asked.

"That's Juicy. Everybody in the neighborhood gets their shit from him. He's the only ink hookup for twelve blocks."

"If you're lying, you're gonna see us again before the sun goes down," Tony warned him.

"I'm not lying! Swear to God, he's my hookup. You're gonna leave my name out of it, right?"

"Never even met you," Marie said. "Congratulations, we're too busy to bust you today. Get out, walk away, and keep walking."

He gave her a hopeful look. "Can I have my shit back?"

She turned in her seat and stared at him.

"Five seconds. Four. Three."

He was out of the car and scrambling down the street before she finished counting.

"What do you think?" Tony said. "Try and sweat him?"

Marie shook her head. "Every time somebody busts an ink dealer, one of three things happens: turns out they're dealing just enough to pay for their own habit and they don't know anything, they're low level and still don't know anything, or they're just high enough on the food chain to be more afraid of their bosses than they are of us."

"And every damn one of 'em gets bailed out, then vanishes." Tony sighed. "You'd think some judge might take that as a hint and start holding them on remand."

"That'd require actual thought. Let's sit on this guy for a while, see if anything interesting shakes out."

It was a smooth operation. A few times an hour, a car would coast up to the corner. Old beaters, family SUVs, the occasional luxury sedan—Juicy had friends all over the city. He'd lean in for ten seconds of brisk conversation and make the money disappear into his coat. Then the car would take the next right, turning the corner and cruising out of sight, while he tapped out a quick text on his phone.

"Figure he's got a partner with the goods squatting on the next block," Tony said. "Juicy never touches the drugs himself so there's nothing illegal on him, just a bankroll. He calls ahead, and the customers slow down just long enough for his buddy to toss the goods through their passenger-side window."

Marie slouched in her seat, studying from a distance. "Probably a kid. These guys like using minors to hold their stash. Slap on the wrist if they get caught."

"Plus," Tony said, "the little shits can run fast."

"There was a convenience store a couple of blocks back, wasn't there?"

"Yeah, why?"

"I need an ATM," Marie said.

She walked him through the plan then she took out a hundred in cash, folding the twenties in a plain white envelope. Then they cruised back up the block. Tony adjusted his silk tie and checked his hair in the rearview mirror.

They stopped at the corner. Marie's window hummed down. Juicy checked them out from the far end of the sidewalk, then slow-shuffled his way over.

"You lookin' for directions?"

Tony flashed a pearly smile. "Looking for ink. Queens is dry, but a brother told me you're solid."

Juicy squinted at him like he had X-ray vision and he was hunting for a badge under Tony's jacket.

"This brother got a name?"

"Nope," Tony said. "Neither do I and neither do you."

Juicy thought about it for a second, then nodded to himself. Weighing risks and rewards. "Yeah, all right, how much?"

Tony glared at Marie. "Girl, get the damn money out already. Don't be wasting this man's time."

Marie pitched her gaze low and pulled her shoulders in tight, making herself look harmless and cowed. Undercover work was an acting job at heart. Selling a character, selling a story, sometimes with nothing but body language. She pulled the envelope of cash from her blazer, keeping her holster carefully out of sight. Juicy took the envelope, peeked inside, and made it vanish.

"Take a right, and drive slow up the next block. Look for my boy in the red-and-white kicks. He'll run it out to you."

He started to turn away. Tony held up one hand.

"Just one thing, my man. Assuming your shit's quality—"

"It's quality, all right," Juicy told him.

"Assuming so, I'm a party promoter, among various and sundry other pastimes. I've got a rave coming up, an under-the-radar deal, and I need to make a big buy. Can you handle a bulk order?"

Juicy had that squint again, like he was counting dollar signs in his head. "How much bulk?"

"Five g's worth."

He blinked. "That's a lot of weight."

"Hey," Tony said, "if you can't handle it, I totally understand."

"Nah, nah, I can handle it, okay? Just not right now, I don't keep that much on me." Juicy rubbed his chin, staring up the street, desperate to keep a fat fish on the line. "But I can get it. Tomorrow. Tomorrow morning."

"First thing? The party's tomorrow night."

"First thing," Juicy said. "You gonna bring cash, right? Small bills?"

"Crisp and clean. And just so we're clear? We're gonna do the hand-off at the same time, got it? I'm not giving you five thousand dollars then driving around the corner and *hoping* I get my shit. This goes right, there's more business in it for you. A lot more. My guy's not reliable anymore, and I'm looking for a new regular hookup."

"Whatever, it's cool. Just be here."

Tony threw the car into drive and cruised around the corner. Halfway up the block, a kid in bright sneakers ran up and pitched a baggie through Marie's open window. He couldn't have been more than twelve years old.

The crystals of ink glistened inside the transparent plastic, spiky and oily-black. Marie tossed the baggie in the glove compartment.

"Right now," she said, "Juicy's deciding if he's the smart kind of dealer—the kind who stands to make a lot of easy money over the long haul—or the dumb kind who's going to try and rip us off for the cash."

"I'm betting on smart," Tony said.

They rounded the corner and circled the block. They found a parking spot at the far end of Juicy's street, watching from a distance. The dealer was pacing, anxious, talking on the phone.

"And that's him calling his supplier," Marie said.

Juicy hung up and started walking.

"And that's him *going* to his supplier," Tony said. "Excellent plan, Detective Reinhart."

"Well executed, Detective Fisher. It's almost like we're partners or something. C'mon, we'd better tail him on foot. He'll notice us creeping up on him in the car."

Even on foot, trailing a block behind, it was dicey. Juicy had one of the most important qualities of a successful drug dealer: a healthy sense of paranoia. They had to duck into doorways more than once as he stopped to check his six. He disappeared down the stairs to a subway platform and they scrambled to keep up, thankful for the bustling crowd while they waited for a train twenty feet away from him.

He got off the train in Bedford-Stuyvesant. Tony and Marie stayed on his tail.

Juicy led them down a tangle of gutted streets and sidewalks strewn with crumpled litter and pigeon spatter. Marie gazed up at towers of crumbling brickwork, the windows shrouded by tacked-up bedsheets.

"I thought Bed-Stuy was going hipster," she muttered.

"Stuyvesant *Heights* is," Tony said, keeping his voice low. "This ain't Stuyvesant Heights."

Juicy squirmed through a torn gap in a sagging chain-link fence. Tony and Marie hung back at the edge of the lot, using the corner of a boarded-up bodega for cover. Beyond the fence lay a razor strip of yellowed grass, a parking lot, and the dirt-brown facade of a storage depot. The weathered sign out front read AJ Shipping and Freight.

From the look of their knockoff logo—a curling AJ monogram in a yellow shield—and the squat brown delivery trucks lining the parking lot, they were taking their best shot at riding on UPS's coattails.

Juicy walked up to the side door and rang a buzzer. He shifted his weight from foot to foot, looking over his shoulder, anxious. The door opened just wide enough for him to slip inside before it slammed shut.

"A shipping company," Marie said. "Opens up all kinds of possibilities for moving product in and out of the city."

"We should call it in."

"Better idea." Marie wriggled her way through the gap in the fence. "Let's get a closer look first and find out how exactly much backup we're going to need."

"What?" Tony whispered. "*No. Marie*—"

She was already off and moving, loping across the parking lot in a low crouch. He sighed and followed her, cursing under his breath as the fence's broken tines scraped against the fabric of his new jacket.

Thirty-Seven

"You keep looking at your phone."

Nessa glanced across the dinner table at Richard. They sat at opposite ends, the gulf of glass and wrought iron marking the no-man's-land between them.

"Expecting a text from work," she said.

"Huh."

She speared a sprig of broccoli on her fork. Her medallion-sized filet was bloody rare, the plate drowning in watery scarlet, and she wiped the broccoli back and forth in the juices before popping it between her teeth. Richard sucked on his bottle of beer and watched her across the gulf.

Nessa hated that table.

He'd insisted on buying it for entertaining guests, once every two or three months. The rest of the time they ate on opposite ends of the dining room, isolated by the span of polished glass. Together, but not.

"You haven't taken your meds," he said.

"I took them before I came down for dinner."

"No," Richard said. "You didn't."

She glanced up at him, arching an eyebrow. "And you know this how?"

He sighed, pushing his chair back. He walked across the room, looming over her, and slapped her pill bottle down next to her plate.

"I counted."

"You...*excuse* me?"

"Dr. Neidermyer called me. He said he didn't think you'd been taking your medication. So I counted. Eighteen pills in the bottle, same as there was this morning."

"I am not a damn *child*, Richard—"

"*Then stop acting like one!*" he shouted. He drew his hand back, her face shadowed by his clenched fist. He froze.

Then he dropped his hand to his side, unclenched it, and stomped back to his end of the table.

"Why are you doing this to me?" he asked her as he dropped into his chair.

She didn't have anything to say, couldn't speak. She was still trapped in a single breath five seconds ago, looking up at his fist. Wondering how close he'd come to using it.

"Take the pill," he told her. "Now. While I watch. If you're going to act like a child, I'm going to have to treat you like one."

Her fingers were numb as she unscrewed the cap. She tapped the pill into her shaking palm. Then she tossed it into her mouth and washed it down with a swallow of Perrier.

"This is how we're doing it from now on," he said. "You'll take your meds in front of me, because I obviously can't trust you to take care of yourself."

She stared at him, still in shock. Her voice came out as a strained whisper. "What is *wrong* with you?"

"With me?" He blinked at her. "What's wrong with *me*? Jesus, will you look at yourself once in a while? I have given everything I have to take care of you. I've stood by you while other men would have walked out years ago—I mean, you really don't know, do you? What about Dad's party?"

"What about it?"

Richard threw a hand in the air and tossed back a swig of beer. "That I had people coming up to me all night, looking at me with pity in their eyes and asking if there was anything they could do to help, you know, with our *situation*. Because my darling wife was standing in a corner, staring at a wall and *talking to herself*."

Nessa shrank in her chair. The room, the table, her husband—everything seemed to loom larger by the heartbeat, towering over her, like she was aging in reverse. Turning back into a helpless little girl with her feet barely touching the floor.

"I wasn't—I mean—I don't talk to myself."

Richard sighed. His anger softened along with his voice.

"No, Nessa. You *think* you don't talk to yourself. You had a twenty-minute conversation with the goddamn wallpaper in the middle of the living room. I saw it. Our friends saw it. Everyone saw it."

Fear and humiliation washed over her in a white-water torrent, so strong she clung to the edge of the glass table. She felt like it might sweep her away forever. Part of her wished that it would.

"How do you think that makes me feel?" Richard asked her.

"I'm...sorry," was all she could manage.

"Hey. Hey. It's all right." He gave her a tired, sad smile. "I just want you to get better, hon. And you will. I need you to trust me, okay?"

"Okay," she said.

"Nobody is going to take care of you," he said. "Nobody but me. And I'm going to protect you, and I'm going to love you. Always. It's just you and me."

"Okay," she said.

* * *

After dinner Nessa sat alone in her workroom, penned in by the black octagonal walls and her half-finished canvases. She held a sketch pad on her lap. The art wouldn't come. Not even a single stroke of her pencil, as she felt a too-familiar fog settling over her brain. Her thoughts wrapped themselves in wooly gauze.

Marie hadn't texted.

She's a detective, Nessa thought. *She works odd hours. Long hours.*

She's avoiding you.

I helped her yesterday, she thought. *She was happy to see me.*

She was faking it. The second you left she and her roommate talked about what a crazy stalker you are and how to get rid of you.

Nessa squeezed her eyes shut. Her fist clenched. The pencil snapped against her palm.

She tossed it aside, broken splinters clattering across the wooden floor, and picked up a fresh one.

As much as her brain wanted her to, she couldn't believe that. She could believe Richard, could believe Dr. Neidermyer, but...not that. Marie was special. Marie was real.

Marie was hers.

She stood and walked to her last canvas. The charcoal sketch of the three faceless women, dancing ecstatically around a bonfire. In the sky above the flames, she began to draw. The curves of a familiar face, the hard angles of a suit of armor. Slow, careful work. It made one little piece of her happy, the tiny chunk of her mind that struggled to rise above the brain fog like a sailor drowning in a maelstrom.

Something wasn't right. The world and her brain weren't lining up. She thought of Dr. Neidermyer, raising her prescribed dosage when she'd been feeling better than ever, and felt a hot flash of angry suspicion.

Which is how crazy people react, she told herself. *That's paranoia. You know this.*

Even so.

She set down her pencil, took out her phone, and sorted through a database of psychiatrists. Somebody with no ties to her husband's family, somebody with a practice nowhere near Neidermyer's. She poked her head outside the workroom door, making sure Richard was out of earshot, and lowered her voice as she cupped her hand over the phone.

"Yes, my name is—" She paused, thinking. "Vanessa Fieri, and I'd like to make an appointment with Dr. Robinson. Yes, I'm a new patient. Tomorrow? That's...that's perfect, actually."

Normally there'd be at least a week's wait, the receptionist told her. Her nine o'clock had just canceled, an illness in the family, ten minutes before Nessa called. A lucky accident.

She returned to her canvas and picked up her pencil. The faceless, shadowy women danced around the fire, charcoal flames crackling as the smoke rose ever higher.

Thirty-Eight

Dora moved by day. No one saw her.

The sun struggled to push through the gauzy Los Angeles smog. Only the heat made it through, sidewalks simmering and the air gritty and dry. Dora ducked into a half-empty diner across the street from the Keller and Sons Auction House and took a seat in the back. She didn't bother ordering, and nobody behind the counter noticed her.

They didn't notice the jar under her arm, either, as she set it on the scratched wooden table before her. It was the size of a thermos, carved from white soapstone and sealed with a silver cap. Letters glittered along the pale surface, runes in a dead and forgotten tongue.

By now, her coven sisters would have their own missions well underway. The Mourner had already sent her pawn to retrieve the knife Nessa would need. Their mother would be using a wayward witch as a cat's-paw, delivering chaos to their mutual enemies and slowing their progress. Now it was Dora's turn. She raked her fingers through her dreadlocks and stared out the window.

There was nothing extraordinary about Keller and Sons. The warehouse had good security and an auction hall up front. It was closed today, though, as they packed and prepared to deliver the goods from yesterday's sales. If she let her vision slide out of focus, the walls disappeared, leaving the people behind. They scurried this way and that, going about their lives, trailing wounds and mistakes and secrets behind them. They couldn't see how they were all joined by invisible thread, their fates conjoined.

Dora could see, though.

She whispered the words of an ancient prayer and reached into her battered army-surplus jacket. On the tail end of her hymn, she drew out a brass key on a slender chain. The lid of her jar unlocked with a faint metallic click, then whispered open on hinges of oiled stone.

A swarm of gnats boiled from the jar, flooding the hash-brown-scented air. The other diners were impassive as the gnats landed on their food and tangled in their hair, not seeing them at all. Dora rose and walked with the swarm. She cradled the empty jar under her arm while the insects buzzed around her face. She pushed open the diner's door and set them free.

The black and churning cloud blew across the street, washing over the auction house, slithering into every crack and open window. Everywhere they touched, the world changed.

*   *   *

Pamela Land had run from Boston to LA. She'd changed her hair, her name, her career—she would have changed her face if she could have afforded plastic surgery on her fourteen-dollars-an-hour paycheck. Every time she moved, he found her. Sometimes it was a few weeks later; once she'd lasted three months on the run. Even after her ex-husband lost his job on the police force, kicked to the curb after violating the restraining order so many times his buddies couldn't cover for him any longer, he kept coming for her.

Last time had been in Michigan. She got fourteen stitches, two broken ribs, and a nose that never healed straight again. He got probation.

It was a hot, muggy day, and her ribs ached. They always ached when the weather changed. She walked the side alley of the auction house, guarding the approach to the loading dock. "Guarding." She almost smiled at the thought. The biggest trouble she'd faced since starting this job was chasing away kids trying to tag the alley wall.

Still, the auction house moved ten million dollars a month in merchandise. If they told her to guard the alley, she'd guard the alley.

"Pamela."

She knew the voice. Knew what she'd see before she even turned around. Her ex-husband stood there, showing her his empty hands, ten feet behind her. Wearing those conciliatory puppy-dog eyes again.

"I'm sorry," he said. "I'm sorry for what happened last time. Look, you just—you just get me so angry sometimes, you know? If you'd just—"

She drew her revolver and shot him six times.

She didn't think. She just did it. Standing outside her body like she was watching a movie, she emptied round after round into his chest. The hammer clicked down on an empty chamber. He hit the alley floor, his glazed eyes staring at the smog-shrouded sun. Pamela stood there, trembling, back inside her own skin.

Dora stepped over to the body. She reached into her jacket, pulled out a tiny .22 with a taped grip, and tossed it onto the pavement next to the dead man's hand.

"He had a gun," Dora said. "It was self-defense."

"He had a gun," Pamela echoed, staring at what she'd done. "It was self-defense."

Dora walked past her, up the alley, unchallenged.

* * *

Inside the cluttered warehouse, thick doors and the whining of forklift engines drowned out the gunshots. A dozen men, their backs stained with cold sweat under their safety vests and lifting harnesses, hauled wooden crates across the floor and ran through shipping manifests. Half the warehouse was being shipped out to lucky bidders; the other half was incoming and needed to be prepped for that evening's auction. The endless circle of work.

The overhead lights flickered, and Jeph, one of the worker bees, sighed. He knew what was coming next.

"How many times, Jeph?" his supervisor shouted from the far end of the floor. "How many times I gotta ask?"

"On it," he sighed for what must have been the twentieth time that week. He wasn't on it. He'd taken to using his electrical-maintenance duties for extended smoke breaks. The building was old, sure, but it wasn't falling to pieces. He needed his cigarettes more than the auction house needed upkeep.

"I mean it," his supervisor yelled back. "You said you had this shit fixed yesterday, and you said the same thing two days ago. I see those lights flicker again, you're getting written up."

No smokes for Jeph today, at least not on company time. He could tell when he'd pushed the boss a little too far. He trudged over to the circuit breaker box and opened it up, trying to estimate the least amount of work he could get away with.

He didn't see the cloud of gnats roiling in the wires, stripping plastic and loosening screws, brushing hot connections together. Or the ones swarming in the employee bathroom just off to his left. The old toilet, as neglected as the wiring, overflowed. Water bubbled over the lid and spilled, rolling out under the bathroom door, the worn grooves of the warehouse floor guiding the stream to form a puddle under Jeph's feet.

"Huh?" he said, hearing his shoes splash. He looked down, distracted, as his hand brushed the metal of the breaker panel.

Later, they'd call it a one-in-a-billion accident. The perfect storm of building fatigue, a near-impossible wiring mishap, and sheer bad luck. As Jeph shook, paralyzed by the lethal current running through his body, the lights flickered one last time and died.

Heads turned as his corpse crashed to the ground.

Workers ran to his side, one dialing 911, another checking his pulse as they gathered around him. In the lightless gloom, their backs turned toward her, Dora strolled by without anyone noticing.

*   *   *

"You left your computer unlocked," was all she said.

Keller, of Keller and Sons, sat behind his desk. He pressed the phone to his ear and faced the unthinkable. He'd never left his computer unlocked. Never.

"You...you invaded my—" he stammered.

"You didn't even bother closing your...pictures," his wife said. "How could you do this?"

"I can explain—"

"*Children*," she said. "It was like you *wanted* me to find it. Like you wanted me to find out what kind of monster I married."

"No, it's not like that. Look, we can work this out!"

"Work it out with the police. I already called them. They're on their way."

She hung up. He set the phone down and sat in stunned silence as his world crumbled around him.

Then he opened his top desk drawer, took out the glossy black revolver he carried for protection, and shot himself in the head. His corpse sagged halfway out of his swivel chair, gun limp in his hand and his blood guttering onto the carpet.

Dora let herself in. She stepped around his body and over to the packing crate on his desk. Her hand lightly brushed against the shipping label. The ink writhed under her fingertips, black text running and marching across the white label like a swarm of ants.

Aubrey Weinstein, Long Island broke up and dissolved. The ink ants marched. When they settled once more, the label read *Vanessa Roth, New York City*.

Dora eyed her handiwork, nodded with approval, and left. The first ambulances were pulling up to the curb as she left the auction house, followed by a pair of police cars. Nobody gave her a second glance.

A couple of blocks away, someone had opened up a fire hydrant, and kids danced and shouted in the spray. The springtime sun fought through the blanket of smog and turned the arc of mist into a rainbow. Dora smiled at the sight. She followed the trail of spilled water into an alleyway. The tail end of the spill spread out in a basin of cracked concrete, forming a dirty puddle. She crouched beside it and waved her hand over the water. It rippled, and her reflection tore away.

The Mourner stared out at her from the puddle, her face shrouded behind heavy lace veils. "Sister," she hissed.

"What's done is done," Dora said. "The Oberlin Glass is getting shipped straight to our girl's doorstep, postage paid. Let's hope she figures out what to do with it. I couldn't exactly send an instruction manual."

"If she is truly worthy of our mother's esteem, her intuition will guide her."

"True. True. Did your pet gangster come through with the knife?"

"My pawn has just begun his work. He will be successful."

"You sound confident," Dora said.

The ivory veils rippled as the Mourner let out a raspy chuckle.

"He hasn't failed me yet. Faust is a resourceful man. Cunning, when cornered. And at the very least, always entertaining to watch from a distance."

Thirty-Nine

Daniel Faust had a routine, and he stuck to it. One drink right before a job. Just enough hard liquor to steady his nerves, not enough to blunt his edge. He nursed a Jack and Coke in a piano bar in Hollywood, some see-and-be-seen joint with polished brass along the bar and leafy ferns dangling from wicker baskets.

He hated Los Angeles.

His phone rang. A familiar Kentucky drawl crackled across the line.

"Sugar," Jennifer said, "you got a problem."

Jennifer was the chairwoman of the New Commission, the biggest crime syndicate in Nevada. Those weren't words you ever wanted to hear coming from her lips.

"Tell me about it," Daniel said. "Lemme guess: the three stooges I took out in the storm tunnels have buddies, and they're sniffing for payback."

Jennifer snorted. "If that was it, wouldn't have even called ya. Woulda just taken care of that on my own. You ain't been in Dallas lately, have you?"

"Nope."

"Didn't think so. Problem is, somebody hit a stash house for ink dealers. Killed everybody on the scene."

"And that's a problem why?" Daniel asked.

"Check the pic."

He tilted the phone, calling up the photo she'd just sent him. Corpses lay scattered across a warehouse floor, throat-cut and sprawled like rag dolls. Black flies nestled in puddles of sticky blood.

Playing cards jutted from their wounds. They were even his usual brand.

"Aw, hell," he said.

"My thoughts exactly. Somebody sure wanted to make it look like you did the deed. Considering you're supposed to be dead, that's gonna put a crimp in things. Hate to add injury to injury, but do I have to tell you who was first on the scene?"

He felt a fist-sized stone in the pit of his stomach.

"Don't say Harmony Black."

"I won't say it, then," Jennifer replied. "I'll just think it real loud in your general direction. Anyway, looks like somebody's setting you two up for a rematch."

His phone buzzed as a text came in. *The Palmer's lobby cameras just went blind*, it read. *You've got one hour.*

"I've got to run," he said, "just got word from Pixie."

"Yeah, when *are* you gonna tell me what you're doing in LA? We hate LA."

He remembered the Mourner's admonition about secrecy. "Private job for a special client. I'll catch you up when I get back."

He tossed back the last swallow of his drink. The empty glass clinked against the lacquered bar. He left a rumpled twenty next to it, folded a newspaper under his arm, and slipped outside. His tailored jacket billowed behind him in a gust of hot wind as he jogged across a clogged intersection. With a coffee-colored sunset at its back, the spire of the Palmer Building rose up like an art deco monument. Built of sandstone and silver, it was a pyramid for the hippest of pharaohs.

The cavernous lobby was a relic from the forties, plush velvet divans edging a kaleidoscope tile floor mural, scarlet and gold sizzling in an endless whorl. The air conditioning was on at full blast, prickling Daniel's skin as he walked across the room like he had every right to be there. Confidence was the most important key to any successful infiltration.

The second most important was having *actual* keys. That morning's recon had taught him that the elevators were locked by electronic access cards. Residents only. He sat on a divan near the elevator banks, unfurled his copy of the LA *Times*, and pretended to read. Three people came and went. None of them was right. Then came lucky number four, stepping off the elevator with his card still in his hand. The bronzed door rumbled shut behind him as he stuffed it in his left hip pocket.

Daniel got on his feet, moving fast, calculating the perfect trajectory. The two men collided halfway across the lobby floor. As their shoulders thudded, Daniel pretended to try to steady his target with one hand, giving him an extra shake and throwing him further off-balance as his fingers dipped into the mark's pocket.

"Jeez," Daniel said, "sorry, sorry about that—"

The man pulled away from him, holding up his open hands. "It's okay."

"Sorry. Wasn't looking where I was going. Sorry."

Daniel strolled to the elevator banks. The stolen card, glossy and black, nestled against his palm.

Finding Andre Lefevre's address had been easy: a twenty-dollar bribe to a studio intern did the job. Another twenty for his limo driver got the down-low on the celebrity chef's schedule, to make sure he wouldn't be home when Daniel came calling. Lefevre was not popular with his staff.

So far, this was a picture-perfect breaking and entering job. That didn't make Daniel happy. He'd been around long enough to know that when everything seemed smooth as glass, there was always something nasty lurking beneath the tranquil waters. Alone inside the mirrored cage, he reached into his jacket and took out a pair of thin leather driving gloves. He slipped them on as the elevator drifted upward.

He got off on the seventh floor and eased down a narrow, dimly lit hall, brass-numbered doors alternating between patches of garish vintage wallpaper. If his info held up, 716 was Lefevre's place. He looked left and right, ears perked in the cold silence, and crouched as he fished out an olive oilskin case. His lockpicks were nestled inside, a baker's dozen with a menagerie of angled hooks and tips.

One by one, the tumblers rolled over for him like a dog doing tricks. The lock let out a satisfying little click, and the chef's door drifted open.

"Mr. Lefevre?" Daniel called across the threshold. "Your door was open. Everything okay?"

Better safe than sorry. No answer, though. He had the place to himself. He shut the door behind him and switched on the lights.

Lefevre had dropped a million on this place, but he was paying for the prestige of the address. His condo was a borderline dump, with cheap wallpaper and clashing colors. Cracks ran the length of the yellowed crown molding. He'd spent some serious cash on the kitchen, though, renovating it with bright white tile, track lighting, and stainless steel everything.

Daniel whistled and popped his head into the refrigerator. He didn't expect to see the knife he was hunting; he just wanted to know what a celebrity chef had in his fridge. Hot sauce, mostly. Bottles and bottles of sauce stood at attention, mingled with brands of imported mustard he couldn't even pronounce and mounds of leftovers stuffed into plastic cubes. He pried up the corner of a Tupperware container to take a peek inside.

It was a human face.

It had been surgically removed, perfectly intact with its eyelashes and eyebrows plucked, and roasted medium-rare. Part of the chin and bottom lip were missing, eaten away. Lefevre had plated it with a small radish-and-cucumber salad.

Daniel put the lid back and stepped away from the fridge. His gaze slid to the long, oversized meat freezer alongside it.

"Aw, hell," he breathed. "Come on. No."

He pried up the freezer lid, took one look inside, and let it fall shut again.

After that he didn't linger. Daniel tossed the kitchen fast, rummaging through drawers and cabinets as he hunted for the Mourner's knife. Lefevre had no shortage of kitchenware—and knives for days, each one of them sharp enough to split a hair right down the middle—but no sign of the right blade.

The bedroom was his next stop, and Daniel approached the scarlet-sheeted bed and closed closet door with a surge of anxiety. Fortunately, the chef kept his murderous habits to the kitchen: nothing but dust bunnies under his bed, and the closet was stocked with a row of tailored suits. He dipped his fingers in pockets and checked inside each jacket, feeling for a hidden sheath or anything big enough to hold the missing knife.

A business card fluttered to the floor. Daniel crouched down and scooped it up. The card was rich cream, with calligraphic text in stark black.

The Hollywood Gourmands' Society

Est. 1923

No address, no phone number. He flipped it over. The back simply read *Admit One*.

He pocketed it. After that he took one last walk-through. He made sure everything was left exactly the way he found it and shut the lights off on his way out the door. Then he went back across the street, back to the piano bar, and had another drink.

For a moment, he thought about chucking the job and going home. He had that old familiar feeling, teetering on the edge of some bad craziness and waiting for the fatal shove before he went tumbling headfirst into it. Then he thought about the Mourner. She wasn't the kind of person who took no for an answer.

He needed backup. He took out his phone.

"Caitlin. Hey, am I interrupting?"

The woman's faint Scottish burr warmed his ear. "Not at all, pet. I'm mired in paperwork, but you make for a welcome distraction.

Are you back in town? I was thinking we could go out for dinner tonight."

"Still in LA, and I don't think I'm going to have much of an appetite tonight. Or tomorrow. Or anytime soon. Hey, you spent some time in Hollywood back in the day. I mean...you know, not recently. A while ago."

"Are you trying to avoid bringing up my age, Daniel?"

"Yes. That is absolutely what I'm doing."

"That's adorable," she said. "But yes, my previous tenure on Earth did see me attend a party or two in that neck of the woods."

"You ever hear of an outfit called the Hollywood Gourmands' Society, would have started up in the early twenties? I'm running on a hunch here, but I'm pretty sure they eat people."

"You'd think I would have, but no. I'll give Freddie Vinter a call."

"Freddie?" He furrowed his brow. "She's in Chicago."

"She also eats people," Caitlin said. "I've found that cannibalism is a curiously social vice. She may network with them. And why are you looking for these...individuals?"

He raised his glass, swirling the liquor around, and sighed before tipping it back. Straight whiskey burned a gasoline trail down his throat.

"Because a crazy witch who lives in a cave told me she wants a magic knife, and I'm expecting that's where I'll find it because the universe hates me."

"Oh," she said, "is that all? I'll expect you home soon, then."

Forty

Night fell over Bedford-Stuyvesant, draping the tattered streets under a cloak of twilight. Marie prowled the edge of the AJ Shipping and Freight office. She kept low and moved from delivery truck to delivery truck for cover, working her way closer to the building. She poked her head out, and Tony's hand, fast on her shoulder, pulled her back. He shook his head, silent, and pointed.

A security camera perched in the eaves at one corner of the mud-brown warehouse, lazily panning its onyx eye across the parking lot.

Marie timed it, watching carefully, holding her breath as she waited for it to sweep away. Then she raced across the open patch of pavement, ducking underneath the camera and darting around the corner. She pressed her back to the rough brick wall. Tony waited for the next pass, breathless as he caught up with her.

Idling truck engines rumbled behind the building. She heard the metallic rippling sound of a loading-bay door rolling open.

"We shouldn't even be here," Tony whispered. "We should call for backup."

Marie glanced over her shoulder. "Either this is a stash house like the one in Monticello or the place they're actually manufacturing the stuff. Either way we're only getting one shot at taking these guys down. We've got to find out exactly what we're dealing with before we call in the cavalry."

She eased along the wall, knees bent, eyes sharp, listening to heavy bootsteps and the sounds of wooden crates dragging along steel. Around the corner, a team of men drifted in and out of headlight beams, lugging boxes from a pair of AJ Shipping delivery trucks and hauling them inside.

Every one of them was carrying a weapon, toting pistols in open holsters or barely concealed under windbreakers. A man smoked a cigarette, headlights at his back, keeping casual watch with a rifle slung over his shoulder. He started to turn, and Marie ducked back into cover.

"*Now* we're leaving," she breathed.

They slipped away in silence, timing their movements to duck under the camera's eye, and skirted the edge of the parking lot. They crossed the street under cover of darkness and found a doorway to crouch in while Marie waited for the kick of adrenaline to wear off.

"We don't just need backup," she said. "We need SWAT."

Tony nodded. "If this is anything like Monticello, these guys are the 'shoot first and ask questions never' type. Did you get a head count?"

"At least seven, all carrying. No idea how many are inside. If these guys even suspect we're onto them, they'll clear out in ten minutes flat. I say we go straight to Captain Traynor, find a friendly judge to get our warrants in order, and see if we can hit this place *tonight*."

"My kind of overtime—" Tony hushed as a square of light fell upon the pavement across the street, a side door whistling open. Juicy came out alone. He wore a cheap canvas backpack, looking fat and weighing his shoulder down.

"You know who *can* tell us how many guys are in there..." Tony murmured.

They tailed him for a block and a half, enough room that his friends wouldn't hear him if he shouted for help. Tony pointed up an alley. Marie broke off and jogged around the long way. Juicy stopped dead in his tracks as she rounded the corner in front of him. Then he turned on a dime, speed-walking back the way he came, stopping a second time when he found Tony standing in his path.

Tony pulled back his jacket and flashed the shield on his belt.

"Don't make us chase you. We get real mean when we have to chase people."

Juicy rolled his eyes, shrugged the backpack to the sidewalk, and clasped his hands behind his head in sullen resignation. Marie walked up from behind. She grabbed one of his wrists and slapped the cuffs on.

"I want a lawyer," was all he'd say, all the way back to the precinct.

* * *

"Lawyer," Juicy said, sitting handcuffed at a battered steel table in the interview room.

Marie slapped her palm against the backpack. Unzipped, with a tidal wave of glossy baggies spilling out, each bag stuffed to bursting with oily black pearls.

"There is *nothing* a lawyer can do for you right now. Don't you get that? You've got a choice to make: you can go down for all this weight, all by yourself, or you can help us put your bosses away."

"Lawyer," he told her.

Sitting next to Marie, Tony leaned back and spread his hands, nice and easy.

"Hey, my man. Trying to help you out here. See, when my partner goes fishing, she wants to keep all the fish. Me? I toss the little ones back. All you got to do is tell us what to expect behind those doors. Sketch a map for us. Tell us how many guns are in play—"

Juicy raised his voice, stretching his mouth as he carefully enunciated for them. "*Law-yer.*"

A knock sounded at the interview room door. Captain Traynor poked his head in. "Detectives?"

They joined him out in the hall, leaving their guest to stew in silence.

"Judge Gaines is moving on the warrants, and I just got off the phone with the Emergency Service Unit," he told them. "We've got a green light. The Apprehension Tactical Team is taking point."

"Bringing the A-Team," Tony said. "Nice. Are we in on this, Captain?"

"You think I was going to bench you? You two are helping with support. I'm setting up a perimeter detail, in case anyone slips past tactical."

Marie nodded at the closed door. "We're not going to get anything out of this guy, but we've got a bigger problem. You know how these people operate: the second he calls his lawyer, the lawyer's going to report back to his bosses. They'll know exactly when and where we grabbed him. By the time we close in on that warehouse, it'll be a ghost town. Happens every time we get anywhere near their operation."

Traynor glanced over his shoulder, then gestured for the detectives to huddle in as he pitched his voice low.

"Take him to holding. Accidentally lose his paperwork on the way back to your desk."

Marie furrowed her brow. "Sir?"

"We made a mistake. He got lost in the system for a couple of hours. It happens."

She stood at attention, sharp. "Sir."

"Once you're done, gear up, see me in my office. Don't tell anyone what you're working on. ESU thinks we need to keep this operation as quiet as humanly possible, and I'm in full agreement. These people have a habit of turning into vapor at the first whiff of trouble. This time, we're not giving them a chance."

*   *   *

A convoy rolled across the Brooklyn Bridge with uniform speed and military precision. No lights, no sirens. A pair of matte-black BearCats took the lead, the armored trucks outfitted with firing ports and battering rams. Next came a heavy rescue truck in blue and white, then a string of unmarked cars. Marie and Tony were halfway down the line. The dashboard squawked as the convoy stayed in contact, laying out the plan of attack.

The staff at Interfaith Medical was on notice. No details, but they'd been told to anticipate a potential number of trauma patients. *Hopefully them and not us*, Marie thought. She held the wheel in a firm, dry grip and stared dead ahead. SWAT was trained to save lives and minimize casualties, but after what happened in Monticello, nobody had much hope for a peaceful surrender. If the gunmen at AJ Shipping wanted to go out shooting, they'd go out shooting.

"Left up here," Tony said. Captain Traynor had laid out a perimeter, his handpicked units covering every approach to the warehouse. If anyone got past SWAT, it'd be their job to close the net. One by one, the support cars broke from the convoy, circling the streets like sharks on a blood trail. Marie turned onto Pulaski Street, found an open spot at the curb, and pulled over.

There was nothing to do now but wait. A quiet tension hung in the air, electric and gathering fast.

Marie took out her phone, her fingertips hovering over an empty text message to Nessa. That same old divide when it came to her job. The things she could talk about, the things she couldn't.

Hey, she wrote, *sorry I haven't checked in. I'm still at work. Long day at the office.*

*   *   *

On the other side of the city, Nessa lay awake in bed. She stared at the ceiling, listening to Richard snore on the far side of the mattress, trying to sleep while her brain fed her a steady list of reasons to hate herself.

The face of her phone glowed in the dark. She snatched it from the nightstand and clung to Marie's words like a life preserver. She clutched the phone to her chest, slipped out from under the covers and padded across the bedroom, the hem of her silk nightgown rippling around her bare ankles. In the safety of her workroom, she tapped out a reply.

I was worried.

Marie's response came back in a heartbeat. *I'm sorry.*

Nessa smiled down at the phone. She held it against her heart, squeezing it like she was giving Marie a hug, then wrote her reply.

It's okay. Catching all the bad guys?

All of them, Marie texted back. *We started with bank robbers and car thieves this morning then worked our way down the list. About to bust the last jaywalker in New York. Ending it with locking up a guy who tore the tags off his mattress. You can sleep soundly tonight.*

My knight in shining armor, Nessa replied.

At your service, my lady.

Nessa glanced at the workroom door. Her smile faded. She could feel Richard's presence in the house like a storm cloud hanging over her head. Part of her was still at the dinner table, cringing in her chair as he loomed over her and drew his fist back.

Marie, she wrote, *will you always protect me?*

*   *   *

Marie listened to the radio chatter, bursts of static humming over the dashboard, and stared at her phone.

Always, she wrote. *I don't know where we're going with this, or what happens next. But I will always keep you safe.*

"TOC," crackled a voice on the radio. "Able and Baker squads are in position and prepared to breach. Breach ready. Over."

Tony cracked his knuckles and craned his neck, looking back down the quiet street. "Here we go."

Gotta go, Marie texted fast, *just spotted that jaywalker.*

She pocketed her phone and shifted in her seat. More instructions, terse and precise, shot back and forth between the tactical squads.

"Probably don't even need to be here," Tony murmured. "A-Team's going to take these dudes down before they know what hit 'em."

"Even so," Marie said.

"Even so."

The final order came down. Teams moving on three. Marie glanced into the rearview mirror. Then she squeezed her eyes shut against a blinding flash as the end of the street erupted in flame.

Forty-One

Gouts of fire licked the starless sky, billowing with an earsplitting crack of thunder. The radio lit up with shouts, screams, voices overlapping and cutting out under the clatter of automatic weapons fire.

"—men down, men down. We've got—"

"—both doors, incendiaries," another voice shouted. "Jesus, it's white phosphorus—"

The sedan's engine roared. Marie slammed on the gas. She peeled away from the curb, hooked a screaming U-turn, and barreled up the street. Tony gripped the armrest as they headed straight for the fire and roiling clouds of smoke.

"They knew we were coming," Tony said. "How the hell did they know we were coming?"

"We're pinned down in the back lot," a voice screamed over the radio, almost drowned out by the sound of gunshots, "in a crossfire, shooters from the building and across the street. We need backup *now!*"

"This is TOC," a crisp voice said. "All perimeter units move in, all perimeter units move in. Emergency services on standby, hold at the staging ground."

The unmarked sedan's lights kicked on, flashing from behind the grill. Marie veered around a taxi, flipped the sirens on, and clenched her jaw tight.

Craig Schaefer

"What are we gonna do?" Tony said.

"Whatever we can."

One of the BearCats was up ahead, a gutted, smoking ruin, white fire crackling through the open gunports. Survivors from the second tactical squad were buttoned down inside its twin as rifle shots pitted the truck's armored hull. Muzzle flare erupted from inside the warehouse, the upper windows smashed out, and from the second floor of a tenement across the street. Marie slammed on the brakes and spun the sedan to a stop in the middle of the road. A pair of unmarked units roared up behind them as she and Tony jumped out. Others joined them, taking cover behind open car doors.

A shot blew out the window an inch above Marie's head, showering her tangled hair in chunks of safety glass. She stuck her gun hand around the side of the door, aimed toward the warehouse windows, and fired. The pistol bucked in her hand as she squeezed off round after round. Someone in the tenement was screaming, a gut-shot howl as the crossfire died. The shooters in the warehouse windows doubled down and alternated their reloads like professional soldiers, flooding the air with lead-jacketed wasps.

One of the loading bay doors slowly rattled upward. Headlights flared against the dark.

"They're gonna make a run for it," Tony shouted, sticking his hand over the roof and firing blind toward the windows.

There were bodies in the street, slumped and broken and bleeding out. Dead cops, their shields gleaming in the light of the burning warehouse.

"The fuck they are," Marie growled.

She popped the trunk and scrambled around the back of the car. A slug slammed into the hood, sparking, another round ricocheting against the pavement. Tony ducked low and looked back at her with his eyes wide.

"What are you *doing?*"

She hoisted a tire-puncture strip over her shoulder. The heavy segmented chain, barbed with steel quills, rattled as it dragged behind her. She answered him through gritted teeth.

"Not letting these assholes get away. Not this time."

Marie broke from cover. She kept her head down and zigzagged across the open black asphalt. The loading bay door rolled three-quarters high now, the delivery truck crouched just behind it like a sprinter at the starting line. Its engine revved, headlights blazing like twin spotlights. Gunshots chewed into the pavement at Marie's feet as she dropped one end of the spike strip, dragging the other while she ran, drawing a line across the parking lot. She dropped the far end and yanked it taut. Spikes erupted like porcupine quills. She threw herself behind the burning wreck of the first BearCat, landing hard and rolling on her shoulder as a fusillade of gunfire tore into the tactical truck's flame-scorched armor.

The delivery truck lurched from the bay. It screamed out and hit the spike strip full-on. The front tires blew out, loud as the gunshots, and the strip tangled up in the axle. The driver didn't take his foot off the gas. Sparks flew from the bent rims, tortured metal shrieking, chunks of shredded rubber scattering in the truck's wake. The truck fishtailed and veered hard left. It jumped the curb on the far side of the street, out of control, and crashed into a boarded-up storefront. Plywood ruptured and filthy glass sprayed across the crumpled hood. The driver launched face-first through the windshield, thrown like a rag doll, landing with a chunk of bloody spine jutting from his broken neck.

The gunfire from the warehouse went silent. One shooter dangled motionless from a window, slumped over the broken sill.

The reverberations from the final shot faded away. Then there was no sound at all, nothing but the crackling flames. The stench of smoke fogged the midnight air, burning metal and the burning dead.

Then came the wail of sirens as ambulances and a fire crew rolled in under police cover, red and blue lights strobing in Marie's dazed, exhausted eyes.

*   *   *

It was five in the morning by the time Marie came home. The first pale threads of dawn kissed the streets of Queens. Marie was only moving on inertia now, fueled by black coffee and her last shreds of raw willpower. Her keys rattled in the door.

Janine jumped up from the futon. She had bags under her eyes and her laptop was streaming a news report.

"You were there, weren't you?" Janine pointed at her screen. A helicopter camera captured long-distance shots of the cleanup, arcs of cold water billowing from fire hoses. "You never came home last night, and you weren't answering your phone—"

"You stayed up?" Marie rubbed a knuckle against one eye. She shut the door and leaned against it, unsteady. "You didn't have to stay up."

"They said...they said eight cops are dead. Five more are in critical."

"I'm okay. Tony's okay."

Janine pulled her into a hug, squeezing tight. Marie let her.

"Do you want to talk about it?" Janine asked, her voice muffled by Marie's shoulder.

Marie patted her on the back. She gently untangled herself from Janine's arms.

"I've got reports, and paperwork, and..." Marie shook her head. "I need five hours of shut-eye. Then it's back to the squad."

"Marie." Janine waved a frustrated, helpless hand at the laptop screen. "Who are these people? Who does this? I mean, ambushing the police? A shootout in the middle of Brooklyn? This doesn't happen in our city. It's not supposed to happen. I took a sick day because I waited up all night, but honestly, right now I'm just afraid to go outside. Or take the bus, or do...*anything*."

"Hey." Marie put her hands on Janine's shoulders. "Hey. Listen to me. That's *why* I'm just crashing for a few hours, then going back on my tour, okay? We all are. The NYPD is thirty-four thousand members strong, and these creeps just picked a fight with *all* of us.

And we are going to do everything we can to keep you safe out there."

Janine forced a nervous smile. "Guess we should both try to get some sleep."

Marie trudged into her bedroom and shut the door. She peeled her clothes off in the dark, then tumbled onto the mattress. Her body had hit its limit, shutting itself down, every part of her going still. Everything but her racing mind. When she closed her eyes she was back on the street, hearing the gunshots, feeling the glass rain down. She put her face against her pillow, but all she could smell was smoke.

Underneath it all, the question driving her was the same one Janine had asked. Who were these people? There was a good reason the city streets weren't drenched in blood every day. That was because most criminals, even the hardcore, dead-end burnouts, still had some sense of self-preservation. They'd rather face a jury than a bullet. Ink traffickers were a different breed. Murderous. Feral.

Richard Roth, her lover's husband, might be one of them.

Eventually she slept. Wandering through turbulent dreams, looking for clues.

Forty-Two

Richard Roth ran his empire from the fifty-ninth floor of a Manhattan high-rise. Floor-to-ceiling windows overlooked the shining skyline, flooding the polished-granite suite with sunlight. He had a curved modern desk and a high-backed ergonomic chair like the captain's seat in a science fiction movie. On a nearby table, an architect's model stood on display. It was a rendition of a proposed development in Tribeca, an entire city block imagined in ivory plastic. His pride and joy.

Today, real estate was the farthest thing from his mind. He paced behind his desk, eyes locked on the grill of his speakerphone, wringing his hands. Scottie burst in through the office's double doors.

"What the fuck, man?" Scottie said. "What the actual *fuck?*"

"I know, I know—" Richard fluttered a hand at the phone. "I've got Westwood on the line. He's got like half the lodge in his office."

"Brother Richard?" echoed the voice on the phone. "Is that Brother Scottie with you?"

"Oh my God." Scottie's jaw dropped. "Will you please quit it with the ritual bullshit for five seconds, Westwood? The ink factory is gone. Our pipeline is gone. You know how many police checkpoints I had to get past just to take the damn subway? The NYPD's deploying Hercules teams all over the city."

"I'm aware of the situation," Westwood said. "We're just trying to figure out how it happened."

Scottie leaned into the desk, fingertips pressed against cold marble.

"I can tell you exactly how it happened. I warned the factory that a raid was coming down."

Richard lifted an eyebrow. "Excuse me?"

"Remember? I've got an inside source. They called me, I called the factory. Passed a warning through the back channels. You know, courtesy from one Network cell to another. Instead of clearing out like they should have, those idiots decided to turn Bed-Stuy into their personal Alamo."

Richard punched a button on the phone, muting the line.

"Weren't we talking about *killing* those particular idiots, so we could get a promotion?"

Scottie dropped his voice. "Yeah, on our timetable. Dead cops, burned-out factory? This is, like, the worst possible way this could have gone down."

"Still. It's *almost* what we wanted."

Scottie's gaze flicked to the phone. "If we play it right. You feel like sharing with the rest of the class?"

"No." Richard tapped the button again. "Brother Westwood, I need to call you back."

He hung up the phone. The soles of his polished shoes rustled against the polished floor as he paced in front of the windows.

"An entire Network cell is gone, and without a flow of product—*their* flow of product—we're basically dead in the water."

"You and me, bro," Scottie told him. "It's all about you and me now. We need to get in touch with somebody higher on the food chain. Screw those other guys. Like Sun Tzu said, in the midst of chaos, there is also opportunity."

Richard faced the window. He clasped his hands behind his back, feeling the warm sunlight on his face.

"We have to be careful. I mean, 'walking a tightrope over a pit of alligators' careful. You know the Network is sending cleaners to fix this mess. And by 'fix'..."

Scottie's shoulders tightened. "They're sending Mr. Smith."

"*Esquire*. It was fine when he was on *our* side, cleaning up that mess in Jersey, but if the cops even glance sideways at us, we're walking dead men. We need to make friends, fast. Get a patron. Somebody to hold an umbrella over our heads while this crap rains down on everybody else."

The office doors swung open. Savannah Cross, swapping her lab coat and goggles for a severely cut pantsuit and sharp cat-eye glasses, strode into the room with a smile.

"I believe I can help with that."

Richard turned from the window. "I'm sorry, and you are?"

"Dr. Cross. And while we haven't met, you basically work for me. Well, you work for someone who works for someone who works for me. Add another five or six steps to that chain of command, and you start to get the idea. I have good news and bad news. The bad news is, the Vandemere Lodge is dangerously close to being considered a liability. And you know how we resolve liabilities."

"But it wasn't our fault!" Scottie said. "We had nothing to do with the place in Bed-Stuy—our lodge handles storage and distribution, period."

"Life isn't fair," Savannah said. "Neither is the Network. The *good* news is that I have a way for you to become very, very essential to our operations. Namely, by becoming essential to me, personally."

Richard squinted at her. "What do you need?"

"For starters..."

Savannah plucked an eyeball from her pocket.

It sat nestled in the palm of her hand, dry and encrusted with scarlet. A ragged string of optic nerve, gnawed off at the tip, dangled between her fingers. She flicked the eye with her other hand. The air above it began to simmer, rippling like a heat mirage. She murmured an incantation under her breath.

Scottie bumped against the desk as he took a halting step backward. "What are you, some kind of witch?"

She glared at him. "I am a *scientist*. Pay attention."

The mirage took form, becoming an image. A faded, sepia-tone memory, frozen in time. A woman's face.

"Her name is Marie Reinhart. A police detective. I want her."

Richard wagged his finger at the image. He walked around it, slow, studying it from every angle.

"I know her," he said. "I've *met* her."

Savannah's eyes lit up. "You have? When?"

"Back when this whole mess started, when we lost the stash house out in Monticello. She and her partner came to my house to question me about it. I got rid of her, it wasn't a big deal." He frowned at the image. "Still. It was weird."

"Weird?"

"Yeah, her and my wife, they seemed to...know each other? I mean, I asked her and she *said* they'd never met, but something was going on there."

Savannah reached into the image. Marie's face rippled as the doctor stroked her fingers against the woman's cheek.

"Tell me," she said, "all about your wife."

*   *   *

At that moment, Nessa was only four blocks away, sitting in a stiff-backed chair. She eyed a picture of wildflowers as Dr. Robinson took a seat behind her desk. The psychiatrist was in her fifties, her black hair streaked with natural gray, and she had an easy, sonorous voice. The kind of voice made for reading bedtime stories.

"If I understand correctly, Ms. Fieri, this appointment wasn't for you?"

"Right," Nessa told her. "I just need some advice. A...friend of mine is in treatment, and I'm concerned that she might be misdiagnosed. Her medication really doesn't seem to be helping her—"

Robinson held up a hand. "I have to stop you right there. If your friend is one of my patients, I can't possibly comment on her treatment. It's both unethical and illegal."

"No, totally different doctor. That's why I chose you. I need a neutral opinion. Part of the problem is that she's taking Seroquel—"

"She's bipolar?"

"That's what her diagnosis says."

The doctor rubbed her chin. "Go on."

Nessa opened her purse, a thin Gucci handbag with a silver chain strap, and fished out one of her pills.

"I went on the Internet, and these pills don't look like what Seroquel is supposed to look like. At all. Is there some kind of laboratory test I can have done to make sure she's getting the right medication?"

The doctor smiled and held out her open palm.

"Nothing so complicated. Pill designs are proprietary. All I have to do is enter the shape, color, and imprint in a database, and in fifteen seconds we'll know exactly what your friend is taking. I'm sure there's nothing to worry about."

Nessa passed her the pill. Robinson set it on her blotter, typed, then froze. She stared at her screen. Then she checked the pill again, holding it close to her glasses and squinting at the faded imprint.

"Doctor?"

"Hold on," she murmured, typing. "I must have gotten that wrong."

Robinson's genial expression faded as she read the screen. She looked across the desk at Nessa, grave.

"Where did you get this?"

"I—I told you, it's my friend's prescription—"

"No," the doctor said. "It isn't. I can tell you with one hundred percent certainty that this did not come from a pharmacy."

"It didn't," Nessa stammered. "I mean, they have an under-the-table thing with her psychiatrist. My friend comes from a wealthy family, and there are politics involved, so they don't want anyone knowing she's in treatment."

Robinson held up the tiny lozenge.

"Ms. Fieri, this is Preloquil."

Nessa shook her head. "I don't know what that is."

"It's a sedative. Intended to be taken before bedtime, as an occasional sleeping aid."

Robinson set the pill on her blotter. Nessa stared at it, her lips parting as an icy, trembling chill trickled down her spine. It spread to her arms, her legs, freezing her in her chair.

"It's a tranquilizer? My...my friend has been taking sedatives? All day? *Every* day?"

"Preloquil was pulled from the market over a year ago. Its FDA approval was revoked."

"So this..." Nessa pointed at the pill. "This isn't for treating bipolar disorder. At all."

Robinson shook her head. "The situation is a little more serious than that, Ms. Fieri. Preloquil was designed as a supplement to a regimen of anti-psychotic medication, in case patients suffered from sleeplessness as a side effect. It tested well, initially."

"Initially," Nessa echoed. Her own voice sounded a thousand miles away.

"You have to understand that there's no such thing as a one-size-fits-all treatment. Psychiatric medications, when they're properly prescribed as part of a regimen of care, can enable people to live healthy, active lives—"

"Doctor? Why was it pulled from the market?"

"There were unforeseen consequences. Some people were taking it against recommendation, as a long term and stand-alone sleep aid. Used *that* way, over a long enough time period, Preloquil caused permanent damage to the serotonin levels in their brains."

"Brain damage," Nessa said. "This drug. It gave them brain damage."

"Not everyone who took it. But, yes, there were cases where otherwise-healthy people manifested symptoms of severe clinical depression, related to their reduced serotonin uptake. There were a number of suicides."

Nessa stared at the pill, so small, so innocent-looking, as her world caved in around her.

"Suicide," she breathed. She struggled to force the words out, her mind racing, storm-tossed. "So. If you wanted someone to be...permanently sedated. To shut them up. If you—if you wanted to give them brain damage, or make them *kill* themselves—"

"Ms. Fieri, please. If someone is giving this to people and misrepresenting it, they're committing a serious criminal act. Do you know this doctor's name?"

"I know his name," Nessa whispered, her eyes misty and her voice jagged. "I know her *husband's* name."

Robinson reached for the phone on her desk, watching, uncertain.

"I think you should sit here with me," she said, "so we can help your 'friend' together, all right? Let's talk to the authorities, you and me, and tell them what happened. Everything is going to be just fine."

Nessa's anguish spiraled inside her chest, a tornado of self-loathing and betrayal and fear and hurt, building until her blood roared in her ears and she thought she might burst.

Then the light shone through. A moment of calm and beautiful clarity.

She wiped at her eyes, sniffed once, and smiled.

"Thank you, Dr. Robinson, but that won't be necessary."

Robinson paused with her hand on the phone. Frozen, as if she physically couldn't push the buttons.

"Ms. Fieri?"

Nessa stood, graceful and serene.

"I have been—I have *allowed* myself to be—lied to, betrayed, used. Treated like an object. Walked on. It ends today. It all ends today."

"What—" The doctor swallowed hard, her hand still frozen in place. "What are you going to do?"

"I'm going to stop being meek," Nessa said. "And I'm going to stop being nice. I'm going to be...me."

Forty-Three

Nessa returned to Inwood Hill.

She found her sanctuary on the tip of the park, her secluded grove by the tree line. She placed the stone pentacle before her and piled it with her mound of beechnut offerings. Her book sat open on her lap, pages turned to "The Game of Finding a Guide." She traced the tangled incantation with the tip of her white-handled knife as she chanted. Each word was a firm call, the spidery syllables winding up to the trees and demanding the universe respond.

The underbrush rustled. The doe emerged, timid, glancing between her and the beechnuts.

Nessa stood. She pointed at the doe with her knife.

"Come here," she said, her voice like razor-edged steel in a velvet jacket. "Come to me. *Now.*"

The doe bowed her head and obeyed, trotting across the dew-damp grass. She nestled right up to her. Nessa stroked her fur, soft and downy under her fingertips, and the doe's deep chocolate eyes gazed up at her.

"I didn't understand," Nessa whispered. "Not until now. You were never my guide."

She giggled. She couldn't help it.

"How could you teach me anything at all?" she asked the doe. "You're *me.*"

The doe trembled under her hand. Nessa understood. She

understood what it meant to live like prey. She understood how it felt to be meek and afraid every single day of her life. She knew how it felt to cringe and apologize instead of standing up for herself. It was wretched to be told by everyone around her that she was strange, unwanted, weak. It was worse to believe it.

Storm clouds passed in front of the sun. The light faded. Darker than it should have been, eclipse-dark, plunging the park into twilight. A strong, cold wind rippled along the wet grass. The trees quivered.

"You were never my guide," Nessa said.

Nessa lifted her head. She looked up to the trees.

A horned owl perched at the edge of a gnarled branch. It gazed down at her with eyes so vast they could swallow the world. Stars shone in their black depths.

"You were my sacrifice."

She slashed her blade across the doe's throat.

The doe kicked and bleated. Hot blood gushed down Nessa's blouse, soaking her sleeves, staining her hands scarlet as she wrapped her arms around the dying beast and held her close. She knelt, pulled down by the doe's weight, gently bringing her to the grass while she whispered in her twitching ear. Nessa thanked her. As the doe kicked one final hoof, the light dying in her eyes, she whispered goodbye.

Nessa rose.

She held out her arms. Her body was drenched in blood, hot and sticky and smelling of dirty copper. She looked up to the trees. The owl tilted its head, locking eyes with her, and she smiled. She saw herself reflected in the depths. Carved from darkness and starlight.

"The doe is dead," Nessa told it. "Call me...the Owl."

The owl unfurled its wings, wide and powerful, as it hurled itself from the branch. It plunged down, razor talons grasping, and landed upon Nessa's left arm. She felt the talons biting into her skin, drawing blood. She savored the pain. It made her feel alive. She laughed, and her laugh became a full-throated cackle, a wild, raw cry of freedom.

At her feet, the spell book was changing.

The pages beyond "The Game of Finding a Guide," fully half of the book, had been a twisted and impossible cypher. *To the true witch,* read the final legible words, *the means to understand are given. Once you have found your Guide, all will be made apparent.*

The ink swirled upon the page. The cypher broke apart and the fractal symbols became letters, the letters became words. Now a new message waited for her.

Welcome, Nessa. I knew you would succeed.

Don't look so surprised. I wrote this book just for you!

We will meet when the time is right. For now, though...

...don't you think you deserve a reward?

There's a new game on the very next page, and I think you'll enjoy playing it.

Nessa crouched and turned the page. She and the owl read the words, studied the magical seals. She broke into a grin.

"Yes," Nessa whispered.

She gathered up the book and strode through the park.

There was no dead doe on the grass behind her. No horned owl perched on her arm. No hot blood spatter clung to her clothes or her face or her hands. She still felt it all, though, and she smelled the blood with every breath she took.

It smelled like magic.

Interlude

All through Carolyn's story, the interrogator took notes. A yellow legal pad sat at his right hand, a mechanical pencil in his steady grip. Across the brushed-steel table, under the hot dangling light, Carolyn Saunders watched him write out a question. Then he double-underlined it. The pencil slashed across the page like a knife.

"You seem agitated," she said.

His hooked nose wrinkled.

"There are certain details we weren't aware of. These three witches, interfering from a distance. The Lady in Red, the Mourner, this 'Dora'...I assume one of them was the author of Ms. Roth's spell book?"

"If *I* was writing the story, that would be the case. I mean, it fits, given how they were shaping Nessa's evolution and pulling strings from the shadows. Also, there's the whole economy-of-characters thing. But there are, sad to say, certain unavoidable truths in play."

"Such as?"

Carolyn shrugged. "First of all, have you *read* my novels? I'm a total hack. But more to the point, reality is always messier than fiction, and there was more than one hand manipulating things behind the scenes. Trying to, anyway. If they'd had any idea what kind of nightmare they'd unleash, once Nessa was finally pushed that last, lethal inch...well. They might have hesitated."

He rapped his pencil against the pad.

"But these witches."

The crow's-feet at the corners of Carolyn's eyes crinkled. "You had no idea, did you? The Network, with all its power and a thousand eyes, vaunted puppet masters—"

"I said we would know if you lied to us."

"And am I lying?" Carolyn asked. Her voice lightly teasing, almost playful.

The interrogator glowered. "No. But there's a difference between a lie and an incomplete truth."

"Dora's task was done," Carolyn said. "The Oberlin Glass was in the mail, cross-country, on its way to Nessa's doorstep. Meanwhile, the Lady in Red was moving her pieces onto the board. Setting Harmony Black and her team on a collision course with Marie. That wouldn't be important until much later, but it'd make all the difference in the end. She was playing the long game, as she always does, and she had covert operatives on the ground in New York. Her servants are few, in this day and age, but devoted."

"Who *is* the Lady in Red?"

Carolyn smiled, silent for a moment.

"The Mourner," she said, "had her own operative in motion. Daniel Faust had been combing the streets of Hollywood on the trail of celebrity-chef-slash-cannibal Andre Lefevre and his Cutting Knife."

"Lefevre," the interrogator said. "He disappeared around that time, as I recall."

Carolyn lifted her eyebrows, her voice bone-dry. "Ah, Andre. You know, I hear he was a man of exceptional taste. Anyway, while that was going on, Marie and her partner were reeling—like their entire city was—from the massacre in Bed-Stuy. Trying to find their footing. More importantly, trying to find the culprit who leaked the news about the police raid and set those officers up to be killed. And Nessa...was finding herself. She'd just crossed a threshold that could never be uncrossed. And she was preparing to cross another."

He narrowed his eyes at her. "That being?"

"Blood will have blood, they say." She leaned back in her chair and spread her hands as far as her cuffs would allow. "Blood will have blood."

Forty-Four

Nessa needed to buy a few things.

She haunted the antique shops in SoHo until she found the perfect pieces. Vintage fabric, an antique needle, thread, and a heavy brass skeleton key. That last was for the "Game of Crossing the Boundaries," one of the new pages in her book. In her workroom, she drew a circle of chalk around the key and a hexagon around the circle, etching seals and symbols as she whispered a fervent chant.

Then she sat in a coffee shop across the street from Dr. Neidermyer's building, waiting for him to go to lunch.

She bit back a surge of fury when she spotted his insipid, smiling face. Her anger rose like hot bile in her throat. She forced herself to hold it down, to breathe deep, to bide her time. She watched him trundle up the sidewalk, out of sight in the downtown crowds, and then she crossed the street.

She took the elevator up and stood at his office door. She'd brought her own way to get inside. The antique brass key tingled against her fingers as she touched it to the lock.

"No man's design will bar my path," Nessa recited under her breath. "No locks, no wards, no hopes, no dreams. I am the shadow behind your back, the whisper in your ear. I am the night wind. I am inevitable consequence."

The skeleton key slid inside the lock, fitting impossibly, perfectly.

"Surrender to me."

The key turned. The lock clicked.

She let herself in.

Nessa's stomach clenched. There was the couch she'd spent hours on, the desk, the chair where Neidermyer sat and pretended to treat her and fed her bottle after bottle of poison. All patience and fatherly wisdom as he slowly murdered her.

And there was his wastebasket. Filled, as usual, with used tissues thanks to his allergies. She picked the crusted tissues out, gripping the edges between thumb and forefinger, and dropped them into a plastic baggie. He'd been cutting his nails in the office; there were fingernail clippings at the bottom of the waste bin. She took those, too.

A few wispy strands of hair clung to the fabric of his chair. She plucked them one by one, adding them to the collection. Then she left and locked the door behind her.

Back at home, safe in her workroom, she laid out her sewing supplies and the vintage calico fabric. She began to cut, to stitch, shaping the outline of a poppet. At her side, her phone lit up.

Marie's voice, tired as it was, felt like a caress. "Hey. Sorry to call, I just...well, I just needed to hear your voice."

"Hey yourself." Nessa tucked her legs beneath her, shifting as she sat on the workroom floor. "Are you okay? You sound exhausted."

"Long day. Are we still on for tonight?"

"Oh, yes." Nessa's lips curled into a hungry smile. "We certainly are."

"I might be a little late. Work is kind of crazy right now."

"That's fine," she said. "Keep me updated. I have something special planned, and the timing has to be just right."

Marie chuckled. "Something special, huh? Should I be excited or afraid?"

"Both, I think. I'll see you soon."

*   *   *

The mood at the precinct was somber. Driven. Phones rang out over the din of low, terse conversations and clacking keyboards. Captain Traynor poked his head out of his office.

"Fisher? Reinhart? In here."

Tony and Marie stepped into his office while he lowered the blinds over his windows. Marie shut the door.

"Lock it," he told her.

They stood, uneasy, as he circled his desk.

"We've got a rat in our house."

"Sir?" Marie said.

"The death toll from the Bed-Stuy raid is up to nine. Flannery died on the operating table twenty minutes ago."

The detectives bowed their heads, a moment of silence for the fallen. Most of the cops who died in the raid were from the Emergency Service Unit, but they had a few empty desks in the squad room today. Flannery's was right next to Marie's.

"Every door to that warehouse was trapped with white phosphorus bombs," Traynor told them, "rigged to blow on a breach attempt. They stationed shooters across the street to stage an ambush. They knew we were coming. Someone talked."

"Sir," Tony said, "with all due respect, we weren't the only people involved. ESU headed things up—"

"And they didn't know who they were hitting until fifteen minutes before the raid. Same with the medical and fire teams on standby. That ambush took time to set up. The way I see it, the only way it could have happened is if someone right here, in our house, called to warn the dealers before we got there."

The captain slid a sheet of paper across his desk. A list of names in stark black type.

"Everyone who knew. Twelve names, not including the three of us."

Marie leaned in. Her eyes widened as she read the list.

"Sir, these...these are solid cops. Nobody on this list has less than five years on the job; most of them have at least a decade. I'd trust every one of these people to have my back."

"And one's a real good liar," Traynor said. "I'll be blunt: the only reason you two aren't on the list is because you found the place and brought me the intel. Wouldn't make sense for you to sabotage the raid you set the stage for in the first place."

"So you want us to sniff around, see if we can dig up a lead?" Tony asked.

Traynor sat down behind his desk. His gaze went distant, fixed on the closed blinds. The muffled din of the bullpen drifted through the glass.

"I don't know what I want you to do. IAB's already on it. They're going to put every last one of us under a microscope, but..."

Marie nodded. "It's a problem in our house. You want it fixed in our house."

"Do what you can," he said.

*   *   *

They left the precinct. There wasn't anything to be done in the grim and dusty squad room, and they couldn't discuss Traynor's unofficial orders in earshot of anyone they knew. Tony and Marie ended up at a fast-food place two blocks down. They ate in the car, reading the list of names over a couple of greasy hockey-puck hamburgers.

"I don't like anyone for this," Marie said. She slurped Coke through a fat straw and gestured at the page. "Evans? Gorski? *Jefferson?* Jefferson's a giant puppy."

"I don't see it either, but the cap's right. They knew we were coming. That's a fact."

"I know it's true," she said, sullen. "I just don't want it to be."

Her phone buzzed. She glanced down at the screen.

"ME's office," she said to Tony. She put the phone to her ear. "Reinhart."

"Detective," the medical examiner said, "I finished the autopsy, and...well, I really hate to say this, but you were onto something."

Marie sat up straight, her spine going stiff.

"Baby Blue? Her body was cannibalized?"

"I wouldn't say cannibalized, per se, but there are unquestionably bite marks. Most of them are covered up by the other forms of trauma, and I wouldn't have noticed them unless I was looking. One bite mark in particular is a standout, though. Lower calf, left leg, *deep*. And yes, the bite is human."

"How clear is the impression?" she asked.

"Oh, it's a beauty. I'm photographing it right now. You find some dental records and I can play matchmaker."

She thanked him and got off the phone. Tony eyed her over his half-eaten burger.

"You got good news?"

"We've got a bite mark," Marie said. "One they can ID if we find a match."

He shrugged. "Not much to go on."

"The DA can subpoena dental records, can't he?"

He set his burger down.

"Don't say it."

"Everything keeps coming back to Richard Roth. His company was linked to the stash house in Monticello. That Five Families hitter was scooped off the sidewalk right by another one of his properties. Roth is connected to the ink cartel, and the cartel is connected to the murders."

"Nothing you just said is wrong." He sipped his soda. "And nothing you just said is proof. No chance in hell a DA's gonna go after somebody's medical records on what pretty much amounts to a hunch. Besides, didn't you say we're looking for multiple killers now, like some kinda cult thing? Even if Roth was there, anybody could have taken that bite."

Marie sighed. She slumped in her seat. Another turn in the labyrinth, another dead end.

"You know," Tony said, "when I moved up to detective, I had a mentor. Day one, he gave me the best advice I ever got."

"What's that?"

"Never have a horse in the race. The second you decide you *want* somebody to be guilty is the second you'll start cherry-picking the facts to fit your theory of the crime. And all the other facts, and the real perp, will skate right on by."

"You think I want him to be guilty?"

"I don't know. You tell me." Tony shook his head and took a bite of his burger. "You've been weird about the guy since we met him. I don't know why you'd have a personal grudge, but you're acting like you want him gone."

Her gaze dropped. She stared at her food.

"I just want the truth," she said.

"So we'll go get it. I'm not saying Richard Roth is innocent. I'm saying he's powerful, he's rich, and he's connected, so we gotta play it smart. Take a shot at a guy like that, you better not miss. Tell you one thing I know for sure."

"Yeah?" Marie asked.

"People are capable of some truly sick, heinous shit." Tony swished his straw around, stirring the ice in his paper cup. "And the more virtuous and squeaky-clean they look on the outside, the deeper and darker those waters tend to run."

Forty-Five

The kid went flying over the padded leather bench. His tray crashed to the ground, tattoo needles skidding across the grimy parlor floor. Daniel Faust grabbed him by the front of his tank top and hauled him to his knees. He cocked his fist back.

"You want to rethink your position?" he asked. "You know, I tried asking nice."

The kid looked up at him, dazed, his lip split. Fresh blood glazed his chin.

"Man, I *can't*. Those people are crazy. They'll freakin' kill me if I rat 'em out."

Daniel shoved him to the floor. Then he snatched up a tattoo gun, dropped his knee on the kid's chest, and started it up. The needle whirred, sharp and gleaming.

"I've been chasing leads and knocking down doors for a day and a half. My feet are tired. My knuckles? Also tired. So are you going to tell me where I can find the Hollywood Gourmands' Society, or do I have to use your face as a canvas? Before you decide, understand this: I am *not* an artist."

"Okay, okay!" His eyes bulged as the needle hovered over his forehead. "It's on Burbank! Little hole-in-the-wall butcher's shop, no name on the place. The door's in the back."

Daniel shut the gun off and tossed it aside. He patted the kid on the cheek.

"Thank you. Was that so hard? Next time, try cooperation. It hurts less."

Standing up, Daniel adjusted the lapels of his jacket. Then he dug in his wallet for a pair of rumpled twenties.

"For the info," he said. "Now forget I was here."

He tossed the money onto the padded bench and walked out the door.

The spot wasn't hard to find. The blue neon outline of a cow hung over the shoebox-sized butcher's market. He strolled through the icy shop without a word to the stone-faced workers behind the counter, right past the glass displays and dangling sides of beef, and pushed through the swinging back door like he'd done it a hundred times before. A tiny vestibule lay beyond, and a second door: this one made of reinforced steel with a sliding metal window about six inches wide at eye level.

He knocked. The window slid open. He held up the card he'd taken from Lefevre's condo, with *Admit One* stamped on the back.

The door swung wide. A waiter in classic black, with an ivory towel over one crisp sleeve, welcomed him inside with a regal sweep of his hand.

It was a restaurant, big enough for maybe two dozen people, draped in red velvet and lit by candlelight. Couples in suits and evening gowns chatted over plates of meat. Their stainless-steel knives sawed into rare cutlets and medallions, served up in strange, lumpy scarlet broths. A woman in a silk halter dress dabbed a cloth napkin at a smear of red on her lips, while her dining companion picked his teeth with a splinter of bone. Soft chamber music drifted across the room, along with an aroma—a floral perfume with a chemical tang—that strained to conceal the odor of offal and blood.

The waiter escorted Daniel to a tiny table off to one side of the room, a two-seater with a lit candle and a menu on crisp parchment for his approval. Nothing on the wine list had a price. Then again, from the vintages he recognized, this was very much a "if you have to ask, you can't afford it" kind of place.

The meal offerings were even less helpful. It was a short list, nothing described, with names like The Third Forbidden Thing, It Still Has Breath, and Flower of Her Regard. This place had its own tribe, its own customs, its own shared language. And they ate outsiders. Outsiders like him.

The waiter hovered, fixing him with an expectant stare.

One item on the list had an annotation: "*prepared tableside by our resident chef." Daniel tapped the menu. "Let's go with...the Forest of Old Desires."

"A challenging dish, sir. And the accompaniment?"

Daniel picked a random item on the wine list, poking his finger at it as he asked a question with his eyes. The waiter frowned, just a bit, and gave a tiny headshake. Daniel slid his finger down to the next wine on the list. The waiter smiled.

"*Very* good choice, sir. Chef Lefevre will be out to greet you shortly."

"Great, and, ah"—he lowered his voice—"is there a washroom?"

The waiter pointed toward the back of the restaurant. "Of course, sir. Just back there, up the short hallway, past the kitchen doors."

"Perfect," Daniel said.

He lingered outside the washroom, using the stub of a hall as cover, and watched the kitchen. He knew Andre Lefevre's face from television. The portly man, his yellow-inked hair worn in slick rooster spikes, merrily rolled out a cart bearing a scattering of knives and a serving dish under a silver dome. His tableside service. Daniel slipped behind his back and into the kitchen.

The kitchen wouldn't have passed a health inspection in hell. Hard electric lights shone down on grimy, yellowed tile, one short wall dominated by a bank of industrial refrigerators. A soup, like a green, oily curry, bubbled in a tall pot on the burner by the door. Daniel walked past it, smelling rich and hearty spices on the steam—then his stomach clenched as he noticed the long black hairs floating on the surface. He turned his attention to the heart of the kitchen and wished he hadn't.

Two corpses, a man and a woman, were laid out on a marble-topped slab side by side and in opposite directions. Heads and feet aligned like puzzle pieces on the stone. They were in the process of yielding up their mysteries to the chef's knife. Chests and genitals opened, ribs cracked and cut away, choice bits already scooped out to roast in the oven or simmer in a stewpot.

There, resting beside the woman's pale and eyeless face, was the prize. Lefevre's Cutting Knife looked exactly like the one in the Mourner's vision. Its wooden handle was cracked and wound with black electrical tape, the dull blade pitted with rust. Daniel snatched it up, wiped it down with a grease-spattered towel, and slipped it into his breast pocket.

He turned just as Lefevre and the waiter stormed through the kitchen doors. They didn't look happy.

"I'm a big fan," Daniel said. "*Love* your TV show."

The chef's gaze shot to the empty spot on the slab, then back to Daniel.

"Also I'm taking your knife," Daniel added. "Sorry. A witch needs it. She lives in a cave, makes people drink tea—y'know, it's really a long and complicated story and I should probably let you get back to work."

"You want a knife, huh?"

Steel rasped against wood as Lefevre slowly drew a fillet knife from a block. The waiter picked up a meat cleaver and circled the slab, moving around to cut Daniel off from the other side.

"Got your knife right here," Lefevre said with a smile. Then he lunged, faster than he looked, spearing the air as Daniel jumped back. Daniel snatched up an iron skillet. The fillet knife jabbed in again and clanged off black iron. Then the waiter raised his cleaver high and charged. Daniel hurled the skillet. It hit Lefevre in the chest, staggering him back and buying Daniel a few seconds to breathe. He turned as the cleaver came swooping down.

Daniel shot his hands up, grabbed the waiter by the wrist, and twisted hard to yank him close and off-balance. Then he slammed his forehead into the bridge of the waiter's nose. The waiter howled as cartilage shattered, hot blood spattering across Daniel's face. The cleaver fell from his grip and clattered on the grimy floor.

Lefevre ran in. The fillet knife lanced across Daniel's shoulder, shredding his suit coat and slicing skin. The wound burned like lit gasoline, but he didn't have time to feel it. Daniel threw a brutal elbow into the waiter's face. His front teeth broke on impact and he dropped, out cold. Then Daniel jumped to the side as Lefevre came at him again. The tip of the fillet knife snapped at his face, missing by an inch.

Daniel leaped onto the slab, clambering over the half-dissected corpses as Lefevre scrambled around the island. The chef was on his heels, bringing back the fillet knife for a lethal slice—and Daniel grabbed the soup pot from the stove and spun on the ball of his foot. A wave of boiling broth splashed into Lefevre's face. The chef shrieked, dropping his knife and clutching at his eyes. Daniel hit him with the empty pot. Then he did it again, forcing Lefevre to his knees as his skull fractured under the stainless steel. And again.

Lefevre twitched like a gutted fish at his feet. Daniel picked up the fallen fillet knife and yanked the chef's head back. Then he forced Lefevre's chin up to bare his throat and finished the job with one quick slice. He tossed the blade aside.

"*Fuck,*" Daniel panted, clutching his burning shoulder, "*you. Seriously.*"

He leaned against the bank of steel refrigerators and caught his breath. Blood trickled down his arm and his back, plastering his dress shirt to his skin. He gently tugged the ripped shoulder of his jacket, eyeing the wound beneath, and winced. Seeing it just made it hurt more.

"Yeah," he muttered to himself, a pulled muscle flaring in his hip as he stumbled to the kitchen doors, "that's probably gonna need stitches."

He pushed his way out through the swinging door and froze.

The entire restaurant was waiting for him. Maybe a dozen people in all, between the waiters and the diners in fancy dress, one big happy cannibal clan. Their hungry eyes glinted in the candlelight, shimmering faintly turquoise. They spread out in a ragged semicircle. Most of them clutched forks and steak knives, looking eager to dig in.

"Okay," Daniel said, nodding to himself. "So, we're doing this."

He opened his hand. His deck of cards launched from his hip pocket in a flurry of pasteboard. The cards riffled into his palm and crackled with anticipation.

*   *   *

Daniel shoved his shoulder against the motel room door and staggered inside. He made it five feet, fell face-first onto the lumpy mattress, and decided to stay that way forever.

Pipes rattled behind the motel wall. His shower turned itself on.

He ignored it. The pipes rattled louder.

"God, *what?*" he grunted, shoving himself off the bed. He shambled into the closet-sized bathroom, the stale air hot and muggy with shower steam. He saw his ghost in the fogged mirror, a disheveled train wreck in a torn and blood-spattered suit.

The Mourner stood at his shoulder. Her ivory veils rippled.

He spun around. Nobody there. Her rasping chuckle drifted from the mirror.

"Were you successful?" she asked him, her slithering voice eager. "Do you have the Cutting Knife?"

"Yeah, I got it. It looks like a piece of crap, just like you showed me. *I'm* fine, by the way, thanks for asking."

"I am pleased you did not die."

He stared at her image. "That's it, huh? That's all I'm gonna get?"

"Return the knife to me at once. I'll have a second task for you once you arrive."

"Are you...have you *seen* me? Is this a one-way mirror? I just need a few hours of shut-eye—"

"Three hours. Then return. I must prepare the knife for its new wielder."

He couldn't see her face—no one ever had and lived—but somehow Daniel knew she was smiling.

"She is about to spread her wings," the Mourner hissed. "And blood her talons. A momentous night."

Forty-Six

It was time for Nessa's appointment.

She didn't take the couch this time. She sat in the chair across from Dr. Neidermyer, her handbag in her lap, hands resting primly on the silver chain.

On her way in, as she shut the office door, she flipped the lock.

"Thank you for seeing me on such short notice, and after your regular hours," she told him.

Neidermyer held up a hand, turned his head to sneeze into a tissue, then tossed it into his wastebasket.

"You should be careful with that," she said.

"Honestly, it's no problem, Vanessa. You're a very important patient—and careful with what?"

She flashed a toothy smile.

"Leaving your bodily fluids laying around like that. You know, back in the olden days, people kept close watch over their hair and nail clippings because they believed such things were still connected, in a supernatural sense, to their own bodies. They feared that witches might steal them. They might use them in their wicked spells, and do terrible, terrible things."

Neidermyer gave an awkward chuckle. "Well, I...I suppose it's good that we live in the twenty-first century, and we know that witches aren't real."

"I suppose so," Nessa replied.

"So, you wanted to discuss your medication? How's the new dosage working out?"

"Oh, it's wonderful," she said. "There's just one problem."

She opened her purse and reached inside. The plastic pill bottle rattled as she set it on the desk between them.

"It appears that instead of medication to treat bipolar disorder, you've been giving me tranquilizers linked to brain damage, depression, and suicide. You're a respected professional, Dr. Neidermyer. Such an odd mistake to make."

He swallowed. Hard. His gaze flicked from her to the bottle and back again.

"Vanessa, before you do anything rash, let's talk about this."

"Oh, I *absolutely* want to talk about it."

She reached into her purse and pulled out a gun. The barrel of the .38 revolver glinted as she casually leveled it at the doctor's face.

"Look at that. My husband's gun somehow fell into my purse." Nessa shook her head. "We're both making such odd mistakes today."

He squirmed, backing up into his chair like he thought he could wriggle through to the other side.

"It wasn't my idea," he squeaked. "Vanessa, please—"

"As much as I enjoy hearing you beg for mercy, is that really how you want to spend your final breaths?"

"It was Richard. He came to me. Put me up to it. He—he paid me to do it."

"Why?" Nessa asked, pinning him under her dour gaze.

"A d-divorce would look bad. He has his family reputation to think of. His father's political ambitions. Couldn't take any chances. He wanted to get rid of you in a way that would make him look...sympathetic."

"So the two of you schemed to gaslight me into killing myself."

"That or..." He swallowed, ducking his head down.

Nessa thumbed back the hammer on the gun. "Or?"

"Worst-case scenario, at least you'd be..."

"Zombified? Trapped in a perpetual stupor? Asleep with my eyes open?"

"Quiet," he said. "So you wouldn't embarrass him."

Nessa stared at him over the barrel of the gun. Her lips curled in a blood-hungry smile.

"I'm not really sick, am I?"

He gave a tiny headshake.

"You're not bipolar," he said. "You do show some depressive tendencies—"

"Which after being on Preloquil for a year, could have been caused *by* the pills, or so I'm told. What else, Doctor? This is our first and only truly honest session together. *Diagnose* me."

"I...I did a write-up for your husband, when I started seeing you. I—" He squirmed deeper into his chair. "Please don't make me do this."

Nessa's gaze flicked to the bubble-domed clock on the wall.

"It's after five on a Friday, Doctor. Most of this building's gone home. Won't be back until Monday. Nobody's going to hear a gunshot. Nobody's going to check on you. You could bleed for a long, long time."

"All right." His hand fluttered. "All right. *Fine.* I told him that your behavior, possibly due to factors of your upbringing, was extremely repressed. That you showed traces of avoidant personality disorder—showing severe inhibition and social anxiety. That you are also...sexually inhibited—"

"Ooh," Nessa said. "Now we get to the juicy parts. Do go on."

"And that you also showed signs of latent and repressed"—he shut his eyes—"sadistic tendencies."

Nessa studied him like a bug under a magnifying glass.

"I'm not a medical professional like you, Doctor," she said, "so let me be sure I understand. Sadism. That means I like to hurt people, doesn't it?"

"It's...it's not classified as a formal disorder anymore. It was rremoved from the DSM because it's largely considered a personality quirk or a sexual—"

She cut him off with an amused chuckle. "Back to sex again. Goodness, it's positively Freudian in here. Here's a question, Dr. Neidermyer: if I get off on inflicting pain...how much trouble are *you* in right now?"

"I'll turn myself in," he said. "I kept records. I can prove what Richard did, what he paid me for. I'll make a full confession."

"I've got a better idea. I think you need a taste of your own medicine."

Nessa nodded at the pill bottle between them.

"Eat one."

He picked up the bottle with trembling hands, shaking out a pill, almost dropping it. He put it between his lips and dry-swallowed it down.

"Another," she told him.

As soon as he put it on his tongue, she raised the gun, aiming right between his eyes.

"Chew it," she said. He froze. She inched forward in her chair, bringing the gun closer. "*Chew it.*"

He chewed the lozenge, wincing as it broke between his teeth.

"Now swallow. Good. Have a third."

"Nessa," he croaked, chewing the third pill as his eyes began to water, "don't do this. Don't shoot me. *Please.*"

Nessa snickered. "Shoot you? How would I do that, Doctor? I don't even have a gun."

He stared at her hand.

There was no gun. Instead, she cradled a poppet of vintage cloth, a crude doll in the shape of a man, stuffed with tissue. Elaborate sigils had been stitched into the fabric, and twists of black thread spelled out his name.

"Are you hallucinating, Doctor? Seeing things that aren't there? Goodness, it looks like you might be suffering from a psychotic break."

"How did you—" He paused, suddenly choking, his next cough guttering out ragged and hoarse. He put his fingers to his mouth. They came away sticky and wet.

"You must have felt so horribly guilty about what you did to me," Nessa said lightly. "I mean, I can only imagine the anguish that drove you to such a cruel method of suicide."

He followed her gaze, down to the desk blotter between them. To his fingertips, sliced and bleeding, one nail hacked halfway off and dangling from its roots by a strand. And to the pill bottle.

It wasn't a pill bottle. It was a tiny wicker basket.

A basket filled with razor blades.

Nessa fished a makeup compact from her purse and casually flipped it open, turning it so Neidermyer could see his reflection in the mirror. The glass captured his horrified, bloody face, his sliced lips. The end of a razor blade where it wedged between his scarlet-stained teeth and dug halfway into his gums.

He clutched his throat, choking, and collapsed to the office carpet. Nessa rose from her chair. She hummed to herself as she stepped around the desk and stood over him.

"Such a man of reason, science, and logic," she said. "So modern and free of superstition. You were never afraid of witches, were you? Never once."

Neidermyer choked up a gout of blood, a crimson splash across the thin carpet. He looked up at her, face contorted in agony, struggling to breathe around the razor blade lodged in his throat. Nessa crouched beside him and smiled sweetly.

"But you're afraid now."

He tried to crawl, to push himself up. His arm gave out from under him as he convulsed. Nessa took out her phone and tapped out a quick text: *Can't wait for tonight. Miss you.*

Neidermyer's desperate hand clenched her ankle. She glared down, irritated, and kicked it away.

Just finishing up some paperwork, Marie replied. *Meet for dinner?*

My place, Nessa wrote. *Don't worry. My husband won't be a problem.*

She leaned in and patted Neidermyer on the head.

"Looks like we're at the end of our session," she told him. "This has been *most* enlightening, Doctor, and I feel like I've made a genuine breakthrough."

He let out one last rattling breath and died. His glazed, terrified eyes stared up at her. She glanced into her compact mirror, fluffed her bangs, and snapped it shut.

"No, don't get up," she said. "I'll see myself out."

Forty-Seven

Richard didn't mind that Savannah Cross had taken over his Manhattan offices. She was a lifeline, after all. Keeping him from being considered a liability and—if they played their cards right—offering a chance for him and Scottie to rise up in the Network. For that he could put up with her eccentricity, her manic bursts, her tendency to carry on four conversations at once.

Her "lab assistants," the silent and pale qliphoth, were harder to deal with. The zombies shuffled here and there on unknowable errands. Some hauled in scientific gear and set up strange machinery, while others came and went in total silence. One had spent the last three hours spreading a handful of rice across the polished marble floor, rearranging the grains again and again.

Dr. Cross herself sat behind Richard's desk, her eyes hidden behind the black curve of a virtual reality headset. Her hands, sheathed in latex gloves articulated with wires, snatched at the air.

"By interfacing directly with my servitors," she said, "I can efficiently multitask. I've also patched into your lodge friends' telephones, so I can access cameras and sound while they comb the city for Detective Reinhart. I'm observing twelve different feeds at the moment. They do know that they're only supposed to follow and observe, yes? No direct action until I give the word?"

"Yeah, Scottie's giving them their marching orders, don't worry about it." Richard glanced over his shoulder. "You know one of your, ah, 'servitors' is squatting in the corner and playing with a bag of rice?"

"Of course I do. It's me. I'm all of them."

The qliphoth raised his pale face and gave Richard a lethargic wave before going back to his work.

"That's a warding ritual to keep your office barred against toxic energy," she said. "My equipment is extraordinarily sensitive to cosmic radiation. If we were in *my* lab, I'd have my extra arms and I could do everything directly. I miss my extra arms."

Richard tilted his head. "Okay."

She froze for a moment, frowning at something she saw inside her headset.

"This...is not right. Mr. Roth, are you a magician? Do you actively study the occult?"

"No. I mean, I participate in lodge rituals, but beyond that I never really had a knack for it. Not like Scottie does. You should see what he can do with a—"

"Is your wife?"

He blinked. "Vanessa? Vanessa's on enough tranquilizers to stun a rhino. She doesn't do *anything*. She also doesn't know anything, trust me."

One of the qliphoth, the construction worker in his bright orange safety vest, shambled over. He held up a printout from one of Savannah's machines. It was an overhead shot of the city, black and white, crisscrossed with streaks of neon red and blossoms of flame.

"This is a heat map of dimensional instability," Savannah told him. "Occult residue builds up over time, creating points of stress. Places where the fabric of reality risks a fracture."

"And?" he asked.

"And as of a few hours ago, when this snapshot was taken, your brownstone is one of the most magically active places in New York City. And these fracture marks are *growing*. Something is happening here, Mr. Roth. Something momentous."

"I haven't even been home today," he said. "I've been with you the whole time."

"Has Vanessa?"

He frowned, thinking. He couldn't remember her schedule at the university. It wasn't like he'd ever had a reason to care.

"Mr. Roth," Savannah said, "these energy patterns are very similar to the eruption caused by Marie Reinhart when she was in close proximity to a late-stage ink addict. Suspiciously similar. And given your mention of an apparent connection between the two women...I may need to study your wife."

He shrugged. "Go for it."

"By 'study,'" she said, "I mean 'vivisect.'"

"When you're done with her, can you make it look like a murder?"

She lifted her VR goggles and rested them on her forehead. They locked eyes with each other.

"A murder?"

"Yeah," Richard said. "I'm just thinking 'grief-stricken widower searches for answers' makes a good headline. You have any *idea* how hard I've been trying to get her to kill herself? I'll settle for an unsolved murder if I have to. Just warn me in advance so I can get a rock-solid alibi lined up."

"You do understand what 'vivisection' means, yes? Just to be clear. You realize that I'll be dissecting your wife. While she's alive and conscious. With no anesthetic."

"Your point being?"

She put her headset back on, swiping at the air as she smiled.

"My point being," she said, "you are exactly the kind of assistant I enjoy working with. No sentiment, full efficiency. I was considering subjecting you to the qliphoth process, but you're actually more useful *with* a complete brain."

"Well...thanks." He eased away from the desk.

"I'll be pulling an all-nighter studying this data. You should sleep. You do require sleep at regular intervals to function, I'm assuming?"

"I...yes." Richard took another step backward. "Why wouldn't I?"

"I keep forgetting, you're *outer* circle. There's a surgery to fix that pesky 'sleep' thing and massively amplify your productivity. Very minor, easy to do—well, easy for me—and most of the Network's upward movers have undergone the procedure. It does occasionally result in incurable insanity, but I'm prepared to have you take that risk."

Richard pointed to the double doors. "I'm going to leave now."

She didn't reply. He was already forgotten, another blip in the endless wash of data.

* * *

Richard's keys rattled in the front door of his West Village brownstone. He held his phone tucked against his shoulder as he let himself in.

"I'm serious, Scottie, I'm not sure if we're better off with this nutcase. Almost thinking we should take our chances on our own and hope that—"

He paused on the threshold. His .38 revolver, the one he kept in his nightstand, was sitting on the credenza by the door.

"I gotta call you back."

He hung up and shut the door. Then he picked up the gun. He tilted it, squinting, like it was an artifact from another world. He hadn't taken it from the nightstand in months. There was no reason for it to be down here at all, let alone sitting out in the open.

"Vanessa?" he called out. "Are you home?"

"In the dining room," she said.

He walked a few feet up the hall and stood in the open archway. Nessa stood there, waiting, utterly casual. She'd changed into a black turtleneck sweater and matching jeans, her lips adorned in that plum lipstick he hated, and a jaunty beret perched on her head.

"What are you wearing?" he said. "You look like a fucking art-school student."

"I'll be wearing what I like from now on, Richard. It's part of my new regimen of therapy."

"New? What do you mean new?"

"Oh, I'm done with Dr. Neidermyer." She chuckled, one of her arms swaying at her side like a reed in the wind. "*Life* is done with Dr. Neidermyer. He told me everything, by the way. Before I graciously allowed him to die."

Richard's grip tightened on the revolver.

"You stole from me." Her voice became a razor carved from ice. "You stole years of my life. You stole my inner fire and tried to snuff it out forever. Tonight I'm taking it back. And to think, this could have all been avoided if your mother had read you fairy tales."

"Fairy..." He shook his head. "*What?*"

"Fairy tales exist to teach children the rules, Richard. For instance, mind the path. For instance, be courteous to strangers. For instance—and this one is very important—never, *ever* steal from a witch."

Richard's eyes went wide. The gun raised an inch in his hand.

"Vanessa." His voice wavered. "What did you do?"

"I picked up your dry cleaning. The shirt you came home in, from your business trip. The one with the bloodstain on the collar. I took it into my workroom and wove a little spell to find out who the blood belonged to."

He pursed his lips, silent.

"Blood...sings to me now, Richard. Blood speaks. It whispers secrets in my ear. I saw her. The girl."

Vanessa's eyes narrowed to murderous slits.

"I saw *what you did*. How many women have you killed? I thought I was your only victim, but your hands are stained far bloodier than mine. You hid it well. Or maybe I just didn't want to see the truth, what kind of a monster you really are."

"Vanessa, you're...you're not well. Okay? You're hallucinating."

"My vision is crystal-clear. Did you ever read Hermann Hesse? 'Whoever wishes to be born,' he once wrote, 'must destroy a world.' I've always liked that line, though I'm not sure I really understood it until now. And back when I believed you loved me, before I knew you were trying to *kill* me...well, you were my world, weren't you?"

He raised the gun. His hand trembled as he aimed down the sights.

"But I'm not going to kill you," she told him. "Oh, I wanted to. And I had every intention, especially after I took care of Dr. Neidermyer. That was *fun*. But here's the thing. I have a lover, Richard. Her name is Marie."

"Marie Reinhart? The cop?" His finger brushed against the trigger.

"Mm-hmm." Nessa folded her arms. Her plum lips curled into an eager smile. "And I will do anything for her. I'll do anything to keep her safe. To make her happy. Marie wants to be a knight, and she wants to slay a dragon. And you...you're the dragon she's been hunting for, all this time. So I'm giving you to her. All wrapped up in a pretty bow."

A fist slammed against the front door, pounding fast.

"Police," shouted a muffled voice on the other side. "Open up!"

*　*　*

Marie had been walking up the stairs from the subway platform, springtime wind ruffling her ragged hair, moonlight in her eyes. That was when she got the phone call.

"Hey, I just got off at your stop. I'll be there in five min—"

"Marie," Nessa's voice gasped. "He's here. Richard came home early. He's—he's gone crazy!"

"Can you get out of the house? Have you called 911?"

She heard wood slamming, like angry fists battering a closed door.

"I'm locked in the closet. He's trying to get at me. Please, Marie! He says he's going to—"

The line went dead.

Marie broke into a run. She sprinted down the sidewalk, barreling through crowds of pedestrians. Horns blared as she raced across an intersection holding her shield high.

Block after block, relentless, her feet pounded the pavement to the ferocious beat of her heart. Pain stitched along her side with every breath, spots in her vision, but she wouldn't let it slow her down. She launched herself onto the brownstone's porch, slamming the door with her shoulder, then hammering it with one hand while she drew her gun with the other.

"Police," she shouted, nearly breathless. "Open up!"

*   *   *

Richard looked between Nessa and the door, baffled.

"You're...you're *insane*."

"Apparently I'm a sadist with a troubled childhood and insecurity issues to work through," Nessa replied. "But I'm told that's not considered an actual disorder, so I'd like to think of myself as 'lovably quirky' instead. Besides, *you're* one to talk. You didn't answer my question: how many victims have you murdered on your little 'business trips'?"

"You can't prove a damn thing."

"You know, you almost broke Marie's spirit. She fought so hard to save that girl, *so* hard. So I'm giving her a present. She doesn't know it, but she needs this. She needs this even more than I do."

His trembling finger slowly tightened on the trigger. "Needs *what?*"

"You're right, I can't prove anything, but that's fine. Once you're gone, I'm sure she'll find all the evidence she needs to prove who you really are and what you've done. She'll find closure. Peace in her heart. That's what I want for her. I didn't lure her here to arrest you, Richard. Marie needs to *slay* a dragon."

She raised her head high, let out an ear-piercing scream, and threw herself backward. The glass table cracked down the middle as she landed on it, buckling, breaking, crashing to the hardwood floor. She crashed down with it and sprawled, bleeding, in a spray of jagged glass shards.

Marie's heel slammed against the front door. The lock gave and the door burst open. She stood in the doorway with her service pistol in a two-hand grip.

Richard whirled to face the sound, with the revolver in his hand and raised to fire.

Marie emptied her gun.

He staggered backward as round after round punched into his chest. Gunfire shredded his tailored suit, puffs of blood billowing like mushroom clouds.

The final bullet punched a nickel-sized hole between his eyes. Richard Roth collapsed to the hallway floor, dead.

Marie dashed into the house. She found Nessa, dazed and squirming in a spreading pool of blood, and knelt down beside her.

"It's okay, don't try to move, I'm calling for help." She pulled out her phone. "This is Detective Reinhart. I have an injured civilian, need a bus to my location *now*—"

Nessa weakly took hold of Marie's other hand. Squeezing it. She looked up at her with stars in her eyes. She had done it. It was over. She had delivered her dragon to this knight, this paladin, this holy crusader.

Her knight.

"You saved me," Nessa whispered.

Marie smiled. She ran her fingers gently through Nessa's hair, picking out tiny bits of broken glass and tossing them aside.

"I always will," Marie told her. She leaned down to kiss Nessa's forehead. "I promised."

Forty-Eight

The ambulance whisked Nessa away, and the house filled with uniforms. They took pictures and measurements. Marie was barred from the scene the second the first car arrived. Out on the front steps, behind a cordon of tape, Captain Traynor took her badge and her gun.

"You have to help me out here, Detective. You have to help *yourself* out here."

"Like I told you," Marie said, "Detective Fisher and I spoke with Vanessa Roth as part of an earlier investigation, and I gave her my card."

"And when her husband attacked her, she called you instead of dialing 911."

"That's correct. I can only assume she felt comfortable with me. We had a good rapport."

Traynor's eyes bored into her like a pair of diamond-tipped drills.

"And you just happened to be in the West Village why, exactly? Last I checked, you live in Queens, Detective."

"My tour was over, Captain. I was on my own time. I wanted to go to the Chelsea Market after work." She nodded up the street. "It's just north of here."

"So it's a sheer coincidence that she called you and you were in the right place at the right time to intervene."

Marie curled her toes until they ached, using the pain to steady her breath and keep her voice even. She'd heard about people doing that to beat polygraph tests.

"I go to the Chelsea Market once a week or so, sir. I like the pastries at Bar Suzette. My roommate can confirm that. So it was really a one-in-seven chance I'd be in the area."

"One in seven." Traynor shook his head. "Detective Reinhart, if you were in my shoes, listening to the explanation you just gave me, how would you feel about it?"

"I wouldn't want to speculate, sir."

"Your last shoot was about as righteous as they come, and you still had to run the IAB gauntlet, you understand that? This one...this isn't. You're an off-duty cop in a place you have no business being, answering a call you shouldn't have gotten, and you just gunned down one of the biggest real-estate developers in New York."

"In fairness, sir, he had a weapon. And I think maybe she called me *because* he's one of the biggest developers in the city. She needed someone he couldn't buy off."

Traynor leaned in, pitching his voice for her ears alone.

"A weapon he never got a chance to fire. And you and I have both been on the force long enough to know how a gun can magically appear in a dead man's hand."

Her eyes went hard. "Sir, if you're accusing me of using a drop piece—"

"I'm not accusing you of anything. I believe you're a good cop, Marie. I know you are. But you need to sit down and have a long hard think about how this is gonna play once IAB gets involved and starts tearing your life open."

He pointed at the open door of the brownstone. An evidence tech circled Richard's corpse, snapping pictures.

"Because, this?" he said. "This raises questions."

Marie stared at the body, silent.

"Go home, Detective. That's an order."

* * *

Detectives combed the brownstone. Securing the scene, studying every angle, documenting a death. Jefferson poked his head out of an open doorway.

"Holy crap, have you *seen* this kitchen? They have a Viking Tuscany range. *Viking Tuscany.*"

Helena Gorski walked past him, rolling her eyes. "Glad you're focusing on the important details, partner. That's some fine detective work."

She spotted Tony on the far end of the dining room, crouched beside the ruins of the glass table.

"You talk to her?" she asked.

Tony shook his head, looking haunted.

"Probably for the best, at least until this shitstorm passes over."

"Lunch today," he said, his voice distant as he walked through his memories. "We were just talking about…"

She put a hand on her hip and frowned. "Talking about what?"

Another headshake. "Nothing. It was nothing."

He headed outside to wait for the medical examiner.

Ten minutes later, Helena was back. She tugged his sleeve.

"I was checking the upstairs," she murmured. "I gotta ask you something. You know I don't like Marie. I've never liked her and I've never pretended to. But I respect her. And I respect you."

He gave her the side-eye.

"Ask what you've gotta ask."

"Is your partner on the level, Tony?"

"Meaning?"

She nodded to the door.

He followed her up the steps to the second floor, the aged wood groaning under their shoes. Helena led him into Nessa's workroom. He stared, bewildered, at her art. The half-finished menagerie of grotesques, the trammeled wings and bound, contorted arms.

"Meaning that," Helena said, pointing to a sketch on a standing easel.

Three silhouettes danced wildly around a crackling bonfire. Clouds of smoke, sketched in charcoal, whirled up and became solid in the sky above. They took on the shape of two women, cradling each other close. A quiet and tender embrace.

One, in profile with a black and wide-brimmed hat, her body shrouded in a cape of starry darkness, was clearly Vanessa Roth. And the mussy-haired woman in her arms, clad in steel plate-mail and wearing a sword on her hip, could only be Marie.

"Fuck," Tony breathed.

Helena snapped a photograph.

* * *

Marie didn't go home. She went to Mount Sinai. She gave her name at the hospital's ER desk, sat down, and waited, stewing in her worries. Her thoughts jumbled around in her head, defying her to make sense of this. She knew she hadn't done anything wrong. So why did it feel like she had?

Two hours later a young man in green scrubs wandered over and said, "She can see you now."

Marie jumped to her feet.

Nessa was in a private room, lying on her stomach in a narrow, railed bed. Her head turned toward the door and she gave Marie a tired smile.

"Fifty-six stitches," she said. "It wasn't so bad."

The back of Nessa's gown was open. Marie stood at her bedside and ran soft fingertips over patches of gauze and tape.

"Does it hurt?"

"I'm on the good drugs," Nessa said. "They said I can go home in a couple of days. Maybe even tomorrow afternoon. Long cuts, but not deep ones. I'm going to have some scars. Is that okay?"

Marie's hand caressed Nessa's cheek. "Yeah. I've got scars, too."

"I know," Nessa murmured sleepily. "I've kissed them. Can you stay with me tonight?"

"I wish I could. I shouldn't...I shouldn't be here with you. You know, because of the...the shooting."

"Are you in trouble?"

"Little bit," Marie said. "I can take it."

Nessa's hand closed over hers. Her slender fingers curled.

"Not alone. You belong to me now."

Nessa closed her eyes. A moment later, she began to snore. Marie gently slipped her hand away, pulled up the stiff, scratchy hospital sheet, and tucked her in.

Forty-Nine

Richard Roth was buried at Woodlawn Cemetery on a bright spring morning.

A crowd of mourners gathered at the gate of the Roth family mausoleum, standing in respectful silence while a priest spoke words of comfort and surrender. Nessa wore a veil. She didn't know most of the attendees, and she doubted Richard knew half of them. In his world, a funeral was just another place to see and be seen. She played the grieving widow and dabbed at her bone-dry eyes with a silk handkerchief.

Alton Roth wasn't playing. The senator's usually stoic lips quivered as he stared at his son's tomb, his eyes bloodshot. A tiny bubble of snot flared at the tip of his hawkish nose until an aide whispered in his ear and passed him a tissue. He hadn't said a word to Nessa since his arrival. Not until now, when she found him sidling up alongside her while the priest droned on.

"You did this," he whispered. "I don't know how you did it, but you're responsible."

She arched an eyebrow, glancing sidelong at him.

"Be grateful," she murmured. "I *didn't* go to the press and tell them how your son threw me through a glass table. For the moment, your golden boy's legacy is intact."

"He *loved* you," Alton hissed. His hands shook. "He called you his angel. I told him when you started dating that you were nothing but trailer-park trash, but he wouldn't listen."

"I have fifty-six stitches' worth of your son's love. Would you like to see the scars? Back off, Alton. It's a simple deal: you don't challenge his will, I don't show up on television talking about how soon-to-be President Roth's son was a monster. Besides, you should be thanking me."

He turned his head, his face twisted in disgust. "Thanking you?"

"Mm-hmm." Nessa folded her arms and smiled beneath her veil. "Now you get to go to the polls as a grieving father. Should be good for a few sympathy votes."

Alton's right hand curled into a fist. His aide tugged at his sleeve, fast, pulling him away.

Nessa returned home after the funeral. It was strange to be alone and know Richard was never coming back. The halls of the brownstone felt wider, draftier. Her footsteps sounded louder when she was the only one there to hear them. She put her music on to keep her company. More than anything, she wanted Marie.

Not until the investigation was over, though. Not with plainclothes officers sitting in an unmarked car across the street, keeping a ham-fisted watch over her. For the moment, for her and Marie's sake, they had to keep their distance.

For the moment.

The doorbell chimed. Special delivery: a cardboard box, about three feet long and six inches thick, from an auction house in Los Angeles. She furrowed her brow as she hauled it into the kitchen, then set it up on a counter and sliced it open.

Inside, nestled in layers of bubble wrap and fistfuls of foam peanuts, an antique mirror awaited her. Nessa purred as she ran her hand over the mahogany frame. The woodwork was exquisite, carved with loops and twists and geometric designs. The oval glass at the frame's heart, speckled with dust, crackled with static electricity under her fingertips. The mirror had been painted over with black pigment and it reflected a world cast in onyx.

It wasn't just static she felt. She peered closer. Subtle symbols hid in the woodwork, seals of the planets and the spirit world. And in the glass, when she let her vision slip out of focus, shadows moved. Shadows that belonged to no living thing.

"Now where," she murmured to the mirror, "did you come from? And who sent you?"

* * *

The ivory plastic skyscraper, Richard's dream of his masterpiece in Tribeca, blasted to shards under Scottie Pierce's fist. Fragments went flying and the broken model skittered across the polished office floor in pieces.

"There is catharsis in destruction," Savannah said, sitting behind Richard's desk with her VR headset on, "but you could take a few lessons from your friend's demeanor. Richard was far less emotional."

He stormed over to the desk, his eyes wet, face mottled and red.

"She killed him. She killed my best friend. That bitch Reinhart fucking *shot* him."

"You're being extremely unproductive right now. Out of curiosity, were you and Richard having sexual relations?"

Scottie walked away, walked back, and jabbed a shaking finger at her.

"I am *not* a *faggot!*" he shouted.

Savannah sighed. Her gloved hands snatched at the air, shuffling invisible data while she studied the world from inside her headset.

"So emotional. I'm only saying that you're exhibiting grief associated with heightened levels of oxytocin. You know, I have a procedure to fix that."

"Why are we waiting?" he demanded. "We tracked Reinhart down, just like you told us to. We know where she works, where she lives. I've got guys watching her apartment right this fucking minute. We can take her *right now*. One phone call and it's a done deal."

"I'm not finished gathering field data. She hasn't been in close proximity to Vanessa Roth for days, thanks to this unfortunate confluence of circumstances. I need to see them up close together. I want energy readings."

"And then?"

Savannah pulled her headset off and looked Scottie in the eye.

"And then, after the next time they meet in person, and after I give my approval, you may do as you please with Detective Reinhart. Just so long as I get whatever is left of the body afterward, for study."

He put his hands on the desk, palms flat.

"There won't *be* much left of her," he said.

*   *   *

Alton Roth sat slumped in the back of his limousine. The world drifted by beyond the tinted glass. Springtime. Birds were chirping, people were smiling. It felt like a personal insult. Didn't they know they should be grieving? The universe should be grieving.

"Vanessa did this." He hooked a finger in his tie, loosening it. "That *whore* killed my boy."

The man who some called Calypso, some called Webster Scratch, sat across from him. Dark fingers smoothed the lines of his caramel-tan suit.

"Your boy had issues," he said.

Alton narrowed his bloodshot eyes. "Watch it."

"Your boy," Calypso said, "was consorting with the Network. Now, I know you're only invested in *human* politics, but my people and their people? We don't get along."

"That's not my problem."

"Noodle it out, baby. Richard was a stone killer, recreational-style. *That* was a problem. We're aiming to sell you as the second coming of JFK; people won't buy into the dream of Camelot if they find out your kid got his kicks on the edge of a knife. Richard was sloppy. And, real talk? You didn't even like him that much."

Alton sank lower in his seat.

"That was before he was..." He shook his head. "I should have spent more time with him."

"I've been around for many, many years, my friend. If it's any consolation, the one real commonality in the human experience isn't love or even hate. It's regret. Right now, in this moment, you're connected to every human who ever lived. Philosophers and kings, baby. Rollin' right alongside 'em."

The limousine rumbled across a pothole. Alton stared at Calypso.

"I want justice."

"Everybody wants something."

"Vanessa and that cop," Alton said, "they killed my son. My *son*. What are you going to do about it?"

"Probably send them a fruit basket with a thank-you note, seeing as they took care of Richard before I had to do it myself. You're forgetting something, Senator Roth."

Calypso smiled. He flashed two rows of curved, jagged teeth. The teeth of a great white shark.

"You already sold me your soul," he said. "You've got nothing left to pay me with."

Alton glowered at him. "*You're* forgetting something. Vanessa hired that cop to murder my boy, so she could get her claws on his money. She set him up."

"That's one theory of the crime. Not the only possibility, though, no matter how badly you want it to be true. What's your point?"

"If we know that, so does that 'lodge' he ran with. You know, those *sloppy* people you were complaining about? And they're not going to let this go any more than I will. So it seems to me, you've got a choice to make: help me take care of this situation in the most controllable, media-friendly way possible, or sit on your thumb until they do something loud and stupid and stick you with damage control. Your job is to get me into the Oval Office. We're one wrong move—somebody *else's* wrong move—from a scandal that could tank the whole deal."

Calypso's fingers played over the razor-sharp fold of a patterned handkerchief poking from his breast pocket. He glanced out the window, lost in thought for a moment.

"I'll concede a point in your favor. How do you see this playing out?"

"Get me some evidence I can use," Alton said. "I'm having lunch with the district attorney. I'm thinking we get Vanessa and the cop indicted. Conspiracy to commit murder. Throw them both behind bars where they belong, and let them rot."

"Turn your life into a true-crime special? That's the opposite of inconspicuous, baby."

"We're already halfway there," Alton told him. "Right now, the official story is that Richard was shot by a cop after he attacked his wife, and I've got two goddamn PR firms working overtime to keep it out of the papers. All Vanessa has to do is go on camera and shed some crocodile tears, and we're screwed."

Calypso nodded, slow. "You want to flip the script. Go all-in on making her the villain of the story, and Richard can play the martyr in memoriam."

"We're going to draw media heat no matter what," Alton said. "I'd rather be the father of an innocent man, murdered by his greedy wife so she could steal his family fortune, than the father of a man who threw his innocent wife through a table and died with a gun in his hand. One of those stories is an albatross. The other makes me a noble, silently suffering victim."

He sat back, grimacing as Nessa's words at the funeral came back to him.

"Should be good for a few sympathy votes," he muttered.

"Talk to your DA friend," Calypso said. "I'll get a few eyes on Vanessa."

* * *

The Chrysler Building loomed over Manhattan, an art-deco monolith seventy-seven stories high. The tower wore a crown, a base and a narrow ledge with radiator caps at each corner, before cascading up in scalloped peaks to a shining, solitary spike. The stainless-steel cladding, ridged with triangles, captured the light of the setting sun.

Calypso sat on the lip of the crown. A cold wind rippled his suit as he dangled one lazy leg over the ledge, glancing to the street nearly a thousand feet below. He could see it all from here, Manhattan and beyond, the crossroads of the world sprawling out to the ocean's edge. Eight million people. Eight million stories. Stories were Calypso's stock in trade.

He unslung his guitar. It was a 1958 Fender Telecaster, cherry and vanilla, just like Muddy Waters used to play. He strummed a single note, rich and deep, letting it ring out across the rooftops. He ran his tongue over his teeth, tasting the sound, like the first sip from a good bottle of cheap wine.

One note became two, then a bar, chords rolling slow and lonely under his guitar pick. In the distance, lightning flashed beyond an ink-black cloud. A storm was moving fast, coming in over the water.

Roth was nothing but a client to him. A vanity project, really. Taking a no-account grifter all the way to the White House was far more trouble than any one man's soul was worth, but it would win him the ultimate in bragging rights. Beyond that, Calypso couldn't care less. Alton Roth was a petty, venal man with petty, venal sins.

Vanessa, though. She was something different. He hadn't told Alton what he'd seen through his own, eternal eyes.

A shadow fell across his guitar. A woman stood on the lip of the roof. Her Louboutin heels balanced on the edge like the claws of a hawk, and she wore her hair in a braided scarlet twist. The wind took hold of her cashmere scarf tail and ruffled it behind her.

"You called," Caitlin said, her voice touched with a Scottish burr.

"You came," he replied. "The delightful Miss Brody."

"I shouldn't be in New York. The locals are territorial and they get nervous when I leave the West Coast. But I don't turn down an invitation from my favorite musician."

He patted the ledge at his side.

She sat down, curling her legs beneath her and smoothing the pleats of her skirt with one crimson-nailed hand. "There's a storm coming."

"That there is." He pointed to the west. "See that?"

Caitlin's eyes flooded with flecks of copper. They swirled and blossomed, as if her irises were filled with molten metal. She leaned forward and squinted.

"Something wicked on the wind," she murmured. "I can taste it. Festering and growing."

"And it isn't *us*. This isn't hell's handiwork."

She frowned. "The Network, then?"

"Those boys are about as subtle as a boot to the head. No, not them either. Something else. Something I've never seen before. And I've been rambling these roads for a long, long time. It's got the faintest tang of the familiar, though. By any chance, were you around back when Franz Ferdinand ate a bullet?"

Her molten-copper eyes twinkled. "Never ask a lady her age."

"There are moments in history," Calypso said, "when a single event changes the world. Times when one profound act sets a string of dominoes in motion. Once the dominoes start to fall, all you can do is roll along, swept up in the tide. Now, at the time, you might not realize what you're looking at. Might not see the trigger event when it happens."

"But in the aftermath," she mused, "gazing upon a transformed world while you're standing in its wreckage..."

"Hindsight is twenty-twenty."

"And you think that's what we're seeing now?"

Thunder rumbled and Calypso strummed a low note on his guitar, meeting sound with sound. He looked out over the darkening skyline.

"The assassination of Franz Ferdinand led to the first world war. One man, gunned down in Sarajevo. That was all it took—the right death at the right moment—to set the entire world on fire."

"But every action rises from another action," Caitlin said. "History is a chain."

"History is a wheel. And I think this time around, the trigger event has already happened. The right death at the right moment. Too late to stop it now."

He gazed into the distance. Off to the west, in his second sight, a shifting, inky blot hung over the city. Dark tendrils of smoke drooled down from the cloud like the arms of a jellyfish, brushing their tips against rooftops and skylights. Searching. Hunting.

"Tonight," he said, "we watch the first dominoes fall. Nothing we can do now but hold on tight."

He strummed his guitar again, picking out the first chords of a blues song. Caitlin leaned close, resting her head on his shoulder, and listened to him play.

Fifty

"It's gonna be *nasty* out tonight," Janine said, craning her neck at the apartment window. She looked over her shoulder, back at Marie. "Did you see these clouds?"

Marie sat on the futon, staring at the paperback in her hands. She'd spent the last two hours trying to read the same page. She'd get to the end of a paragraph, her thoughts would drift, and she'd find herself starting over again.

The woman in green-steel armor, the story read, *sank to one knee on the black basalt floor. Around her, she heard the rattling of dead, dry bones as she put one hand to the key at her throat.*

"The elders of the city have forsaken me," she said, fighting through her tears, "and my order has cast me out. They deny the coming darkness. They refuse to see. But I am still a knight in my heart. And a knight is nothing without a liege."

The witch-queen sat upon her bloody throne, a hungry smile rising to her lips.

"You seek to wage war upon darkness," she said. "To triumph, would you embrace mine?"

Janine craned her neck to read the cover. "Carolyn Saunders? Again? You know, we got her new book in at the library."

Marie blinked, her listless, looping train of thought broken.

"Oh, *The Killing Floor?*" She shook her head. "I couldn't get into that one. She brought in some new characters and it was kinda weird. Anyway, this is...you know. Comfort food."

"Yeah." Janine nodded at Marie's phone, resting silent on the futon's armrest. "You hear from 'George'?"

Marie had to smile, just a little bit. "No. I told Nessa we need to be careful while Internal Affairs is investigating me."

She sat back and closed her book.

"But I don't want to be careful."

"So...I hate to ask, but how much trouble are you in?"

Marie looked to the window, and to the gathering storm on the borough's edge.

"Well, my police union rep told me the odds of keeping my job when all is said and done, and he wasn't smiling when he said it."

Janine held up a finger. "Hold on."

She scurried into her bedroom and came out with a long, slim box wrapped in garish birthday-cake paper. She thrust it at Marie.

"It's not my birthday," she said, taking it from Janine's outstretched hands.

"It was the only wrapping paper I had. This is an award for being my best roommate."

"I'm your only roommate."

"So that's why you keep winning." Janine waggled her fingers at her. "Go on, open it!"

The paper peeled away in long, winding strips. Marie opened the cardboard box inside. A baton, like an umbrella handle with a sleek black finish, dropped into her hand. Marie blinked at it. Then she flicked her wrist. The inner core of the baton snapped out, expanding and locking in place.

The tactical baton—two feet long now, with a steel-headed tip—slashed through the air in Marie's grip.

"Janine...this is an ASP."

"Yeah," she said, beaming. "I mean, they took your gun away, and I know you don't like being unarmed, so I figured it was a fun *and* practical gift."

"No, I mean, you're a civilian. Civilians can't own tactical batons in New York. It's kind of the law."

Janine held up her open hands. "I don't own it. You do. So we're all good."

Marie stood, bracing the steel baton in both hands, then took another practice swing. She'd trained with an ASP back in her uniformed days, learning how to restrain or disable a suspect with pinpoint strikes, and the muscle memory came back fast.

"Seriously," she said, "where did you get this?"

"From the guy who sold me my stun gun, on Canal Street. Same guy I get my fake handbags from."

"Janine."

"What?" She shrugged. "You know I can't afford real Coach."

"Stun gun. Also illegal for a civilian to own."

"I'm a *naughty* librarian."

Marie's phone lit up. Tony calling in.

"I have to take this," she said. "But our discussion is not over."

"I'll be in my bedroom," Janine said, sauntering off. "Doing *crimes. Crime stuff*, Marie."

"We have to meet," Tony said before Marie could get a word out.

"That's a bad idea. Tony, IAB is all over me right now, and I don't want any of this stink rubbing off on you."

"It's not really an option." She heard the sounds of traffic in the background. "Come over to that coffee shop on Broome."

"In Nolita? That's nowhere near the precinct."

"Exactly," Tony said. "I'm on the move. See you there."

* * *

Marie sat across from Tony in a hipster coffee joint just north of Little Italy. They advertised authentic Greek yogurt made from the milk of grass-fed cows. Marie ordered a small coffee and kept it black. Tony sat behind a folded-up page of the *Times*, in a spot far from the windows.

"What's with the cloak and dagger?" she asked, lowering her voice as she eased her chair closer.

"Because it's not just me you're meeting with. Captain Traynor is here in spirit. He wanted me to pass on a message."

"What'd he say?"

"To me? Nothing directly." Tony set down his newspaper, glancing around to make sure nobody was in earshot. "It's what he didn't say. He called me into his office, pulled an email up on his computer, and said he had to go answer a personal phone call. He told me he'd be back in exactly two minutes, get me?"

"Deniability," Marie said.

Tony nodded. His eyes were grave.

"Marie, the DA was giving him a heads-up. Nothing's been handed down yet, but...they're considering an indictment. They're talking about charging you with Richard Roth's murder."

Marie's shoulders clenched. The white walls of the coffee shop closed in around her, claustrophobic, penning her in.

"I didn't do anything wrong! He had a gun—"

Tony cut her off with a wave of his hand. "I know. I know, all right? But look how it plays. Vanessa Roth stands to inherit millions off his death. They subpoenaed your logs from the phone company, Marie. They know you were in communication with her. Witnesses put you two together at her college. Then you just happened to be in the exact right place at the exact right time to blow her husband away? We've sent people to prison on less evidence than that."

"How long do I have?"

"I don't know. A day, a month, a year? I just know Richard's old man is pushing hard and he's got serious political reach. He wants Vanessa locked up, and you—going by his theory—were her hired gun."

"If she's in prison," Marie said, "he can contest Richard's will."

"That's *my* theory. Only thing I don't have is the truth." He stared into her eyes. "Marie, we've been partners for years. I have always had your back. You've always had mine. Off the record, you and me, tell me what's really going on here."

Wisps of steam drifted from Marie's coffee cup. She gently rapped her short-cropped nails against the porcelain. The truth felt like a maze of razor wire. The more she tried to untangle it, the more she bled.

"I'm in love with her. The last time her husband was out of town, we...spent the night together."

"Damn it," Tony sighed, slumping back in his chair. "You know how that's going to play in front of a jury, right?"

"Tony, I swear to you, I'm not lying. She called me. He was attacking her. I kicked the door in, he brought his gun up, and I was one second faster on the draw. I told the truth. I didn't do anything wrong."

He took that in, silent for a moment as he weighed the evidence.

"And I believe you, partner. But you're in one hell of a mess. How are we going to get you out of it?"

Marie stared into her coffee. Studying the amber depths, like a fortune-teller trying to read the future in a teacup.

"It's slim, but there's one shot," she said. "It all comes back to this ink cartel. Look, we're in agreement that Richard had something to do with the drug trade."

"Sure, we just can't prove it."

"And we know Baby Blue and the other victims were killed by these dealers. Some kind of ritual murder."

"I'm with you," he said.

"And we know there's a rat in the house. Somebody leaked the details on the Bed-Stuy raid."

"Long list of unlikely suspects, and zero leads."

"You're going to need the captain's help," she said, "and the medical examiner's, but I think they'll go for it. Remember that perfect bite mark on Baby Blue's leg? You've got a match."

"We do?"

"No. But you're going to leak that you do. Make sure every single person on that list 'accidentally' overhears that the investigation just hit a breakthrough and that bite mark is the key piece of evidence that's gonna crack the whole cartel open. Now, imagine you're the rat, and you're on these sick bastards' payroll. What do you do?"

Tony's face broke into a smile. "I panic and try to destroy the evidence."

"Bingo. Watch the morgue. When they show up, take them down."

"But how does that help you?"

Marie shrugged. "This rat's responsible for nine dead cops. I'm guessing they'll give up everyone and everything they know for the faintest whiff of a deal. If we can prove Richard Roth was part of the ink cartel and a serial killer? Well, it makes my version of events look a lot more reasonable, doesn't it?"

"This is a Hail Mary pass, you know that, right? You're counting on a whole lot of maybes."

"You got a better idea?" she asked.

"No." His chair squeaked on the tiles as he pushed it back. "Okay, you need to stay out of sight. Go home and hunker down. And don't go within ten miles of Vanessa Roth."

"Tony, I have to. If there's an indictment in the works and Senator Roth is targeting her too, she needs to be ready for it."

He squinted at her. "I'm not going to be able to stop you, am I?"

"Nope."

"I didn't tell you about the email from the DA," Tony said. "I also didn't tell you that there's an unmarked prowl car parked outside Vanessa's house around the clock. So if you do go to see her, which I don't recommend, you should meet up elsewhere."

"You're a good guy, you know that, Tony?"

Tony shook his head as he stood to leave.

"Just watch yourself out there. If I have to drive all the way to Westchester County to visit your incarcerated ass for the next twenty years, I'm gonna be a little salty about it."

Fifty-One

Marie called. Nessa answered and summoned her to the edge of Broadway. Even the lights of Times Square, blazing a couple of blocks away, could barely stand against the storm clouds blanketing the city. They hung like a roiling, rumbling shroud of smoke, flickers of lightning in their depths. The air was bone-dry and crackling with static electricity. Pregnant with the promise of a downpour to come.

Marie skirted the lobby of the Iroquois Hotel, making her way to a cocktail lounge in the back. Lantern's Keep was small, elegant, dimly lit, and appointed with rich dark wood like a turn-of-the-century parlor. *It's very Nessa in here*, she thought. Her lover was sitting at the six-seat bar, and she'd saved the stool on the end.

Marie leaned in as if to kiss her, then paused and pulled away. Nessa did the same a second later. They shared an awkward glance.

"I'm not sure how we do this," Marie said. "Are we the kind of couple that kisses hello? I mean, in public?"

"I think the best thing about a new relationship is discovering what kind of couple we are. At any rate, we should probably be circumspect while you're under investigation." Nessa took her handbag from the empty stool and patted the cushion. "Sit."

Marie sat alongside her, casting a glance over her shoulder. The bartender came over and she ordered a Tom Collins. A little something to steady the nervous flutters in her stomach. Nessa lifted her cocktail glass, some kind of amber liqueur with a tiny black shadow at the bottom.

"Bobby Burns," she said. "Named for the poet. My signature drink. Scotch, vermouth, Benedictine, usually garnished with an orange peel, but I like mine with a cherry. That way you end the drink with a sweet little *pop* between your teeth."

"My partner, Tony, he—he heard something. Nessa, they might arrest us. For killing Richard."

Nessa's expression was naturally dour, tinged with gloom even when she smiled. She pushed her owlish glasses a bit higher on the bridge of her nose. Thinking, as she took the news in.

"This wasn't supposed to happen. You were supposed to have plausible deniability."

"Plausible..." Marie trailed off. A dark suspicion uncoiled in the knot of her stomach.

Nessa met her gaze, silently waiting.

"Nessa...is there something you want to tell me? About the night Richard died?"

"Yes," she replied. "Richard was a serial killer. He murdered that girl, the one called Baby Blue. And others. He confessed to it, right before he died."

A cold chill rippled down Marie's spine. *I got him*, she thought.

"Can—can you prove it? I mean, that's what me and Tony suspected, but if we can *prove* it—"

"No," Nessa's fingers curled in frustration. "I can't. I had hoped that once he was dead, once he couldn't cover his tracks any longer, the evidence would naturally come to light. You weren't supposed to get in any trouble. I wanted this to be good for you."

"Nessa...you're saying this like you...like you arranged it. Like you planned for me to kill him."

Nessa weighed her words in silence for a moment.

"The gun was real," she said. "It was loaded. And if you hadn't arrived when you did, he most certainly would have murdered me.

Is there anything else you really want to know about that night? Ask me any question, and I'll tell you, with absolute honesty."

Marie turned to the bar. She drank her Tom Collins.

"No," she said. "That's all I needed to hear."

Nessa raised her glass. "Alton Roth's hand is behind this. And his influence. Which makes me wonder…"

She sipped her cocktail.

"Nessa?"

"If Alton is pushing for an indictment, maybe Alton needs to go away."

Marie knitted her brow. "Go…away?"

"He's trying to kill us, Marie." She eyed her over her drink. The amber glinted in the circles of her glasses. "That would make it self-defense. Everyone has a right to self-defense."

"We can't—" Marie shot another glance over her shoulder as she dropped her voice to a whisper. "We can't *murder* him."

"And why not? You shot Richard. Do you feel bad about it?"

"No." Marie shrugged. "He was hurting you. He was a killer. He deserved it."

"You know my general opinion of the human race, Marie. A *lot* of people deserve to die, or at least don't deserve to live. But let me put it another way. Are we in this together? You and me?"

"Until the end," Marie said.

"Then do you plan to lie down and die? To wait until your former brothers-in-arms show up at your door with handcuffs, then let an unjust system railroad you into a prison cell? Or will you *fight*?"

"Of course I'll fight," Marie said. "I'll do anything I can. But…I'm a police officer. I promised to uphold the law."

"You promised to protect me."

Nessa tossed back the last of her drink, swallowed the cherry garnish, and set the empty glass on the bar.

"Come with me. I've made my decision. It's time."

"Time for what?" Marie asked. "And where are we going?"

Nessa brandished a room key.

"Upstairs," she said. "Behind closed doors. It's time to get your priorities straight."

*   *   *

Nessa led Marie into a suite with a view. The lights of Times Square shoved back against the rumbling storm front overhead. An electrical war. Nessa pointed to the middle of the carpet, gold edged with crimson, and snapped her fingers.

"Stand there."

Uncertain, Marie moved to the spot while Nessa shut the door and flipped the deadbolt. She left the lights off.

"You have every right to be angry," Nessa said. "You *should* be angry."

"About?"

Nessa flung her hand toward the window, taking in the world. Thunder rippled in the starless dark.

"Everything. We live inside a narrative. A series of carefully constructed boxes engineered to keep us in line. From birth, we're taught the rules of being a woman. Smile. Be quiet. Be pretty. Smile more."

She circled Marie slowly, a shark in black waters.

"Men play their stupid games, and what are we meant to be, hmm? Prizes. Trophies. And you see what happens to any woman who wants more than that. They tear us down. We're even taught to tear each *other* down. The entire system is rigged. Constructed to keep us in chains from the cradle to the grave, and make us forget that we have the power to change the world."

She stopped, standing in front of Marie, eye to eye with her.

"Look out the window," Nessa said. "Turn on a television. This is the world they've built for us. There is no justice. The wealthy, venal, and stupid are *rewarded*. The powerful are *never* held to account. Men like Richard, men like Alton Roth—they plunder, and they steal, and they are celebrated for it. It's funny. I think back to what I taught my students, and I'm not sure I fully understood it at the time."

"What's that?" Marie asked.

"To be a witch," Nessa said, "is to be an outlaw. Humanity has spent centuries trying to impose order upon the wild. To pave over the forests with cities, to replace nature in all of its beautiful chaos with rules and regulations that serve only the powerful and keep everyone else in chains. But a witch cares nothing for the authority of men. We undermine. We poison. We bring *change*. And that is why they hate us."

Marie saw her own shadowed image reflected in Nessa's glasses. Nessa moved closer, close enough for Marie to feel hot breath on her cheek.

"They used to fear us, too, but they've forgotten what fear feels like. I think it's time to remind them. I squandered so many years of my life, Marie. Being meek, being afraid. I was wrong. I didn't know my own power. And now I embrace it. All of it. Senator Roth, and all of his kind...they're the ones who should be afraid. Because the Owl is here. When my work is done, they'll call me a villain. But that's all right. I don't mind. Women who refuse to submit have always been called that and worse."

Her lips brushed Marie's cheek. Then her earlobe.

"If the only way to rise up in this world is to be a villain," Nessa whispered in her ear, "then I will be a villain. And I will have my way."

The storm broke. A torrent of water lashed the window as the rain roared down, drenching the city streets. Lightning flickered like a sea of flashbulbs. In the sudden roar, Marie could barely hear her own voice.

"Nessa...what are you going to do?"

She stepped back and flashed a toothy smile.

"Terrible things. But let's talk about you, Marie. Let's talk about you. You're standing at a crossroads. You dedicated yourself to the law. And how was your loyalty repaid? They want to lock you in a cage, like an animal, for the rest of your life. Even if you don't go to prison, they'll never give your badge back. Is that right? Is that how things should be?"

"No," Marie said. Her hands clenched at her sides. "I didn't do anything wrong."

"You must be thinking that your storybooks lied to you. They told you that you could be a knight. A champion of the right and the just. And look what happened when you tried to live like your imaginary heroes."

Marie closed her eyes. Her jaw tightened.

"Don't mock me," she said.

Nessa's hand touched her cheek. "I'm not mocking you. Open your eyes and look at me."

Nessa's fingernails dug into Marie's cheek, light pressure becoming sudden sharp pain, until her eyelids flicked open. Nessa stared at her, fervent.

"The stories didn't lie. You just misunderstood."

"What?" Marie shook her head. "What didn't I understand?"

"I know what I want. And I know what you need." Nessa prowled around her again, watching her as Marie stood petrified. "I want you at my side. I want you at my feet. I want your love. I want your obedience. I want you to adore me, fear me, fight for me. I want you to carry a torch in the heart of my darkness. Give yourself to me, utterly—and I will break the world for you. Do you understand what I'm telling you, Marie?"

Marie's lips parted as Nessa stood before her, and she struggled to speak. Her heart hammered against her ribs.

"Say it," Marie whispered.

"King Arthur is dead, and the Round Table isn't hiring. So tell me, Marie...would you like to become *my* knight?"

Marie's hands cradled Nessa's hips and slid down her legs slowly, as she knelt before her lover. Her fingertips dropped to touch the golden carpet. Marie's forehead rested against Nessa's knee.

"I swear my sword to you." Marie's voice trembled, on the edge of breaking. "I swear my heart to you."

"Yes," Nessa said. Her fingers ran through Marie's ragged hair, stroking her head.

A single joyous teardrop fell, splashing on the toe of Nessa's shoe.

"I swear my life to you," Marie breathed.

"*Yes*," Nessa said.

Her fingers curled in Marie's hair. Holding on tight, as the rain thundered down.

Fifty-Two

The storm raged.

A silver Rolls Royce prowled through the streets of Manhattan. The antique limousine circled the block as its sole passenger, the Lady in Red, reclined in the back seat. She stared out at the rain as it pounded a staccato beat against the windows.

A makeup compact, inlaid with vintage pearl, nestled in her palm. She flipped it open. Mercury shadows danced in the mirror's depths.

"Fair is foul, and foul is fair," she murmured. "You've done well, my daughters."

Dora's voice echoed from the mirror. "Did I just feel what I think I felt?"

"Nessa and Marie have embraced their natures."

"Meaning," the Mourner's voice slithered from the foggy glass, "without knowing it, they have turned the hourglass. And when the sand runs out...they die."

"Normally, yes," said the Lady. "This may be their one and only chance to break the cycle. As it stands, all of the pieces are on the board. I believe their first doom already approaches."

"You gonna help 'em out?" Dora asked.

"No. Nessa and Marie need to learn what they're capable of. To explore their own depths. If I intervened to save them now, they'd never have a chance against the greater perils ahead. They'll stand on their own two feet, or die."

"Our enemies," the Mourner hissed, "have no such qualms. They'll do whatever it takes to destroy them."

The Lady chuckled. A dark, melodic sound.

"Then our newborn witch and her servant will be tested and tempered, won't they?"

                                    *   *   *

On the edge of Bloomington, Illinois, another storm brewed over a lonely cornfield. Carolyn Saunders—not knowing she was due to be abducted not once but twice in the near future—sat behind her old, bulky monitor in the office of her cluttered ranch house. She worked away on her latest pulp-fantasy potboiler. A fresh mug of coffee steamed beside her right hand, alongside a half-empty bottle of Jameson whiskey.

Ghouls! she typed. *Donatello Faustus had faced defilers of the living, the blood-drinking fiends of Nefada, but these were no mere vampires. The cave was filled with shambling half-human nightmares, and their fangs tore into the bloody, chained limbs of a fresh victim. The master thief's blade snicker-snacked from his—*

She stopped typing. *Jesus,* she thought. *Sticking in a random Lewis Carroll reference for no reason? Hack much, Carolyn? Maybe I should go back and—*

She froze. Rain was lashing the office window. Last she'd noticed, the storm had been off on the horizon.

Also, it was dark out.

She checked the time. It was nine in the evening. Her coffee, untouched, sat cold as a stone at her side. The day was just *gone*, hours lost in the blink of an eye. Then she looked to the screen. She'd been busy. She scrolled up and read what she'd written in her fugue.

"*This* shit again," she muttered under her breath.

She shoved her chair back and trundled over to the wall behind it, curling her arthritic fingers around the edge of the cheap wood paneling. The panel popped loose, exposing the closet-sized nook concealed behind it. And her paranoid's wall, a map of Post-it notes and photographs, news clippings and maps, all linked with colored lines of string. A spiderweb of conspiracies, connections, suspicions.

She ran her finger down a list of titles, like cards in an alien tarot. The Paladin, the Enemy, the Scribe, the Thief. And halfway down: the Witch and her Knight.

Beside the words, she scribbled "*IN PLAY*" and pushed a blue thumbtack into Manhattan.

She carried her mug and her bottle into the kitchen. Cold coffee splashed into the sink over a pile of unwashed dishes. She used the empty mug to pour herself three fingers of Jameson, neat. Then she raised her drink to the kitchen window, to the rain, in a wry salute.

"Here's to reunions, short-lived as they may be. Good luck, kids. You're going to need it."

*   *   *

Lightning crackled outside the floor-to-ceiling windows of Richard's office. Savannah rose from the dead man's desk, striding to a table where Richard's plastic models had been replaced by machines. One long steel box screeched with static, the death shriek of an electronic beast, as a needle scribbled wild lines across a rolling sheet of graph paper.

"This is exceptional," she gushed. "Absolutely exceptional."

Scottie shook his head. The readout might as well have been written in hieroglyphics.

"What is?"

"When the subjects came together, the energy output *spiked*. I think...yes, I think we're ready for the next phase of the experiment. Call your people watching the Iroquois and tell them to follow Marie once she leaves. I want to take the two of them separately. Safety concerns, after all. I'm still not sure what they *are*."

"I'll have my guys grab her and bring her to the zoo."

Savannah fluttered her fingertips at him, shooing him away. Her heels clicked on the marble floor as she returned to Richard's desk.

"Unnecessary," she said. "I want to get up close and see what she's capable of."

She put on her VR headset. Her gloved hands plucked at the air, pressing invisible buttons. As one, her pale and dead-eyed minions snapped to attention.

"I'll be capturing her personally."

*   *   *

A crosstown train rumbled through dark winding tunnels, making its way back to Queens. Marie sat alone at the edge of a nearly empty subway car, hugging herself, smiling like a loon at her reflection in the scratched-up window.

She was a little scratched up herself, under her cold and rain-drenched clothes, and aching in all the right ways. Nessa hadn't let go of her hair when she knelt—tugging her to her hands and knees and then over to the bed—and their second time had been better than the first. They were more confident now, more certain of each other's bodies.

"Do you have a safeword?" Nessa asked her.

She giggled, nervous, as the stroke of Nessa's hand sent ripples of pleasure down her spine. "Do I need one?"

"Mm-hmm. For instance, if things got too intense for you, or if I were to do this—"

Her fingernails pinched. Marie tossed her head back with a sudden gasp, a spike of pain mingling with the waves of delight. Transforming the sensation.

"—or something like that, and you didn't like it, I would know to stop."

"I didn't say I didn't like it," Marie whispered.

Nessa's giddy laughter filled the room. The sound wrapped around her like silken chains.

"Your safeword," Nessa said, "is symmachy. A word I'm fond of. It means 'fighting together against a common enemy.'"

"Symmachy," Marie echoed.

For a while the world had faded and there was nothing but the sound of the rainstorm and their bodies. Marie hovered in the afterglow now, cherishing every second of the memory, even as reality dampened her bliss. She was still facing the end of her career. Still facing the threat of an indictment.

And Nessa, her lover, her liege, was thinking about killing Alton Roth. Maybe it was just the cocktail talking. Was Nessa really capable of committing premeditated murder?

If Nessa asked her to, was she?

This train of thought led her down tunnels darker than the subway, and she didn't notice the new arrivals making their way into the car. Not until they filled the aisles to her left and right, cutting off both of the doorways. Marie glanced from side to side. Six of them in all. An elderly woman, a construction worker, a skinny teenager—just a random crowd from a random street. All they had in common was bloodless skin and pale, unblinking eyes. Eyes fixed on her.

"Can I help you?" Marie asked.

The six, moving as one, lifted their left feet and lurched one step closer.

Marie smiled. "This is a flash-mob thing, right? Lemme guess, you're all about to start dancing."

Now their right feet. One more step toward her, penning her in.

"Okay," Marie said, her amusement fading. "You're starting to weird me out a little. Whatever it is you're trying to accomplish here, you might want to know that I'm a cop. You know. Just take that into account."

The teenager's jaw slowly yawned open, and he wriggled the root of his severed tongue at her.

One by one, like a rolling wave, the other five did the same.

Marie jumped to her feet. She whipped the black steel handle of the ASP from under her coat. With a flick of her wrist, the tactical baton snapped out to its full length. She held up her other hand.

"You need to move back. *Now*."

They charged.

The kid was first, hurling himself at her. She dropped low, ducking under his hand and unleashing a pinpoint strike to his kneecap. His knee shattered under the steel and his leg fell out from under him. He went down like a puppet with its strings cut, in utter silence. A man in a red checkered shirt was already moving in, too fast, and his fist slammed against Marie's left eye. She staggered backward. Another man behind her got his arms under her elbows, trying to restrain her. Marie raised her leg and drove her heel down onto the arch of his foot. He lost his grip. She shoved away from him and lunged, the steel baton whistling through the air.

It connected with the construction worker's skull and crushed it like an eggshell.

His skin and bone ruptured, collapsing inward, half of his head turned to confetti and one eye dangling from a dried out optical nerve. His exposed brain was a gnarled lump of gray tissue the size of a baby's fist, wildly pulsing as he grabbed her by the shoulders.

Marie swept her arm around, breaking his grip and shoving him aside. Then the elderly woman jumped her from behind. An arm curled around her throat, squeezing tight, cutting off her air. As spots flared in her vision and her heart pounded, Marie threw an elbow into the woman's ribs. Then another, feeling the brittle bone shatter under the impact, loosening her grip.

She'd carved an opening. The aisle to the right was clear, even as the downed teenager was silently pulling his way toward her. He dragged himself on his shattered kneecap, clawing at the air, still in the fight. Marie jumped over him and ran. She threw open the door at the end of the subway car, then the next, barreling up the length of the train.

The brakes squealed as the train slowed down, rumbling into the next station. The pneumatic doors hissed open. Marie leaped out, running, her feet pounding the platform stairs as she raced for open air. She didn't even know where she was, hadn't registered the announcement.

She'd just seen the impossible, and she wanted to get as far away from it as she could.

Fifty-Three

Back at home, Nessa had taken the Oberlin Glass up to her workroom. The antique mirror, with its face painted jet black, perplexed her—she had no idea who had sent it, and nobody at the auction house was answering the phone—but it wasn't long before she saw the possibilities. When she'd tried her scrying experiment with Marie, her bowl of ink had shattered under the strain. Whatever the message was, the magical recording warning her of danger, her simple tools hadn't been able to handle that level of power.

The glass, though...that might do the trick. From the carvings hidden along its ornate wooden frame, it had clearly been intended for some kind of witchcraft.

"Why not mine?" she asked the empty room and lit a black candle.

By the flickering candlelight she opened her book to the pages of "A Game for Conjuring Distant Sights." The now-familiar chant slithered across her tongue. Her face faded from the glass. Then came the fall of shadowed snow, like rippling static, and there was...Marie. Making a mad dash through the rain, her eyes wide with panic, in the clothes she'd worn earlier that night.

The sight jarred Nessa's concentration. The spell broke, the image dissolving into nothingness. She was already snatching up her phone and dialing.

"Nessa," Marie gasped in her ear. "I was on the subway. They...fuck, I don't even know who *they*—I got away."

Nessa's back muscles clenched and she squeezed the phone until her knuckles turned white. "What happened? Are you safe now? Are you hurt?"

"Nessa, they weren't—they weren't human. I know how crazy this sounds, but they weren't human."

"Come to me. My house. Now."

"It's too dangerous," Marie said. "The police are watching you, remember? If they see us together—"

"Chance worth taking. Come to the back door. Be quick and clever."

Weren't human. Nessa mulled it over as she glided down to the kitchen, putting on a kettle of hot water. She knew magic was real, obviously. And she had anticipated almost every way her father-in-law might seek revenge for his son's death...everything but that one.

She was almost amused as she rummaged through a cabinet, digging for her stash of tea bags. *Do you have pretensions to occult power, Alton?* she thought. *Did you conjure something up to punish my lover, keeping your hands distant and clean?*

What a dreadful mistake.

As the kettle whistled, Nessa turned her head. There came a soft knocking at the kitchen door. She ushered Marie inside fast and shut the door against the storm.

"Had to take the back alley," Marie said, holding up her dripping arms. "Sorry, I look like a drowned rat."

"I'll get some towels," Nessa called over her shoulder as she swept from the room. "Tea on the counter—it's chamomile. Pour a cup for me, too."

Later, with two mugs of steaming tea and a fluffy towel wrapped like a turban around Marie's head, she told Nessa her story. Nessa took it in, frowning as she listened.

"These creatures don't match anything I can remember from my books," she said. "I see only one option. You remember our little experiment with the ink and water?"

Marie cast a nervous glance upward, toward the workroom. "The message. You sent yourself a message from the future, saying you were in danger."

"Mm-hmm. We need to hear the rest of it. We need to know the truth."

"Do...do I need to be there?"

Nessa reached out and touched her arm, rubbing softly.

"I'm admittedly going on instinct," she said, "but I think it needs both of us to unlock it. I understand that you're nervous. You've seen things—the first time you scried with me, the subway tonight—that most people don't believe are real. *You* didn't believe. And seeing, well...that changes your world forever."

"I just keep wondering," Marie said, shaking her head as her gaze went distant. "Wondering how deep this goes, you know? It's like I've spent my whole life standing on the tip of an iceberg, and I'm just getting my first glimpse below the waters."

"Magic is real," Nessa said, her eyes twinkling behind her glasses. "You can choose to embrace it. Let it in. Starting right now. Besides, there's a practical consideration to think about here."

"Oh? What's that?"

Nessa reached up with one finger and lightly bopped the tip of Marie's nose.

"You're the servant of a witch. I'll handle the magic, but you'd best not be gun-shy around it, or your job's going to be a difficult one."

They finished their tea and went upstairs.

They sat cross-legged side by side, their knees and hands touching. Nessa framed the mirror with a pair of black candles. The shimmering lights swam in the dark of the glass.

"I'll lead the chant," Nessa told her. "You just breathe deeply. Four seconds in, four seconds out. Try to empty your mind of everything but your breath. Fall into the vision. Surrender to it."

Her fingers stroked the nape of Marie's neck.

"Surrender to me."

The words of the chant seemed to take on form and weight, spiraling around the glass in spidery lines as the candles blazed higher. The flames turned a vivid orange, and then a deep midnight blue.

Within the black mirror, a figure emerged. Nessa. But not quite her: her face was a little different, the angles off. She sat cross-legged too, hovering in the air with her open hands on her knees. Her wrists had been cut. Blood wreathed from her arms and twisted around her in twin streamers, like a scarlet DNA helix. This Nessa's eyes were blots of solid crimson, marbles of wet blood.

She was in a stone chamber, dark, hard to see. A few feet away, a girl—maybe fourteen, with a heart-shaped face and a worried look in her eyes—held a heavy book open.

"*My name is Nessa Fieri,*" the mirror-Nessa said. "*Maybe yours is, too. I'm—I'm not certain how all this works. But if you're receiving this, then listen and understand: you are in terrible danger.*"

Another figure had emerged from the shadows, creeping up to witness the ritual. Marie— again, not exactly her, but close enough to be her sister—in a rough linen shift. Mirror-Nessa's head swiveled around like an owl's.

"*Marie. Go back to sleep.*"

Mirror-Marie's face went slack, curiosity turning to sudden lethargy. She turned and stumbled off. Mirror-Nessa swiveled her head forward again.

"*I haven't told her. She carries all of my burdens. This one I think I can carry for her. I believe I've found a way to break the cycle, but...*" Her hands clenched. "*If you're seeing this message, clearly I failed.*"

"This isn't from the future at all," Marie whispered, staring wide-eyed at the Nessa beside her. "It's from the *past*. But I don't remember this—"

"Neither do I," Nessa said. Her gaze stayed fixed on the glass, on her bloody-eyed doppelgänger.

"*As a precaution,*" her twin said, "*I'm reaching into the Shadow In-Between and carving a message there. A permanent warning, in the hopes that one of us finds it. Maybe forewarned is forearmed. I have to try. I'm creating this message from the bowels of the Black Archives. My apprentice, studying her histories, found some very disconcerting records."*

She took a deep breath, looking paler by the minute. The teenager narrowed her eyes at her.

"Mistress? Do we need to stop?"

"No." Mirror-Nessa shook her head, then looked back to the glass. *"You need to understand. I don't know why this was done to us, or who did it, but you—you meaning me—and Marie are under a curse. We have been locked in a cycle of reincarnation for...I don't even know how long. I shudder to guess. The point is, we are reborn each time, possibly in new worlds if what I've read is true, with our memories burned clean. You learn the arts of witchcraft. You meet Marie. You...learn to tolerate her presence."*

The teenager glared. *"Mistress."*

"Fine, Hedy." She took a breath. *"You fall in love with her. And then, shortly after...you die. Sometimes you're both murdered. Sometimes you're murdered, and in her grief, Marie takes her own life. And then you're placed in new bodies, with your minds scoured, to do it all over again. And again. And again."*

Marie's hand tightened around Nessa's.

"This is our hell," the mirror-twin said. *"For the first time in our lives, we find love. And then it's torn away from us. Then we start over, only to suffer anew. A curse more cruel than any I have ever woven, I assure you. Make no mistake, Nessa: someone did this to us. Is it a punishment? A sick joke? I don't know. But if you're seeing this, then my quest ended in failure. Now I'm you, and it's your turn to suffer, unless you can accomplish what I could not."*

Hedy spoke up. *"Mistress? I don't know how much longer we can sustain the projection."*

"Listen to me," mirror-Nessa said. *"Find Wisdom's Grave. It's the wellspring of magic. The resting place of the first witch who ever lived. If there is any weapon, any spell capable of shattering this curse, that's where you'll find it."*

"Never even heard of it," Nessa murmured.

Her twin's eyes blazed, the floating streamers of blood boiling as her voice broke.

"*You are our only hope, Nessa. You are my vengeance. You are the Owl now. Allow no mercy into your heart. Not one shred of compassion. Terror and madness are your tools: use them. Spread the shadow of your wings across the world like a living nightmare, because that is exactly what you are. Then break this curse and find the architects of our pain. And when you finally track them down?* Make. Them. Bleed."

Her fury faded. She stared out from the glass, her voice weak now.

"*And keep Marie safe. She's the only good thing that ever happened to us.*"

The vision erupted into a flurry of burning ash. A cloud that swirled and fell away into the depths of the black mirror.

Then nothing more.

Nessa wanted to say *this can't be real*, but she knew better. She sat there, frozen as a statue, holding Marie's hand.

"Wisdom's Grave?" Marie asked.

"I don't know," Nessa said.

"What about those other things she said? The Shadow In-Between? The Black Archives? What are—"

"I don't *know*," Nessa snapped. She let go of Marie's hand. Then she grabbed it again, squeezing hard. "We'll figure it out. I'll figure it out. We need a plan."

Then it hit her. She turned to Marie, eyes wild in the candlelight.

"Let's run away."

Marie blinked. "Run? Where?"

"*Away.*" She scooted around on the floor so they were sitting knee to knee. "You were attacked tonight. The police are closing in. Alton Roth is after both of us. We need breathing room. So let's just *leave*. We can figure it out on the road."

"But this is our home," Marie said. "I've lived in New York almost my entire life."

"Marie," Nessa said, "your career is over. Your old life is gone.

Is there really anything worth staying for? Worth the risk of being killed or thrown in prison for?"

She didn't have an answer. Nessa leaned closer.

"Run away with me. Tonight."

"Okay," Marie said.

Nessa pulled her into a tight hug.

"But I have to stop at my apartment first," Marie said.

"I will *buy* you new clothes, Marie. I must admit I'm looking forward to refining your fashion sense."

"I still need to pack an overnight bag, at least. And I have to say goodbye to Janine. She's been my friend for years, Nessa. I can't just vanish on her. I *won't*. And if people might come around looking for me, I have to warn her."

Nessa pursed her lips, thinking fast.

"Fine," she said. "That's fair. While you do that, I'm going to get all the cash I can lay my hands on. The banks are closed, but I've got a few cards—mine and Richard's—I can hit an ATM with. Meet me at Grand Central. We'll leave by train."

Marie had to smile. "Escaping on a train together? That's almost romantic."

Nessa darted in and kissed her, hummingbird-quick.

"It'll be very romantic. Now *go*. Do what you have to. I'll be with you soon."

Fifty-Four

She didn't want to spend the money, but Marie jumped into the first taxi she saw. After her last attempt to make it home, getting back on the subway wasn't an option. The storm had subsided in spots, the sky still basalt-black but the monsoon tapering off to an icy drizzle.

"Crazy weather, huh?" the cabbie asked her.

"Whole world's crazy," she said.

There were no anchors anymore. No safe places. She'd told Nessa that learning about magic felt like standing on the tip of an iceberg. Now she realized she was wrong; she hadn't been standing on it, she'd been climbing it. The ice buckled and broke under her fingers, sending her tumbling down to the lightless waters below. Now the water had her, pulling her under, giving her a good look at the world's hidden face.

Her phone rang. Tony.

"Hey," she said, "any news?"

It took him a second to answer. His voice was muffled, like he was cupping his hand to the phone.

"Yeah. I...damn it, Marie, I wish I didn't have to make this call."

"Tony? What's wrong?"

"Twenty minutes ago," he said, "a warrant was issued for your arrest. Vanessa Roth's, too. They're charging you with murder."

She sagged against the cold vinyl.

"No," she breathed. "Tony, I'm innocent. I didn't do anything wrong—"

"I know that. We know that. But Alton Roth's got friends in high places and a lot of money to throw around. I talked to the captain. I'm supposed to ask you to come to the precinct, right now. Turn yourself in, so...you know."

"So you don't have to drive me downtown in the back of a squad car."

"No perp walk, no cuffs if we don't have to, we'll make it as easy as we can. You'll be in protective custody until your bond hearing. And probably after."

Protective custody. A solitary cell. Only safe place to put a police officer who landed behind bars. *People go insane in solitary,* Marie thought, imagining the windowless door slamming shut. *People go insane after a month. I'm looking at maybe twenty years. Or the rest of my life.*

She bit back a dizzy surge of panic. She wanted to throw the taxi door open and jump out, anything to breathe fresh air, to stop feeling like a wolf with her leg caught in a steel trap.

"Marie?"

She took a deep breath.

"I can't do that, Tony."

"You know there's only a few ways this can end," he said. "You can make it a lot easier if you come in. On you. On all of us."

"I can't clear my name from inside a cell."

"I don't see how you can do it as a fugitive, either."

"Can you stall for me? Just buy me a couple of—"

"Stop," Tony said. "Stop talking. Don't tell me what you're doing, don't tell me where you're going. I don't want to have to lie when they ask me about it. If you're going to run, run."

She closed her eyes.

"Thanks, Tony. You're a good guy, you know that?"

"You were a good partner, Marie."

There wasn't anything left to say, nothing they could give voice to.

They hung up. Marie shot off a quick text to Nessa: *Warrants have been issued. If you're home, GET OUT. If you made it out, be careful. See you at the place we talked about.*

* * *

Nessa checked her phone as she strode through the cavern of Grand Central Terminal and knitted her brows. *Safe for now,* she texted back. *Hurry.*

Even this late, the mammoth train station was bustling, sound bouncing off the warm, glossy marble and stone. A carry-on bag rolled at Nessa's side. She wore her sun hat from the funeral—black, with a wide, floppy brim—and a long black cloak against the rain. She'd worn the cloak exactly once before Richard had banned it from her wardrobe, saying it made her look like she was "going to a goddamn renaissance fair."

Come to think of it, he'd hated the hat, too. Nessa had to smile, just a little. It was good to live on her own terms.

It was good to live.

And if we want to keep doing it, she thought, *we'd best be cautious.* Her gaze flicked to the clock. *And get as far away from here as humanly possible.*

The crowds were her cover and a source of suspicion all in one. Her eyes fell on anyone not carrying luggage, anyone who seemed to be more interested in the passengers than the trains. A pair of men were loitering by the stairs, their jackets bulging. Their clunky square-toed shoes screamed *cop.* Maybe not looking for her, probably not, but the nervous prickling at the back of her neck warned her not to chance it.

She turned and walked the other way. All the way to the opposite stairs, navigating toward the lobby of the Grand Hyatt Hotel. She'd find a lounge or someplace she could perch, close but not too close, and wait for her lover's return.

* * *

Across town, in the antiseptic stillness of the morgue, a shadow moved under cold, dead lights. It pulled back a shroud, exposing the battered face and mottled skin of Baby Blue. Gloved hands rolled the dead woman onto her stomach. In the light of a cell phone, the figure studied her left calf. There it was: one perfect bite mark, untouched by the cuts that ravaged the woman's flesh.

The shadow reached for a scalpel.

As the blade touched the edge of the bite, the overheads flickered on and flooded the morgue with harsh white light.

"Funny," Tony said. "When I do that in the kitchen at home, the roaches always run for cover."

With a phone in one hand, scalpel in the other, Helena Gorski slowly turned around.

"Would it help?" she asked.

He stepped from the far corner, where he'd been lurking in hopeful silence, and gestured at the body.

"It was you. You were the cartel's errand girl all along. You ran interference for Richard Roth, you tipped them off about the Bed-Stuy raid. Helena...how could you do this?"

She gestured with the scalpel and slipped her phone into her pocket. Freeing up her gun hand.

"Wouldn't have had to do anything if your partner could just take a hint. I gave her my blessing to interview Roth because I *thought* she'd back off once she saw there wasn't any evidence to go on. Turns out she isn't just batshit insane, she's a fucking dyke who fell for the man's wife. Oops. My bad." Helena's face fell. "Then you two go off hunting dealers. Why do you think I wanted to take lead on the ink investigation so badly? It wasn't about stealing all the glory for myself; it was about making sure nobody stepped on the wrong toes. And you just had to put on your tap shoes, didn't you?"

"It's called doing my damn job," Tony said. "Nine cops died in that raid. People you knew and worked with every single day. How can you live with yourself?"

"My son had lymphoma. You can't imagine. My little man, suffering, wasting away. He's eight years old."

He shook his head, not following. "So, what, they gave you money for chemo or something?"

"You don't get it." Her eyes went wide. Fervent, like a new convert stepping up to address the congregation. "He *had* lymphoma. You think you're dealing with drug dealers and killers. They're magicians, Tony. I don't mean top hats and pigeons, I mean black masses and ritual sacrifice. Magic is real. And it works. They made my son's cancer go away."

"That's impossible."

"You want to see the medical records? Our doctor called it a miracle. Sure was. A miracle bought with blood. And then they dropped the hammer on me. See, they took his cancer away. They can also give it *back* with a snap of their fingers, anytime they feel like it. They told me if I slipped up, if I wasn't loyal, I wouldn't pay the price: my son would. That was the deal. My treason for his life. Of course I said yes. Any mother would have done the same."

Her free hand edged dangerously close to the gun under her blazer. Tony kept his eyes locked with hers, his own hand inching toward his shoulder holster.

"I didn't want anyone to die." Her eyes brimmed with tears. "They were supposed to clear out when I warned them. God knows I've spoiled twenty other busts. I've made evidence disappear. I've leaned on witnesses. This time, this *one* fucking time, they decide to make a stand and go out in a blaze of glory. I had no idea, not until the fireworks started. Me and Jefferson were *there*, remember? We could have gotten killed too."

"Was Jefferson in on any of this?"

"No. Just keeping him distracted was a full-time job."

"You're coming with me," Tony said. "You're going to tell the truth about Richard Roth, and you're going to help clear my partner."

Helena gaped at him. She blurted out a laugh.

"Clear her? Sweetheart, your partner is guilty as sin. Do you think I planted that picture at the Roth house? Or altered Marie's phone records? Richard Roth was a world-class, grade-A scumbag, but his wife still set him up to be killed and your partner still pulled the trigger."

"It was self-defense."

"Yeah." Helena's lips curled in contempt. "You go on believing that. Anyway, you're wasting your time. Marie's never going to see the inside of a courtroom. Richard's buddies are looking to dish out some payback, and she's just been green-lit. By the time they're done with her, there won't be enough left to fill a shoebox."

Tony's face tightened. "Then that's ten cops you helped murder."

"I won't see the inside of a courtroom either. Can't let you take me in, Tony. I do that, my son's good as dead. I'm sorry about this. I always have respected you. I wasn't lying. But the only way he survives is if I walk out of here or die trying."

Her hand trembled, easing toward her holster. Tony squared his footing. He stood like a gunslinger, five seconds from high noon.

"Helena, don't do this. Don't go out this way."

"It's like I said," she told him. "Any mother would have done the same."

They drew at the same time.

Fifty-Five

Twin muzzles flashed. Helena's bullet tore through the meat of Tony's left arm, spattering scarlet across the tile wall behind him. His slug caught her in the gut. She buckled to the floor, wheezing. He gritted his teeth and fought the white-hot slash of pain as blood drenched his torn sleeve. He ran in, kicked her trembling gun hand, and pinned it under his heel.

"Let go of it," he told her.

Helena shoved weakly against his leg with her free hand. She squirmed, slipping in a spreading puddle of her own blood. Tony twisted his foot and ground his heel down on her fingers.

"*Goddamn* it, Helena, let *go* of it!"

Her fingers unclenched. He holstered his weapon. Then he scooped her gun off the floor with his good arm and tossed it onto the slab. He fished out his handcuffs and wrestled her wrists into them, biting back the pain as a torn muscle shifted in his wounded arm. The stench of gunpowder and spilled blood battled with the industrial antiseptic.

"Finish it," she groaned. "Fucking *finish* it, kill me already."

"Not doing that." He patted her down, plucked a .22 from a holster on her ankle, and set it next to the other gun. "It's a gut shot. Hurts like hell but you're going to live. And you're going to prison."

Helena sucked in deep lungfuls of air and coughed them out again. Tears glistened on her pale cheeks.

"Tony, they'll kill him. They'll kill my son—"

"We'll get an order of protection for your kid. He'll be fine."

"You *can't hide from them*," Helena croaked. "And your partner is *dead*. If she's not dead now, she's on her way. They're coming for her."

*   *   *

Marie dashed through the apartment door, barely pausing long enough to slam it behind her. Janine jumped up from the futon.

"Marie? What's going on? You've been gone all night. I was about to go to bed—"

"Hotel." Marie rushed past her and darted into her bedroom. "You're going to a hotel tonight. I don't want you anywhere near this place."

She rummaged through her closet, digging past a few years of clutter and clothes. She found her old rolling suitcase at the bottom of the pile and threw it on the bed.

"Marie?" Janine hovered in the doorway. "You're kinda freaking me out right now."

Marie turned to her, fumbling for words that wouldn't come. Her anger and her fear and her guilt all collided somewhere in the back of her throat, a flaming wreck that stopped her voice from getting through.

"I have to go away," she managed to tell her.

Janine studied her. Her intuition connected the dots.

"The police are coming, aren't they?"

Marie nodded, miserable. Janine rushed across the tiny room and hurled her arms around her roommate's shoulders. She squeezed tight and whispered.

"It's okay. If you've gotta run, run."

"It's not just that," Marie said. "People might come around looking for me. It's complicated. You wouldn't believe me if I told you—"

"How long have you known me? I believe a lot of things."

"Trust me." Marie gently wriggled free from Janine's arms and opened her dresser drawer. "*I* barely believe me. Just understand that this wasn't my choice. And whatever they say about me when I'm gone, I'm innocent."

Janine put a hand on her hip. "Yeah. No duh. Are you taking George with you?"

Marie had to smile, despite everything. "We're going to...I don't even know what we're going to do. We'll figure it out on the way."

"I want an invite to the wedding. Actually, forget that. After everything I've had to put up with, I'd *better* be your bridesmaid, bitch—"

A heavy fist hammered at the front door. They froze.

"Ignore it," Marie murmured. "They might go away."

More pounding. "Open up," shouted a gruff voice. "NYPD. We've got a warrant—you can open up, or we're coming in."

Janine put a finger to her lips. "I'll get rid of them. You stay in here and pack. *Quietly.*"

She hustled out of the bedroom. Marie tossed clothes into her suitcase, no rhyme or reason, just whatever she could fit—and then Janine screamed.

Marie burst through the doorway. Their visitors weren't the police. Janine wrestled with a man in a ski mask as he threw her against the kitchenette counter. A glass fell and shattered on the tile floor. Two more men in masks were right behind him. One pointed at Marie.

"That's her!" he grunted.

Suddenly, Marie was five years old again, the night her home was invaded. The night her parents were taken from her by men in black masks. Her muscles turned to stone, pinning her where she stood.

"Marie," Janine shouted, "*help!*"

No. Marie was here now. She wasn't trapped—not in her memories, not in reality—and she wasn't helpless.

She was a knight, and she knew her duty.

She whipped out the ASP and locked it at full length as one of the men charged her. She sidestepped, lashed the baton across his shoulders, and sent him crashing into the coffee table. A knife appeared in the second man's hand. He lunged in and she leaned back, his blade chopping air. The baton whistled. His wrist shattered under the steel shaft and he dropped the knife, howling behind his mask.

The first one rolled onto his hands and knees. He crouched in the splintered ruin of the coffee table and leaped at her. He hit Marie from behind, wrapped his arms around her waist, and hauled her down to the carpet.

Janine reached behind her, her fumbling fingers grabbing the edge of a dirty plate, and swung it across her attacker's face. The porcelain burst into razor shards. He let go of her and stumbled back, his shoulders thumping against the refrigerator as he clutched his bleeding cheek. Janine yanked open a drawer, searching fast. He came at her again—then he went rigid, trembling, as Janine shoved the business end of a stun gun against his abdomen.

She let go of the trigger. He hit the floor. She leaned in and jolted him again.

"You like that?" Janine panted. "You want some more? *Never* fuck with a librarian."

Marie wrestled across the carpet, rolling, while the man who'd downed her climbed his way up her body and his gloved fingers clawed at her face from behind. She rammed her elbow into his gut, but he wouldn't give up. Then she saw the fallen knife, a foot away.

She snatched it up, turned, and drove the blade through the man's sternum. His eyes went wide behind the mask. Blood sprayed from the wound, splashing across Marie's face and shoulders, a battle baptism. She shoved the dying man off her and wrenched the knife free.

The killer with the broken wrist staggered out the door. The one on the kitchenette floor was already coming around, groaning as he tried to crawl away. Marie rose in a crouch, her mind feral now, swallowed in an adrenaline haze.

He reached under his windbreaker and pulled out a gun.

Marie knew a dozen moves with the ASP to disarm and restrain a suspect. If she were still Detective Reinhart, she would have used them. Nessa's knight cleared the space between them in a scramble and brought the knife down. The point speared the palm of his hand and impaled him to the linoleum. He was still screaming when the tactical baton hit his throat with a full-force swing, crushing the cartilage like a cheap carton of strawberry milk.

"Oh shit," Janine breathed. She put one hand to her mouth. "You killed him. You killed two of them."

Marie's head swiveled, taking in the carnage. "Where's the third?"

Her roommate pointed a shaking finger at the open door.

"I'm going after him. Stay here."

"Marie, *wait*—"

"Can't let him warn his friends," she growled. "They attacked my home, they attacked *you*. No. He's not getting away."

Marie smelled blood on the stale air as she barreled down the hallway, taking the stairs two at a time. She felt alive. All her old oaths, the rules she lived by, the chains and weights she'd draped herself in, were gone. The terrified little girl, hiding under her bed while men in masks tore her world apart, was gone. Detective Reinhart, servant of the law, was gone. She was becoming something new, something wild, and free, and true to herself. Nessa's knight.

She shot out the foyer door and into the shadowed street, searching for signs of her prey. He'd tell her who he was, and then he'd tell her who sent him. If he was on Senator Roth's payroll...well. The night was young. She had to protect Janine—*a knight defends the innocent* raced through her fevered mind—which meant making sure there was nobody left to hurt her once Marie had fled the city.

Something on the left caught her eye. Wet red spatters marred the sidewalk. She loped in pursuit, eyes intent on the tracks, darting past an alley mouth—

—and a beefy arm hooked around her throat. She kicked backward, flailing, as a needle bit into the side of her neck. Blood roared like wind in her ears, whistling high and shrill, and the world went black.

*   *   *

Janine paced by the window. She'd doused the lights, half to try to spot Marie down on the street, half so she wouldn't have to look at the two corpses her roommate had left in her wake. They were just misshapen lumps in the dark now, pieces of human-shaped debris.

Her fingers fumbled against her phone. She managed to misdial 911 twice. Then she gave up and hit her contact-list entry for Tony Fisher. It rang through to his voicemail.

"Tony, it's Janine. Call me back, okay? Call me back as soon as you get this. Marie was here, and I don't even—"

Her voice trailed off. Down on the street below, a panel van idled at the curb. The side door rattled as it slid open. She watched a masked man haul Marie's limp body from the alley, tossing her into the van like a sack of groceries.

"Marie's in trouble," Janine said. "Just...call me. Please."

The door slammed shut. The van's headlights flared as it rumbled down the street.

She could trust Tony to do the right thing by his partner. As far as anyone else in the NYPD was concerned, Marie was a murder suspect with a warrant out for her arrest. Even if they could save her, they'd just be putting her in handcuffs and dragging her off to a different doom.

There was only one other person she could trust.

"My name is Janine Bromowitz," she told the university's answering service. "I need to get a message to Professor Roth. As soon as possible, please. It's about a family emergency."

Fifty-Six

Nessa strode through the apartment door, her dark eyes shrouded by the brim of her hat. She paused on the threshold and gazed upon her knight's handiwork.

"Marie killed them?"

Janine nodded, mute. Nessa's lips curled in a tiny smile, a little rush of pride.

"Then what happened?"

"I saw them throw her into a van," Janine said. "She wasn't moving, like she was knocked out. I couldn't see the license plate."

"Any designs on the van? Logos? A name? A number?"

"Nothing. Just...white."

Nessa leaned in close, scrutinizing her.

"That won't do at all, will it?"

She pushed past Janine and made a beeline for Marie's bedroom. Her mind was on her book and the new pages she'd deciphered. So many new games to play, but so few of practical use, save for...yes. "The Game of Sympathetic Location." She flicked on the bedroom light, taking in the open dresser drawers, the half-packed luggage on the rumpled bedspread. She thought back to the last time she'd been here, and her gaze drifted to the framed print on the wall.

"That book." She snapped her fingers at the picture. "Her favorite, yes?"

"*Swords Against Madness*," Janine said. "She's read it twenty times. Why? What does that have to do with—"

"Where is it?"

Janine ambled over and ran her fingers along Marie's overstuffed bookcase. "Should be here somewhere. She doesn't alphabetize her shelves. Physically pains me."

Nessa frowned. Her instincts drew her to the suitcase. There it was. The yellowed paperback, its cover crinkled with age, rested at the bottom under a jumble of underwear and T-shirts. It was the first thing she had packed. The book tingled against her palm, laden with the residual energies of Marie's thoughts, her imagination, her hopes and dreams. The pages were a palpable connection to her lover's heart.

"This will do nicely," she said, turning to leave. She fished her phone out as she walked. Janine followed on her heels.

"What are you going to do?"

"I'm calling a Lyft," Nessa said. "I don't own a car."

"No, I mean *after* that."

Nessa turned, fixing Janine with a glare so intense it drove her back a step. It washed across her face like a burning backdraft, a tsunami of raw anger and hate, though Nessa's voice was frozen-calm.

"Oh. After that. After that, I'm going to find Marie. And I'm going to find the men who took her from me. And I am going to explain to them, in explicit and *most* painstaking detail, exactly who they just fucked with. Stay here. Lock your doors."

"I could—" Janine swallowed hard. "I could come with you. I could help."

Nessa's cheeks tightened, her cold fury cut with wry amusement.

"You're a good friend to her, Janine. But Marie would never forgive me. You can help her by staying safe."

"What if more of them come looking for her?"

Nessa drifted past her. She paused on the threshold.

"There won't *be* any more. Because I'm going to murder every single one of them."

*   *   *

Lemmy had been a ride-share driver for three months, a little extra cash to supplement his on-again, off-again bartending job. The gig economy, they called it. Tonight he'd barely picked up a single fare, and he spent most of his shift white-knuckling the wheel of his rust-spotted Hyundai as he fought through streets washed blind with rain. At least the storm was letting up. The deluge had turned into a cold and steady drizzle, though the black skies above still rippled with lightning.

His GPS pointed him to his next fare. She was on the corner up ahead, standing in the rain under the curve of a burned-out streetlight. He pulled curbside and rolled down his window.

"Hi," he said, "you called for a—"

He froze. The woman smiled at him. The horned owl, perched on her outstretched arm, stared unblinking. His gaze shot to the windshield as the rain became thicker, heavier.

Scarlet. The drizzle, spattering his windows and rolling down in long, slow rivulets, had turned to blood. He looked back to Nessa, his eyes growing wide as the crimson rain matted her hair and rolled down her cheeks. She delicately cleared her throat.

"I need a car," Nessa told him. "I don't need a driver. Get out."

*   *   *

Captain Traynor paced his office floor. He stared at the phone on his desk like he could make it ring by sheer force of will. It sat stubbornly silent.

He had two decorated detectives in the hospital, each one with a wound from the other one's gun. Detective Fisher was already out of the ER—his was a through-and-through—and Detective Gorski was still getting Fisher's shrapnel dug out of her small intestine. Detective Reinhart had gone fugitive, fleeing her arrest warrant, and as for the Roth woman—

Jefferson stuck his head into the office, popping open the door and then knocking.

"Captain? You wanted to be notified if there were any developments?"

Traynor stopped pacing. "They found Reinhart?"

"No, sir. And the roommate is standing by her story that she saw Marie driven off in a panel van. Sir...I believe her."

"Jefferson, your partner allegedly tried to kill Detective Fisher after he caught her destroying evidence. I'm questioning your prowess as a judge of character right now. Is that all?"

He ducked his head. "No, sir. There's something else. We just got a ten-twenty-two about a stolen vehicle. A Lyft driver called it in, and the description matches Vanessa Roth."

Traynor's eyes narrowed. "She was armed?"

"No...no, sir. He, um...*gave* her his car."

"She threatened him?"

Jefferson cringed. "No, sir, not in so many words. He said she had an owl on her arm and he was afraid it was going to eat him. Also, it was raining blood at the time."

Traynor stared at him.

"Once she drove off," Jefferson said, "he realized he might have hallucinated the whole thing. Though he insists he wasn't on drugs. Not tonight, anyway."

Traynor dropped into his chair. He rested his forehead against his palm.

"I'm sure he does, Detective. All right, get the make and plate number out to all surrounding jurisdictions. If whoever took Detective Reinhart is leaving the city—*if* she was taken—it's a safe bet that Roth is on her trail. We find one of them, we find them both."

* * *

Nessa drove north, and the storm clouds followed.

She rode the curves of Interstate 87 with Marie's paperback sitting on the passenger seat. She kept one hand on the wheel and one on the faded cover. She felt it pull against her fingertips, jerking like puppet strings, telling her where to go. *Like calls to like,* her spell book had taught her, *and beloved things carry the residue of their owners.*

This knowledge can be used to find you, to hound you, and to cast workings against you, the book warned. *As such, you must never love anything you cannot destroy in a heartbeat. Care for nothing you cannot discard. Better still, care for nothing.*

Hell with that, Nessa thought. Being a witch meant following her own rules and nobody else's, not even her anonymous teacher's. If the author of the book knew her so well, they must have known that much. Marie was the one thing she couldn't leave behind.

Stay alive, she thought. *I'm coming for you.*

Fifty-Seven

Marie slowly stirred from a chemical haze. The world swirled around her, woozy, lurching, spinning like the nausea in the pit of her stomach. She tried to move her arms. No give. Her wrists and ankles were trapped in bracelets of burning ice.

No. Not ice. Cold stainless steel. She squinted as her double vision swam into focus.

She sat in a stiff-backed chair, bound by steel restraints. She felt a strange pressure on her temples and followed orange wires to an oblong machine on a table at her side. Electrodes. Two more were pasted to the backs of her hands, and her blouse had been unbuttoned far enough to stick another pair just below her collarbone.

The humid air smelled musty, the odor of wet straw and dung. It reminded her of her last trip to the zoo. That was it. The monkey house. Her vision sharper now, the artificial brown painted walls of an animal enclosure rose up around her. The animals were long gone, though. Just her, the softly humming machine, and the woman in the pristine lab coat and goggles who stepped into her field of view with a tablet in hand.

"So finally we meet," Savannah told her. "You've posed quite the conundrum, did you know that? And more than a small share of trouble."

"So let's fucking *kill* her already," growled Scottie Pierce, stepping up behind her. He fixed Marie with a lethal glare.

"Not until I get the answer to a most vexing question." Savannah tapped the side of her goggles. Sapphire-blue lasers streamed across Marie's face. "Can you tell me what you are, exactly?"

It took Marie a second to remember how to talk. The drugs slurred her words, and her tongue felt like a dead slug in her mouth.

"NYPD," she said. "Detective Reinhart. You just kidnapped a cop."

"That's who you are." Savannah walked over to the machinery-laden table. "*Who* is easy. I knew the *who* days ago. Look at this."

She plucked a gadget from the table, a rectangular box on a handle with a pair of protruding antennae. She waved it across Marie's face and chest. It sat silent.

"According to my ethereal spectrometer—which I built, yes, it's brilliant, thank you—you *don't exist*. You literally are not here, not in any human sense. Yet you seem, for all intents and purposes, to be a living human being. Why?"

Scottie frowned at her. "Maybe it's busted."

Savannah turned. She pointed the gadget at him. It lit up, emitting a stream of excited electronic squawks.

"Maybe," Savannah said, "you should be a good helper monkey and not second-guess me."

A portly man in a three-piece suit, his face etched with worry, stepped into the enclosure. He whispered in Scottie's ear before scurrying off.

Scottie threw up his hands. "Well, that's just great. Vanessa Roth flew the coop, nobody's got any idea where she is, and my police informant got caught red-handed."

"Good!" Savannah's eyes lit up behind her goggles. "Inside every crisis, an opportunity to learn. Now we can test a theory of mine. I believe that Detective Reinhart and Mrs.—excuse me, *Ms.* Roth are linked on some deep, primal level."

She glided over to the table and traded her gadget for a syringe.

The drug inside was black as tar. She held it up to Marie for inspection.

"You're familiar with ink, of course. I invented it. Well, not alone, it took a team of subordinate researchers and innumerable test subjects, but most of them are dead so I feel comfortable taking credit at this point."

"So you're the kingpin behind the cartel," Marie rasped. "You started a drug epidemic. Does the money help you sleep easier at night?"

Savannah laughed. She clutched the syringe to her chest and gave Marie a delighted smile.

"Oh, Detective. You misjudge me. It's not about the money. It never was. Well. Okay. Maybe it's a little about the money, but I'm a salaried employee. Ink's value as a recreational drug is strictly to lure in the rubes. To fill the cheap seats, if you will. A little opiate, a tiny dash of lysergic acid, cook it just right and you've got a tasty concoction that literally melts on your tongue and livens up the dullest of dinner parties."

She moved in, standing over Marie, and held the syringe closer. The oily liquid slowly bubbled and churned inside the syringe, as if it was a living thing.

"The *real* payload is an alchemical compound, magically charged and designed to turn habitual users into psychic antennae. And it's been doing its job masterfully, with minimal hiccups, until you and your lady friend came along."

"Turn them into..." Marie shook her head. "*Why?*"

"Please. I'll be asking the questions here. Enlightenment would be wasted on you. Now, street-grade ink is very heavily cut with various nontoxic additives. Generally about twelve to twenty percent pure." She flicked her fingertip against the syringe. "This is the real deal. One hundred percent pure. Seeing as ink users seem to have a strong reaction to your presence, I want to see how *you* react to *it*."

Marie squirmed in her chair, fighting against the steel straps as

Savannah forced her sleeve up. The needle stung like a wasp, sinking in, the ink burbling as the plunger slid down.

"We'll start with a small injection, two CCs. Still enough to send many human subjects into a fatal overdose, but I'm betting you're no ordinary subject."

The world dissolved into points of starlight.

The drug burned lit-gasoline trails through her veins, spreading across her body. It was a serpent of fire, coiling up her spine and nestling at the base of her brain. She felt like a stranger in her own flesh, and then it wasn't her flesh anymore. She saw the world as an unbroken line of overlapping lenses, slices of reality laid on top of one another. And as the machinery of the universe churned, cosmic gears clanking and galaxies spiraling, the lenses came apart one by one.

She perched on a wagon in her ragged, makeshift clothes, leading tumor-ridden horse-beasts across a cracked and endless wasteland. Then another lens flicked out of place.

She crouched in a crude fighting pit, her breath drawing curlicues of frost in the air. She gripped a pair of wooden batons as a man-mountain covered in tattoos shambled toward her with a sledgehammer. The crowds in the stands screamed for blood, their shouts drowning out the roar of her heartbeat.

She strode down a burning slum street, windows bursting and screams echoing around her. She wore jet-black armor, a sleek carapace of ceramic and steel, and a helmet with a visor that painted her vision in strokes of neon light. Women in matching armor—*my Valkyries*, she thought with a sense of dark pride—strafed the buildings with gouts of fire from flamethrowers shaped like insectoid shells.

She was Marie Reinhart, strapped to a chair and feeling the sting of the needle. Savannah stood over her and made notes on a clipboard.

"Pupils dilated, heartbeat accelerating...fascinating. Now, Detective, I need you to do something for me. Call to your friend. Call to Ms. Roth."

Marie barely heard her. She was lost in a memory of her childhood. Huddling in the ruins of a burned-out shack, hiding from the bioluminous searchlights and listening to the wet squelching sounds as the Unkind Ones dragged their bloated bellies down the street on twisted elephant-stump limbs—

No. That wasn't her childhood. *My name is Marie Reinhart,* she told herself, fighting to keep her identity from tearing apart at the seams. *I was born in Cooperstown, New York, on the twelfth of May...*

Savannah clapped her hands twice, sharp, in front of Marie's face. "Detective? Cooperate, please. Call to her. Call her name."

"What are you trying to accomplish here?" Scottie asked her.

"We want Vanessa, don't we? They're linked. Magically, mentally, on some level I haven't begun to discern. If Marie cries out to her, under duress, her lover will come for her. And we'll be ready."

Scottie folded his arms, glowering. "She's not under *nearly* enough duress."

"My thoughts exactly. Let's increase her stress levels. A natural flood of adrenaline and endorphins might amplify the effect."

Savannah stood by her bank of machines. Marie was a million miles away. "She's not here," she breathed.

She felt like she was falling. Tumbling backward into an endless black pit. Nessa wasn't there. Part of her was missing, part of her had been missing her entire life—and she never knew it until they met.

"Detective?" Savannah snapped her fingers. "Focus, please. I'm going to have to use enhanced interrogation techniques on you now. Please understand that I'm doing this for the purpose of advancing scientific thought. It isn't personal."

She turned a dial, and now the endless pit was lined with razor blades. Marie thrashed in her chair and let out a ragged scream as power lanced along the wires, the electrodes lighting her skin on fire.

"That isn't electricity that you're feeling," Savannah explained. "This is a nerve induction synthesizer. It interacts directly with your nervous system and simulates damage ranging from the mild to the catastrophic. For instance, this—"

She pressed a series of keys and flipped a switch. Marie bucked in the chair, her mop of hair flailing as she shook her head wildly and groaned behind clenched teeth.

"—this is the exact sensation of having your right arm snapped in two places. If you'll be so kind as to look at your arm, however, you'll see that no actual injury has taken place. I'm afraid that won't make the pain go away: your brain simply won't be able to reconcile what you're feeling with what you're seeing. I'm told it's quite unpleasant."

Her hand hovered over the keyboard. She waited patiently as Marie sagged in her chair, her groans subsiding to heavy, labored breaths.

"Now then," Savannah said. "This next sequence, which I've already queued up, will perfectly simulate what it feels like to have all ten of your fingers broken, one at a time, from left to right. I don't *have* to proceed. Would you cooperate and call out for Vanessa, please?"

Marie raised her head, slow. Cold sweat matted her bangs to her forehead. She looked to Savannah and spat her words. "*Fuck. You.*"

Savannah sighed and shook her head. "As you wish. You forced me to do this, Detective. Your choice, not mine."

Marie's little finger shattered like glass. An explosion under her skin, every nerve screaming and her voice screaming with it. Then the finger beside it. Then the next, a perfectly timed symphony of pain with every starburst of agony flaring brighter than the one before.

Through her scarlet-fogged vision, eyes blurry with tears, she saw a figure approach. Impossible sunlight shone at the woman's back, bright and strong, her hips gracefully swaying while her boot heels clicked on the straw-scattered floor.

She was perfect.

She wore a vest of sleek black brigandine accented with cold brass studs, over a blouse and leggings in nightingale blue. A wolfskin cloak clung to her shoulders, furred at the neck and draped low at one shoulder. It was pinned with a brass chain and a brooch bearing the stylized image of a horned owl. Twin sickles dangled from her belt, their curved blades honed to a killing edge.

In the space between bone snaps, Marie breathed, "You're a knight."

She crouched down before her chair.

"I'm you," the other Marie said. She stroked Marie's arm with fingers sheathed in black leather. "I *was* you. And you were me."

"I don't remem—" Marie's words broke into a howl as her thumb shattered.

"Shh," the Other said, her voice gentle, penetrating the wall of pain and confusion. "I'm here to help you. Focus on my voice, okay?"

"O-okay," Marie managed to gasp.

Scottie frowned. He pointed at Marie, sitting alone in her chair, and looked to Savannah. "Who is she talking to?"

Savannah shrugged. "Likely delirious. Detective? Can you hear me? Call out to her. All you have to do is cry your lover's name, and the pain will stop. Please?"

Silence.

"As you wish," Savannah said. She flicked a switch. "Let's move on to your toes, then."

Fifty-Eight

Nessa's hand jerked from the paperback and she nearly lost her grip on the steering wheel. She'd felt a sudden, flaring pain, like a deep paper-cut slashing across all of her fingertips at once, then nothing. Her intuition told her exactly what it meant.

They're torturing her.

She gritted her teeth until her jaw ached and stomped down on the gas pedal.

Her mind was like the storm clouds roiling in the midnight sky. A seething torrent of rage and hatred and grief and fear, all swirling together and ready to rain down upon the entire world. She wanted to find the men responsible for this nightmare. She wanted to take the fear in her heart—her fear for Marie, her fear of losing her forever—and put it where it belonged. Inside of *them*. She wanted to savor every moment as they begged for their lives.

And then, later, when they begged her for permission to die.

"We've always failed," said her own voice from the back seat. Her voice but older, more weathered, wizened by age. "We always lose this battle."

She looked into the rearview mirror, somehow not surprised to see a passenger there. A woman sat huddled in cloaks of gray moth-eaten wool, shroud upon shroud draped over her frail body. Her face was shadowed by a heavy, tattered hood.

"You fight for all of us tonight," the woman said. "Life after life, we've felt the glow of hope, only to have it crushed under our enemies' heels. Love destroyed, life taken, sent back to the beginning to start all over again."

"How many times?" Nessa asked her. "How many lives have we lived? How many times have we done this? A dozen?"

The shrouded woman held her silence.

"A hundred?" Nessa asked. She swallowed against a lump in her throat. "Hundreds?"

"All of our hopes are with you tonight," the woman replied, "but we have so little hope left to share. Do this for us, Nessa. Do this for your sisters, all who came before."

"Do it for *yourself*," said a new voice.

Another woman sat in the back seat. A picture of elegance and wealth, in a black tailored suit with a baroque cut reminiscent of Renaissance gowns. When she met Nessa's gaze in the rearview, her left eye glittered. It was artificial, robotic, with a scarlet iris that swiveled like a camera lens. She lifted a cigarette in a long ebony holder and snapped her fingers to conjure a spark of flame.

"You're the center of your world, Nessa, the only thing that's ever really mattered to you. And why shouldn't you be? This world and everyone in it were *meant* to be your playthings. You're a witch, and 'witch' is just another word for 'goddess.' Power and pleasure are your birthright. Start acting like it. Sure, go and rescue your servant. Enjoy the slaughter. But don't get weepy over poor little Marie. She exists to serve you, nothing more."

"Lies," said the woman suddenly sitting at Nessa's side. She recognized the mirror-Nessa, the one from the warning vision, by her blue peasant dress. Her face was hidden behind a mask of white bone, intricately carved to resemble an owl's face. Her eyes peered out through small ovals, bright and piercing.

"You disagree?" Nessa asked her. She realized she was chatting with a hallucination, but the idea didn't bother her.

"Do it for both of you," her masked twin commanded. "And do it for her. This is who we are, Nessa. She fights for you. You fight for her. We and she. The Witch and her Knight. This is the story. *Our story.*"

"But the story always ends the same way," Nessa said.

"Then *change* it. You have what none of us had. Open eyes. You have what we were all denied: a fighting chance. This may be our last and only hope to break the cycle and win our freedom. If you fail tonight, you doom us all. And you doom her with you."

"Marie," Nessa breathed. Another lance of pain shot up her arm. Somewhere in the back of her mind, she heard Marie screaming. Her eyes welled with tears.

"You're much like me, you know," the mirror-Nessa said. "I used to be a teacher, too. We Owls enjoy teaching."

Her eyes glinted wickedly behind her mask.

"So go, and know that we are with you. Find Marie. Find her tormentors and teach them. Teach them the true meaning of fear."

* * *

One of the worst things about the nerve induction synthesizer was how it forced Marie's mind to war with itself. She could look down. She could see that her left foot was perfectly fine. That it wasn't a mangled and bloody stump, the toes twisted, broken and black. But nothing could convince her brain of that. Nothing could stop the endless, searing pain dragging hoarse screams from her ragged throat.

Her Other was with her. The knight crouched at her side, stroked her sweat-soaked hair with her soft leather gloves, and sang strange lullabies in her ear.

"Well?" Savannah asked. "Would you like to cooperate now, or do we move on to your right foot? No? Nothing? Right foot it is, then. You know, Detective, we haven't *started* to get creative yet. This is really more of a warm-up. You can spare yourself what's coming. All you have to do is call her name. That's all I'm asking. I don't think I'm an unreasonable woman."

She twisted a dial, and Marie's world whited out in raw agony.

"I can't," she heard herself stammer, somewhere deep inside her mind. "I can't do this."

"You have to," her Other said. "Marie, listen to me: *Nessa is already coming for you.* She'll be here soon. These fools have no idea. But if you call to her, they'll expect her and lay an ambush."

"She's coming?" Marie's fevered thoughts raced. "You promise?"

"I promise." Her Other kissed her tear-soaked cheek. "She would never abandon you. But these men outnumber you both and they have weapons. She needs the element of surprise. Can you endure a little longer? Can you do it for her?"

Marie managed to lift her head high.

"I'll do it for Nessa."

Scottie stood at Savannah's shoulder, watching as she worked the synthesizer like a musician. "Can you really simulate anything with this?"

"Any physical sensation, yes. For example, here's one of the more distasteful patterns, though a highly effective one." She flipped a pair of switches and turned another dial. "This setting perfectly replicates the feeling of having the left arm degloved from shoulder to fingertip, peeling back and removing the upper layers of flesh—"

Marie didn't hear the rest. She didn't hear anything but her own ear-splitting shriek, lasting on and on until her throat and her breath gave out.

* * *

Tony wasn't supposed to be out of bed. Then again, he reflected as he stumbled through the hospital corridors, nothing was the way it was *supposed* to be tonight. He wasn't supposed to be dressed in a paper gown with his ass hanging out and his arm in a sling, the pain of his stitched-up wound cutting through a Percocet fog. His partner wasn't supposed to be the target of a manhunt. If what Janine said was right, after she finally got through to his hospital room, Marie wasn't *supposed* to be abducted by blood-hungry drug dealers, either.

He wasn't supposed to be standing on the threshold of the room where they were keeping Helena Gorski, the woman's wrists handcuffed to the side rails of her bed. But there he was.

She looked over at him, squinting, groggy from the surgery and the morphine drip. "Fisher?"

"Your buddies took my partner."

"Told you...told you they would. Forget it, Fisher. She's dead. Or she wishes she was. You're too late."

He crossed the room and stood over her. His face was a mask of stone.

"Where did they take her, Helena?"

She shifted on the mattress and winced. "So they can kill my whole family when they find out I talked? Piss off, I'm not telling you anything."

"I'm not giving you a choice."

Now she was awake.

"Tony, what...what do you think you're gonna do? There are two uniforms sitting right outside this room. If I so much as raise my voice—"

"No," he said, "there aren't. They just went on an extended coffee break. I told 'em I'd keep a lookout while they were gone."

His hand closed over her dangling IV bag and gave it a squeeze. The trickle of solution, running down a tube to her handcuffed arm, moved a little faster.

"Thing is, I'm a little groggy from the drugs, so if you happened to have an accident? Well, you could be stone dead before anybody comes to help you."

"Tony—" Her eyes went wide. "What are you *doing?*"

"Get this through your fucking skull. Nine police officers are dead because you sabotaged that raid in Bed-Stuy. Four more are in critical condition. You *tried* to kill me. Do you really think any uniform in this building is going to lift one finger to save you?"

"You can't do this," she stammered. "You're a good cop—"

"I'm a cop whose partner is fighting for her life tonight, and I'm looking at the perp who knows where she is. Don't ask if I'll kill you,

Helena. You'd better damn well know I will. After everything you've done, I want you to look in my eyes and ask the real question here."

He loomed over her. His fingers tightened around the IV bag.

"Ask yourself if I'll lose one minute of sleep over it."

*   *   *

The hospital-room door swung shut at Tony's back. Captain Traynor was marching up the hall, a pair of plainclothes detectives trailing in his wake.

"Fisher? What were you doing in—"

"She's fine," Tony said. "Listen, these ink dealers, Richard Roth's buddies, they took Marie."

Traynor's eyes went hard as flint. "Where?"

"Vandemere. It's an abandoned zoo, a couple of hours upstate. According to Gorski, there's at least a dozen of these creeps holed up there and they're armed to the teeth."

"I'll get on the horn with the locals and have them send SWAT."

"Captain," Tony said, "they've got my partner. Fugitive or not, she's still one of ours."

He leaned in close.

"Send *everybody*."

Fifty-Nine

Marie sagged in her chair, slumped against the stainless-steel restraints, her head bowed. Her breath came out in slow, ragged gasps. Savannah studied her, frowning.

"Why won't you *break?*" she murmured.

Marie's voice came out as a rasping croak, her throat raw from screaming. Through the worst of the torture, in the scant moments when she was able to draw breath, she'd been repeating the same fervent litany over and over again.

"...will hold in my heart the virtues of a knight. Mercy toward the poor and oppressed, and none for their oppressors. Humility. Honor. Absolute faith in my liege, and absolute trust. I will—"

Scottie shook his head at her and shot Savannah a look. "Maybe you're taking the wrong tack here."

She arched an eyebrow. "You have a better idea?"

"Maybe. Lemme run this up the flagpole. I'm no tech geek, but I know a little magic—"

"Magic *is* a science, Mr. Pierce."

Scottie waved a hand at her. "Tomato, tomahto. Point is, we do rituals here. And they work. I'm thinking I should round up the boys—who are getting restless anyhow—and we can get our lodge's patron involved."

"Patron?" Savannah asked.

He held up his fingers and curled them into claws as he flashed a perfect smile.

"The King of Wolves," he said.

"You want her to run your little obstacle course, I take it? Like the prostitutes you abducted?"

"Hey," Scottie said, "you *know* the Kings are real. They *built* the Network."

"Their chosen emissaries did, but close enough." Savannah tapped her index finger against her chin. "So you think he might be drawn to the sacrificial energy and...end result?"

He shrugged. "Who knows? That's what makes it fun. Call it an experiment."

Savannah turned, studying Marie in silence for a moment.

"I've just about wrung all the data I can out of her using conventional methods," she mused. "All right, permission granted. Just one thing? I'll be studying the energy output. I realize you gentlemen are...excitable. But please make an effort to kill her as slowly as possible."

Scottie stared at Marie. He ran his tongue across the tips of his teeth.

"Bitch shot my best friend," he said. "Trust me. You don't even need to ask."

*   *   *

The men of the lodge lined up, in order of seniority, to claim their weapons from the Hunting Wall. Scottie bit his lip as he saw Richard's bokken hanging on the rack, the wooden training sword stained with the blood of his last victim. Never to be swung again.

Well, maybe one last time. He left his own bokken on the rack and picked up Richard's, resting it across his shoulder like a baseball bat as he strolled away to start the show.

Normally he or Richard—he felt another sudden pang remembering his friend's face, how happy he always was on lodge nights—would lead the sacrifice out personally. Of course, that was when they were dealing with petrified street rats who had been kept in a cell and starved for a few days. Marie might have been trembling and pale from her torture session, but she was still a trained cop with years of experience on the street. Better safe than sorry. He took a seat behind the console in the zoo's security room and tugged a microphone over.

Finally, he thought, *a fucking challenge for a change. The King's going to reward us for this one.*

He tapped a button on the console. On a flickering black-and-white screen, the steel restraints on Marie's chair popped open.

"Get up," he said into the microphone. "Door's open."

He could smell the suspicion wafting off her, it showed in her body language, but she did it anyway. The door led out of the monkey house, out into the cold and overcast night. In the distance, a storm front was rolling in.

He called up a second camera feed, watching Marie as she stood uncertain and alone at the edge of the abandoned zoo.

"Here's what happens next," Scottie said into the microphone. "You're going to run. We're going to give you a thirty-second head start. And then me and twenty of my best pals are going to hunt you down. All of whom were buddies with Richard, just so you know. You remember, the guy you murdered for his whore of a wife? Now, when we catch you, that's when the real fun happens. Let's just say it's going to be like everything Dr. Cross made you experience, but worse. And very real. And it's going to take a long, *long* time for you to die."

He couldn't resist. He flipped a switch on the console. Across the park, a spotlight shone like a beacon of hope.

"Fair is fair, so here's a bonus offer. See the spotlight? Right in the middle of that tall grass, on a pedestal, there's a revolver waiting for you. Six bullets is a hell of an equalizer—but of course, if you go for it, we'll spot you. Risk it or don't, it's your choice."

His lips hovered an inch from the microphone.

"Either way, you're going to die tonight. See you soon, *Detective.*"

He started the automated countdown. The zoo speakers crackled to life all over the park, trembling with a booming bass-horn drone. Then came the electronic voice, ticking off the seconds to Marie's death: "*Thirty. Twenty-nine. Twenty-eight.*"

* * *

Marie ran.

Not toward the light. She knew a rigged game when she saw one. Her hunters would spot her from halfway across the park if she stepped into that spotlight and she couldn't trust that the gun was even loaded. She went the other way, sprinting up a dark path toward the old aquarium habitat. She cast a quick glance at a cartoon signboard that showed the park's layout.

It was a big zoo. Lots of places to hide. Not that she was in any mood for hiding.

Now she understood—this was the fate of Baby Blue and the victims they'd kidnapped before her. They'd been held here, forced to run this gauntlet of madness—and died trying to escape.

These were the men responsible for the murders. They needed to be held to account. To be forced to stand and face judgment.

They needed to be punished.

As the timer counted down, she darted behind the filthy white walls of the aquarium. A short muddy incline led down to the outer wall of the zoo. She glanced up and despaired. The wall was a good ten feet, no handholds, and topped with concertina wire. She wasn't getting out that way.

"Coven knight," hissed a voice from the shadows. A woman was crouching there, her eyes burning in the dark.

Herself, again.

This Other wasn't like the knight who held her steady through her torment. This version of Marie had a sun-chapped and blistered face, with elaborate ritual scars across her forehead and chin. Geometric designs and unreadable glyphs puckered her flesh.

"Where'd the other one go?" Marie whispered, crouching beside her. This Other wore ragged, loose leggings and a tunic of deerskin, clasped with ornate pewter. Her feet were bare and caked with black mud.

"Your heart calls to the memory you need. And this was much like the night of our initiation." The Other flashed a yellow-toothed smile. "Many salarymen short-sold our stock, thinking we'd die in the rushes. Oh-ho! Come morning they were poor. Downsized! And the profit was ours. Recall the ordeals you endured in the *cah-pe-tol*. Recall your training. You were taught how to fight this way, one against many."

"I don't—" Marie shook her head, her fury battling with her helplessness as the countdown reached its end. "I don't remember, I'm sorry. I know that I'm you, I mean, that you were me once, but I don't remember."

The Other poked a broken fingernail at Marie's heart.

"Doesn't matter. We are all inside of you. The knowledge is there. Trust your intuition. Adapt to your surroundings. And *fight*."

As the countdown hit zero, a new sound drifted through the frigid night air. Laughter. Howls. Whoops of delight as the doors opened wide and the men of the Vandemere Lodge went on the hunt.

The Other was gone. Marie was alone now.

Her mind raced. She needed a weapon. First, she needed to live long enough to lay hands on one. She looked at the mud, dug her hands in, and slathered it on. She smeared it over her face and hands, her hair, the white of her blouse, coating herself in earthy muck. Along the dark and winding paths of the abandoned zoo, it might be enough crude camouflage to give her an edge.

Marie held her breath and listened. The sounds were moving, splitting up, the men scouring the park in small packs. She waited just long enough for them to spread out.

If they wanted a hunt, she'd give them one.

Sixty

Tucker and Westwood prowled alongside what used to be the tiger habitat. On the other side of a low safety wall, the enclosure plunged down a twenty-foot drop to artificial rocks and a dried-up fake riverbed. The tigers were long gone, but the smell of musk and manure permeated the painted stone. Tucker's head was on a swivel, his eyes wide and anxious as he gripped his machete like a baseball player going for a home run.

"I'm telling you, you never should have let Richard or that asshole Scottie into the lodge," he was saying.

"*We,*" the older man said, flexing his hands around a tire iron, "voted on it collectively, Brother Tucker."

"I'm just saying, look what happened. We're totally screwed. We've gotta think about where we're going from here. *Collectively.*"

Westwood took the lead along the curving path. "I'd rather we focused on the here and now, if you would. Tonight's sacrifice is going to be slippery, and I'm tired of coming in second place. Also, this one is likely to put up a fight."

"She's just a woman. Badge doesn't make her any different from the rest. What are you so worried—"

Tucker paused, feeling a tap on his shoulder. He looked behind him.

All he saw was the crudely sharpened end of a branch spearing toward him, a split second before it punched through his left eye. He fell to his knees, clawing at his face and shrieking as the branch jutted from the ravaged socket and ocular juices dribbled down his cheek like egg yolk. Marie snatched up his fallen machete and charged at Westwood.

He was faster than he looked. The machete clanged against the tire iron as he brought it up to parry her swing, and a second later she ducked as the iron whistled over her mud-caked hair. She lunged in, thrust with both hands, and drove the blade half a foot into his belly. Air gusted from his lungs, followed by a gout of blood that rolled down his chin like a closing curtain. Marie ripped the machete free, grabbed him by the belt, and shoved him up and over the wall of the tiger habitat.

He screamed all the way down. Then his body broke on the painted rocks below. His eyes were wide and lifeless, staring up at the oncoming storm.

*   *   *

Scottie heard the screams. His feet pounded as he ran toward the source, five men at his back and another two coming up from the western footpaths. He stalled in his tracks as he looked down at Tucker's body. The branch still jutted from his eye socket.

"Shit," one of his lodge brothers shouted. He pointed down into the tiger enclosure. "She got Westwood, too!"

They were worried about two dead idiots. Scottie was worried about Tucker's empty hands. The cop had a weapon now.

His grip tightened around the lacquered hilt of his wooden sword. *Good*, he thought. *Only makes this more interesting. The ending stays the same.*

*   *   *

With her face slathered in dried mud and her eyes narrowed to hard slits, Marie crouched low in a scraggly clump of bushes. The brambles bit into her skin, scratching welts, but she forced herself deeper into the makeshift hiding place.

She watched shoes thunder past, slapping the dirt-strewn path as they charged toward the fading screams. She had let the first one, the one whose machete she'd taken, live. Not as a mercy. She'd slashed one of his arms from wrist to elbow as a parting gift, opening an artery and writing his death sentence if the wound to his eye wasn't enough to kill him—but she made sure he'd keep breathing, and keep crying out to his friends, while she ran for cover.

He had stopped screaming now. Marie guessed he'd stopped breathing, too. Two down, eighteen to go.

The last hunter passed her by. She watched him disappear around a bend; then she slithered her way from the underbrush. She'd deliberately lured the entire pack to the eastern side of the park.

The gun, sitting out in the spotlight, was west.

She rushed to the edge of the pool of light and froze. The gun was a nice piece, a .45 with a magazine loaded. Of course, no way to tell if it had any bullets in it. That wasn't what gave her pause, though. Her senses were in overdrive, taking in every sound, every whisper of the wind and distant shout, adrenaline coursing through her veins. Her intuition told her that something was very, very wrong here.

The grass. She realized that while the zoo had obviously been closed for years, someone was still tending to the landscaping. Everywhere but here. The ring of tall grass in the spotlight was overgrown, choked with weeds. *Only* the grass in the spotlight.

She dropped down to her knees, getting low and sliding her fingers across the edge of the grass. They brushed metal. She touched the jagged, rusty teeth of the bear trap hidden in the overgrowth.

No way to tell I'd come from this direction, she thought. *There have to be other traps hidden in the grass. Lots of them.*

She could use that.

*   *   *

A fresh scream, shrill enough to shatter glass, turned Scottie's head. He raced ahead and followed the sound. It led him to the edge of the zoo's swan lake, a kidney-shaped dugout that had been drained years ago. Now fallen leaves floated on a few inches of brackish, stale water, runoff from the last rainstorm.

A new storm was here. Black clouds, thick as smoke, blotted out the stars. Faint, slow drizzle came down, trickling fingers of ice along Scottie's neck and dancing on shallow puddles. A threat of things to come.

One of his lodge brothers was down in the dirt, sucking air through his teeth as his two hunting companions tried to pry the jaws of a bear trap from his broken leg. Scottie turned, fast, navigating by memory as he sprinted up a flight of stone steps to the old food court. Surrounded by shuttered and dusty booths, he crossed the faux cobblestone and leaned over the far railing. The elevated perch gave him a perfect view of the spotlit circle of grass.

The gun was still there. She must have weighed the risks and the reward, realizing how long it would take her to ease her way across the trap-studded grass and back again, and decided against it. *Smart girl*, he thought.

Not smart enough. This was his dominion. His hunting ground. He ran mental fingers over a map of the zoo, working out her movements.

You went for the fence first. They always go for the fence, until they get a good look at how high it is. You didn't jump for it, didn't slice your hands up on the wire. No. You hid. Waited. You took out Westwood, bled Tucker so we'd follow his screams—thank you for that, guy was a prick—and used the distraction to make for the gun. You didn't take the bait. You did take a couple of traps, though.

A couple, specifically. Those traps weighed almost twenty pounds each and they'd slow her down. No way she could haul off more than two or three, tops.

So why take them? Desperation, he thought, *any port in a storm, any weapon in a fight. You dropped them on the way, hoping you might get lucky and whittle us down. So where are you going?*

Marie had run from the spotlight to the lake's edge. Only one path, and the bear trap was dead in the middle of it. Scottie guessed the second trap would be a little farther up. Not too far. Speed was her best ally right now. That and the machete she'd taken off Tucker's body. If she followed that path north...

"The gates," he said out loud. "She's running for the main gates."

He'd picked up more hangers-on, seven of them now, looking at him like wide-eyed wolf cubs. Annoying. He hunted with Richard, or he hunted alone. All the same, they might be useful. He snapped his fingers at one of them.

"You. Head along the lake path and try to find any more traps before some other idiot loses his damn foot. The rest of you, follow me. We're going to circle around and cut her off at the carousel."

* * *

Savannah huddled over her bank of consoles, staring at readouts, measuring and collating. It was a shame; she would have liked to capture both of the women, to study them under controlled conditions, but she'd have to settle for what she could get. Marie lit up the zoo like a beacon on her screens, a scarlet smear of magical energy rushing along a secluded trail. Savannah could have told Scottie and his friends exactly where the detective was hiding. She'd even offered to, just to be efficient. He'd replied with some nonsense about "the rules of the hunt" and how they had to conduct their sacrifice "the right way" or the King of Wolves wouldn't be pleased.

"Ridiculous and unproductive," she murmured as she studied the readouts. "Religious claptrap is no substitute for rigorous methodology."

Her screens flickered. A needle went wild, drawing erratic arcs across a rolling spool of paper. Savannah recognized the energy signature in a heartbeat; it was the same burst of occult power she'd observed when the detective and the Roth woman were together at the Iroquois Hotel. Somehow, without Marie's help, Vanessa Roth had found her way here. And the entire lodge was scattered across the zoo, with no one standing guard.

"Oh," she said. "Oh, no."

She tugged on her goggles and ran for the door.

* * *

Just south of the main gates, at the heart of a paved boulevard that cut through the belly of the zoo, a carousel rotted away in the dark. Icy drizzle rained down on the peeling paint, the burned-out lights, the upturned faces of wooden horses and zebras frozen in mid-prance under a tattered and broken canopy. Marie ran in a desperate, loping crouch, trying to minimize her profile as she skirted the carousel's edge and—

—skidded to a dead stop in the middle of the boulevard. Scottie strolled up to meet her, his wooden sword resting casually against his shoulder, and the six men at his back spread out to cut off her advance. She heard footsteps running up behind her, from the paths to the left and the right.

The carousel square filled with leering, hungry faces. At least fifteen men, sealing every avenue of escape. Every eye on her. On her body, as they brandished their clubs and knives. Marie's throat tightened.

"Now comes that fun part I mentioned," Scottie told her.

She should have been terrified. Instead, she found a strange quiet in the center of her heart. Tranquility in the eye of a storm. Freezing raindrops kissed her face and rolled down the blood-slick blade of her machete. She turned the weapon in her hand, appraising its weight.

"Vicky Wagner," Marie said. "Lottie Holmes. Letisha Franklin—"

Scottie shook his head. "That supposed to mean something?"

"The names of the women you killed here. The ones I know about. How many other victims were there?"

"You think I counted? We kill a lot of people, and I don't write their names down. Far as I'm concerned, they don't have any." He spread his open hand, taking in the gathering of men. "Don't you know where you are? These are the hunting grounds. Only hunters have names here. You? You're nothing but meat."

"I have a name."

She held the machete before her. The rain upon the bloody steel caught her image and shone it back at her, her burning eyes reflected in every drop. Multiplied a hundred times over.

"My name is Marie Reinhart. *Knight*. Servant of the Owl. You call yourselves hunters? I've been hunting you for months. And now I stand at the end of my quest."

"Jesus." Scottie blurted out a nervous laugh. "Savannah's torture machine really scrambled your brains, didn't it? Either that or you were always a whackjob and just better at hiding it. So here you are, oh brave and mighty knight. What now?"

"Now?" Marie said.

She pointed the tip of her machete at Scottie's face.

"Now I'm here to avenge the dead and fight for the living. To make sure you never ever hurt another innocent person again. And we both know there's only one way to do that."

She lowered the blade and drew a line across the ground between them.

"You want me?" Marie said. "Come and *get* me."

*   *   *

Savannah ran alone along the empty walking paths. There was the carousel, about a hundred yards to her right. She saw the pack of men, circling, hemming the detective in. That was good. She saw the glint of the bloody machete in Marie's grip. That was...suboptimal. Still, the lodge had the advantage of sheer numbers; it was a battle Marie couldn't hope to win. More importantly, a battle Savannah didn't have to get involved in. Her focus was on the padlocked gate to her left and the pressure she felt building in her sinuses with the speed of a runaway train. Something was coming. Something powerful. Relentless.

Something angry.

A peal of thunder rippled across the ink-black sky. The gate exploded. Savannah threw herself to the dirty pavement as a shredded padlock and a length of bike chain whipped above her head, debris from the blast. One half of the gate hung open, swinging crazily on twisted hinges. The other was completely torn free, knocked flat in a billowing cloud of dust.

Nessa's cloak flared out behind her as she strode into the hunting grounds. The wide, floppy brim of her hat cast half of her face in velvet shadow.

"I believe," she said, "you have someone that belongs to me."

Sixty-One

A lodge brother charged past Scottie's shoulder and ran at Marie, holding a mallet high above his head. Marie darted inside his reach and slashed a line from his belly to his shoulder, and he went down screaming. A sledgehammer whistled through the air and she ducked low, diving under the iron head. She didn't have time to retaliate, not with another attacker on her left, swooping in with a butcher knife and aiming for her throat.

Their blades clanged together, edge against killing edge. She thrust, punched the machete's tip through the crotch of his pants, and twisted. Blood spatter flew in an arc like a string of wet rubies, mingling with the icy rain as she ripped the blade free and spun to parry the swing of a claw hammer.

She needed space. There were too many of them, pressing in too close. Marie jumped up onto the dead carousel and ran. She darted and weaved between the painted horses, trying to break up the pack on her heels. A man with a bad toupee and a Louisville Slugger jumped out at her from the left. She ripped his throat open with her blade, felt his hot blood spray across her hands, and never stopped running.

She came full circle, face-to-face with Scottie.

"*Enough*," he roared, louder than the thunder. Behind her, the lodge brothers froze. So did she.

"Can't trust you idiots to find your asses with both hands and a map," he snapped. "Richard was *my* friend. This bitch is *my* sacrifice."

The wooden katana spun in his grip, so fast the blade left after-trails in Marie's eyes as he carved the air between them. He raised his other hand, hooked his fingers in a ritual gesture and whispered a sibilant incantation.

Blue-hot flames rippled along the blade like a trail of lit gasoline. His mad eyes glowed in the light of the burning sword.

Then he bellowed a warrior's shout, and lunged in for the kill.

* * *

Nessa and Savannah slowly circled each other, ten feet of cobblestone between them.

"Your lover wasn't very forthcoming, Ms. Roth. I encouraged her to cooperate. Is that how you found us? Did you sense her distress?"

"So you're the one who hurt her," Nessa said.

Savannah nodded. "It was necessary. For my work. I don't suppose you could tell me exactly what you are?"

"What...am...I. Let's see. Once, I was a doting wife. A socialite, when I was forced to be. A college professor—"

"Irrelevant," Savannah said.

"Agreed," Nessa replied. "What's past is prologue. You want to know what I am now."

Thunder pealed in the sky. The flickering glow of chain lightning lit up the smoky clouds.

"Lucky you. You're about to find out."

Savannah twined her fingers, her elbows swaying, and whispered a ritual chant. "Three and three establishes the grid lay three numbers crosswise to establish celestial concordance then divide by the lunar hour to determine trajectory and speed—"

As she hissed her equations, a sphere of air around her began to shimmer and harden. It took on a reddish tinge, like she was standing in a thin bubble of stained glass. Raindrops bounced off the magical shell. Nessa watched her, unimpressed.

"I'm aware that you're some sort of witch," Savannah said. "You'll find no victory here. I've done more than master the craft of magic. I've *modernized* it."

"And you're proud of that? There's no poetry in what you do."

Savannah squinted at her. "Poetry? Poetry is pointless. All that matters is matter. Anything that can't be measured, quantified, and optimized is a waste of time. My magical technique is inherently superior because I've stripped away all the old chaff and dead weight, refining my spell-work down to the absolute essentials."

"Seems like a lot of joyless tedium. You could have just waltzed through a cloud of fireflies instead."

"Fireflies," Savannah said, "aren't magical. They're insects with bioluminescent properties."

"And if you dissect one, that's all you'll learn. But watch the fireflies dance around you on a warm springtime night while you walk at your lover's side. See them sparkle and ignite, feeling the soft skin of her hand in yours, savoring the curve of her nervous smile. There's magic to be found."

"Spare me." Savannah rolled her eyes. "Romance is nothing but oxytocin plus delusion."

"Mm. Well, if you don't enjoy the kinder side of my art, perhaps you'll like this better."

The shadows thickened around Nessa's cloak. They congealed and glimmered like long feathers of onyx, as she slowly raised her arms.

"A child wanders into the woods, though he's been told not to stray from the path. He's lost now. The sun is setting. He's cold, and frightened, and so very alone." Nessa's visible eye narrowed, the other half of her face veiled in shadow, as her lopsided smile grew. "There's magic to be found there, too."

Savannah wavered under her stained-glass dome, suddenly uncertain. "What are you—"

"The pounding heart of the prisoner being marched to the execution pyre. The hollow sympathy of the doctor as he reads your lethal prognosis, telling you what you already knew deep down inside: you're going to die, in pain, and there is nothing you or anyone in the world can do to save you."

The feathers became blades of shadow, razor-edged wings that stretched out at Nessa's back like a cloak of swords. They turned, glinting, trembling at the sound of her voice.

"You asked what I am," Nessa told her. "I am fear. I am despair. I am the punishment you have most definitely earned. Let's keep it simple and just say I'm a walking nightmare. And considering you hurt my Marie...I'm *your* nightmare."

She slashed her arms downward and the blades of razored shadow launched toward her prey. Savannah's scarlet bubble shattered, her wards sundered, and the shadows sliced bloody rents across her shoulder and her hip. She cried out, dropping to one knee, and quickly twirled her hands. Her ritual gestures were mechanical, millimeter-precise.

"Let Z-one be Z squared plus Z," she hissed, "and Z-two be Z-one squared plus Z—"

The air took on new life around them as Nessa's shadows fell under Savannah's command. They formed a barrier, swirling, losing their organic shapes and becoming hard-edged fractals that blossomed like black snowflakes. The geometric patterns echoed in Nessa's eyes, hypnotic, overwriting her mind like a virus. She felt Savannah's spell slipping in through the pores of her skin, lighting her veins on fire, drowning out her thoughts and her mind.

"The prime constant calls to you," Savannah's voice said, somewhere inside Nessa's inner ear. "An orderly world has no place for the likes of you, witch. Become one with the universe, now. *Dissolve.*"

*   *   *

Marie ducked low as Scottie's flaming sword sliced the air above her head. The bokken slammed against a carousel horse, knocking its wooden head from its shoulders and leaving a pitted black scorch in its wake. He spun the blade above his head and unleashed another brutal swing. Marie held her machete in both hands, bringing it up to defend herself. The impact sent them both staggering back a step, but Scottie rallied in a heartbeat, coming at her with a curse on his lips.

The flames dazzled Marie's eyes, leaving white smears across her vision as she struggled to fend off blow after blow. He drove her back, step by step, her footing shaky on the rusted steel of the carousel. She felt the other lodge members around them, silently watching the duel, but she couldn't spare a breath on anything but parrying Scottie's furious onslaught. He was relentless, more rage than technique, so fast she couldn't even try to fight back.

A wild slash caught her across the collarbone. The tip of the bokken ripped her blouse and scored a shallow gash in her skin, the flames cauterizing it black. She gritted her teeth, eyes watering, and pressed her sleeve to the smoldering fabric. She jumped back to escape another sweep of the sword, and the carousel shuddered under her feet.

Weak metal, she thought, *rusted out. Careful, you could put a foot through this thing if you land hard in the wrong spot.*

Then she knew what to do.

Marie took another halting step back and fell. Stumbling, she landed flat on her back at Scottie's feet. He stood over her for a moment and savored his triumph. The crackling flames gleamed in his eyes. Then he raised the flaming sword high and drove it down like a spear.

Marie's feigned fear vanished, replaced by cold determination. She rolled to one side as the sword came down and punched through the rusted metal flooring. She sprang up to one knee, using her momentum, and lashed out with the machete.

Scottie had bought the ruse. He was off-balance, wrestling with his trapped sword, and barely saw the blade flashing toward him. He felt it, though. It cleaved his hand, slicing flesh, shattering bone.

Three of his fingers tumbled to the carousel floor.

Scottie howled in pain and horror, clutching the mutilated stumps of his fingers. The magical flames guttered out. He staggered back from the blackened, smoking shaft of his bokken, squeezing his hand to his chest. Marie watched with grim satisfaction as he turned and ran, howling into the dark.

Now the others, she thought, rising to her feet.

They never gave her a chance. A baseball bat crashed across her shoulders, knocking her back to her knees with a grunt of pain. Something slammed alongside her head and left her ears ringing. The next thing she knew she was down, curled fetal as shoes stomped down at her from every direction. She felt a rib buckle and snap. The men's feral shouts drowned under the roar of blood in her ears. Her vision grayed out, a welling darkness that threatened to pull her under.

*   *   *

Nessa felt herself coming apart at the seams.

Savannah's magic encased her in a shell of cold logic. The shadow-fractals burned into her skin like hot wires, carving her into puzzle pieces. A soul dissection.

Sweat beaded on Savannah's brow. Her mechanical hand gestures spun faster, fingers weaving and stirring the currents of occult energy as she doubled down on the attack.

"*Submit*," she rasped, her voice hoarse with the strain. "The order and authority of the universe commands you. *I* command you."

I'm dying, Nessa thought. Her body crumpled to the dirty cobblestone, the force of the onslaught pushing her down. She knelt, enmeshed in burning gears that ground her mind to pieces with cruel precision.

Fingers curled around her left hand. Then her right. In her vision—fading now, along with her heartbeat—she saw her sisters. They held her, standing firm in a line that stretched farther than she could see. Hundreds of them. Hundreds upon hundreds.

Hundreds of lifetimes in which she'd had hope, joy, *love* dangled in front of her like a carrot on a stick, only to have it ripped away from her. A sick, cruel joke.

"*No more*," she whispered.

Rage blew open the furnace doors of Nessa's heart. Her past echoes took up the call. They fed her their rage, their grief, their lament, stoking the fires until they burned hotter than the sun.

Savannah's hands began to tremble. "The order and the authority of the universe command you—"

Nessa's head snapped up. Her sisters lifted her up. She rose to her feet.

"No," she said.

The spell sputtered and died. The shadow-fractals shattered on the stone at her feet. Savannah staggered back a step, winded, and shook her head in stunned disbelief.

"What? How did you—"

Nessa strode toward her, slow, like a lioness stalking her prey.

"I *reject* order," she growled. "I am the *nemesis* of all authority. And the universe? The universe is chaos. You can try to impose your rules, your petty sense of order, safety blankets to make you feel like you have some semblance of control. But you don't. At the end of the night, chaos always wins. *And I am chaos.*"

Nessa raised her open palms to the storm-cast skies.

"Let me show you."

Savannah looked up. Her mouth hung open, fear dawning in her eyes. A swarm was coming. Dark shadows roaring down from the storm clouds.

Owls.

Hundreds of them, small and large, tawny and ice-white, screeching, blanketing the sky over the zoo. Two landed on Nessa's outstretched arms, wide-eyed witnesses while the flock flew low, their wings battering the air around them. Savannah threw her arms over her face as an owl buffeted her, razor-sharp talons clawing at her scalp and drawing blood. She batted it away and it carved into her arms, slicing jagged rents in her coat sleeves. A smaller one clamped down on her shoulder, digging into meat and bone, and gnawed at her throat.

Savannah shrieked as she fell. There were owls on her back, on her legs, clawing and tearing as she tried to crawl away. Death by a thousand cuts. She held out a trembling hand to Nessa, pleading with her eyes.

"Now what would ever make you think," Nessa murmured, "that I have anything resembling a shred of mercy in my heart?"

She strolled past her, leaving Savannah to die. She didn't look back.

*   *   *

Somewhere along the line, the men's victorious shouts had turned into howls of pain. Clinging to the edge of consciousness, Marie realized they weren't stomping on her anymore. She groaned, forcing her head up, and stared bleary-eyed at the carnage.

Owls swirled around the carousel like the winds of a tornado given talons and lethal intent. The last survivors of the Vandemere Lodge were swinging wildly at the birds as they dove and clawed and bit. Some men were on the ground, dead or dying, pecked bone glistening under ravaged, bloody flesh. One man stumbled past, shrieking himself hoarse. His eye sockets were ragged black pits.

The last man fell. The last choking death rattle faded into silence.

The owls departed, one by one or in small flocks, winging off into the dark. One took a long, slow turn around the carousel, flapping its wings in a farewell salute. They left her alone with the dead.

Marie pushed herself to her feet. Even breathing hurt. At least she could walk. She leaned on a painted horse, then staggered to the carousel's edge.

Nessa emerged from the shadows. Somehow, despite it all, Marie found the strength to run to her. Nessa met her halfway. They held each other tight.

"I'm supposed to be the one who saves you," Marie whispered.

Nessa pulled back, gazing at her in quiet awe, the faintest glimmer of tears in her eyes.

"You did," Nessa told her.

The storm broke. Light shone on the horizon, the first rays of dawn. Dawn, and the distant wail of police sirens.

"Time for us to leave," Nessa said. "We're still fugitives, unfortunately, and...I don't think we can come up with any acceptable explanation for what happened here tonight."

"We're really doing this," Marie said. "Running away."

"Together," Nessa said.

They had time for one last kiss.

Sixty-Two

Heavy, bare feet trod across the battlefield. They came to a stop beside the corpse of Savannah Cross.

No. Not a corpse, even though her skin hung on her body like bloody rags. Her chest torn open, her rib cage splintered. The fingers of her left hand, stripped down to the bone, gave a tiny twitch. She stared up, with one eye and what little of a face she had left, and took deep, shuddering breaths. The last reserves of her magic wove a shimmering net around her, denying her the release of death. It wasn't a kindness.

Adam, the master of the Network, crouched down beside her. The big, bare-chested man furrowed his crude brow and shook his head.

"Doctor," he rumbled, "I send you on one tiny errand, and look what mischief you get up to."

His lips, too fat and wide for his face, curled into an ugly smile. Savannah's torn mouth trembled. She was trying to speak.

"Shh," he said. "Save your strength. You know that the Network has no patience for failures. Still, you've done us great service in the past and I don't want to seem ungrateful. So I had an idea."

He held up his hand. His beefy fist clenched a trio of syringes, each filled with black, bubbling tar. Savannah's creation, pure and uncut.

"Let's leave it up to chance," he said.

Then he drove all three needles through her broken breastbone, straight into her heart. He pressed down on the plungers.

Savannah arched her back and let out a strangled wheeze as the ink flooded her system. It glowed like black neon under her skin and raced through her veins. The pupil of her eye blew out, blossoming, driving all the color from her iris as it grew.

"Sometimes," Adam mused, "a taste of one's own medicine is the best cure."

Her body was healing. Skin knitting itself, the new flesh mottled and gray. Ropy strands of ink congealed in the cracks of her exposed bones, resetting and adorning them like black gold.

"And how do you feel, Dr. Cross? Still clinging to mathematical certainty? Do you remain devoted to your vision of a structured and rational universe?"

She stared past him, fixed on some infinite plane.

"I see...*worlds*," she rasped.

"Thanks to these women, these two *mortal* women, Dr. Cross, the Network's investments in New York have been all but destroyed. We've lost years of progress, millions of dollars. Damage control is going to be a nightmare."

He loomed over her, leaning close.

"I want them. You have full authority over Network resources for the duration of this operation. Find them. Capture them. Bring them to me. Don't fail me, Doctor. You've been given a rare second chance. There won't be a third."

*　　*　　*

Helena tried to turn in her hospital bed. The handcuffs rattled, stopping her short. She kept forgetting she was cuffed to the side rails. Then it all came back to her, the sick realization of what she'd done, and what lay ahead for her, and she had to breathe slow until the wave of nausea passed.

She wasn't alone. She looked to the door, to the man with the forgettable face and the bland gray wool suit.

"Helena Gorski." He inclined his head. "My name is Mr. Smith, Esquire. I've been appointed as your attorney."

"I know what you are. I know who sent you."

He seemed almost apologetic as he approached her bed.

"Then you know why I'm here."

She nodded, weak. "Tell me. My son..."

"The Vandemere Lodge has been destroyed. They cannot harm him. Insofar as the Network goes, we see no reason to close your son's account. *He* isn't a loose end."

She closed her eyes. "Thank you."

"You're quite welcome."

They fell into a companionable silence.

"Well," Helena said. "Do what you gotta do."

The tip of a needle bit into her arm. She felt herself convulse, heard the hospital machines shrill as she went into cardiac arrest, but there wasn't any pain. She let go and tumbled into the darkness.

*   *   *

A desert sun rose over Nevada. Alton Roth sat behind his desk, staring at a pile of paperwork, not really reading a word. He had to come back to work eventually. There was nothing to keep him in New York. His boy was in the ground.

Calypso leaned against Alton's bookshelf, his arms folded. The tall, lean man gave him a discerning eye. "I smell some dangerous distractions floating around in that noggin of yours. You've got places to go and babies to kiss. Better focus up."

A sheet of paper crumpled in Roth's trembling hand.

"My son is *dead*. His murderers are out there, running loose, and you expect me to—"

His intercom chimed.

"Sir." His receptionist's tinny voice echoed from the speaker. "There's a visitor here to see you. She says her name is Svetlana Tkachenko, from the Sunlight Bail Bond Agency? She's not on your calendar."

Calypso checked his watch. "I figured you'd need a little encouragement. Don't be a square, big daddy. Open up your heart and let her in."

Roth blinked. He tapped the intercom button. "Er, thank you, Norma. You can send her up to my office."

His visitor was a blonde goddess in black leather. Her sleek clothes hugged her curves like a second skin, and she wore her almost-ivory hair in a braid that dangled past her waistline. Her eyes were shrouded behind a pair of black Wayfarers. She gave Alton a hungry smile, her words dripping with a thick Russian accent.

"This one is pleased to make your acquaintance, Senator Roth. It is always good to make new friends, especially in high places. This one's mother has spoken well of you."

Alton looked between her and Calypso. "I'm not entirely sure what's happening here."

"Get hip to this," Calypso replied. "See, your daughter-in-law and her lady love are slated for a one-way ride to Crashville. I'm calling in a few favors on your behalf, so you can relax and concentrate on your work. As of about...oh, fifteen minutes ago, a contract on Vanessa and Marie went live, and it's being circulated from New York City to the Frisco Bay."

"A contract?" Alton squinted at him. "You hired...what, bounty hunters? Hit men?"

"A little of both." Calypso nodded at the new arrival. "You can let your hair down and use your real name, baby. We're all clued-in around here."

A cloud passed in front of the sun. All the light seemed to drain from the room, the window at Alton's back going dark, as his visitor took off her sunglasses.

Her eyes were swirling orbs of molten copper. Twin wisps of steam rose up, twining above her hair like the ghostly impression of jagged horns. Her grin grew wider, but now she had the teeth of a great white shark, the razor tips stained permanent crimson.

"All hell will hound them," she said, "all the way to their doom. But you may rest assured that this one will have the honor of the kill. Nyx does not fail."

Sixty-Three

Tony had spent plenty of time in interview rooms. Usually, though, he was the one asking the questions.

"And your last point of contact with your partner was...?" his interrogator asked.

The hospital had cut him loose with a sling for his arm, a prescription for Tylenol 3, and an appointment at a rehab clinic. IAB had been on his heels ever since, trying to get to the bottom of his shoot-out with Helena. This time, though, the questions were coming from a higher authority. Special Agent Harmony Black had requested a few minutes of his time. The tone of her voice made it clear that refusal wasn't an option.

"As I said, I called her the night a warrant was issued for her arrest, asking her to turn herself in. This was done with the knowledge and approval of my captain—you know, I'm *really* feeling like I should have my union rep in here."

From the other side of the table, Harmony's eyes bored a hole right through him.

"You aren't being accused of anything, Detective Fisher. We're just trying to get the facts straight. Now, did Marie or Vanessa ever mention being in contact with a man named Daniel Faust?"

Tony shook his head. "I only met Mrs. Roth once, and no. I don't know who that is."

She opened an unlabeled folder and showed him a photograph. He knew the picture. The canvas in Vanessa's workroom, the sketch of her and Marie—her in a cape of starry darkness, Marie dressed like a knight from one of her fantasy novels—in a tender embrace. Agent Black tapped the bottom of the sketch where three women, their forms indistinct and faceless, danced ecstatically around a bonfire.

"Do you know who these women are?"

"Answer something for me," Tony said. "We've got a zoo full of mutilated bodies, and from the ones they managed to put back together, it looks like the vics were some of the most elite moneymen and financiers in New York City. Old money, new money, all kinds of money."

"Correct," she said.

"Then why isn't it on every TV station? I checked the paper this morning. *Nobody* is reporting on what happened up there. I called the medical examiner, asking what his ruling is gonna be. He got ten shades of nervous and said he's not supposed to talk about the Vandemere Zoo. He said if I was smart, I wouldn't either."

Harmony stared at him across the table, silent for a moment. Appraising him.

"You should take his advice," she said.

He looked in her eyes.

"Agent Black...you're not really an FBI agent, are you?"

"Can I be blunt with you, Detective?"

"That's how I like it."

"Sometimes," she said, "people make a wrong turn in life. They open a door that should have stayed closed. They hear a secret that should have stayed unspoken. And by no fault of their own, they find themselves in over their head, in a world they are not remotely prepared to face. I believe your partner made a wrong turn. Now, dealing with situations like this is my job. Sometimes I'm able to save people. To bring them back from that other world."

"And when you can't?" Tony asked.

"The best thing you can do right now," she said, "is put everything that happened, and everything you may or may not have seen, out of your mind entirely. I've spoken with your internal-affairs department. Following a cursory psychological evaluation, you should have your badge and your gun back by the end of the week. Desk duty, until your arm heals, but you'll be fully reinstated."

"Sounds like there's an unspoken price tag on that gift. Something along the lines of 'if you shut up and play nice.'"

Harmony pushed her chair back and closed her folder. She tucked it under her arm as she stood.

"If you heard it," she told him, "I don't need to say it."

* * *

Tony's next stop was Marie's apartment. Janine met him at the door, heavy bags under her eyes. She pulled him into a gentle hug, careful of his sling, and waved him inside.

"Just put on coffee, want some?" she asked. "I've been living on coffee since...since it all happened. Any news?"

"Nothing. Marie's in the wind and I'm getting stonewalled."

Janine trudged over to the kitchenette. She rummaged in the cupboard, bringing down two mismatched mugs. She frowned over her shoulder at him.

"Stonewalled? Doesn't everybody *want* to find her?"

"Some seriously weird stuff is going on here. And I've pretty much been told by everyone from my captain to the feds that I should pipe down and forget I ever knew her." He took a deep breath. "I'm calling bullshit on that. I'm still suspended for the time being, and seeing as I've got plenty of time on my hands...well, I'm going after her myself."

Coffee splashed over the lip of Janine's mug. She turned to face him.

"Going after her?"

"She's my partner." Tony shrugged. "I know her better than anybody, except maybe you. So I'm gonna work the case. Marie is in trouble. More trouble than anybody can handle on their own. She needs my help."

"Our help." She set the coffeepot down, looking wide awake now. "Give me ten minutes, I'll pack a bag."

"Wait, what?"

"You said it yourself, Tony. We're her best friends. I can help. I want to help. Let me come with you."

"You aren't a police officer," he said.

"And this week, you aren't either. In fact, I have seniority here."

He arched an eyebrow. "How do you figure?"

"You're on suspension. I, on the other hand, am a veteran employee of the New York Public Library System. Which makes me a higher-ranking civil servant than you at the moment."

"Not sure that's going to help us." He shook his head. For the first time since the night Marie vanished, he had to smile a little. "But yeah. Sure, what the hell. Let's do this."

"I'm useful!" She disappeared into her bedroom, calling out over her shoulder. "And you don't have a weapon right now, so clearly I have to be the muscle on this team. I'm packing my stun gun."

"You...do know civilians aren't allowed to own those, right?"

She poked her head out of the bedroom.

"Something you ought to know about me by now, Tony. I'm a dangerous woman. I do *crimes*."

"Probably something you should keep to yourself."

She disappeared again. "I'm also bringing my road-trip mix! I hope you like Journey."

Tony sighed. He wandered over to the doorway of Marie's bedroom. He looked to her open dresser drawer. The suitcase, half-packed and abandoned. His gaze drifted to the print on the wall. He took in the image of the knight in green armor, standing alone with her lance as she prepared to battle the shadowy behemoth on the horizon.

Partner, he thought, *I don't know what you got yourself into, but it sure looks like you've picked one hell of a fight. We're coming. And when you need us, we'll be there. That's a promise.*

* * *

Scottie Pierce paced his momentary home, an eight-by-eight holding cell. The cops had flooded the zoo, blocking every way out, and some local yokel caught him trying to staunch his bleeding in one of the old public toilets. He told them he was a victim. He'd lost three fingers, for Christ's sake. They told him they needed to take him into custody until they got everything sorted out.

He stood by the bars, looking up the short, empty hallway. "Better be calling my *lawyer*," he shouted for the fifth time in the last hour.

He wanted to get everything sorted out, too. No idea what had happened out there, but apparently his tactical retreat had saved his life. He was the sole survivor of the Vandemere Lodge.

Just without his good hand. The stumps of his fingers, swaddled in gauze, stung almost as much as his wounded pride.

The lights flickered. Then they died.

"Hey," he called out. He shook the door to his cell, making the bars clank. "Hey, you got a power outage back here—"

The words died in his throat as a pale gray glow lit the cell at his back. He turned slowly.

A woman in luminous rags crouched before him. Ashen bandages wrapped around her face like a mummy. Her hands were talons, mottled and gray with black, curving nails. They clutched at the air as she writhed from side to side. Her movements were sinuous. Chaotic. Organic. A dance with no steps and no music.

"Scottie," Savannah whispered. Her spine made clicking sounds as she rose to her full height, like dice rattling in a wooden box. "How nice to see you again."

He pressed his back to the bars.

"Dr. Cross? I...I thought you were dead."

"I'm going on a *hunt*, Scottie." Her arms swayed at her sides, the dangling shawls like the wings of a plague-stricken bird. "I want you to *come*, Scottie. I'm changing my methodology."

She edged closer to him. Her foot bones clicked.

"I've seen what they are now. The witch and her knight. To hunt the witch, I must become the witch. And that means I require a knight. Will you be mine?"

"A knight? Y-you mean like...like a samurai?"

Savannah tilted her head. Her neck cracked. A strip of bandage fell away, baring a single eye. Wide, mad, and black as midnight.

"Sure," she said.

He swallowed, hard.

"I guess I can do that."

She waved her clawed hand. He fell backward as the cell door swung open, unlocking on its own. She brushed past him without a word, her walk jittery as her bones shifted and clacked under her skin.

Interlude

The floor of the interrogation room rumbled again. *Engines*, thought Carolyn. *We're on a ship.* Across from her, the interrogator sat in sullen silence. It had been a while since he'd taken any notes.

"So," Carolyn said, "let's tally up the scorecard. Vanessa and Marie fled New York with a price on their head and hunters on their trail. Specifically, the NYPD, the FBI, the black-bag government agents *posing* as the FBI, Senator Roth and a handful of bounty hunters from hell—literally—and...you people, via your not-at-all-terrible decision to send the reborn Savannah Cross and her murderous frat-boy samurai henchman. Oh, and Mr. Smith, Esquire, as their personal cleaning service. For as long as that partnership lasted, anyway."

The interrogator stared down at his notes.

"So they knew about the cycle of reincarnations at that point," he said. "But they didn't know *why*."

"No. That came next, when they met me. But I'm jumping ahead. They had a few ordeals to face before I came into their lives, and more than a few bullets to dodge. Again, literally. They didn't know it at the time, but their final destination was on the other side of the country. Las Vegas, Nevada. Two thousand, five hundred miles on the open road, with the entire occult underground *and* the authorities gunning for their heads."

"How did they survive?"

Carolyn didn't answer right away, suddenly cagey.

"Magic," she said. "You know, I've been talking for hours and my throat isn't what it used to be. Before I tell you about the road trip...perhaps you could get me a glass of water? Maybe with a little bit of lemon?"

He narrowed his eyes. "I'm not concerned about your comfort."

"Will you be concerned when I can't talk anymore? You can torture me all you want, a sore throat is a sore throat."

He pushed his chair back.

"Torture," he said as he rose, "is still an option."

"Have I spoken a single lie?"

He stared down at her. His hooked nose twitched.

"Stay put."

She held up her cuffed wrists as he walked past her. "And I'm going to go where, exactly?"

The interrogation room door slammed. She heard a deadbolt slide shut.

She tugged a pendant from the neck of her sweater. It was a small antique key on a brass chain. The tip of her thumb rubbed against its ornate curves. It might have looked like a nervous habit. Or a gesture of prayer.

"All right," she breathed, "let's get to work."

Sixty-Four

Nessa and Marie sat in a greasy spoon on the Jersey side of the Hudson River. The aroma of scrambled eggs and black coffee hung thick in the warm morning air. Marie could see the span of the George Washington Bridge from the diner window. And beyond it, the spires of her city. Her home.

"We'll come back again," Nessa told her. "Someday. We'll find a way."

Marie shifted in her seat and winced. She was a mess of bruises, with a big purple splotch on her jaw, and her ribs were taped tight under her blouse. The pain she could live with. She would heal.

"Did we break the cycle?" she asked Nessa. "Are we free?"

Nessa glanced to the window. She shook her head.

"I don't think it's that easy. If it was, we—I mean, one of our previous us-es—would have done it already."

"So what do we do?"

Nessa sipped her coffee.

"We go west. You remember what I told you about magic, Marie? When you let it into your life, it changes everything. Your old world is gone forever and there's no going back."

Marie nodded. She pushed hash browns around on her plate. She couldn't find the appetite to lift her fork.

"Well," Nessa said, "your new world—*our* new world—is right outside that door. I've read rumors, in my books. America has secrets of its own. On the highways, the back roads, in small towns and big cities. There are legends, mysteries, wonders. Terrors."

"Magic," Marie said.

"The mirror-Nessa said that if we're going to have any shot at surviving this, we have to find Wisdom's Grave. The wellspring of magic. So let's go and find it."

"Sounds like an adventure," Marie said.

Nessa gave her a lopsided smile and a mischievous wink.

"You're damn right it does."

They set off hand in hand and hit the open road. New York City faded in the rearview mirror. Marie waved it goodbye with a pang of heartache. Still, she believed in Nessa. And if she said they'd come back home someday...they'd come home. For now, the witch and her knight had a new quest, and the fight of a lifetime ahead of them.

The fight of a thousand lifetimes.

That was all right. Marie didn't mind a good fight. And as she watched the warm spring breeze catch Nessa's hair in its fingers, the glow of the sun on her pale face, she knew exactly what she was fighting for. The odds were grim, but that didn't matter.

They had each other. They couldn't lose.

Afterword

The *Wisdom's Grave* trilogy was born from a happy collision of ideas. When I began work on the four-book *Revanche Cycle* back in 2014, I fell in love with a certain traumatized bounty hunter and the owl-masked witch on her trail. I wasn't the only one, it turned out, as Mari and Nessa quickly became reader favorites. I didn't want their time to end with the series; I believed they could carry an entire story on their own, given the chance, I just had to figure out how.

At the same time, I was starting to unravel the cosmic aspects of my ongoing urban-fantasy series, laying clues about a handful of people who had been cursed to continually reincarnate and relive their tragic stories again and again. An idea sparked. I drew the connection, spent an entire day frantically scribbling notes and ideas down, and laid a foundation. Three years later, here we are, and our (anti)heroines' adventure has just begun. As I write this, on a cold winter morning with my supply of coffee looking dangerously low, I'm a fair distance into the manuscript for book two. It's tentatively titled *Detonation Boulevard*, and I can tell you there's one heck of a wild ride ahead. I hope you'll join us for it!

In any event, thank you so much for coming this far. I'm grateful you took the time, and I hope I was able to keep you entertained. Of course, if I did, I didn't do it alone. I have to give thanks to my editor, Kira Rubenthaler; my cover designer, James T. Egan; Susannah Jones, my amazing audiobook actress; and Maggie Faid, my steadfast assistant. Maggie is always a great help, but this time around she was able to lend her psych background to several scenes and become Dr. Cassidy's real life stand-in. Susannah also gets an extra heaping spoonful of thanks for showing this wide-eyed traveler around New York City, and introducing me to many of the real-world locales that appeared in the story. (If you go to Kashkaval Garden, heed Nessa's wisdom and order the tapas.)

And special thanks to the bartender at Lantern's Keep — I'm so sorry I didn't get your name! — who stepped up when I needed him most. I told him, "I'm looking for a signature drink for a West Village socialite who might be planning to kill her husband." Without missing a beat, he said, "I've got you covered." One minute later, I was sipping a Bobby Burns with a cherry garnish.

Want to know what's coming next? Head over to http://www.craigschaeferbooks.com/mailing-list/ and hop onto my mailing list. Once-a-month newsletters, zero spam. Want to reach out? You can find me on Facebook at http://www.facebook.com/CraigSchaeferBooks, on Twitter as @craig_schaefer, or just drop me an email at craig@craigschaeferbooks.com.

Printed in Great Britain
by Amazon

62740539R00255